D0945236

THE
MONSTER
HUNTER
FILES

BAEN BOOKS by LARRY CORREIA

Monster Hunter International
Monster Hunter Vendetta
Monster Hunter Alpha
Monster Hunter Legion
Monster Hunter Nemesis
Monster Hunter Siege

Monster Hunter Memoirs: GRUNGE (with John Ringo)
Monster Hunter Memoirs: SINNERS (with John Ringo)
Monster Hunter Memoirs: SAINTS (with John Ringo)*

The Monster Hunter Files (edited with Bryan Thomas Schmidt)

THE GRIMNOIR CHRONICLES
Hard Magic
Spellbound
Warbound

DEAD SIX (with Mike Kupari)
Dead Six
Swords of Exodus
Alliance of Shadows

*Forthcoming

THE
MONSTER
HUNTER
FILES

Featuring stories in the world of Larry Correia's
Monster Hunter International

Edited by
Larry Correia &
Bryan Thomas Schmidt

A Baen Books Original

Baen Publishing Enterprises
P.O. Box 1403
Riverdale, NY 10471
www.baen.com

ISBN: 978-1-4814-8275-2

Cover art by Alan Pollack

First printing, October 2017

Distributed by Simon & Schuster
1230 Avenue of the Americas
New York, NY 10020

10 9 8 7 6 5 4 3 2 1

Pages by Joy Freeman (www.pagesbyjoy.com)
Printed in the United States of America

For the reader fans,
who so enthusiastically await
every new MHI story and book,
and the writer fans who came along for the ride.
We hope you enjoy reading this
as much as we enjoyed putting it together for you.

CONTENTS

THE
MONSTER
HUNTER
FILES

INTRODUCTION

The following reports have been compiled from the archives of Monster Hunter International, as well as items which are believed to have leaked from the United States Monster Control Bureau, MI4 and the British Supernatural Service, the Blessed Order of St. Hubert the Protector, Special Task Force REDACTED, other miscellaneous monster hunting organizations, and individual records.

Though I can't verify all of them, I believe that these accounts are for the most part accurate and should be useful for all of our Hunters in the field. But as always, when dealing with unearthly forces it is best to tread carefully. Like Earl Harbinger says, keep a flexible mind.

—Albert Lee
Cazador, Alabama

Monster Hunter International is the premier private-sector monster eradication company in the business. In addition to being MHI's Finance Manager, Owen Zastava Pitt is widely believed to be the "Chosen One." Owen vehemently denies this rumor.   —A.L.

Thistle

Larry Correia

"Hello, little girl."

"I'm not a little girl," she answered, not looking up from the picture she was drawing. A nurse had brought her a stack of paper and a box of colored pencils to keep her occupied. They had told her that somebody from something called Child Protective Services would be coming to take her to a new home. That was silly. She didn't need protecting, and she didn't want a new home. She wanted her old home back, like the way things had been before...

Before the monsters came.

"My apologies, miss," the man said as he pulled up a chair and sat on the other side of the table. He was wearing a suit and tie, and seemed very polite. "The doctors say you can leave the hospital now. I'm here to take you somewhere safe."

She didn't answer. There was no such thing as safe as long as the monsters were out there.

"I'm terribly sorry about what happened to your parents. I'm a good listener. Would you like to talk about it?"

"No," she muttered, scribbling furiously. She was compelled to draw the battle while the memories were still fresh. She would never allow herself to forget. "I'm drawing monsters."

The man picked up one of her pictures. The page was covered in streaks of yellow and green, with bursts of purple. Yet there were black claws amid the golden lines, and beneath the chaotic

3

swirl were dismembered stick figures, single-line arms, legs, and circle heads with Xs for eyes scattered around. She had scribbled over all the body parts with red.

"You're very talented."

"I know."

"What's going on in this one?"

"Good guys fighting bad guys. The good guys tried super hard, but father and mother died anyway."

"Well, thankfully you're here." He slid over another picture to look at. One stick figure was bigger than the others. Red fire shot out the end of an angry cartoon gun. Over the figure's chest she had drawn a happy face with horns, and then colored it green. "Who is this?"

"His name is Owen. He kills everything."

"Owen Zastava Pitt?" the sheriff called out. He looked like an old cowboy.

"Yes, sir," I answered as I approached the wooden barricade blocking the road.

"Figured it was you. The lady on the phone told me you were a really big fella."

The lady in question was my wife. Julie was back in Cazador conducting business. It was the full moon so Earl had stayed home, too. That left me in charge. The rest of my team was parked down the hill in our air-conditioned rental SUV until we got the go-ahead to poke around the crime scene. I couldn't blame them. Arizona in July is hotter than hell.

"Monster Hunter International, at your service."

I shook the sheriff's hand. Appropriately, it had calluses like he had spent a lot of time roping horses or whatever it was cowboys did nowadays. My hands were about the same, but that was from weapons, weights, and a few years of beating the ever-living snot out of the forces of evil.

"Monster Hunter International..." His eyes were squinty and suspicious beneath his cowboy hat. "I still can't believe that's a thing."

"Since 1895. The Feds read you in, I'm assuming."

"They did...and were assholes about it. I'm supposed to blame this string of killings on *mountain lions*. Can you believe that shit? This is our fourth attack in two weeks, but they went on and on about the need for secrecy, and I don't feel like getting prosecuted for violating national security"—he nodded in the direction of the yellow police tape—"which is why we're talking over here, while all my men are over there collecting bits and pieces of my constituents."

We were pretty far from the nearest actual town, but somebody had set up a roadside fruit stand at the intersection of two roads. It had been flattened and there was dried blood all over the plywood. Deputies were placing little plastic numbers next to the scattered body parts and taking photos. There were a *lot* of little plastic numbers.

"How many bodies are we talking about, Sheriff?"

"This time? Three, I think... It's kind of hard to tell where one ends and the other begins, though. And lots of parts are missing."

"Eaten?"

"Looks that way." He spit on the ground. "You don't sound surprised."

I shrugged. "You get used to it."

"So MHI has seen this before?"

"Well, we don't know what it is yet, but this is the sort of thing we deal with."

"Often?"

"Every damned day, sir. Every damned day."

When MHI had gotten the call, the closest regional teams had already been booked. So it fell on the Cazador team to fill in. This latest attack had happened while we were in the air. As far as the sheriff's department was concerned, we were *wildlife consultants*. The county was paying us a hefty fee just to show up, and assuming we caught whatever was killing people, we'd collect PUFF on it, too. I loved getting paid twice for the same job. I'm still an accountant at heart.

We were down two regulars, but Albert Lee had volunteered to come along. Since he'd gotten severely injured, he had mostly worked as the company archivist and researcher, but knowing we were shorthanded, he'd said he could still drive a truck or guard a base camp. He and Holly Newcastle were off interviewing some of the witnesses to try and figure out what we were up against.

That left the rest of us at the latest scene. Trip Jones got a copy of the medical examiner's report from the prior attacks from one of the deputies and started reading. Milo Anderson had been doing this sort of thing for decades, and was by far our most experienced

Hunter, so he went poking around in the splintered wreckage of the fruit stand. I wasn't exactly CSI, and had no idea what I was looking at, but I tried to help. All I could tell was that whatever had done this had really messed these people up. I'm talking arms *pulled* off. And gashes through muscle and bone that looked like they had been inflicted with one of Ed's battle axes.

Speaking of Edward the Orc, he was just sort of doing his thing—meaning he was standing there awkwardly, staring off into the distance, wearing a ski mask and hood even though it was a sunny one hundred and six degrees, and making the sheriff uncomfortable. I'd told everybody to keep it low-key, so we were wearing normal clothes and had left all of our gear in the truck. Sadly, Ed's idea of low-key meant carrying *only* one sword.

The sheriff looked at Ed—who had gotten on his hands and knees to sniff the dirt—and shook his head. "Wildlife consultants, my ass."

"At least he isn't stealing anyone's chickens," Trip said, not looking up from the reports.

"You say so." The sheriff just looked perplexed. "The victims are the proprietor, who I knew, and two customers. Not locals. No ID on them yet. Their cars are all over there."

There was one old pickup, and a Honda with out of state plates. The area around us was rugged low hills, lots of rocks, yellow grass, and scrubby plants. There was a hot wind that tasted like dust. Judging by the traffic turning around back at the roadblock, this was a pretty busy road for people driving between small towns, but very few people lived near here. There were only a few houses in sight, solo trailers mostly. If our monster was on foot, then its range—and victim pool—would be limited. But in this job, you never assumed. For all I knew, it could drive a car. Or fly.

Trip was thinking the same thing I was. "Sheriff, where were the other attacks?"

"First was three miles north of here, then five miles west. Last was about eight miles south, toward town."

"Sounds like hunting grounds. I don't think it's passing through." Trip said. "I know there has been a lot of activity recently, but have people turned up missing in this area before?"

He frowned. "Well, once in a while. This is a pretty quiet place, but the terrain is rugged and unforgiving. We'll have a hiker disappear every few years. Usually they get lost and fall off a cliff, but sometimes they just up and go missing and we never find a body. Every now and then we find abandoned cars on the highway, and we can't track down the owners. But as far as the actual number of missing persons, that I couldn't tell you for sure."

"How come?"

"Illegals, son. I don't know how many people I've got walking north across my county any given day. They don't exactly declare at the border and get their passports stamped."

Most predatory monsters were clever enough to pick off targets who wouldn't be missed. It was possible that whatever this thing was, it could have been active for a lot longer than the last few weeks. It might have just gotten sloppy lately.

"Anything special happen around here about the time the killings started? Construction projects? Earthquakes? Weird lights?"

"Human sacrifices?" Trip added. "Raining frogs?"

"Now you guys are just messing with me."

"Pandemonium! Dogs and cats living together!" Milo's voice was muffled from beneath the collapsed stand.

"Nothing particular that I can think of. There's always wildfires this time of year, but nothing close by. Big heat wave rolled through around then, that's about it."

I made a mental note to have Lee check the area's history. Maybe we had some sort of monster that got riled up when it got really hot. If it was, of course the friggin' thing would decide to live in Arizona.

"Found something." Milo crawled out from beneath the splintered wood. I helped him up, and Milo dusted off his cargo shorts. He'd put on latex gloves, but I didn't have the heart to tell him that he'd gotten something white in his long red beard. I think it might have been brain tissue. "In addition to fruit, they were also selling fake topaz jewelry, pot, and what I think are illegal Mexican fireworks."

"I can respect capitalism," I said. "You know what we're dealing with?"

"No clue. Claw marks indicate they're long and sharp, four fingers, but I didn't see any hair, so not a werewolf. Chupacabras suck bodies dry, but don't rip apart corpses like this. Daytime rules out some undead, especially vampires. Speed it got in and out without being seen by cars rules out most of the others. That takes care of our usual suspects."

The sheriff crossed himself.

"But whatever it is, it's prickly. Scratches on the wood and paint wherever it rubbed."

"It's got spikes?" I asked.

"My guess, thorns." Milo held out one glove. "And it left these behind."

It was a purple flower, partially crushed and splattered with blood. As far as flowers went, it was spikey and aggressive-looking. "I'm not a botanist, Milo. What is it?"

"It's from a bull thistle, a nonnative, invasive species. Eurasian origins, but all over the US now. They'll grow anywhere a little moisture can collect above five thousand feet," Trip explained. We all looked at him funny. "What?"

"Nerd," I said.

"I only know that because there was a note in here." Trip held up the police report. "They've been found at every attack... You're just mad that I win at Trivial Pursuit sometimes."

"Only because of the sports questions!"

The sheriff stepped forward and took the flower. "Yep, every time. When I thought I was dealing with a regular old-fashioned murderer, I figured maybe it was some sort of ritual or something, but they're just kind of left there, like litter."

"Do you think it could be some kind of plant monster?" Trip asked.

"I hope not. I didn't bring my flamethrower." Milo quickly turned to the sheriff to explain, as if he was embarrassed to be caught without a flamethrower handy. "Rush job. No charter available so we flew commercial. The TSA *hates* flamethrowers in checked baggage. Actually, long story, but I'm the reason for that rule!"

I looked around. There was a clump of the nasty thistles just across the highway. Most of the prickly things were about four or five feet tall, a couple of feet wide, and chock full of scratchy unpleasantness. The tops were covered in those same bulbous purple flowers. Turning slowly, I realized there were patches of the thistle in every gully and ravine around us.

"They're camouflage."

Ed had quit smelling the ground, had wandered over to a patch of thistles about a hundred yards away, and politely raised his hand. I realized that I didn't know how long he'd been standing there waiting to get called on, but Ed didn't like butting into human conversations. I walked over to see what he was looking at. The dirt by the fruit stand was packed so hard that there hadn't been any tracks, but down here the ground was sandier and softer. Ed had found a trail.

The imprint could have been mistaken for a bare, human footprint. It was much smaller than my size fifteen boot. Except the toes ended in sharp points, and there might have been a hook or spur of some kind on the heel.

"Good work, Ed."

The orc just nodded, then pointed up the ravine. *It had gone thataway.*

"Any chance you know what this thing is?"

Ed just shook his head in the negative. Then he walked a few feet into the grass and thistle. It raised a cloud of insects. It was so dry that everything just crumpled to dust as he hit it. It made my nose itch.

"Smell..." He didn't talk much, so when he did, it was probably important. "Little human." He mumbled something in Orcish. "Girl child." Ed bent over and picked something up. It was hard to tell, but from his reaction, I think it shook him a bit. He held up his find.

It was a baby doll, new and clean enough that it hadn't been out in the weather for long.

"Girl drop." Ed growled. "Monster...carry girl away."

The creature had taken a kid.

This had just turned into a rescue mission.

We searched the surrounding hills from morning until the middle of the night. The sheriff offered to bring in the volunteer search and rescue posse, but until we knew what we were dealing with, that might have just given the creature more victims. But we did accept the offer of dogs. Except like Ed's sensitive snout, they didn't have any luck tracking the creature by smell either. Ed said that the creature smelled like "dust under sun" which wasn't particularly helpful.

Lee and Holly joined us. There had been two witnesses to the earlier attacks, but they weren't much use. The MCB had already given them the intimidation speech to shut them up, so they'd been hesitant to talk at all. It sucks that we're on the same side, but the MCB's stupid regulations hinder us from doing our job in a timely manner, which just leads to more witnesses for them to intimidate, which makes their mission harder, but that's how the system—nominally—works.

However, Holly was persistent and charming—or possibly threatening, I didn't ask—enough that the witnesses told her what they saw. But they hadn't gotten good looks. All we got from them was that it was humanoid, around six feet tall, green and yellow in color, and *really* fast. Now, fast is a relative descriptor, and considering everyone on my team had dealt with vampires, we were a little jaded when it came to the concept of fast movers, but both locals insisted that it was at least track-star-on-steroids speed. And that was when it had been seen leaving the scene, with a belly full of innocent victim, so presumably a little bit on the sluggish side.

We had visited a bunch of houses in the vicinity. There were a few, little, clean and respectable farms, but most of them were poor or run-down, lots of single-wide trailers, even one dude who lived in an old school bus, that sort of thing. Nobody had seen anything. Nobody knew anything. A couple of places no one answered the door. For those I was under the distinct impression that if someone was home they were probably cooking meth, and we weren't getting paid to get shot at. It was that kind of neighborhood.

We had reserved hotel rooms in town, but I decided we would set up camp in the hills near the fruit stand in the hopes that it would come and attack us during the night. That way we could just kill the thing and get it over with. Sometimes making yourself a target is just part of the job.

It only got down to about eighty degrees that night, so our camp didn't get a fire. Milo was a little disappointed, because that man was always looking for an excuse to make s'mores. We set watches, and most of us turned in.

I was too uncomfortable and spun-up to sleep, so I used Google Earth on my tablet, trying to figure out, if I was a monster who had kidnapped a child, where would I be hiding? There weren't any caves or mine shafts close. We'd hit all the houses the sheriff had known about, but there were a few things on the maps that looked suspicious, like abandoned shacks, rusted-out cars, that sort of thing. So I flagged those. Only for all I knew the critter just slept out under the stars. We were in the desert and it probably needed water to live, but we'd already hit everything bigger than a puddle in a ten-mile circle. But then again, maybe it just drank blood, and that little kid was the equivalent to a canteen. Sometimes the supernatural scoffed at our knowledge of biology.

Lee limped over to join me. I was sitting on the dirt, resting my back against a truck tire which was still uncomfortably warm. He tossed me a water bottle from the cooler. I absently caught it. With a sigh, Lee sank down against the other tire, leg brace creaking. He saw what I was looking at.

"I hate to say it, Z, but we might not be able to save this one in time."

"Yeah, I know. We're still going to try though."

"Damned right we are." He popped the top on a can of beer. "Eating people is one thing. Eating children offends me."

"Tomorrow we'll break into teams of two and hit all these spots. After that we'll work outward in case this thing can cover more ground that we expect. Any luck on your end?"

"Maybe. I've found two times in the last thirty years where heat waves correspond to a higher than average number of people vanishing during the summer. Could be our monster, or it could just be people getting lost and dying of dehydration. But no specific monster legends—American, Mexican, or Indian—seem to match up. There used to be a weirdo separatist hippy cult out here, sun worshippers believe it or not, kept to themselves mostly, but the locals think they all moved away years ago. Maybe they played with some black magic and summoned something? I've left a message with the county clerk to see what parcels they used to own."

"It's worth a look."

"It's a crapshoot." Lee took a long drink. "I just don't even know how much I don't know."

I put down the tablet and rubbed my face. It was covered in grit and sweat. "Don't beat yourself up. You've been doing good work."

"It's a work in progress. I'm collecting every monster story I can, from us, from other companies, Feds...when they'll talk. Every scrap, tall tale, and sea story, and I'm going to put them all together so eventually guys like us can know what the hell we're doing. Eventually we're going to have books of these, ready to go, like a Hunter's guide of how to smoke anything."

"Sounds great, Al."

"Sadly, today is not that day."

I didn't like breaking up the team, especially when we didn't know what our monster's capabilities were, but we needed to cover more ground. Flying solo was a great way to get killed, so I settled on teams of two hunters. The sheriff loaned each team a single deputy to act as an escort and to keep us from getting lost. Ed and Milo were on four-wheelers looking for more signs in the hills near the fruit stand. Trip and Holly would take everything I'd flagged to the north, and Lee and I would take all the flags to the south. We were supposed to check in periodically via radio. Though surprisingly, I was getting decent cell phone coverage out here, too.

It had been a fruitless few hours. We were driving up a steep dirt road toward one of the parcels of land that had been owned by the weirdo church Lee had looked up. Our cop escort was behind us in his 4x4. On both sides of the road were patches of thistles, dying and crinkly, their purple flowers fading.

There was the possibility that this case could be a total bust. If the monster only came out once a decade for a heat wave and the worst was past, it could go back to doing whatever it normally did, and we'd never know. Not every monster hunt ended in a big PUFF bounty and victory party. Sometimes people died, Hunters spun our wheels, and the bad things got away.

I really hoped this wasn't going to be one of those.

Lee was driving. "I couldn't find anybody who knew much about these people. They lived off the grid, kept to themselves, that sort of thing. Basically they were creepy introverts, and everybody in town assumed they spent their time doing drugs and dancing naked in the sun."

"Great way to get skin cancer."

"They were dedicated. Supposedly they worshipped the sun."

"That's some hard-core, old-school religion right there." And I had once nearly been sacrificed to an ancient squid god, so that was saying something. As we crested the top of the hill, the road dumped us out on a flat spot. It was covered in tall yellow grass and lone thistles standing like sentinels. There was a burned-out wreck of an old barn ahead, but surprisingly there was an RV—which still looked mobile—parked next to it. That hadn't been on my satellite view.

"An out-of-the-way spot like this, what's your bet?" Lee asked. "Campers, coyotes, or cultists?"

The RV was an old beater, rusty, dusty, but the tires were

still inflated. We parked a hundred yards away and waited for our escort to catch up. It was better to let the local authorities deal with people. We were just contractors.

The deputy parked his truck next to ours. His name was Campos. Young guy, but seemed levelheaded and professional. Like Lee, he'd been a Marine, so they had bonded. I didn't know how much the sheriff had told him about us and why we were here, but he was fired up about our search for the missing kid.

Campos rolled down his window. "Squatters?"

"Beats me. We need to search those ruins for any sign of demonic summoning, but human beings are your jurisdiction, Deputy."

"Don't worry," Lee added helpfully. "If that RV from Breaking Bad is giving you any creepy vibes, I've got a machine gun in here I can cover you with."

"Wildlife consultants, my ass," Campos muttered as he got out of his truck.

"Your boss said the exact same thing yesterday morning." I got out, too. Because we were mostly wandering around and talking to people, I was just wearing jeans, a T-shirt, a pair of sunglasses, and two concealed handguns. It was kind of impolite to show up on somebody's doorstep wearing body armor, not to mention it was too friggin' hot. Though judging by those claw marks, if we ran into our monster I would probably regret that decision.

Campos walked up the lane. I followed about twenty feet back. Lee, having volunteered to *cover us*—which actually meant staying in the air conditioning—remained with our rental. The sun was beating down on my head and I was kicking myself for not bringing a hat. It was stupid hot. Sure, our home base in Alabama this time of year was like breathing through a wet sock that had been pulled out of the dryer too early, but this gritty, dusty, no oxygen, standing-in-an-oven feeling was somehow worse. As we got closer, I could see that the RV had New Mexico plates.

Campos went up to the steps, stood a bit off to the side, and knocked on the camper's door. It made a hollow metallic rattle.

I kept looking around. There were thistle plants all around us, a few solitary but most in clumps. There was no wind. The plants were still except for the insects buzzing through the stickers. The grass was deep enough that you could hide a lion in it.

The hair on my arms was standing up.

One of the curtains moved in the old RV's side window. Campos saw it, too. He knocked again. "Sheriff's department."

And then one of the solitary thistles *moved*.

I pulled my .45, but the deputy was between us. I didn't get too good of a look right then—humanoid, but wrapped in spines and prickly leaves—because it leapt at Campos in a flash, tackling the deputy, sweeping him from his feet. The two of them crashed in a cloud of dust.

They were thrashing and rolling. Claws were flying. The monster wasn't making any noise. Campos was screaming. Walking forward, I punched my gun outward, focusing on the front sight, monster blurry behind it, but had to wait an agonizing second so I wouldn't plug the deputy. An arm raised to strike, it lifted its body...and for just an instant I had a clear shot.

The bullet smacked into the monster's head in a puff of dust. It lurched back. I nailed it twice more before it rolled off.

The door of the RV flew open. I shifted focus, but the woman leaping from the doorway was human. There was no time to see what she was doing, because the monster was moving again. I swung the STI over and opened fire.

It was on its belly, face down, arms and legs splayed wide, claws black as obsidian ripping through the dirt, and it scuttled forward like a crab. I kept blasting. Dust and dried fragments of leaves flew from it.

You can go through fifteen rounds really fast when you're motivated. The slide locked back empty. As I reached for a new magazine, it lifted its head, displaying an all-too-human face, only with black holes for eyes. It opened its mouth, and inside was nothing but a circle of black spines. It let out an unholy shriek.

There was a chain of impacts as Lee ripped off a burst from his rifle. The first was low, spitting up dust and gravel, the next couple slapped right into the creature, and the last was high, the ricochet making a buzzing noise as it continued down the road. One of those rifle rounds punched a hole through its cheek in a spray of black sap.

I dropped the slide and shot it fourteen more times. Lee kept on shooting, too.

By the time the dust cleared, there was a broken, riddled, oozing husk of a thing lying there. It wasn't moving, so I went to the wounded deputy.

"Oh man! Oh man!" Campos' cheek had been sliced open. His uniform shirt was hanging in tatters and the vest beneath was shredded. Everything that had touched the creature had been scratched. That was a lot of damage inflicted in the span of a heartbeat. There was blood running into the sand, but I couldn't tell where it was coming from. "Oh man!"

"Hang on." I ripped open the Velcro strap on his vest and pulled it aside. One of the claws had gotten through. I couldn't tell how deep the laceration down his torso was, but it was bad. I wiped away the blood, saw red muscle through the hole, swore, and then used his vest to put direct pressure on it. "Lee! Grab the med kit!"

The other Hunter had driven the truck up closer, climbed out, and was covering the downed monster with his short-barreled AR-10.

"Hold on. It's not dead yet."

I realized that the monster was still twitching. *Shit.*

Only Lee had already retrieved something else from the truck. There was a hissing pop as the incendiary grenade went off right next to the creature. The prickly leaves it was wrapped in were so dry that they instantly ignited. With a *wumpf,* the whole thing went up. The intense heat caused the monster to blacken and curl into a fetal ball. That ought to do it.

Lee grabbed the medical bag from the truck and hobbled over. "Did you see the runner?"

There was no sign of the lady who'd bailed from the RV. "What about her?"

"She was carrying a little kid."

Campos was all fucked up. We were out in the middle of nowhere. Waiting for an ambulance meant he might bleed to death. So we'd gotten the bleeding under control as best as we could, then I carried him to the police truck. Lee put the hammer down, and the two of them were headed for the hospital.

I radioed for help, paused long enough to grab my vest and Abomination from the SUV, and then I'd gone after the kid.

At first I'd hoped that the runner was human, just some regular person minding her own business, when some dudes had started shooting a crazy thistle monster outside her RV, who had grabbed her child and fled in terror...but a hundred yards up the ravine I found the shredded remains of an abandoned sundress, and a fresh footprint in the sand with toes that were way too pointy.

So it was a shapeshifter. Whatever these things were, they looked like people. Or maybe they were people, but turned into *something else.* Now that I had a second to think about what I'd seen, I wasn't so sure that it had been wearing plants as camouflage, so much as they had been growing from its body. It was hard to tell though, since it had all happened so fast. Even if I'd had time, I couldn't have examined the body, since it was still sending up a cloud of oily black smoke below. There was nothing on the tables for this monster, so I would have to request a government PUFF adjuster to figure out the bounty.

Or somebody else would, if this one killed me. Or if I had a heart attack or died of heatstroke up here.

I was breathing hard. The air was too thin. Every shifting, gravel-crunching, rock-slipping, uphill footfall was sending up more dust and dried pollen, which just made it even harder to breathe. My chest hurt from the exertion. I was covered in sweat. Running as fast as I could, I got out of the gully, but stayed parallel to it, hoping that if I stuck to higher ground I might spot my target.

The problem was that there were thistles everywhere. It could be hiding and waiting for me. These things were ambush predators, and I was blundering along after one without a clue. One of the first things we learned in Newbie training was that solo hunting was dangerous. Avoid it whenever possible. Like Earl said, no matter how tough you were, you can only look in one direction at a time. Even if we hadn't needed to evacuate Campos, with Lee's bum leg there was no way he could have made it up this rocky mountainside. The smart thing would have been to wait for Trip and Holly. But I wasn't feeling smart, I was feeling stubborn.

I hated losing people.

There were at least two monsters, but there could be fifty more for all I knew, but I had a full-auto shotgun and a bad attitude. At the next spot that was relatively clear of brush it could hide in, I stopped to catch my breath and look around. I had to take my shades off to wipe the sweat from the glass. There was no sign of the monster or its hostage. I checked in on my radio and gave Trip my location. He knew it would be a waste of time to tell me to wait for them. Good thing Holly hadn't answered, because she would have yelled at me.

Then I heard the singing.

Well, singing was the best way I could describe it. It was an alien, keening sound, and it certainly didn't come from a person or an animal. It was like a hot wind through dry leaves. It was angry and bitter. Sad. Lonely even. I turned around and realized that from up here there was a great view down to the RV, and the blackened, smoking circle we'd left.

It was *mourning*. I think we killed its mate, and now it was singing a funeral hymn.

The sun was directly overhead, beating down like a hammer. Maybe Lee had been onto something. Maybe these things were the result of the old sun worshippers or, hell, maybe they *were* the sun worshippers, changed somehow, drawn back here for some reason. Black magic was malevolent like that.

I set out toward the song. Upwards again, through the densest, scraggliest high desert plants yet—of course, because it can never be easy. Another hundred yards and my arms and face were scratched everywhere. Stickers had worked their way through my boots and were lodged in my socks, irritating my skin.

The song stopped. It must have known I was close. I paused to listen . . . and picked out a new sound. A little girl crying.

I didn't know what its senses were like, but I tried to come in stealthily. Only that was a job better suited for Ed, because everything I put my foot down on either cracked or caused little bits of rock to scrape and crunch. *To hell with it.* I was way better at blundering headlong into trouble anyway.

"*Hello!* Can you hear me?"

The crying turned into a frightened sob. I couldn't imagine what that poor kid had been through.

I pushed through the last of the brush and reached an uneven, rocky clearing. There were tall tufts of grass and low scrub breaking through the loose surface. And of course, more of those damned purple thistles. The kid was huddled next to a rock, skinny little arms wrapped around her skinny little knees, crying her eyes out. I guessed she was about six. Dirty, scratched, blond white kid, but currently so lobster-red that she was going to have one hell of a sunburn . . . if she survived.

I shouldered Abomination and approached cautiously. Either the creature had just dropped her here and kept running, or she'd left her out in the middle to lure me into a trap. But I reached the girl without anything trying to kill me. Keeping my head up, I knelt next to her. "Hey. It's going to be okay. I'm here to rescue you."

But she was out of it, rocking back and forth, scared out of her mind.

"My name is Owen."

There was a sudden gust of wind. One of the thistles shook. I spun and fired a round of buckshot through it. The little girl screamed and slapped her hands over her ears.

It was either sit up here with who knew how many monsters stalking me, or get the hell back down to where my friends would be arriving. With an innocent involved, that was an easy tactical decision, but the little girl didn't look to be in any shape to walk. Her knees and elbows were scraped to hell, and she was shaking like a leaf.

"I'm going to carry you out of here. You just need to hold on tight, okay?"

She shook her head and mouthed the word "no" repeatedly. Poor thing was scared out of her wits. Keeping Abomination in my right, I picked her up with my left. She didn't weigh much, probably just forty pounds or so, but the hill was steep. She was squirmy and made me even more top heavy than usual, and I really didn't want to slip and roll down the mountain with the kid. I'd probably squish her. I'd have to be careful.

We started back down as fast as I could go without losing my footing.

I made it nearly a hundred feet before the monster hit me.

I hadn't even seen it coming.

It passed behind me in a yellow blur, so fast its hands made a *snap* in the air. There was a ripping noise as claws ran across my back. I spun, ready to fire, but it had already disappeared back into the weeds.

"Shit!"

Luckily it hadn't pierced my vest. Even as hot as the damned thing was, the vest had just saved my life. The little girl was crying in my ear. It was making it hard to listen. "It's okay. It's okay."

I kept moving. A bush shook. I put a round of buckshot through it. It could have been the monster, or it could have been a squirrel. Better safe than sorry. I began sliding downward again.

Unfortunately, I was heading back through the thicket. Somehow I'd wound up on a narrow deer trail. I could only see a few feet ahead. The monster we'd killed had demonstrated that it could low-crawl like a boss, and there were a million places one of these things could be hiding. My mouth was painfully dry.

The monster came out of nowhere.

That time its claws got a little bit of skin, but worse, it knocked me through the bushes, off balance. I tried to throw myself flat on my back so I wouldn't crush the kid. I raised Abomination and shredded the bark on a bunch of bushes, but the friggin' thing had already disappeared again.

"Are you okay?" I checked the girl for blood, praying she hadn't gotten hit with a claw. *Nothing. Good.*

It was a long way down. This hit-and-run stuff was the monster's game, not mine. It wanted to hide? Fuck that shit.

The sheriff had mentioned wildfires. They were a plague this time of year. Everything in these mountains was flammable right now. I just needed to find a spot where I could burn this place down without getting roasted in the process. There was a pile of rocks about twenty yards to my left. It was an island in a sea of knee-high weeds. I scooped up the girl and ran that way.

Somehow I made it before the monster took another shot at us. I reached the pile of rocks. There was a rattling noise and a snake lifted its head. I didn't have time to dick around so I just shot the rattlesnake with Abomination. The buckshot pretty much just turned it into a red cloud, but it wasn't anything personal.

"Stay here! It's going to get hot, and it's going to be hard to breathe, but no matter what, don't climb down." Then I gently put the sobbing girl down on the rocks.

I pulled out my Zippo. I'd been so jealous of Earl's that I had gotten myself one with the MHI logo engraved on it too, and I didn't even smoke. But you never know when you'll need to commit arson. I held the flame beneath some dried stems and they went right up like they were soaked in oil. I began walking in a circle, lighting plants as I went.

The fire began spreading rapidly, crackling and popping. It was amazing how many flying insects suddenly appeared, fleeing. The creature must have known I was removing its ability to hide. I was forcing its hand. Fight or flight time.

Apparently, it went with *fight.* I had made half a circle around the boulder pile when the monster flew through the smoke and slammed into me.

Claws flashed. Abomination roared.

I fell on the rocks, but the creature was already gone. Damn, these things were like vampire speed, though I was pretty sure I'd nailed it. Unfortunately, I'd lost my lighter. Not that it mattered, since my little fire was rapidly spreading out of control.

At least the fire would make a great signal for the others to zero in on ... or at least tell them where to collect my body. I keyed my radio, only to realize that the plastic housing had been ripped in half by a claw. Wires were dangling from it. So much for communications.

At first the smoke was heading away from us, but then the wind shifted and it was blowing right back in my face. Since my lungs were already half closed off with pollen and dust, and I'm an asthmatic, let me tell you, that was unpleasant. I started coughing so hard that it was making me dizzy.

This time the monster flanked around ... and attacked *over* the rocks. It leapt past the kid, hit me in the back, and knocked the shit out of me. The only reason it didn't just rip the back of my head off was that we were lucky enough to topple *into* the fire.

I rolled one way, scattering ash. It rolled the other. The thistles sprouting from its back immediately burst into flames, but it still came up, desperate and swinging one burning arm. I raised Abomination and swatted aside the claws, then kicked it in the stomach. The creature flew back into the fire again.

"Weren't expecting that, were you?"

It was screeching, igniting as readily as the ground around it. It began running away, but I aimed Abomination low and opened fire, cutting its legs out from under it. The monster crashed back into the burning weeds. It began clawing its way forward, toward the rocks, trying to get away from the fire.

Now I was really pissed off. The fire had reached a big bush. I don't know what it was, but it went up like a rag soaked in kerosene as soon as the fire touched it, roaring like a bonfire and blasting us like a furnace. The little girl screamed as she saw the flaming monstrosity reaching for her. I walked after the monster, wrapped my hands around its shattered ankles, and dragged it away from the rocks. Stickers and pokey leaves cut my palms as I pulled it toward the flaming bush. It kicked at me with its other damaged leg, and the black spur on its heel embedded itself deep into a plastic magazine full of shotgun shells on my chest. *Too little, too late, monster.*

With a roar, I swung the creature around and flung it right into the flaming tree. It disintegrated in a shower of sparks.

A couple hours later I was sitting on the tailgate of a sheriff's department truck, drinking my third Gatorade. I was sunburned, heat-exhausted, had inhaled way too much smoke, and I don't think I'd ever been this dehydrated before in my life. I had sweated out water that my ancestors had drunk.

The sheriff joined me. "Well, Pitt, the firefighters are really mad at you. Didn't you ever hear Smokey the Bear say only you can prevent forest fires?"

"Yeah, well Smokey wasn't up there getting his ass kicked." If Smokey had been a Monster Hunter, he would have been in favor of napalming the whole mountain.

"Can I assume we're done with *cougar* attacks for now?"

"I think so. My guess it was a pair of... Hell, I don't know. This is one for the MCB to figure out." Lee hadn't read any stories about these either. He'd probably want me to write it up for his collection of monster stories. "How's Campos?"

"He should be okay. Thanks to your friend blowing through town at a hundred and twenty miles an hour. And the girl is at the hospital, too. Doctors say she's damned near catatonic, but I'm not convinced that's a bad thing right now. We still haven't identified those other victims from the fruit stand, but I can only assume they're her parents. Seeing what happened to them? That's a hell of a thing."

"Give her time. People are tough."

"Because of you, that little girl gets to grow up. You MHI guys are okay in my book. That said, I truly hope I never have to see you here again."

The man put the drawing down. "You're very talented."

"You said that already, mister."

"I'm not talking about your artwork. I'm talking about who you are. The doctors couldn't see it because you're not all grown up yet, but I understand. You see, I collect stories, from every time and from all over the world, so I always know to be on the lookout for things that are special. Like you."

She was suspicious. This one knew too much. "Father said never to talk about how we're different."

"But your parents are gone now."

"The monsters got them." *As she said the words, she could see them, wilting and twisting as they were consumed by the monster's fire, and a sudden rage filled her. She slammed her pencil down so hard that it penetrated the table and stuck there, right through the happy face with horns.* "Why wouldn't they just leave us alone?" *she shrieked.*

The man remained calm. "Because people fear what they don't understand. Plus your pops got caught ripping some people apart. Society frowns on that."

"Those humans were a blessing of meat. Father says when the hot time comes the sun grants the blood feast to those of us who sing the black hymn."

"Yeah, whatever, kiddo. Theological differences aside, it sure didn't help matters. You were too weak to do anything about it this time, but you won't always be. You're too young to control your power, but with some time and a little guidance, you'll be dangerous as hell. But until then, I know how to keep those monsters away."

She looked up and really studied the man for the first time. He was wearing glasses with orange lenses that hid his eyes. "Why is your skin so white? Does the sun not favor you? Father said our family is cursed. Do you bear a curse?"

"Sort of. I made something very powerful very angry once. You can call me Stricken." *He reached into his pocket and pulled out a silver object. He held it out for her to see.* "This is called a PUFF exemption."

"It's shiny."

"When you have one of these, you're off-limits. It means monsters like Owen aren't allowed to hurt you anymore, no matter how different you are." *She reached for it, but with a malicious grin, Stricken snatched it away.* "Not so fast. There are rules. You have to earn it first."

"How?"

"By doing what you were born to do, but only when I tell you to. Can you do that for me?"

She held out one hand. Her palm split open and a spikey purple flower grew from it.

"I'll take that as a yes. Come on. You'll like your new home."

Here at MHI it is easy to get so caught up in the big things that Hunters often forget all of the hard work that goes on behind the scenes to keep this company running. You can't do the job without your support staff.   —A.L.

Small Problems

Jim Butcher

"Here they come again," said Fred, scratching at his potbelly nervously. "Now keep your head down and your mouth shut, Sid."

I didn't say anything back to Fred, who was not the boss of me. I just kept working on getting the old electrical outlet out of the wall.

Monster Hunter International headquarters in Cazador was a right solid piece of work, but it wasn't exactly new. I mean, some of it was. Any time something got destroyed by monsters, I guess they built it back as new as they could. But this particular hall back to the trainee barracks must have been left alone by the forces of evil, because it was pretty run-down.

I got the cover off and the central bracket screw undone and started working the outlet box out of the wall. It was a tight fit, and I had to pull hard enough to sit me back on my butt when it finally came free.

My shoulders went back and bumped into the legs of a trainee named Don something or other as he walked by. He had his buddies, Tweedles Dee and Dum with him. They never gave me their names, so I had to make do.

Don was just coming back from the range and smelled like expended propellant. And sweat, of course. Summer in Alabama means sweat. Don was one of those good-looking fellas who had always been bigger and stronger and faster than everyone around

23

him, and figured that meant he could treat them however he liked and get away with it.

"The fuck is wrong with you, dummy?" Don said.

"Excuse me," I said about the same time.

Don swatted the back of my head. Which I did not appreciate. I turned to look at him, and he was squared off over me.

"You could have injured my knee. Maybe you don't get it," Don said, "but I'm the talent around here. You're a goddamned janitor."

"You stink," I said. "Should maybe take a shower."

Fred winced.

The Tweedles snickered and Don's face turned red. Redder. Summer in Alabama means sunburns, and plenty of them.

"I'm about tired of your mouth," Don said. "Get up."

I squinted at him and said, "You want to fight me."

"It isn't going to be a fight," Don said. "I'm going to teach you some respect is all."

"Uh-huh," I said.

Well. Don was about six inches taller and maybe sixty pounds heavier than me, and he was a trained soldier and about to be a Monster Hunter and all. So I didn't feel too bad about whipping my fist up into his balls.

It wasn't a real hard hit, the way I was sitting there, but Don made a funny noise and staggered, and that gave me room enough to come up swinging. I got picked on a lot when I was a kid. Bullies like giving it to the little guy. But they don't like it so much when you paste them a few times, and I'd learned about that.

I fetched him a good one on the nose, drove my shoulder into his stomach, and pushed him across the hall and into the other wall. Once he bounced off that, I went to work on his belly like it was the heavy bag. That was going pretty well until the Tweedles grabbed me and pulled me off.

There were two of them and one of me, and they knew how to work together. I hear they teach the Marines that now. I got in a punch good enough to hear someone's nose break, and after that it was my turn to be the heavy bag. Don staggered back in about the time it was down to my getting kicked and stomped on. It doesn't take much of that to make for a good beating.

"What the hell is happening here!" demanded a sudden voice, a woman's, cracking like a whip.

The beating stopped. I'd curled up in a ball to take most of it on my back and shoulders, which didn't feel good but was a lot better than taking kicks to the ribs, guts, and groin. I hurt, plenty. I had an eye that I could see out of and lifted my head to see a genuine Monster Hunter bracing the trainees.

Miss Holly wasn't particularly big, but there was something about the woman that told you that you really didn't want to get on her bad side. She'd been a showgirl or some such back before she'd gotten into the life, but these days she was something fearsome who happened to look like she did. She'd squared off against the three trainees like a mountain lion sizing up three spikehorn bucks and deciding which one to eat first.

"Boys, boys, boys," Miss Holly said, "that isn't how things are done around here."

The three trainees had the good sense to look ashamed. Well, the Tweedles did. Don looked like he might have had trouble standing up without the wall to help him.

"He started it, ma'am," one of the Tweedles mumbled.

Miss Holly gave him a look that would have peeled paint. "One of him, and three of you, and you expect me to believe he started it?"

"He *cheated*," Don wheezed.

That drew a bright, scornful laugh out of her. "What are you expecting out there? Marquess of Queensbury rules?" She eyed Don up and down and said, "You need a hospital?"

"No."

"You better hope he doesn't," she said, gesturing toward me.

"Or what?" Don asked.

Holly gave him a smile that would have made a wise man uneasy. Too many teeth. "Don—it's Don, right? You ever hear of the hot-crazy quotient?"

Don glanced at the Tweedles for support, but didn't get much. "Uh. Yeah, I guess."

"Well, Harbinger has what you might call a competent-asshole quotient," she said. "Attempting to rough up the staff makes me think you might be on the wrong side of that quotient, from Earl's point of view. What do you boys think? Do you want to get on the wrong side of that valuation in the boss' eyes?"

The mention of Earl Harbinger had what my books would have called a salutary effect on the trainees. He's that kind of fellow.

"No, ma'am," they mumbled.

"Well, then. Hit the showers."

One of the Tweedles gave Don an arm, and the three of them shambled off toward the barracks.

Once they were gone, Miss Holly sighed. "Why is it always the good-looking ones who are assholes?" She turned to me and shook her head. "Damn it, Beauregard. Don't you have anything better to do than get yourself beaten up?"

She gave me a hand up, and passed over a bandana. I cleaned off as best I could with it.

"What happened?" she asked me.

"Nothing to worry about now, Miss," I said.

She lifted an eyebrow. "If I'd come down that hall five minutes later, they'd have kicked your guts out."

"Maybe not," I said. "But you did come. And it's over now."

"Yeah? What happens the next time they run into you in a dark hallway?"

"Don's the big dog in that pack, and I reckon he'll remember he got some bruises, too," I said. "Look. This wasn't personal. This is how some folks are. They have to test the boundaries. Now they know how far they can push me."

"They know?" Miss Holly asked. "Or you know."

I had to smile at that, because she had a point. "Well...let's say we are all gonna be more comfortable with one another now. Someone will buy someone a beer later. It will be fine."

"Men," Miss Holly said. "You going to be all right?"

I rubbed at the back of my head. There were bruises forming under the hair, and one eye was swollen shut, but an ice pack and aspirin would help that some. I wasn't going to be comfortable for a couple of days, that was certain. "Sure," I said.

"You know, Earl isn't going to appreciate hearing about you roughing up his trainees," Holly said. "He does need them, you know."

"Mister Earl is a good man," I said. "He'll understand."

She shook her head and looked after the trainees. "Three of them and one of you. And you gave about as good as you got."

"Well, Miss Holly," I said. "I cheated."

She snorted and put out a fist. I bumped it with mine. My knuckles were a lot more swollen and bruised and cut up and scarred than hers were.

"I'm looking for Fred. We're still having a problem with rats. Have you seen him?"

I looked up and down the hallway. My fellow janitor was nowhere to be seen. Fred had a big belly but he didn't have much of a stomach for fighting. "I see him, I'll be sure to tell him, Miss Holly."

"It's just Holly," she said.

"Please, Miss. I'm Southern."

That reply drew a smile, and it made her look as fine as a frog's hair split four ways. "Your first name is Sid, right?" she asked.

"Thucydides," I said. "Sid to my friends. Which I reckon you are, after today." I offered her the bandana back.

"Keep it," she said. "You want to head to the infirmary, have them check you out?"

"Naw," I said. "I got some more work to do."

"Okay, tough guy," she said and strode off. "Try not to pick a fight with Z before the end of the day."

"No, ma'am," I said. And I meant it.

Owen Zastava Pitt wasn't the sort who needed to test boundaries.

I got back to work on the wall outlet—and found it lying on the floor.

Now that was strange. It should have been wired up. Maybe the wires had been so old that they'd broken off. I picked up the outlet and checked. It was an old one all right. All the fittings and screws were tarnished with age—except for the screws on the connections themselves, which were shiny where they had been loosened . . . recently.

I squinted. That old box hadn't moved in years. And yet someone had undone those screws in the last few days.

From the *inside* of the wall.

I got the little flashlight out of my toolbox and peered into the opening in the wall. The wires weren't there. Apparently, whoever had unscrewed them had taken them, too.

Huh.

Now that was damned peculiar.

A few days later, Mister Milo had dissected some damned thing and it was time to clean up, so Fred and I were on the scene.

"What the hell kind of monster is this, do you think?" Fred asked me as we got to work with the mops and buckets.

"A messy one," I said. The strands of the mop were sticking to some kind of thick, tacky ichor that had drained onto the floor around the operating table. I tried pulling it away and the strands just ripped away from the mop.

The corpse was a sort of sickly gray color, speckled with flecks of purple. There were several dozen tapered tentacle-looking limbs, sort of flopping everywhere, and two pairs of heavy crab-like claws that poked out from beneath a shell that swirled and humped without any apparent pattern. It must have weighed half a ton if it was an ounce. I knew because I'd loaded it onto the reinforced autopsy table with a forklift that morning.

And it smelled. It smelled like rotten compost mixed with dead fish sitting in the back of a car on an August afternoon.

"What's the PUFF on something like that, you think?" Fred asked.

"Gotta be over twenty thousand," I said. I poked a series of gouge marks on the shell with the end of my broom. "See there? Bulletproof."

Fred snorted and nodded toward the shredded mess where the thing's head had once been. "Not everywhere."

"I heard Pitt was right underneath it before he started pulling the trigger," I said. "Can't imagine that's going to be a popular tactic for the teams."

"They think killing things is hard work," Fred spat. He wrenched his mop, grunting, until he managed to rip it free of the ichor. He eyed the half-ruined mop head and sighed. "They should try *this* part of the job."

I grunted and nodded. "Cook it away, you think?"

"Probably just make us have to chisel it off again, but it's worth a try. I'll get the flamer."

Fred hurried off toward the supply shed, and I started clearing everything out of the immediate area around the autopsy table. Mister Milo was more or less the senior technician, which at MHI means that he worked with a lot of experimental guns and ammunition. It would be a little awkward to set a few barrels of propellant on fire while we were trying to clean the place up. I was getting cases shut away in storage closets when I heard a sound behind me.

I'd only caught a little hint of it out of the corner of my eye, but it looked like the thing on the table had moved.

Standard training seminars in other companies mean you learn about team building and sexual harassment and five-year plans. At MHI, you get drilled on how to survive a spectrum of weird things that might happen which your average corporate HQ just don't got to worry about.

And part of that training is specifically what to do if you think something just might, *might* be an active hostile.

You run like the dickens and find someone with big guns to shoot it until it isn't active no more.

I went for the door like a shot and as I did, something came flying off the table and right at me. It wasn't much bigger than one of those little handbag dogs you see people with sometimes, but it was moving fast, faster than I could much see. I just got an impression of something reddish smeared with black, with eyes like tiny burning coals and teeth too numerous and too large for its mouth.

It hit me like a medicine ball thrown by a real big guy—it was too dense and heavy for its size, too. I was already trying to fall out of the way, so it hit me hard enough to knock me the rest of the way down and knock half the wind out of me before skittering off my chest and hitting the wall of the workshop. It rang the metal wall like a great big bell and left a dent in it the size of a bowling ball—and I got a good look at it for the first time.

It was built long and low and wide, like some kind of desert lizard. Its head was too damned big, something between a tiny alligator and a pit bull, and its front legs were about twice as big as the back ones and equipped with a couple of talons each that left deep scratches in the steel wall as it thrashed its way to its feet, focused on me, and let out a furious hiss.

Well.

I ain't much afraid of a fight, but I ain't a damned fool, either. I didn't wait around to give it a chance to come at me again. It might have been little, but it was quick, and it was armed well enough to cut steel. I figured it wouldn't have much problem with my coveralls, or the flesh beneath. I was on my feet and running before it had fully gotten its balance back, out the door, into the sunlight, and smack into Fred.

We both went down and I felt a sudden hot pain in my leg. Fred was carrying the flamer, which was basically an insecticide sprayer we'd rigged up with more flammable fuel and a propane pilot light. That's what had burnt my leg. I seized the flamer from him and hoped he'd taken the time to pressurize it before lugging it up. I turned the wand to the door of the workshop and squeezed the handle.

Fred had gotten it ready. Flame washed out into the doorway.

The critter, whatever it was, must have hit the fire because it let out the most god-awful scream I've ever heard—high-pitched enough to make my fillings ache. I kept the spray of fire aimed at the door until the screaming stopped, and then I kept it there for a few moments more.

By the time I let up and lowered the wand, there were a couple of tufts of dried grass and weeds on either side of the workshop door that were burning, but the critter, whatever it was, was gone.

"What the hell, Sid!" Fred stammered. "What the hell was that?"

I shook my head and rubbed at my chest, where the thing had hit me. I had a feeling that I had gotten real lucky. Like, if that little critter had gotten its claws into me, it would have just buzzsawed its way right on through.

And there would still be the original mess to clean up, sure as anything.

Some days, this job is just one damned thing after another.

"Sid," Mister Pitt said a while later, in his office. "We swept the entire workshop, but we didn't find anything."

I sat across from him. Mister Owen Pitt had his own office and it was surprisingly small and surprisingly neat. Pitt didn't exactly look like a small, neat guy. He was about my age, right around mid-twenties, and one of the bigger, meaner-looking cusses I'd seen in a life thick with big, mean cusses. He was educated, too. Accountant for the organization—and he could handle a shotgun like Fritz Kreisler could play a fiddle.

"It was there," I said.

He lifted both hands. "We found the marks on the wall. I believe you." He rubbed a hand back over his hair and sighed. "Milo thinks it might have been some kind of parasite in the mirelurk."

I smiled slightly. "Mirelurk, huh?"

"I killed it, I name it," Pitt said. "We'll have everyone keep their eyes open, but we're dry. Maybe it crawled off and died."

"Maybe," I said. I straightened my coverall a little and said, "You didn't call me in here to tell me nothing got found."

He cleared his throat uncomfortably and said, "Yeah. Look, Sid. Some things have come up missing."

I frowned for a minute and then said, "I'm not a thief."

"It's just that," he began.

I stood up and said, louder, "I'm not a *thief*."

Pitt rocked back in his chair and his eyebrows went up. "Sid," he said, in a level tone, "you've got to be kidding me. You're a buck fifty. Maybe."

"So?"

"So I'd break you in two," Pitt said.

"Unless I got lucky, yeah," I said. "You call me a thief again and I guess we'll see."

"Christ, Scrappy," Pitt said. "Take it down a notch. I'm not calling you a thief."

I felt a little bit foolish. I took a deep breath and then I sat down. "Sorry."

"And I thought I walked in here with a chip on my shoulder," Pitt said.

I was quiet for a minute and then said, "Me and big guys haven't gotten along. Sorry."

"Sure," Pitt said, and exhaled. "I guess Holly is right about you."

I tilted my head at him. "Miss Holly said something?"

"She said you were the wrong kind of stupid to be the thief. That it wasn't how you'd do it."

"Well," I said, "I'll allow that I can be powerful stupid at times."

"You and me both," Pitt said. "Thing is, some things have gone missing all over. Food from the commissary, a computer from the locker room, some varmint ammo from Milo's workshop, a couple of supplies from the infirmary, some sheet metal from the metal shop. There are only three people in the whole place with keys to all of them—Earl, you, and Fred."

I grunted. "Maybe it isn't Mister Harbinger."

"Maybe not," Pitt agreed.

"Fred isn't a thief," I said. "He works slow and he maybe isn't too bright. But he isn't the kind."

Pitt spread his hands. "Sure. I can go with that. It's not even that much money involved. And I'm not accusing anyone of anything yet. But we have to know what's going on. You know?"

I subsided a little and said, "Guess you gotta do your job."

"Yeah," Pitt said. "Exactly. Which is running numbers and killing monsters and not necessarily in that order. So I'm doing what all good middle management does. I'm sharing the grief. This is your problem now."

"What?"

"You're around. You're capable. Find out what's going on. Let me know what you learn."

I grunted, warily. "I can keep my eyes open, I guess."

"Good," Pitt said. He looked at me for a minute and said, "Trainees worked you over pretty good."

"Had worse," I said.

He eyed me. "Where?"

"Cash fights."

"MMA?" he asked.

"Warehouses mostly," I said.

He snorted. "How'd you end up here?"

"Took the wrong money. Wound up in a cage match with a goddamned zombie."

Pitt puffed out a breath. "Unarmed?"

I nodded.

"You went bareknuckles with a zombie and won?"

"Well," I said, squinting. "I cheated. I wasn't supposed to walk out, but Earl was there. Offered me a job after. Seemed like I'd taken my fight career as far as it was going to go."

Besides, I hadn't had anyone to be with or anywhere else to be. I guess Harbinger picks up quite a few strays.

"So now you make minor repairs and clean up messes," Pitt said.

"Not as exciting," I said, "but there's more time to read." I stood up and asked, "Anything else?"

"Oh. Dorcas said something about rats again."

I pursed my lips.

Huh.

"Fred's on it," I said.

"Fine," Pitt said. "Good job surviving today. Find out what's going on. Try to stay out of trouble for a while."

"Will do," I said.

The next morning, I came out of my quarters, a single-room miniature apartment in the subbasement of the HQ building... and found Don's dead body.

The trainee had fallen on his side and curled into a fetal position—or at least that's what I thought he'd done until I got out my flashlight. Once I had, I could see that I'd been right about everything except which way he had curled. His body had bent backward in such mortal agony that it looked like maybe he'd broken his own spine. He was lying in a pool of congealing blood, thick and black and sticky like some kind of terrible pudding.

From the throat down, he looked like sausage fresh from a grinder, covered in so many wounds that it was hard to tell when flesh ended and shredded clothing began. It was eerie to see his handsome, horrified face on top of those injuries, clean and neat except for where a bit of tissue had been stuck to a shaving nick.

The smell was intense. My stomach heaved. But I hunkered on my heels and looked at him, because finding a dead man that you'd quarreled with a few days before seemed to be the sort of situation where you'd want to know as much as possible before going on about your day.

The wounds were fine, fine things, like someone with X-Acto knives for fingers had just gone to town on him.

Or maybe something not very big, with very, very sharp little claws.

I heard a little skittering sound, and my flashlight beam began to quiver.

The light to the hallway was right over my head, but the switch was all the way down the hall, by the stairs up. I turned it out every night because it was easier to sleep without the light spilling under the old door to my room. I'd have to cover twenty feet to get it on, by which point, if Don's killer was still there, it would have had ample time to get me. Until that time, there would be only dim and indirect light from the staircase, and my handheld light.

I flicked the flashlight beam left and right, trying to paint the entire hallway before I started moving. I caught a flash of movement at the end of the hall—nothing more than a low shadow, vanishing swiftly around the corner that led back to the emergency generator and the storm shelter. I thought I saw maybe a bare tail, a flash of brown fur.

Then nothing.

I held my breath for a few seconds, listening. But there was only silence.

I had just let my breath out again when the door down the hallway opened and Fred emerged from his own apartment, ready to head to breakfast in the mess hall and start the day. I heard his breath catch in his throat, and then go fast as he fumbled for his flashlight and shone it at me.

He let out a high-pitched squeal and bolted.

"God damn it, Fred," I sighed.

Mister Pitt didn't look too happy with me.

It was one thing to face him in business casual clothing in his small and neat office. It was something else to do it when he was dressed in fatigues and body armor with a miniature arsenal strapped to him and that monstrous Frankenstein's monster of a shotgun called Abomination in his hands.

"Damn it, Scrappy, what did I just say not twenty-four hours ago?" Pitt demanded. "I specifically told you not to do something exactly like this."

"He didn't check with me," I replied.

"What a goddamned mess," Pitt said.

There was the sudden *whup-whup-whup* of rotors thundering over the building, and we both looked up. The sound tripled and then quadrupled.

"God damn it," Pitt muttered. He patted absently at his chest, frowned, and opened a secured drawer in his desk. He took a couple of round, smooth balls of steel painted military olive and with his team's logo in bright red—a little smiley face with horns. He clipped the grenades to one of the belts strapped across his torso where there was a little room as he spoke: "The timing for this just could not be any worse. Those birds are taking us down to Bayou Sauvage. Every Hunter here."

"You didn't check with me either," I said.

Pitt snorted, as his brow furled, thinking. "Earl has to call this in. We can't have the staties or the Feds running around this place, so you can expect MCB to show up in a few hours," he said.

My innards already didn't feel too good. The mention of the federal government's Monster Control Bureau didn't help them feel any better. "What should I do?"

"Do *not* try to fistfight any of them when they get here," Pitt replied. "That's the first thing."

Pitt's radio chirped and Earl Harbinger's voice said, "Pitt, what the hell?"

Mister Pitt made a frustrated sound and clicked the radio's send button a couple of times in acknowledgement. "Sid. Did you kill him?"

I looked him in the eyes. "No, Mister Pitt."

Pitt frowned and nodded. "Yeah. Milo says it was maybe the same thing from the workshop. Look, MCB does not give a flying fuck about justice. They just clean up messes. They'll ask questions, and when they find out you two fought a few days ago..."

He left it hanging. The implication sort of dangled around next to my guts, somewhere way below the rest of me.

"If it was me," Pitt said earnestly, "I'd want to have something's body to hand them, all wrapped up in a bow. Makes their paperwork easier. They like that. Find that thing."

"How am I supposed to do that?" I asked.

Pitt's radio chirped again. "Pitt! Do you want dead Boy Scouts? Because this is how you get dead Boy Scouts! Move your ass!"

"I'll hold off telling Earl until we're in the air," Pitt said, heading for the door. "Give you as much time as I can. Sorry, Sid. Best I can do."

And with that, he pounded down the hall at a dead run.

I sat there for a minute, just sort of stunned.

The Monster Control Bureau made people vanish. With most of the organization out on a mission, I was going to be on my own.

I'm not a real smart guy, but at least I know it. I mean, fixing things, sure. That's easy stuff. But dealing with the courts? Talking my way around federal guys? I was more about fistfights and a beer later.

What the hell was I going to do?

Well. I guess I could start with the scene of the crime. That's what Spenser or Travis McGee would do. Look for clues.

Sure. That would work.

They'd already moved the body up to the infirmary for Milo to get a look at it, so what was left was just an ugly leftover biohazard.

In other words, a mess. I'm good at messes.

I try to think positive.

I got down close to the puddle of drying blood and fluids. The smell wasn't as bad now, though it wasn't what I would call pleasant. I didn't see much. So I went down the hall and turned the light out. I went back with my flashlight and shone it sideways across the surface of the blood.

There were indentations in it. Not big ones, but there was definitely something there, as if something light had skipped across the surface of the drying blood in little hops, leaving small dents in the dried blood without breaking the surface. One, two, three hops, and then gone.

I squinted at the line and went around to the side of the puddle and took a line on the row of jumps. Then I turned the lights back on and followed that line down the hallway.

It ended at a power outlet.

On a hunch, I pulled out my multitool, extended the blade, and flipped at the plastic cover. It came right out of the wall and landed on the floor, leaving an open hole behind it. I picked up the cover. Someone had filled in the outlet holes with plastic and apparently painted fake slots onto it. They'd gone so far as to saw off the bolt that would hold it on, and glued the head of the screw onto the exterior to make it look normal.

"Sid," I said to myself. "This is a door."

But a door for what?

I shone my light inside.

Two little jewels glittered red, way back in the hollow space behind the wall, and then vanished.

"Hey!" I said. "You know how much of a pain it is to run new wire to an outlet once the wall is up?"

Only silence answered me.

Rats again. Maybe. But no clue about little buzzsaw monsters. Nothing to hand to MCB, that was for sure.

I was screwed.

My smartphone buzzed. Me and Fred both had one, so that we could get called around the place when we were needed. I took it off my belt and found an anonymous text message on it:

MISTER SID. WE SHOULD TALK. YOUR QUARTERS.

I stared at the phone for a while, bemused.

"Well, Sid," I muttered. "Why not."

My quarters were what a poetic person might call Spartan. I had a bed and a dresser and a small bookshelf. A little table, a small fridge for snacks. And a big bookshelf. And a second big bookshelf. Most of the books were tattered and old and second-hand, but I'd read them all. I didn't always understand them but I was working on it. Books were good.

I checked carefully and found nothing in the room. Then I got out my phone and carefully texted: OKAY. I AM HERE.

The answer came back quicker than I could have typed it on the tiny screen. My fingers are kind of thick. PLEASE SIT AT THE TABLE, MISTER SID.

I squinted at the phone. I examined the table and chairs but didn't find a bomb there or anything. So I sat down, warily. I still didn't know who was texting me or whether they wanted me to wind up like Don.

No sooner had I sat down than there was a rattle from a wall vent and it fell outward onto the floor.

My phone buzzed again: STAND BY. DO NOT PANIC, PLEASE. WE MEAN YOU NO HARM.

At that, my eyebrows went up. "Well," I said aloud. "Come in, I guess."

THANK YOU, MISTER SID, said my phone.

And then the damnedest thing happened.

In a column five across, tight across the space of the vent, came marching out rats. Big rats. A whole damned *lot* of rats. They didn't hurry and . . . and the damned things were carrying *shields*. Roman-style legionary shields, on their backs. And strapped onto every shield with what looked like fishing line was a scalpel or an X-Acto knife. At least a hundred rats marched out into the middle of the room, formed into a legion square, and at a squeak from a rat in the first row, all stood up on their hind legs and sat there, staring at me.

That was one of the damned creepiest things I ever felt—the attention of a *crowd*, all concentrated into a space maybe five feet by five in the middle of my floor. Every single little critter there stayed focused on me with an unnerving intensity, not moving, holding still with military discipline.

"Huh," I said.

Then there was another stir at the vent and four rats came out carrying a smartphone on their shoulders. Behind them marched a white rat in a rough breastplate that had been hammered out from some sheet metal and fastened on with more fishing line. He bore an X-Acto knife marked with a stripe of what might have been red duct tape, and his red eyes were focused on me firmly as he walked forward.

The rats with the smartphone stopped behind the legion and set it up at a forty-five degree angle, holding it on their backs, and the white rat went to the phone, set down his spear, and began tapping quickly on the surface of the phone.

GREETINGS, MISTER SID. MY NAME IS JUSTINIAN MALLEUS, AND I OWE YOU AN APOLOGY.

I sat there for a moment. Then I put my chin on my hand and said, "You're going to have to give me a second here, to adjust."

Justinian typed his answer and then stood at attention, his paws clasped behind his back. VERY WELL. I AWAIT YOU.

I took a few deep breaths and then said, "All right. I guess. You're rats. And you can type."

SPOKEN ENGLISH REMAINS PROBLEMATIC, Justinian typed. WRITTEN COMMUNICATIONS SEEM MORE PRACTICAL.

"Uh," I said. "Sure. That makes sense. You're the ones who have been thieving, I take it."

I REGRET THAT IT WAS NECESSARY TO PROTECT OURSELVES AND TO ESTABLISH COMMUNICATIONS. I WILL TAKE FULL RESPONSIBILITY FOR YOUR LOSSES ONCE THE CURRENT EMERGENCY HAS PASSED.

"What emergency?" I asked.

THE BEAST, Justinian typed. THE CREATURE. THE ONE THAT ATTACKED YOU YESTERDAY.

I narrowed my eyes. "You know about that?"

IT HAS BEEN HUNTING MY PEOPLE. WE HAVE PREPARED OUR-SELVES TO DO BATTLE, BUT ITS STRENGTH AND SPEED SEEMS OTH-ERWORLDLY.

I eyed the rat warily, because it struck me that a couple of hundred intelligent rats with X-Acto knives could do that to poor Don if they had a mind to . . . and were crazy enough.

Justinian peered at me and began typing. IF I WANTED TO HURT YOU, MISTER SID, I WOULD NEED ONLY TO HAVE REMAINED SILENT AND WAITED FOR YOU TO SLEEP.

"That ain't hardly comfortin'," I said. "But I take your point." I squinted up at the other vent to the room, high up on the wall. "I heard some ammunition went missing, too."

Justinian seemed to consider his answer before typing. MY FIRE TEAMS HAVE ORDERS TO SHOOT ONLY IF YOU ATTACK US. THEIR WEAPONS ARE CURRENTLY NOT AIMED AT YOU.

I mused on that for a moment, studying the other vent. I was careful to stay relaxed in my seat, because it seemed prudent. "Justinian Malleus," I said. "You are more than a little intimidating."

I ONLY WISH MY PEOPLE TO SURVIVE. THAT IS WHY WE ARE HERE.

"Where the hell did you come from?" I asked.

A GOVERNMENT FACILITY. IT HAD NO NAME. WE WERE CREATED THERE. TORTURED THERE. WE WILL NOT RETURN.

Justinian cheeped something, and the other rats whipped out their spears and planted their steel butts firmly on the floor in a surprisingly sharp, short shower of impact.

"Well, I don't much care for the government either," I said. "Why here?"

FILES SPOKE OF ONE NAMED HARBINGER. THEY SPOKE OF HIM WITH ILL FAVOR. IT IS OUR HOPE THAT THE ENEMY OF OUR ENEMY MIGHT BE OUR FRIEND.

Oh, crap. Only someone working in the same circles at the MCB would have information on Harbinger's operation. And the MCB was on their way.

"Well," I said. "I guess anything's possible. But we got to get some things straight, right now."

ACKNOWLEDGED, Justinian typed.

I got the steps to the door fixed in my head, in case my question set Justinian off. Creatures clever enough to steal weapons and manufacture their own arms might be smart enough to make some kind of zip gun, too, and I didn't want to be a sitting duck. "Did your people kill the man in the hall last night?"

Justinian stared at me, and his expression was grim. He typed slowly. WE DID NOT. BUT WE WITNESSED HIS DEATH. WE WERE NOT YET PREPARED TO DO BATTLE, AND I ORDERED MY PEOPLE TO REMAIN CONCEALED.

I leaned forward excitedly. "But you saw it?"

YES. IN MY JUDGMENT THE WARRIOR HAD COME TO MAKE PEACE WITH YOU. THE BEAST STRUCK HIM FROM ABOVE AS HE CAME TO YOUR DOOR. IT TORE HIS THROAT FIRST, SO THAT HE COULD NOT SCREAM.

I shuddered. Damn. Poor Don. He was an arrogant ass but he hadn't deserved to go like that. "Christ almighty. Then it's smart."

HIGHLY, Justinian typed. THIS IS HIS COMMUNICATOR. IT TOOK ME TIME TO LEARN TO OPERATE IT AND TO FIND YOUR SIGNAL CODE.

"Hell, took me weeks to work mine," I said. I rubbed at my jaw. "Do you know where it is? The beast?"

WE BELIEVE IT IS COMING FOR YOU.

Well. That made my heart go skippity-skip, let me tell you. This conversation felt pretty unreal in the first place. Adding a spike of adrenaline to it didn't make me feel any more grounded, you know?

"Why do you think that?" I asked a little numbly.

WE BELIEVE THE BEAST IS A SOLDIER AS WELL, FOLLOWING THE BIDDING OF ANOTHER. LAST NIGHT, IT HAD COME FOR YOU.

"And Don just walked into it," I breathed. "What's controlling it?"

NOT WHAT. WHO. Justinian squeaked an order, and the rats holding the smartphone wheeled it around to face me, and then group-marched closer until they were near my feet. Justinian came along with them, pacing gravely, the butt of his X-Acto spear thumping on the ground. Once they reached me, the white rat flicked nimbly through several screens and called up the phone's photo records. I was treated to a view of what I presumed was Don's erect former penis, accompanied by the text "Hi, Holly!"; a couple of shots of a neatly cored-out bull's-eye in a target from the range; and then a movie.

Justinian hit play and stood back.

I watched a view from the vent in my room, focused on the trash can next to my bed. The slats in the vent gave me only a partial view, but it was enough to see someone enter the room. They padded quickly to the trash can, and rummaged in it. They came out with a rumpled cloth—the bloodstained handkerchief Miss Holly had given me to clean up my face with.

I sat back slowly, working through the implications.

Justinian took the phone back and typed rapidly. IN SUPERNATURAL MATTERS, IS THE BLOOD OF A SUBJECT NOT OFTEN USED AS A MEANS TO DIRECT UNNATURAL FORCES AGAINST HIM?

"Yeah. I reckon it is," I said.

THEN YOU SEE THE DANGER. YOU MUST CONFRONT THE THIEF.

I felt my jaw harden. "Yeah. And there's more trouble than that coming." I explained to him, briefly, about the approach of the MCB.

That shook the discipline of the legion. Rats looked at one another in restless agitation.

Justinian squeaked at them, and a couple of larger centurion rats squeaked themselves and restored order to the ranks.

IT APPEARS WE BOTH HAVE A PROBLEM. AND A CLEAR OBJECTIVE.

"We do."

If we lend you our aid, can you secure a place for my people here?

"I can't promise you that," I said. "But if we help each other out of this, and I can't convince Mister Earl, I'll leave and figure out a way to make one for you on my own. How's that?"

Justinian studied me gravely. Then he typed, nonoptimal, but acceptable.

"Done," I said. "One last question."

Justinian nodded.

"Why me?"

Justinian simply pointed at my bookshelves, one at a time. Then, the damned little thing saluted me, putting his fist to his heart.

The rest of the legion followed suit in a chorus of tiny thumps.

I shook my head. A legion of warrior scholar rats. This was the weirdest job I'd ever had. And I'd once gotten paid to beat a zombie to death.

Justinian began typing again. The thief is—

I waved a hand without reading the rest of the text. "I know who he is. I recognize his boots."

I walked into the empty mess hall, shut the door behind me, and said, "What the hell were you thinking, Fred?"

Fred was seated at the table nearest the kitchen. All the chairs were up on the table. He was supposed to be waxing the floors, but the machine was sitting to one side of the room, unplugged. A stack of donuts left over from breakfast was sitting in front of him and he was chewing on one of them thoughtfully.

"Fucking Thucydides Beauregard," Fred said. "The high and mighty. You know I had it pretty good around here until you showed up."

"The hell are you talking about?" I asked.

I would have preferred to charge him, knock him down, and start rabbit-punching him. But I needed to kill a little time—and the doorway to the mess hall was the place that would give me the most lead time if some little claw critter came skittering up to tear me apart.

"You and your kissassery," Fred spat. "Rushing everywhere. Getting everything done just right. Crossing all your fucking *i*'s and dotting all your *t*'s."

"God. I know I'm not a damned genius, Fred, but you are just a dumbass."

That got to him. Fred slammed his fists down on the table and scattered donuts everywhere. "You're just trying to make me look like an idiot!"

"I'm not trying," I said. "Fred, that's how you work a damned job. You get into it and you do it right. You work hard, and you do better."

"Oh, bullshit!" Fred seethed. "You just want to be my boss!"

"So you call up a goddamned demon?" I demanded. "How petty can you get?"

"I didn't have to call it up," Fred spat. He rummaged in his coverall pocket and came out with a small leather-bound book. "See there? Ray Shackleford wrote it himself. Some kind of journal. He opened that big damned door to the Outside all those years ago—but what no one realizes is that it's got a big-ass crack underneath it. And sometimes little things get through. Little things that you can make do things for you if you know how." He shook the book. "It's all in here."

I rolled my eyes. "Jesus, Fred. What could possibly go wrong with that plan?"

"I've cleaned up shit my whole damned life!" Fred screamed. His face was red and he was breathing hard. "My job is shit now, but I'm not letting you fuck it up for me, Sid! You got lucky in the shop! And that idiot jock got in the way last night! But now you're a goddamned dead man!"

And, from somewhere above, there was a brassy, chilling shriek.

My belly turned to jelly. Oh, hell. The little monster was coming.

"I said the words and drew the star and it's *your* blood it wants!" Fred screamed. "You're a dead man, Beauregard!"

And from a ceiling vent the tiny terror exploded. It sailed down onto a tabletop and slammed its claws and its tail down at the same time, stopping it cold. It opened its overlarge jaws, still stained with Don's blood, and shrieked again.

"Now!" I shouted.

There was the sudden sound of a high-pitched whistle being blown—and four ground vents in a square around the mess hall slammed down and disgorged precisely fifty rats apiece. Justinian's Legion rushed forward, screaming high-pitched war cries.

Fred looked around, his eyes wide, and stumbled back from

the table. He pointed at me and shouted something in a panicked, high-pitched voice—and the tiny terror on the table whirled toward me and flung itself forward, bounding down from the table and rushing across the floor.

I whipped a wrench and a claw hammer out of my tool belt and held my breath, trying to track the thing. It was coming like a fastball. I forced myself to wait for a fraction of a second and then swung the wrench—and connected. The critter let out a shriek of nine parts fury to one part pain, and even so it clawed the wrench out of my hand with terrible ferocity as it went. It flew to one side, hit a chair and knocked it from the table, and tumbled down beneath the table with a squall.

The Legion rushed forward, circling the thing and coming to their feet, shields raised, suddenly presenting a bristling fence of scalpel-sharp...scalpels. And X-Acto knives. The critter whirled around, bigger than any three rats but outnumbered and, kept from leaping by the table overhead, let out another scream.

"What the fuck!" screamed Fred. "What the fuck is that?"

"Rattus ex machina," I snarled. "Give me the book, Fred."

"Fucking *rats*," Fred snarled, drawing a petite revolver from his pocket.

Well. I could have run. But that would have left Justinian and his people alone against a demon summoner, as pathetic as he was, and a monster. They had shown up to fight for me, so I couldn't do less.

I charged a man with a gun.

Fred shot at me, screaming. I'm not much of a gun guy, but I know that screaming while you shoot isn't good. He got off three shots as I came toward him. I flung my hammer at him. It whirled through the air and forced him to duck. The handle bounced off his shoulder and he wasted a second screaming, "Ow!" That bought me a few more steps before the next shot, and something hot ripped across my left arm and it went numb. Then I slammed into Fred, lifted him off his feet, God was he heavy, and slammed him into the wall behind him.

The gun didn't fly out of his hand like it always does in movies. He started to bring it to bear on me, and I had to reach across his body with my right arm and grab his wrist. He didn't panic or keep pulling the trigger until it was empty, like they always do in movies.

I'm pretty strong for a guy my size, but Fred was bigger and heavier, if not exactly stronger—and he had two functioning arms. He slammed his left fist against my head a few times, but he didn't know how to punch right—starting with the fact that you don't punch a guy in the skull if you can avoid it. It took him until the third hit to figure that out, when he started wailing and cursing in pain.

I slammed my head against his chin. He responded by latching onto my ear with his teeth and biting hard.

Let me tell you, that hurts. Even by my standards.

We spun around a few times as I tried to keep the gun pointed away from me. Fred finally bit through and ripped some meat away from me. I screamed, lifted my foot, and stomped hard on the inside of Fred's knee.

Fred screamed, and we fell.

The gun went off as we hit the ground, and this time, Fred *did* drop it. It went skittering away.

I started slamming my skull against Fred's. That's not a great idea, but I wasn't giving it everything. I wanted to scare him with the ferocity of it, force him to try to get away. I screamed as hard as I could as I did it, and managed to spatter blood from my mangled ear into one of his eyes.

Fred did one of the only smart things I'd ever seen him do—he got his weight on top of me, despite the attack. He pinned my good arm down with his left forearm, and started punching the left side of my neck with his right hand.

Necks aren't built to take that kind of thing for long. A couple of hits later, I felt like I'd been kicked in the groin across my whole damned body. I managed to get my shoulder up and to turn a little, and I shrugged the next couple off, but I was failing.

And then there was a trilling, tiny shriek, and Justinian Malleus flung himself forward, leaping up Fred's planted arm, his X-Acto spear held in both hands, and drove it with all the force of his charge into Fred's neck.

That got him off of me. Fred rolled away screaming, clawing the X-Acto knife out of his neck, and batting the white rat away. Justinian flew off and slammed into a table leg, spinning several feet further, then laying still.

I.

Hate it.

When.

The big guy.

Hurts.

The little guy.

My vision went red and I kicked Fred's legs out from under him. He fell. I rolled into a mount as he hit his back, and started slamming punches down at him with my good arm—and I know how to hit. I crushed his nose flat and pounded his head right through his uplifted arms. The hits didn't hurt him—but the way his head kept hitting the floor beneath him every time a punch came down would scramble his brains pretty quick. My hand took too many hits and went half numb, so I shifted to slamming my elbow onto him until he stopped moving.

Another shriek made me look up to see the critter slamming its way out of the encircling knot of the Legion, bleeding black blood from a dozen fine wounds. It scattered the last few rat legionaries out of the way and rushed toward me across the open floor.

Right into the field of fire of the Legion's artillery teams.

Three teams of two rats were in position. One rat held a piece of steel pipe on one shoulder, aiming it, while the second rat drew back a nail, an improvised firing pin, that had been fixed to layers of twisted rubber bands. An officer rat with them squeaked, and the miniature gunmen opened fire at the critter.

The little zip guns barked, twenty-twos maybe, and one of them scored a hit on the critter's hindquarters. It spun the thing partway around, and it let out an unholy squall as it did, its rear legs suddenly going limp. It rolled across the floor, snapping its jaws in such mindless rage that it bit off its own tongue and sprayed the air around its jaws with a black spray of blood.

I looked around wildly and spotted my claw hammer a few feet away. I seized it in my numbed fingers, whirled around through a hellish pain in my left arm, and brought the thing down on the critter, hard.

There was a crunching, wet, splattery sound.

Then the rat legionaries caught up to it and went to town with their spears.

Pitt was good to his word. He didn't tell Earl about what had happened until they were done blowing up an infestation of mirelurks in Lousiana. As a result, the teams and MCB arrived at about the same time.

A big, ugly MCB agent stood at the end of my infirmary bed in a big cheap suit, scowling, while another one took my statement. I scowled back at the ugly one and answered in a calm voice. I told them about Fred and the critter. Fred and the thing's body had already been taken into custody. I did not tell them about Justinian or his people, because fuck the government.

I'd had a rough day.

Once I was done, the big guy walked up next to the bed and poked my bandaged gunshot wound. I tried not to wince, but clenched my teeth.

"Thirty-two wound," noted the ugly guy. "Pussy."

"Don't you got anything better to do?" I asked him.

"The other pissant janitor," said the ugly guy, "says there were rats."

"It's rural Alabama and we don't keep cats," I said. "Duh."

"Says there was an army of them," said the ugly guy.

"That guy's a fuckwit," I said.

The big ugly guy leaned down, getting too close to my face. "You're lying."

You know. Any other day, maybe I would have taken a swing at the guy. I mean, it's kind of my thing.

But maybe I didn't have anything to prove to the jerk.

"Can't really hear you," I said and closed my eyes. "I'm down to one ear. Shock and blood loss. Whatever, fuck off."

The MCB Agent, Franks or Hanks or something, made a sound in his chest that sounded like the kind of growl you'd hear from a patch of deep shade somewhere in Africa.

"There a problem here?" asked a new voice from the door.

I opened my eyes. Mister Earl had arrived. Mister Pitt loomed large behind him, splattered in enough sticky gore that I started laughing. It came out sort of jerky and unsteady, and really sounded more like I might have been choking.

Agent Franks held up the little leather-bound book and stared hard at Harbinger. "Fucking Raymond Shackleford's journal."

"One of them." Harbinger stepped forward. He was a man of middle years, not of remarkable size, but balanced and quick-looking. He wore jeans and a leather bomber jacket, and there wasn't a speck of grime or blood on him. "He had a couple dozen.

What, you never found at least five of them, right? Now you've got one less to worry about."

Franks growled again.

"Some idiot stumbled onto it in one of the subbasements," Earl said. "You're lucky it was a damned barely literate janitor." Earl nodded toward me. "My man needs rest. You get his statement?"

Franks said nothing.

"Then I guess I'll see you later."

Franks stared at Mister Earl for a moment, and I thought that something might be about to happen. Then Franks grunted at the other agent and lumbered out. He smacked his shoulder against Pitt's and knocked him aside like a large child. Then he was gone.

Pitt stared after him and muttered, "Slimed you. Take that. Prick."

Earl waited until Franks had been gone a while and then eyed me. "Talk. Everything."

I told him.

"Rats," Harbinger muttered. "Goddamned rats, now."

Pitt's shoulders were quivering.

"They won't cost much and they can earn their keep," I said. "They just need some startup."

"Earn their keep? Doing what?" Mister Earl growled.

"Taking care of small problems," I said. "That thing that killed your trainee? According to that book, one of them comes through every year or two. Mostly they just wander off—but Justinian's people can shut them down at the source. It's in a crack in the foundation, by the way. You'd have to dig up the whole place to get to it. I figure if they save one trainee every ten years, you're coming out at a big profit."

"For the love of all that's..." Mister Earl looked like he'd had a long day and wanted to take it out on someone. He whirled on Pitt and said, "This is on you. You do it."

Pitt blinked. "Do what?"

"Whatever," Mister Earl growled. "You put this guy on the job. This is your fault. Deal with it."

And with that he stalked out.

Pitt looked at me and sighed.

"Justinian has a badly broken leg," I said. "Some of his people got cut up pretty good. They need a vet."

"The rat...needs a vet," Pitt said.

"Rats. About twenty."

"Oh, for crying out loud."

I squinted up at him from my hospital bed. "We gonna have a problem now, Pitt?"

Pitt threw up his hands, turned to leave, and said, "For crying out loud."

I sort of hazed out for a few minutes. Then Miss Holly showed up. She was still in her battle gear and looked great. Then I saw that she was carrying a tray of food and she looked even better.

"Hail the conquering hero," she said and put the tray down on my lap. "Hey, how come Owen is looking for a vet?"

Darkness Under the Mountain

Mike Kupari

The narrow ribbon of highway cut a straight line through otherwise uninhabited terrain. Rocky desert stretched out as far as the eye could see in every direction. The rugged, uneven terrain was broken by steep hills and barren cliffs. My nose was clogged with fine, talcum-powderlike dust even though the road was paved. The sights and smells brought back memories. It had been a long time since I'd last been to Afghanistan, but at that moment it was like I'd never left.

I sat in the passenger's seat of a white Toyota Land Cruiser, part of a five-vehicle convoy speeding down the lonely Afghan highway. At the wheel was Cheng, our driver and interpreter. I guess he was fluent in Pashtun and English as well as his native Mandarin. His English was perfect, as a matter of fact, with no hint of an accent. He'd been provided by the Chinese mining company that was paying for this little expedition. He seemed personable enough, but I was positive he was a spy for the Chinese government.

Behind me was my old buddy Barb. His real name was Anthony Vincent Barbarino, and I knew him way back from Naval School, Explosive Ordnance Disposal. We'd come up through Air Force EOD together.

"This is kind of weird," he said, scanning the horizon through Oakleys.

I nodded in agreement. "It's weird being back here after so long."

"For you, maybe. I deployed to the 'Stan again after you went back to your weekend warrior bullshit. I was just here a couple years ago. I meant it's weird driving down an Afghan highway in an unarmored truck."

"Yeah." Both of us were habitually scanning the edges of the road, looking for the telltale signs of hidden IEDs.

Cheng looked over at me briefly, the horizon reflected in his mirrored aviator sunglasses. "Mr. Cooper, I assure you this road is quite safe. We haven't had any problems with terrorists in almost a year."

We were in a remote part of Afghanistan that had been quiet throughout most of the war. The road we were on had been originally paved by the International Security Assistance Force, paid for mostly by American tax dollars, but now was maintained by the Chinese. The region was rich in minerals and several Chinese-owned companies were pulling ore out of the ground, following the veins deeper and deeper into the earth.

"It is not dangerous malcontents that you need to be concerned with, Mr. Cooper," Cheng continued. "There are worse things skulking about."

"Yeah," I said hesitantly. Talking to anyone who wasn't a Hunter or MCB about this sort of thing made me uncomfortable. It was all authorized, of course. The job I'd been hired for was approved by both the State Department and the Monster Control Bureau, but I didn't know Cheng.

"I was there, too," Barb said. "It was crazy. Zombies—actual, no shit zombies. Coop's team and mine were both in this village with an Army platoon and a company of ANA. It was this big operation to clear out the Taliban. There were insurgents and IEDs all over the place."

"A lot of guys got killed," I said grimly. "Mostly Afghans, but a few Americans, too. Then shit started to get weird. The next morning the dead insurgents were gone. Most of the villagers were, too. Then this woman in a burka attacks an ANA officer, bites his throat out."

"She started eating him, right there in the road!" Barb said.

"The ANA freaked out and ran. The Army guys shot her to pieces. She didn't stay down until they hit her in the head."

"We had been dropped off by a helicopter, and after the Army platoon leader reported what happened, they wouldn't send another out to get us. We were told to find a defensible position and maintain radio silence until we were contacted. They left us out there for two fucking days while zombies killed off most of the remaining villagers. By nightfall of the second day, the compound we were holed up in was surrounded; there had to be hundreds of them. There were more of them than there were villagers in that town, so it must've been more widespread than that."

"It would seem that you managed to escape intact," Cheng said. "You were fortunate. I have read reports of this incident. Your government's attempts to cover it up weren't as effective as they might think."

"Yeah, after they got us out they carpet-bombed a few villages. Just leveled them with B-52 strikes. They wouldn't do that to the Taliban for risk of civilian casualties, but they'd do it to zombies. It was bullshit."

"Were you recruited by Monster Hunter International shortly after this incident?"

"No. We all got debriefed by some asshole from the government. Monster Control Bureau, actually, but we didn't know that at the time. We were told it was classified and that any mention of the incident would land us in prison."

"How did you come to be recruited by MHI, then?"

"The zombie attack wasn't my last encounter with weird things. I was on a road trip after getting home and...the darkness found me again."

"Someday you need to tell me that story," Barb said.

"Someday." The winged, batlike thing I'd encountered on a lonely stretch of highway, holed up in a rest stop, used some form of psychic manipulation to lure unsuspecting motorists into its lair. It still gave me nightmares. It didn't just get a look into my mind; I got a look into its, and the cruel malice of the thing shook me to my core. I didn't like talking about it. "But yeah, that second incident got me a job offer. The first one was hushed up. I don't even think I'm supposed to be talking about it now, but fuck 'em. Barb here stayed in the Air Force. I went back to Reserve duty after getting home."

"Are you still in the military?" Cheng asked.

"No, I left the Reserves a couple years ago. Barb just separated. Got sick of the bullshit, just like me."

Barb shrugged. "So what are we up against here? When Coop called me for this, I figured it was zombies again. Is it zombies again?"

"It would seem not," Cheng said. "You'll get a full briefing when we get in. I trust it won't be anything you can't handle. Monster Hunter International has a very good reputation, and you worked for them for several years."

"I'm freelance now," I said and left it at that.

Cheng actually smiled. "All the better. More money for you." He pointed ahead to a lonely, rocky mountain in the distance. "That is our destination."

The sun was sinking toward the western horizon as we arrived at the mine site at the base of a lonely mountain. The China Metallurgical Group Corporation had a sprawling complex in the shadow of that rocky peak, an entire town built to house hundreds of Chinese workers and engineers. The grunt work was done by Afghans from the nearby villages, but few of them were in evidence at the boomtown.

Barb and I found ourselves sitting alone in a conference room, wondering when Cheng was going to get back with our briefing. We'd seen no sign of him for over fifteen minutes and were getting sick of waiting. One wall of the conference room had a flat screen TV, thankfully muted, that was showing the news from China.

"How are things with Amber?" he asked, after a long silence. "You haven't said one word about her on this whole trip. You guys okay?"

I took a deep breath. "She moved back in with her mom a couple months back. We're still, you know, married, but I don't hear from her much. I expect to have divorce papers waiting for me when I get home."

"Shit, dude, I'm sorry. I guess...well, you guys got married kind of on a whim. You'd known her for what—a week? It was Vegas. It probably wasn't going to work out."

Barb didn't know what Amber and I had gone through together. We weren't supposed to talk about the incident at the Last Dragon Hotel in Las Vegas, even though the MCB hardly managed to contain that mess. She was younger than me by a few years, a UNLV student who worked at Hooters part-time.

"It's my fault," I said glumly. "The company...Monster Hunter International...had me assigned in Seattle. After the, uh, mess in Vegas, I was supposed to go back. Amber didn't want to pack up and move. She was in her third year of nursing school. I requested a transfer to the Vegas branch. They said no, so I quit."

Quitting MHI was one of the hardest things I'd ever done. Even more so than the military, I'd considered those Hunters to be my brothers. Being honest, I hated Seattle, and my team leader, Esmeralda Paxton, wasn't my favorite person (the feeling is mutual, I'm sure), but monster hunting is the best job in the world.

"What happened, then?"

"You have no idea how hard it is to go from monster hunting to working a day job. I found work doing range clearance at Nellis. Decent money, nice and safe, and I was home every night. I guess I wasn't happy, though, and Amber could tell. We started to fight a lot. She said I wasn't the same person. She said I shouldn't have quit my job, and I told her I quit it for her, and she got mad at me for throwing it in her face."

"Ouch."

"Yeah. So I started looking for freelance hunter jobs. I... look, people don't usually quit MHI. It's a family-owned company. Tight-knit bunch. I couldn't go begging for my job back, so I looked at the market. Paranormal Tactical out of L.A. is hiring, but fuck those guys. Also, I kind of got into a fistfight with their lawyer."

"*You* got into a fight?"

"He was a UFC fighter, I guess. I held my own." Okay, that was a lie, I got my ass kicked, but Barb didn't need to know that.

Before I could say anything else, Cheng walked in, followed by two other Chinese. One was a middle-aged man in a plain, tan suit. The other was a very attractive woman, probably mid-thirties, in a tight-fitting business suit. Her skirt was a little short and her heels were a little high for typical office attire. Cheng was still dressed in an olive green shirt and tan cargo pants.

"I apologize for making you wait, gentlemen," he said. "This is Mr. Wu and Ms. Liu, with the China Metallurgical Group."

Wu and Liu. Hilarious.

"Thank you for coming, Mr. Cooper," Ms. Liu said in heavily

accented English. "You as well, Mr. Barbarino." She pronounced Barb's name as *BAR-bree-no*.

"I hope you can help," Mr. Wu said. "Production has all but stopped due to the . . . the . . . creatures."

"Tell me everything," I said, taking out a notepad and pen, and Wu started to tell his story. Like dwarves, it seemed the China Metallurgical Group had delved too greedily, and too deep, because they stirred up some shit that was now terrorizing the locals. I was shown a cell phone picture of a creature that looked feminine and humanoid, but hideous. Its skin was gray and its eyes were shiny and red.

"Our security personnel managed to wound this one," Wu said. "We thought it dead, but when we came back later to recover the body, it was gone."

"You didn't use silver-core ammunition," I said. "They heal quickly unless you use silver."

Wu nodded and continued. After the creatures appeared, the Afghan miners refused to work. A local militia had showed up to try to protect the villages in the area from the things that came in the night, with limited success.

"These . . . things . . . seem to prey mostly on women and children. Several pregnant women in the surrounding villages were attacked, viciously. They have claws and fangs like steel. They . . ." Cheng paused, tapping on the screen of his iPad briefly. "Well, see for yourself."

"Holy shit," Barb said, looking at the gory mess on display.

My stomach turned. "Jesus Christ, is that . . . is that what I think it is?"

"I'm afraid so," Cheng said. "They rip the fetuses out of the wombs of mothers. They have also carried off children. Have you ever seen anything like this?"

Barb looked at me, wide-eyed. "Yeah, have you?"

I frowned. "No, but give me a second." I retrieved my laptop from my pack and pulled up the monster encyclopedia on there, glad I didn't erase it like I was technically, legally required to do when I quit MHI. I typed and clicked for a few moments, then turned the laptop around so the others could see. "I think this is what we're dealing with."

Ms. Liu turned white. Mr. Wu started to sweat. "What is that . . . that thing?"

"It's called an Al. They've been reported in Afghanistan, Iran, and as far west as Armenia for centuries. There are several variations on the legend, and as with most monsters, none of the legends quite get the facts right. The Persian legend, for example, says that the Al have hog- or piglike features, including fur and tusks, but that isn't the case. What is true is that they attack women, especially pregnant women, and prey on children."

Ms. Liu looked horrified. "But why?"

I shrugged. "Who the hell knows? I don't pretend to understand the why of any of this. One legend has it that God created the Al as Adam's first consort, but he couldn't deal with her inhuman drama or whatever, and they've hated human women ever since."

"That's preposterous," Wu said.

"And yet here we are, talking about monsters that attack women and eat babies. So, what now?"

Wu and Liu looked at each other nervously. Cheng said something to them in Mandarin, then looked at me. "Please forgive my compatriots. This is, you must understand, a touchy subject. Officially, the Communist Party of China denies that the supernatural or paranormal exists. Discussion of such things is, you might say, strongly discouraged."

"I'm guessing that's why I'm here and not a Chinese hunter team?"

"Something like that," Mr. Wu said. "Political considerations. We are . . . if I may be forthcoming, we are trying to handle this in-house. If production is halted much longer, I'll have no choice but to call back to China for help, and there might be . . . well, I'd like to avoid that."

"I imagine so."

"Our miners seem to have opened a nest deep beneath the earth, where these things may be coming from. The ground here is full of natural cave systems, and it is not known how deep or widespread they are."

"If they can travel underground in caves and dig their way out, that would explain how they're sneaking up on these villages," Barb said.

Now he was thinking. I'd make a monster hunter of him yet. "I think you're onto something."

Cheng nodded. "Agreed. One report said the creatures climbed out of a well in a village several kilometers from here. They only come in the dark of night, and can reportedly move quite swiftly over open terrain. We need you two to find their nest and kill them."

"Well, we'll do our best, but that will be a challenge with just two guys."

"You'll have the assistance of our security personnel."

"That's good," I said, "but the hard part will be finding the nest."

"We suspect it's in one of the caves that connects to our south tunnel," Cheng said. "It was during the expansion of this tunnel that the creatures first appeared."

"Wait," Barb said, looking confused. "You think they were just hiding underground for however long until this mining operation found them? How could they survive down there? Where did they come from?"

"You need to understand..." I trailed off, looking at everyone in the room. "You *all* need to understand. We are dealing with unearthly forces. They spawn and multiply in dark places. They come from other...realities, other dimensions, whatever you want to call it. Someplace else. They're not beholden to the laws of nature, and they are not a product of natural evolution. They're not like wild animals; they are malevolent. They are evil. They seek out people to hunt and kill, and for all that we've learned about them, we don't really understand their motivations aside from the fact that they seem to enjoy it. You'll go crazy trying to wrap your brain around this stuff. Don't overthink it. All that matters is that they're mortal, and they can be killed. They feel fear, too, and we're going to show these things what it's like to be hunted." I looked up at Cheng. "I'll need a little bit of time to get a plan together. I need maps of the mine tunnels, too."

"We have used seismic refraction and other techniques to map out the cave systems to some extent," Wu injected.

"Good, I can use those too. Cheng, I'll come up with a plan with my partner here, and when I'm ready, I'll brief the security guys that are going with us. Can you be there to translate? Do they speak English?"

"I will be there, Mr. Cooper," Cheng said. "I'm going with you as well. I have been assigned to protect you. That assignment doesn't end when you go underground."

"Okay then, you'll want to stay for this. Were they able to get the equipment I requested?"

"Most of it, yes," Cheng assured me. "Including the flame-thrower. The silver-cored ammunition was the most difficult item to acquire, I'm told."

My own gear had been flown to Afghanistan with me. Being on an officially sanctioned international hunting job made getting certain things through customs more feasible than it would have otherwise been, even if it did entail an ungodly amount of paperwork. Getting the necessary approval from the MCB, the State Department, Customs, and the ATF had taken months. "Good. Have a sit-down and let's get started."

If you've never been underground, you've never experienced true darkness. The mine tunnels, cool and slightly damp, offered no natural light. They were lined with electric lighting for the workers, but in areas that light didn't reach, the darkness was foreboding. *Oppressive.* Abysmal in a way you never experience aboveground.

It wasn't just the natural unease that comes from being in a deep, dark place. After you hunt monsters for a while, you begin to get a feel for the places they like to lurk in. It's a combination of experience, subconscious cues, and gut instinct that helps keep you alive. An experienced explosive ordnance disposal technician gets a similar sense for improvised explosive devices and areas where they might be placed.

Long story short, this tunnel was giving me the professional heebie-jeebies. The air was musty, but beyond the natural smells of earth and stone I caught a whiff of something fouler. Just a hint, then it was gone.

The other members of my ersatz monster hunting crew seemed to share the sense of danger as well. Cheng, dressed in fatigues, armor, and sporting a Chinese clone of an M4 carbine equipped with a bright weapon light, seemed calm but on alert. The four Chinese security contractors with him were decidedly out of their element. Three of them were equipped with weapons similar to Cheng's, and the fourth had a flamethrower with a backpack-mounted fuel tank.

Barb and I were kitted out, too. I'd had us both fitted for new purpose-designed monster hunting armor vests. They didn't provide the level of coverage that MHI's suits did, but were lighter, offered you better mobility, and most importantly, were a lot cheaper. They were made of a combination of flexible ballistic and stab-resistant materials, protecting you from claws, teeth, blades, and gunfire. In front and back were hard plates that would stop a .30-06 round, spears, knives, or just about anything else some unholy beastie might come at you with. Over the armor we wore load-bearing vests covered in magazine pouches, first aid stuff, you name it.

We had both brought our personal weapons with us. I scrounged up a few boxes of silver-cored .45 for Barb's 1911, and I had plenty of the MHI-issue .308 stashed away for my SR-762 rifle. Barb had some kind of high-end custom AR carbine. Both of our weapons were equipped with Aimpoints and bright lights. Our packs were both loaded with explosives, a mix of military-grade Semtex and good old-fashioned TNT, provided by our hosts. They had been a little hesitant to provide it, fearing we'd cause the mine to cave in or something, but I wanted every possible tool in my toolbox.

We were in a huge, semicircular main tunnel, reinforced with wood and steel and bathed in amber lighting. It was easily big enough to drive a five-ton truck down. We were probably almost a mile below the surface now, and the tunnel was still angling downward slightly. Down its center ran narrow-gauge railroad tracks, presumably to haul ore out to the lifts that made the long climb to the surface. The tunnel ended abruptly about fifty meters ahead of us. A truck-sized contraption on steel tracks was parked at the very end. As we came to a halt, the contractors fanned out to provide security from both directions of the tunnel.

"That is the borer," Cheng observed. "This is where they ceased operations on this tunnel. It was after those things were discovered."

"There's nothing here," Barb said.

"There wouldn't be," I pointed out. "I can almost guarantee they know we're here. They can hear us breathing and smell us a mile away. They wouldn't hang around in a well-lit area like this. They'll be waiting in some dark corner. Keep your eyes open, and don't forget to look up. Some tunnel-dwelling critters like to drop down on unsuspecting marks from above."

Barb nodded his understanding. "Where do we go from here?"

Cheng studied the screen of a tablet computer for a few moments. He looked up and pointed. "That way. There is a side tunnel, and an exploratory shaft, that extend off to our right for about a hundred meters. This tunnel ends where the miners found the cave system. They were attacked and fled."

"Just how many of these things are there?" Barb asked.

"We don't know," Cheng admitted.

"Super," I muttered. "Let's go then." I paused as I came to the mouth of the side tunnel. It was smaller, just big enough for three men to walk down abreast, but was pitch-black. "Cheng, what happened to the lights?"

"I don't know. The last report said that the lights were still..." He fell silent. "Did you hear that?" I had. It was a scratching sound, like claws on stone, coming from the darkened tunnel. Cheng, Barb and I brought our weapons up simultaneously, flooding the tunnel with bright white light.

There were three of them. They scuttled up the tunnel at us on all fours, but froze when the light hit them. Red eyes shined back at us. Their skin was gray and leathery. Black, matted, ropelike hair hung from their heads, accentuating their vaguely feminine features. Each had an unnaturally wide jaw, hanging open in a ghastly smile, filled with pointed teeth. Their hands and feet were tipped with long yellow claws.

Cheng swore in English, which I thought was odd. One of his security contractors screamed. I brought my rifle to my shoulder and opened fire on the closest one. Heavy, silver-cored .308 slugs tore through her. Black ichor splashed on the tunnel walls as she screeched a death rattle. Barb and Cheng opened fire an instant later, their smaller 5.56mm weapons adding to the head-rattling sound of gunfire in the tunnel. Barb fired upward; one of the Al had been crawling up the ceiling like some kind of enormous bug. It shrieked and dropped to the floor as it died. The last one was hit several times, but stood up on its legs and bolted into the darkness.

Just like that, it was over. Fifteen seconds, maybe, from contact to cease-fire. Echoes of gunfire rumbled throughout the tunnels for a moment longer; then it was quiet. My hearing was amplified by electronic earpro, but all I could hear was the ragged breathing of my teammates.

"Everyone okay?" I asked, removing the half-empty magazine from my rifle and placing it in my pocket. "Cheng, check your men. I think they crapped their pants." I slammed a fresh magazine home and turned to Barb. "You okay, bro?"

He was wide-eyed and still had his carbine pointed down the tunnel. His light, bobbing slightly with his breathing, was fixated on the two dead Al, and the trail of black blood the third had left as it retreated down the tunnel. "Y-yeah," he managed, looking at me a moment later. "That was intense."

I grinned. "Hell, yeah, we're in the shit now. Congrats, bro, you just got your monster hunting cherry popped." I turned to Cheng. "Your guys okay?"

He nodded in the affirmative. He had been berating Flame-thrower Guy, the one who screamed.

"Okay, tell 'em to move out. I want three pulling rear security, and Flamethrower Guy up here with me. Tell him if he sees anything moving ahead of us in the tunnel, burn the mother-fuckers. Don't hesitate, don't wait for me to tell him to fire, just burn 'em. Okay, follow me. We got us a trail, hopefully lead us back to their lair."

We proceeded down the side tunnel cautiously, lights illuminating the way. I had Barb snapping chemlights and leaving them on the floor, leaving a visible trail should we somehow get turned around or lose our lights. Using bright lights and fire easily gave our position away, but they were an advantage. Cave dwellers like the Al can see in the dark. Their eyes are so sensitive that our lights would blind them, hopefully get a deer-in-the-headlights reaction like we did before. Plus, almost all foul, unearthly things feared fire.

We were still descending as well. The exploratory shaft angled downward a few degrees. It was cold enough down there that our breath misted. The electric lights strung along the shaft had all been ripped down, probably by the Al. Up ahead, illuminated by very bright tactical lights, I could see the end of the tunnel, where it opened up into a natural cave system. As we approached, the air changed, becoming damper and fouler. We were definitely close. Somewhere, echoing off in the distance, the sounds of water running could be heard, or maybe felt through the stone. There was an underground river down here, somewhere, probably undiscovered by man until now.

The entrance to the cave was barely big enough for a man to pass through. There was another, smaller boring machine parked at the end, left where it had been abandoned. "All right," I said, turning to the team. "This is the perfect place for an ambush. Do you guys smell that? I think that's their lair."

"How do you wish to proceed?" Cheng asked.

"Do your men have grenades? Good. Tell them I want two frags tossed in, one right after the other. Then, I want Flame-thrower Guy to stick the muzzle of his Zippo in that hole and give a good long burn, sweeping side to side. As soon as he pulls back, crack open a couple flares and toss 'em in. Then I'm going in first. Barb, I want you right behind me. Cheng, you next. Take one of your guys. Leave the other two out here for rear security. Leave the dude with the flamethrower, he's bulky and might get hung up on the rocks in there." Cheng quickly relayed my instructions to his team as I took off my pack and set it down. "Everybody ready? Let's do this."

Cheng's men moved with precision. Two from the rear came forward, fragmentation grenades in hand. The first shouted what I'm assuming was Mandarin for "frag out" and tossed his grenade in. The second followed suit an instant later. We all turned away from the opening to the cave. *BOOM BOOM!* The double concussion of the blast rocked the tunnel, kicking up dust and causing dirt to fall from the ceiling. Even with hearing protection in place, it left the ears ringing just a little.

Flamethrower Guy didn't miss a beat. He stepped forward and, leaning downward a little, let off a long blast from his weapon into the cave. A high-pitched, unearthly shriek came from inside the cave, enough to chill a man to the bone. We'd gotten at least one of the damned things anyway.

"He says he burned one!" Cheng told me, as he tossed a couple of red flares into the cave entrance.

"Outstanding," I said, readying my weapon. "Let's do this. Barb, you come in right after me. Move, move, move!" You can't hesitate in a situation like this. Whatever things were still alive in there, hesitating only gave them time to regroup or retreat. If they crawled away into the cave system, we might never find them. I crouched down, weapon first, and jumped down into the cave. The entrance was a couple of feet above a damp stone floor.

It was quiet, save the snapping, crackling, and popping of the burning Al on the floor a few feet ahead of me. The stench, the smoke, the burning hair and flesh, the unnatural stink of unnatural things, it was enough to make even an experienced hunter gag. One other Al was dead on the floor, closer to the entrance, but as I swept the cave with my weapon light, those two were all that I could see.

Barb slid down into the cave a second later, taking up a position next to me. "Nice entrance, Leeroy Jenkins." He was followed by Cheng, who gagged at the stench.

The cave itself was big, probably fifty feet across. There were several other exits, leading off to God-knows-where under the earth. "This is definitely their lair," I said, studying the ground by fire, flare, and flashlight. "Look." There were mutilated corpses of both people and animals. Bones covered the floor, many of which looked gnawed upon. Some of the bodies were strung up, as if being saved for later.

"Did...did they make ropes out of their hair to hang the bodies with?" Barb said, a look of disbelief on his face.

"Looks like it."

"Where did they all go?" Cheng asked. "We can't have gotten them all." Two of his contractors had followed him in.

"No," I said, scanning the room, trying to shine my light into every nook, cranny, and tunnel entrance, "I don't suspect... we..." I panned my light up to the roof of the cave, some twenty feet above us. "Fuck me." *I forgot to look up.*

The rock of the ceiling was just as porous as the rest of the cave. There had to be a dozen of the things up there, big ones and small ones, looking down at us with shining red eyes and glinting white teeth. One was right above me, grasping the roof of the cave, her head turned all the way around like an owl. Black, ropey hair hung from her head. I raised my weapon just as she let go, and all hell broke loose.

The Al hit me like a hundred-pound sack of flour. I fell flat on my back from its weight, and the ghastly thing landed right on top of me. My rifle was pinned to my chest, between the Al's body and mine, and I couldn't bring it to bear. It took both hands to force her face away from my throat. Her jaw was nearly twice as wide as a human's and she snapped hungrily at me. The creature was spindly and effeminate, but was a hell of a long stronger than it looked. She tried to bite my face off. It took all of my strength to keep her at bay, and I was quickly tiring.

I couldn't tell what was going on around me as I struggled for my life, wrestling with the thrashing beast. Gunfire roared in the cave. A blast of fire from the flamethrower. Men screaming. Al shrieking. More gunfire, shouts in English and Chinese. A terrible clacking sound as the Al on top of me snapped its jaws like an alligator, its hot spittle dripping on my face.

At least I was wearing goggles. There was no way I was going to win this fight and I knew it. The thing was stronger than I was, and I was getting tired. The rest of my team was getting slaughtered all around me from the sounds of it, and there was no time to lay on the floor and get my face eaten! Grunting, gritting my teeth, I used all of my strength to push the thing away from me, my gloved hands up under its chin, until I could lock my elbow out. I dropped my left hand down to my side, finding the butt of my sidearm on my left hip. I pulled the revolver, a Ruger GP100, clear of its holster and stuck the end of its five-inch barrel under the Al's chin. *BOOM.* A contact shot from a full-power .357 round was enough to blow the Al's head open. Black ichor and brain matter splattered all over the cave and poured onto my face. It had the texture and smell of wet, sloppy swamp mud.

I sat up, spitting the foul ooze out of my mouth, and pushed the Al off of me. Lining up the revolver's glowing tritium sights, I put two rounds into an Al that was charging for me, dropping it. I swiveled to my right just in time to see Barb shoot the last one to the ground with his .45.

He ran over to me a moment later. "Holy shit, dude, are you all right?" He helped me to my feet. My load-bearing vest, goggles, and armor were all spattered with the black blood of the Al.

"I think so," I said, patting myself down. I turned on my headlamp and checked for blood. "No bites. What about you? Are you bit?"

"No," he said, eyes wide. "Why? Will...will I turn into one of them?"

"What? No. No, no, you just might get a nasty infection. Al don't multiply that way. We don't actually know how they multiply." I shook my head, remembering to focus. "Cheng? You all right, man? Who's left?"

Cheng stepped forward, out of the darkness, a moment later. He, too, was covered in black ichor. His hand was clutching a bleeding wound at his neck, but he seemed otherwise okay. "I'm here. I'm afraid I've lost two of my men."

Scanning the room, I saw them. Amongst the dead Al were two humans, Flamethrower Guy and one of the other security contractors, facedown in pools of blood. One of them had his arms ripped off, and it was all I could do not to vomit. My knees were shaking. "Well then," I managed, turning away. "Did we get them all?"

"No," Cheng said. "Some escaped through there." He pointed at one of the tunnel entrances at the far end of the cave. It was little more than a crack, barely wide enough for a person to slip through. I noticed then a slight breeze moving through the cave, toward the crack, and realized then that that was where the sound of water was coming from.

"I'm not about to chase these things all the way back to hell," I said, "but we can take a quick peek through there."

Once again, I was the first one through the breach. I found myself on a rocky precipice, overlooking an unbelievably huge cave. Shining my light around, it extended as far as I could see. It was so vast that I couldn't even guesstimate how big it was. It was too dark and there was no frame of reference. On the far floor, hundreds of feet below me and maybe a quarter mile away, there was a strange cluster of rocks, angular and cyclopean. They were the size of buildings... and looked unnatural. An unearthly glow, pale and blue, emitted from... something... in the center in the cluster of—it hit me then—*structures*. This was a city. And underground city! *My God...*

"What... what is it?" Barb asked, stepping up next to me. "Where is that light coming from?"

I shook my head slowly, in awe. The source of the light was obscured by the structures, some of which went all the way to the ceiling of the cave, hundreds of feet above me. The main cluster of them sat on the island in the middle of a great underground river. "It's a city, man. An ancient, subterranean city."

"That doesn't make sense," Barb said, the realization hitting him. "This far belowground, there's no way ancient people could have dug this deep."

"It wasn't built by people," I said. "It wasn't built by people at all. Hey, Cheng," I said, turning around. "What—" I fell silent. Cheng's two surviving security men had their M4 knock-offs pointed at Barb and me.

"I'm sorry, Mr. Cooper," Cheng said. His carbine was slung, but he had a pistol in hand. "I'm afraid you've just stumbled upon what will inevitably be declared a state secret. It's nothing personal, I hope you understand."

I glanced down at the cliff behind me. It was hard to tell in the dark, but the rocky outcropping seemed to jut out above the underground river. *Is this it?* I thought to myself. *Either get murdered or Butch and Sundance it off a cliff into a city of the Old Ones?* Not for the first time, I found myself questioning my career choices.

BLAM BLAM! Two shots rang out, startling me. My head snapped up in time to see Cheng's two men hit the floor, each having been shot in the head. Cheng stood over their bodies, Glock 19 in his hands and blood on his face. *Did he just shoot his own guys?* Barb and I leveled our weapons at him instantly. *A Mexican standoff between two Americans and a Chinese. Hilarious.*

"Just take it easy," Cheng said, raising his hands over his head. He didn't drop his gun. "I'm on your side."

"What the fuck is going on?" I asked, keeping my rifle trained on him.

"I'm with the CIA," he said calmly. "I'm also a liaison between the CIA and the MCB. Please, lower your weapons."

I didn't lower my rifle. "Why did you shoot those guys?"

"Because they were going to kill you, Mr. Cooper," he said, holstering his pistol. "Don't you get it? This is what they were looking for."

"This city?"

"Yes. There are reportedly rumors of it, found on tablets on the Plateau of Leng in Northwestern China. Look, we don't have much time. We need to get out of here. The Chinese have been looking for this for years."

"Why? What's down there? And why would they hire me if they're looking for a secret underground city?"

"The mining company doesn't know what they're looking for, either. They think it's just about ore. We don't have time for this! Will you please come on?"

"You're outgunned now, buddy," I said coldly. "Start talking."

"Without me, you'll never get out of here alive, Mr. Cooper," he said, turning his back to me. "Now come on. We have to use the explosives you brought to collapse the tunnel. Between that and the workers refusing to come back, it'll buy us time. Come with me or stay down here. Either way, I'm blowing the tunnel."

So that's the long and short of it. Using all the explosives we had, including some that Cheng had been carrying, we collapsed the cave entrance and, as near as I could tell, most of the exploratory tunnel. On the long lift ride back to the surface, Cheng warned us not to speak a word of this to anyone. He said it fell under the normal jurisdiction of the Monster Control Bureau regarding open discussion of the paranormal, and he warned that bad things would happen if we didn't keep our mouths shut. He confiscated our phones to prevent us from calling anyone before we got home. He wanted to make sure the CIA and the MCB had a monopoly on this particular bit on information for the time being.

What he didn't find was the Roshan network phone I'd bought in Kabul shortly after landing in-country. Network access across Afghanistan was spotty and international calling was costly, but the thing worked. I'd paid cash for it, so it wasn't linked to me in any way. The first thing I did, once I was able to get away from Cheng, was send Amber a text, telling her I'd lost my phone, but was otherwise okay. I hadn't heard from her since arriving in-country and wasn't sure why I was bothering, but I sent it anyway.

The next thing I did was dial a number from memory. It took a few seconds to connect. A woman answered the phone.

"MHI," she said simply.

It was Dorcas. "I need to speak with Earl Harbinger."

"Who is calling?"

"Cooper. I used to work for MHI."

"I see," she said, sounding bored. She always was an ornery old goat. "I'm going to have to take a message."

"Dorcas, you tell him that we found a city of the Old Ones buried under Afghanistan and the Chinese are about to find it and I need to talk to him right fucking now!"

She was clearly unimpressed. "One moment."

After a few seconds, a rough male voice came on the line. "Harbinger," he said simply. "Calling to beg for your job back, Cooper?"

"No. Listen, you need to know this before the CIA and MCB quash it. This could be huge." So I told him everything as quickly as I could. He asked very few questions, but I could tell he was writing things down.

"Good work, Cooper," he said after I'd finished. "You get out okay?"

"Yeah, my partner and I are safe. We've got a flight out in a couple of days. The CIA asshole was at least nice enough to see to it that I still got paid, so this wasn't all for nothing."

"Listen, kid. Get in touch with me when you get back to the States. There might be an opening in the Vegas office."

I told him I'd think it over and would be in touch, and thanked him. After hanging up, I noticed that I had a text from Amber.

I miss you, baby.

I miss you too, I texted back. *How are you?*

I've been thinking about a lot of stuff, she replied. *Please come home. We can work it out.*

I love you, I texted back hopefully.

Almost a minute went by before I got a reply. *I love you too. Come home.*

I'll be on my way home soon.

For most of us who end up in this life, it was because something horrible tried to eat us. But sometimes regular people have encounters with unearthly forces in unexpected ways.   —A.L.

A Knight of the Enchanted Forest

Jessica Day George

It turns out that if you blow up your school, they expel you. Even if no one was hurt. Even if it was only the science classrooms, not the whole school, like the newspaper claimed.

Even if you only did it because your biology teacher was a werewolf.

And it turns out that if you get expelled for blowing up your school, your father decides to quit his job to homeschool you. And if your father decides to quit his job to homeschool you, he is going to insist on doing it in the middle of nowhere, in order to get you away from the friends who led you astray and helped you blow up the school.

And it turns out that if your father quits his job to homeschool you in the middle of nowhere, you have to give up your nice house with the antique porch swing, and live in a trailer park in something called a double-wide.

It was like some terrible rejected sequel to *If You Give a Mouse a Cookie.*

"You're really going to love this place, Glad," her dad said. "I rolled the dice, and when they landed, I *freaked.* You're going to freak, too. I swear!"

Glad nodded, but she didn't say anything. She didn't "freak" about things nearly as much as her dad did, because her dad was

69

the world's youngest hippie, and she...wasn't. Glad's mom had been a hippie once, too, but when Glad was three, had shaved her legs, bought a suit, and become a real estate agent.

"*Mom* is gonna freak when she finds out where we're living," Glad muttered.

"I let the dice pick the park, even the unit we'll be renting," her dad went on. "The dice know." He rattled the medicine bag around his neck, which was filled with multisided dice from various roleplaying games.

That was how her dad decided everything. He would list his choices, number them, then reach into his medicine bag, pull out the first die his fingers found, and roll. That was how he'd become a sixth grade teacher, and why his hair had exactly twenty dreadlocks while his arms had exactly fourteen tattoos.

Apparently, it was also how they'd come to move into the—

"*Enchanted Forest?*" Glad said. "The Enchanted Forest Trailer Park?"

"See!" He pounded the steering wheel as they passed the sign.

At one point it had been painted in cheerful colors and redcap mushrooms with happy faces dancing below the name. But the paint had faded and the mushrooms looked leprous. There was kudzu growing all over the sign, and Glad sank lower in her seat.

"What happens if you give a mouse a magic mushroom?" she muttered.

"Could anything be more perfect?" her dad enthused. "Just look at all the gnomes!"

Glad scooted back up and peered out over the top of the door. It was true: there were a *lot* of lawn gnomes. She had always imagined trailer parks being decorated with plastic flamingos, but the patches of weeds and debris around the broken-down trailers all had gnomes half hidden in the overgrowth or peeping from behind piles of junk and broken-down cars.

She wasn't sure how that made anything perfect, though. Her dad thought the pointy-hatted lawn ornaments were hilarious, but she'd always thought they were super creepy. They were so *smug*, and their eyes followed you as you walked by. The sunlight glinted on a particularly horrible-looking one that had been made to look like a rapper, with black clothes and a bunch of gold chains. As they drove past, Glad could have sworn that the gnome winked at her, but when she looked back, it had sunglasses.

"I really hate this," she said.

Glad felt sick. The place looked like a junkyard—an abandoned junkyard. They hadn't seen a living soul. The gnomes were laughing at her. Everything was horrible.

Her dad's face crumpled. He steered the station wagon carefully to the side of the road, put it in park, and turned off the Volvo engine, which coughed a little as it always did when it stopped.

"I know you do," he said. He kneaded his medicine bag. "But I didn't know what else to do." He looked at her. "I'm trying . . . but I need you to try, too."

"Dad," she said. "I'm sorry."

"I know."

"But he really is a werewolf!"

"Oh, Glad," her father sighed. "I know you love Harry Potter, but—"

"Let's not point fingers about loving fantasy books too much," she retorted. "I'm just lucky I'm not a boy. Frodo is a horrible name."

She sucked in air and let it whoosh back out. She'd laid out her case for her father carefully and methodically. Glad knew what she'd seen: Mr. Stinson *was* a werewolf.

But no one believed her.

The moon had been very full and bright, and all the parking lot lights had been on as well as she came out of band practice. The thing, which was not a wolf or a bear but looked like something in between, had bounded across the asphalt and jumped right on top of Mr. Stinson's Toyota. It threw back its head and howled, and she could clearly see the tie around its neck, shaped like a trout. Mr. Stinson loved that tie, and he wore it every Thursday. Glad had shrunk back into the shadows, one hand pressed over her mouth so that she wouldn't scream. It had sniffed the air, and she'd been sure she was a goner, but a dog had howled across the street and the werewolf had set off in pursuit.

Glad had run all the way home to sob out the story to her dad, but he'd just made her drink some nasty tea and go to bed. The next day Hadleigh Jaffetts had been in tears, talking about how a wild animal had eaten her beloved husky Nanook. Hadleigh had been too distraught to play her flute and had gone home from band practice early. It had come out that other kids had missing or dead pets: two cats and a dog (besides Nanook) had gone missing the night before. The last batch had been a month ago.

When the next full moon brought another rash of pet deaths, Glad decided it was time to take action. She didn't know where to get silver bullets, or a gun, or how to shoot a gun anyway, and she wasn't sure she could actually kill someone, even a werewolf. But a childhood spent playing Mousetrap with her grandmother had taught her a great deal.

She just hadn't known that her school was so...flammable.

Which brought her here, to the Enchanted Forest. And a rundown double-wide that at least didn't have any gnomes standing around its square of dusty grass. It also didn't have curtains.

Glad stood and stared at it in despair while her dad unlocked the front door and started to carry their things inside. He didn't talk, just let her have her space, which was one of the things that she liked about living with her dad. Her mom would have made her state her feelings out loud so that she could "clear her mind and move on," which would mean helping to unpack.

Glad sighed and got her suitcase.

Everything inside the trailer was rectangular. Glad had never before realized how many shapes there were in a normal house. Every countertop, room, cupboard door, and window here was a rectangle. And it was all...

"Poop brown," she said. "Everything here is feces-colored."

"Don't worry! We'll add color," her father said, walking past her with a box.

"No, Dad, no!" Glad ran after him. "You didn't!"

But he had. She could see them. Random pieces of cloth were hanging out of the top of the box. She wished she'd seen the box earlier. She could have dumped it out on the freeway.

"It will brighten this place right up!"

Her dad dropped the box in the middle of the floor and began taking out lengths of tie-dyed fabric. He happily pinned them over the windows with the thumbtacks he found already stuck in the fake wood paneling.

"Daaaaaad," Glad moaned. "All the local stoners are going to come here looking for pot. And hookahs! And shiny crystals to stare at while they smoke hookahs!"

"Y'all got them hookahs and things?" said a voice with great interest.

There was a grungy-looking guy in a stained wifebeater and a feed store cap standing in their new doorway. He scratched his stomach and grinned at Glad.

"No, we do not," she said firmly.

"That's okay," he said.

"I'm Winston," Glad's dad said, rushing forward to shake the man's hand. "Your new neighbor! And this is my daughter—"

"Glad," she interrupted. "My name is Glad."

"Glad like the plastic wrap?" the man asked.

"Yes," she said.

"And Winston like that round-faced feller in England?"

"Like Winston Churchill, yes," Glad's dad said.

"I liked him," their neighbor grunted. "I'm Elmo."

"Like the Muppet?" Glad blurted out.

Her dad nudged her with his elbow, but she didn't care. Elmo had just compared her to sandwich wrap.

"Yeh," Elmo said. "Somethin' like that. Muppet. Yeh." He snorted.

"So . . ." Glad's dad said. "Would you like to help me unload the U-Haul?"

"Oh, no," Elmo said. "I just came to see if you was all right."

"Yes, we're great," Glad's dad said. "Thanks for checking on us."

"I wasn't checking on you," Elmo said, and his good-natured manner dropped away. "I was *checking* on you." He leveled a stare at Glad's dad and then at Glad herself. "We don't want no trouble here. This is the Enchanted Forest and we like things nice."

"We're very nice," Glad's dad said, holding up his hands.

"But *you're* an asshole," Glad said. "Get out of our trailer!"

"*Galadriel*," her father said, still with his hands up.

"Nah, I respect that," Elmo said, holding up his own hands. "Y'all have fun movin' in." He walked out of the trailer.

"How is this better than home?" Glad demanded.

"I cannot believe you just called our new neighbor an asshole," her father said. "This just proves that we need to get you away from the influences back home."

"You mean *Gran*?" Glad demanded. "The only person I hung around with, aside from other band geeks, was *your mother*. And all we did was watch *Wheel of Fortune* and eat Oreos."

"Exactly," her dad said. "TV and processed sugar! It's no wonder you hallucinated werewolves."

"I wasn't...Never mind."

No one would ever believe her. Even Gran had just patted her hand and told her the full moon made everything seem strange. Hearing this from her grandmother had been the worst part of the whole ordeal. Gran had always been her confidante, her supporter. And even she thought Glad was just seeing things.

Glad *had* been seeing things. She'd been seeing her pervy, mouth-breathing science teacher turn into a werewolf. And then eat the pets of the students he didn't like.

And no one believed her.

Glad and her father unpacked the U-Haul in silence.

They spent the next few days setting up house. It didn't take long. Most of their stuff was books, and her father had given away their TV and any other electronics. He'd let Glad keep her phone, but only so she could text Mom. He'd deleted her apps, except for Cupcake Mania. She was on level 239, and Winston respected her accomplishment.

Any time Glad stopped moving—stopped shelving books, stopped tacking up a plain purple sheet for a curtain in her own room—her dad was there, suggesting something else she could do. The curriculum that he'd ordered hadn't arrived yet, and he seemed to think that if she wasn't learning or cleaning or flattening boxes, she'd blow something up.

But finally, on the third day, when they'd completely run out of trail mix and granola and apples, her dad had to go to the grocery store and run some other errands. He looked like he was going to make Glad come with him, but then it seemed to dawn on him that she needed to be left alone, and he probably did as well. So he told her to stay out of trouble and left.

And she'd tried to stay out of trouble. She'd alphabetized all her books. Then the spices in the kitchen, which just made her hungry. Then she'd taken some boxes outside for the recycling and had a look around while she was there.

There was a gnome on their square of dirty grass.

It was the ghetto one with the chains and glasses. Glad stared at it for a long time. She looked around, but no one else was around, and she didn't know who could have put it there. Or why.

Maybe it was a gift. Maybe it was some sort of stalkery message. Either way, she wanted it gone.

She picked up the gnome, which was surprisingly heavy, and...

warm. And squishy. Glad had meant to hide it in the weeds by the side of the trailer just behind theirs, but it was so creepy that she sort of threw it instead. It rolled, arms and legs flopping, and disappeared under the rickety porch of the neighboring trailer.

Glad let out a little scream, which failed to cover the profanity that came from the gnome itself. Glad ran to the other trailer and peered underneath, but she couldn't see anything.

Panting and sweaty, Glad leaned against the wall of the trailer. Her stomach growled. Clearly that was the reason why she'd thought the gnome was alive. She was hungry, it was hot and muggy, she was in a strange new place. Yes. That was why.

The windows of the trailer were open, and the TV was on. The unmistakable sounds of *Wheel of Fortune* came wafting through the screen. Someone was about to buy a vowel.

"Idiot," Glad muttered. "If you have to buy a vowel, you're jacked."

"Who there?" A woman demanded.

Glad ducked to run back to her own trailer, but she tripped over some debris in the weeds and landed on her face. The screen door slammed behind her, and there was a flapping sound. A pair of puffy ankles in bunny slippers walked into her line of view.

"Whatchu doin'?" The woman had a raspy smoker's voice.

"Um, nothing?" Glad turned over and looked up.

The completely round woman standing over her was wearing a flowered muumuu. She had dirty blond hair wound up in pink curlers and a suspicious look in her blue eyes.

"I don't *like* them gnomes," she said. "I seen yew with one." Her voice and eyes were accusatory.

"I don't like them either," Glad protested. "Someone put it in our yard, but I thought it was yours."

Glad staggered to her feet, trying to dust off her jeans. The round woman was very short, though she was nearly as wide as she was tall. She was holding a Zinger in one hand. Glad's mouth watered.

"I love those raspberry coconut ones," Glad said.

The woman put half of it in her mouth. She chewed slowly while Glad watched, the dry granola in her stomach feeling like a wad of dust and hair.

"Yew watchin' *Wheel* through my window?" the woman said, swallowing.

"I wasn't... trying to," Glad said.

"I thought yew was some kina hippy dippy didn't like TV," the woman said, eating the rest of the Zinger.

"My dad is," Glad said. "I...I just...I like to watch game shows with my grandma, but she lives in Indiana."

And to her embarrassment, Glad burst into tears. The fat woman drew back slightly, then she pushed out her lower lip. She had beautiful, bright blue eyes almost hidden in folds of fat, and they filled with sympathetic tears as she patted Glad on the back.

Glad wiped her nose on her wrist. "I'm sorry," she said.

"Yew wanna come in and watch *Wheel* and have a snack?"

"Yes!" Glad almost shouted. "Please, I mean."

"Ah got more Zingers," the woman said, leading the way into the trailer. "An' I'ma order some pizzas in a minute here. Yew like ranch with pizza? For dipping?" The woman paused on her way across the broken-down porch. Clearly this was an important question.

"Yes," Glad said, fervently and honestly. "Pepperoni pizza and ranch dressing is the food of the gods."

"Atta girl," the woman said.

They passed a couch that smelled like pee and dogs, and a recliner that was the exact orange of the one Glad's gran favored. Glad touched the arm of it as they passed to go into the trailer, and her fingertips tingled. She hoped that didn't mean she'd gotten fleas. Gran's recliner was a sight cleaner than this one.

Inside the trailer wasn't a whole lot better. Still, it was more messy than dirty, Glad noticed with relief. Glad moved some magazines over and sat on the green couch. It was very soft and smelled like French fries and faintly of cigarettes, which also reminded her of Gran.

"Watchu called?" the woman asked.

"Glad."

"You can call me Yer Majesty the Queen," the woman grunted and settled into a recliner.

She snapped her fingers at a box of Zingers. Glad jumped up, got herself one, and then when the fat fingers kept snapping, she handed one to the woman as well. There was a lidless cooler full of sodas and beer next to the Zingers. Her Majesty snapped her fingers and Glad got her a Bud Light, taking a grape soda for herself. Glad settled back on the couch with her treats, feeling more relaxed than she had since the school incident.

"*Wheel*'s over," Her Majesty said. "But *Jeopardy*'s on!"

"Do you—do you mind if I yell out the answers?" Glad asked tentatively.

"Yew go for it, gal," the woman told her.

For the next half hour, Glad ate junk food and drank soda and shouted out the answers, or questions, rather. The contestants were particularly dumb in this episode, and Glad was right more often than they were. Her Majesty laughed in delight whenever Glad beat them.

The pizza man arrived with her father.

"Glad!" Her father pushed past the pimply boy holding his armload of pizzas. "Where have you been?"

"Right here," Glad said, leaping up. She looked down helplessly at the wrappers and cans she'd accumulated.

"Yew the hippie next door?" The woman gave Glad's dad the once-over.

Then she waved an imperious hand at the pizza boy, and he put the pizzas down and left. Glad wondered if she had an account with Domino's or something because she hadn't paid. He bowed as he backed out of the trailer.

"I'm so sorry that my daughter has been bothering you," Glad's dad said. "It won't happen again."

"Shoot, she ain't botherin' me," the woman said. "Whyn't y'all sit down an eat?" She pointed to the fridge. "Get the ranch, hon," she told Glad.

"Thanks, but we have to get home." He grabbed Glad's arm and hustled her out of the trailer.

"Yew can come tomorrow for *Wheel*," the woman called after them.

"Thanks," Glad called over her shoulder. "I will."

Her dad jerked her along into their trailer. There was another, more normal-looking gnome on their square of dead grass. Glad tried to give it a kick, but it shimmered like a mirage and was out of range of her sneaker. She shrieked.

"Don't," her dad said, still dragging her along.

"What did *I* do?" she demanded when they got into the trailer.

"I came home, and you weren't here," her dad said. He was rubbing his medicine bag, clattering the dice inside.

"I took some boxes to the recycling pile, and the queen invited me in."

"Who?"

"Our neighbor," Glad explained. "She said to call her Her Majesty the Queen."

"The queen of what?" her dad muttered.

"The queen of the Enchanted Forest," Glad shot back. "Isn't that great? There's a queen for our new, fancy, enchanted forest!"

"Now, Glad, calm down," her dad said. "I know that this isn't ideal. In fact, I think the dice may have been wrong about this one." He looked so mournful that Glad bit back her snarky response. "That's why I was in town so long. I was talking to Mom, looking into some other places. We don't have a lot of money, but it's not *that* bad."

He pointed outside the window. One of the tie-dyed curtains was pinned back, and it gave them a nice view of at least six rusted heaps on cinder blocks that used to be cars. Possibly. And an absolute shitload of gnomes.

"What is *with* the gnomes?" Glad said, distracted. "I swear, there are like, fifty more since we moved in. One of them was on our lawn. That's how I met the queen."

"Glad, are you listening to me?" her dad demanded. "Your mom is looking for something else for us. A realtor friend said that there's a wild space called Natchy Bottom—"

Glad snickered, but she didn't take her eyes off the gnomes across the way. She was almost certain one of them was looking back at her. It had binoculars.

"*Natchy Bottom*," her dad said, in full teacher mode, "is a hotbed of urban legends, but very disturbing ones. Disappearances, violence, it's most likely a hiding place for some sort of drug ring."

"And it's right outside the Enchanted Forest?" she asked, dragging her attention away from the gnome, which hadn't moved.

Because lawn gnomes did not move. They were not squishy and warm, and they did. Not. Move.

"Yes," her dad said. "So, let's pull those boxes out of the recycling, and just stack them over there." He pointed to the corner of the room where any normal person would put a TV. "I don't want to pack again just yet—we need to start on your lessons—but as soon as your mom can find something, we will."

"But I *like* the queen," Glad said.

"You like being given processed sugar and watching TV," her dad said with a frown.

"Whatever happened to peace and brotherly love?" she said. "And trust? And treating me like an equal?"

"That ended when you almost killed someone."

Glad went to her room. She had nothing else to say to that. Her dad knew her arguments, and she knew his.

But they didn't reckon on the queen.

Glad started lessons with her dad, where they found that if they stuck to the curriculum he'd ordered, they didn't argue. After school hours, Glad was supposed to practice her clarinet and then use a YouTube tutorial to learn to knit, which the curriculum said promoted concentration and small motor skills.

But promptly each day at five P.M., Elmo knocked on their door and asked if Glad could visit the queen. It turned out that he worked for her or was some kind of relative. He'd seemed shocked at the very idea that he was her son, which Glad's dad had first asked.

"That would be presumptin'," he'd said. "But she done take a fancy to your gal, and she wants her to come watch her shows."

"I could take my knitting," Glad had said, holding up the mess of wool and bamboo needles.

"Her Majesty useta crotchit," Elmo said. "Mebbe she could teach ya."

"Crochet is good for your hands, too," Glad had said hopefully.

But her dad had said no, and shut the door on Elmo's surprised face. But the mulleted hick would not be deterred, and so he appeared the next day, and the next. Then a woman with a massive ball of heavily backcombed and sprayed hair, wearing extremely tight jeans and an extremely cropped top had come by. She'd dropped off cookies and said it was a real shame that Glad couldn't visit that nice lady next door.

"Yew prolly remind her of her girl, Tanya," the woman said. "She done run off with some hunters."

"Oh." Glad said, blinking at this.

"I'm so sorry," her dad said stiffly, holding the plate of cookies as though they were a bomb. The plate looked none too clean, but Glad had to admit that the cookies smelled amazing.

"She'll come home one a these years," the woman said comfortably. "Tanya were wild, but she done knew her place." She nodded as though that meant something. "Her Majesty like to have a gal around, remind her a Tanya. She weren't black or nuthin', but she had that sassy look yew do," she told Glad.

"I'm biracial," Glad said. "My mom is white."

"Good for her," the woman said, oblivious to any insult. "Anywhoo, it ain't nice to tell the queen 'no.'" And she left.

"This is freaking me out," Glad said. "Slightly."

"Me too," her dad admitted. "I'm gunna—going to—call your mother and see if she's found anything."

Glad went back to her knitting, but she kept lifting the corner of the curtain behind the couch to peer at the queen's trailer. There were a couple of old dogs sleeping on the couch on the porch, but other than that, nothing was moving.

Nope. The gnomes. The gnomes were moving.

There hadn't been gnomes there the last time she'd looked, and now there were three. One of the dogs kept lifting its head and growling.

"Dad," Glad called.

"Shh, honey, just a minute," he said, holding the phone away from his mouth. He plugged his other ear. "Uh-huh, Uh-huh . . . right this minute?"

"Dad!"

"Glad, I'm on the phone!"

But then he ended the call and grabbed his wallet and keys. "Come on," he said. "There's an apartment in town in our price range, but someone else is looking at it, so we need to go right now."

"Dad, the queen really hates gnomes, and there's a bunch in her yard," Glad said, putting on her shoes. "We should move them."

"Glad, we don't have time to do that," her father said. "This thing with the gnomes is even more reason to move!"

"Because they're freaky?"

"Because *you're* freaking out about them," her dad said.

But as they stepped down off the porch, even he paused. It was hard to deny that there was something going on. There were dozens of gnomes around every trailer. Three stood between Glad and her dad and their car.

"It's probably just a practical joke," her dad said in a whisper.

"Who would do this?" Glad demanded. "I'm the only kid living here! And the queen hates them: so who would risk her wrath by doing this?"

"I don't know, but we definitely need to get that apartment," her dad said. "Come on."

"No," Glad said, to her surprise and her father's. "I'm going to get our boxes and get rid of them." Her voice came out very shrill. "I want them to go away."

"Well, maybe later—" he began.

Elmo came slamming out of another trailer, saw the gnomes, swore, and ran for the queen's trailer. Glad bolted past her father after him. When she was through the screen door, she turned and made a shooing motion at her dad. He sighed, but got into the station wagon and left. Apparently his need to get them into a decent apartment was greater than his need to keep Glad from collecting gnomes and probably bingeing on Twinkies while she did it.

When she turned around, she saw Elmo and the queen staring at her. The man was goggling, but the queen was giving her a narrow-eyed look, sizing her up.

"What the *hell* is with all the gnomes?" Glad demanded.

"Yew just run on home, girlie," Elmo said. "I got this."

"No," Glad said. "They're *watching* me, and I don't like it!"

"That's some imagina—" he began, but the queen cut him off with a gesture.

"What if I tole you them things is alive?" she said.

"I would totally, one hundred percent believe you," Glad told her. "Why?"

"Because my teacher was a werewolf, and no one believed *me*," Glad told the fat woman. She hesitated. "And I can't stop thinking about the one I tried to put in your yard," she admitted finally. "It was *alive*," she finished in a whisper.

"Them gnomes been gunnin' for my land," the queen said. "Since they hear I'm on gubmint pay and ain't doin' magic no more."

"It ain't them B'ham gnomes," Elmo said. "That's a mercy. These're fresh off the boat, lookin' for turf. I'ma handle it fine mah ownself."

"Um, what?" That did take Glad a minute.

"I hurt ma back," the queen went on, ignoring Elmo to speak directly to Glad. "The gubmint done put me on the disability, but I cain't do no more spells." She said this all slowly, as though it would make more sense that way. "Them gnomes tryna take over."

"So the gnomes *are* alive?" Glad said, just to make sure they were on the same page.

"Yep."

"And you ... used to do magic?"

"Still do," the queen said, lowering her voice. "Just to keep mah hand in. Just don't tell the gubmint."

Glad locked her lips and threw away the key, but she still looked at Elmo for an explanation.

"This here's Queen Ilrondelia of the Elves," he said with pride. "I know yew wasn't proper innerduced."

It was then that Glad's brain registered what her eyes had been seeing since day one: the ears. The queen's hair was always wound around pink curlers, which made it hard to miss her ears, which were very, very pointed. So were Elmo's. In fact, they stuck up on each side of his trucker hat, like goal posts.

"Oh. My." Glad breathed in and out loudly. "You're *elves*."

"That's what we been sayin'," the queen said. "Now, Elmo here's ma best diviner, what with Tanya gone off with the Hunters."

Elmo rolled his eyes.

"Too many of the young'uns done up and left the Enchanted Forest," the queen said mournfully. "So it were real nice of y'all to move in and sit with a lonely young queen like myself." She sat up in her recliner, and suddenly, even without the ears, Glad could see that this was no ordinary woman. The curlers might as well have been a crown. "Now. Yew gunna help?"

"Yes, Your Majesty," Glad said. "I know just what to do." She looked at Elmo. "Have you ever played the board game Mousetrap?"

Elmo's eyes gleamed. "Sure have."

"We're going to need a lot of boxes, rope, and sticks," she said. Then she looked at the queen. "Your Majesty? Do you have . . . could you do a spell that would make us invisible?"

The queen threw back her head and laughed. "I like yew, I knew I did!"

Elmo and Glad got to work. They weren't invisible, but thanks to the queen, the eyes of the gnomes slid right past them, giving them time to set traps.

They were stupid, really: boxes propped up with sticks, with a twine tripwire to drop the whole thing. Glad had gotten an A on her assignment to build a better mousetrap in sophomore science, so really, Mr. Stinson had no one to blame but himself for what had happened.

Of course, stealing her band teacher's keys so that she could sneak into the school and set the trap for Mr. Stinson had been a criminal act. And the box she'd rigged to trap him catching fire on a Bunsen burner and torching the science wing had been impossible to predict.

"What do the gnomes want?" Glad asked. "Beside the Enchanted Forest, I mean?"

"Beer," Elmo said with a shrug. "Cigarettes. Same as us."

Glad was slightly taken aback. She was having a hard time, as they strung wires and propped up boxes around the oblivious gnomes, with reconciling the elves of the *Lord of the Rings* movies with the actuality around her. She was willing to accept that they were real, that the gnomes were alive, that her teacher was a werewolf... but still... They wanted beer and cigarettes?

"Ooookay," Glad said. "Well, we're going to need some. For bait."

"Done and done," Elmo told her.

They baited the traps with beer, cigarettes, and cookies. It turned out that the woman with the big pouf of hair was also an elf named Lara. She provided cookies. And skepticism.

"Ain't they gunna know we's tryna get rid of 'em?" she asked as she put another plate of cookies next to a pack of cigarettes and then backed out from under the hanging laundry basket. "They ain't that dumb."

"These are *tomte*, right?" Glad asked.

Elmo nodded.

"Well, then, they should go for it," she said. "My dad's been teaching me all about European folktales. The *tomte* guarded farms, but only if you laid out food for them. They'll see this and think that it's their just desserts. Literally. In fact, they'll probably be excited. If Neil Gaiman can be believed—and if he can't, what's the world coming to?—then they were brought to this country by believers from Europe, and then abandoned."

Lara just looked blank, but Elmo nodded.

"These're pure Norroway *tomte*," he said to the woman. "They'll think they done gone to Valhalla. Not like them city gnomes." He slapped Glad on the back and nearly sent her face first into a pile of cookies laid over a noose.

With everything in place, they went back to the queen's trailer and she took the spell off them. She looked pale and sweaty from the effort, and Elmo called for pizzas while Glad got Her Majesty a cold Coke and some Ho Hos.

A few minutes later, there was an almighty clatter and the sound of profanity. Glad grinned.

"Well, ain't yew just my bright gal," the queen said, and gave her a Ho Ho.

A battered Volvo station wagon pulled up in front of the MHI headquarters. Two people got out, seemingly oblivious to the weapons that had just been pointed at them. There was a guy in his early forties with graying dreadlocks and a teenage girl with a crinkly cloud of dark hair and gray eyes. She waved cheerfully at the gates as the man opened the back of the station wagon and began unloading cardboard boxes with holes punched in them.

"What the hell are you people doing?" Owen demanded, jogging over.

"Z, I'll take this," Holly said, putting a hand on her arm. "Honey," she said to the girl, "who are you and what is this?"

"Oh, hi!" The girl stuck out her hand and Holly shook it, bemused. "This is my dad, Winston, and I'm Glad." She kicked one of the boxes, and a stream of profanity issued from the holes. "And these are the gnomes that just tried to invade our turf."

More profanity while Owen stared at the dozen or so boxes that the guy was still pulling out of the Volvo.

"The queen told us to leave them with you," the girl said. "She's pretty pissed. If you have any more questions, though, you'll have to come to the Enchanted Forest.

"You can ask for Sir Galadriel, the Knight Protector of the Enchanted Forest." The girl beamed. "That's me."

The British Supernatural Service is as tight-lipped as our MCB, so this one is difficult to verify, but during the Cold War years we know they messed around with a lot of unearthly forces. That always comes back to bite you eventually.   —A.L.

The Manticore Sanction

John C. Wright

When Her Majesty's government decreed that he must murder his fiancée before New Year's, Madhouse Harry thought it only reasonable.

Sir Henry "Madhouse" Adrian Scrope, 24th Lord Scrope of Wormsley Hall, had served the Crown loyally for thirty years in hidden wars against unearthly horrors. MI4 was Manticore—Metahuman, Abnormal, or NonTerrestrial Invasive Cryptozoological Organism Research and Extermination—and it did not officially exist. In Serbia, he had lost his right arm, not to mention the Enfield revolver his grandfather had carried in the Boer War, in the teeth of a creature that also did not officially exist: an invulnerable lioness the size of a lorry. He still missed that piece.

Scrope knew the risks. The girl he loved did not; she must never know. It was for that reason he intended never to carry through with the engagement. He had spent fifteen minutes, no longer, raging and refusing. Less than that would have seemed suspicious.

His partner, William Fox, now stood next to him in the lift. Both wore sunglasses and overcoats. There the similarity ended. Fox had fifty pounds more muscle than Scrope, was five inches taller and five years younger. And he had both hands.

One of those hands was in his overcoat pocket, holding the pistol that would put a bullet through Scrope's back at the first sign of hesitation.

As they were passing the tenth floor, Fox drew out Scrope's Webley-Fosbery and passed it to him.

"MI18 delivered the cartridge," he said. "Only one shot. The target is drugged. Just put the barrel to her head."

MI18 was Special Weapons. They did not design silver hollowpoint Teflon bullets filled with holy water, or their other contrivances, just to kill normal humans.

Scrope held up the pistol and worked the action lever awkwardly with his one hand. The cylinder-barrel section broke and tilted forward, exposing the chamber. He proffered it to his partner. "You mind?"

"Not at all," said Fox.

Fox took a single cartridge out of a cedar box incised with Viking runes; it was a coppery-greenish segmented shape more like a stubby worm than like a bullet.

"Hard business, this," muttered Fox.

It was a sign of weakness.

"It's the business we are in," said Scrope calmly, putting his hand casually in his overcoat pocket. "No hard feelings. We can go for drinks after."

There were three things hidden inside his coat pocket lining. The first was his cellphone.

The second was a Luftwaffe-designed, out-the-front gravity knife, meant for paratroopers to cut tangled chute shrouds one-handed.

The third trembled when he touched it. It was a flat disk of stone with the hole in the center, small as a Chinese coin.

Fox did not look up from loading the pistol. The green bullet seemed to be slippery. "The Spaniard's? She deserves a proper wake. Nice girl."

Without taking his hand from his pocket, Scrope flipped open his phone and pushed the speed-dial for his partner. The phone in Bill's pocket rang.

A second sign of weakness. Procedure was to turn off all electronics during a mission. But, no doubt, Fox was hoping for a last-minute reprieve.

One cannot hold pistol, bullet, and cellphone and still block a blow. Scrope flicked the blade of the paratrooper knife open with the same semicircular motion that caught Fox right under the chin.

Dimly through the walls, he heard church bells ringing, fireworks igniting, automobiles honking horns, the roaring of countless people crowing and cheering the New Year. It drowned the gargling, whistling shriek William Fox made as he died.

The hour had struck. The witching hour. Scrope knelt, drew out the small black stone and placed it in the mouth of the corpse. The forbidden words were few and terrible and burned his throat.

The dead eyes flicked open. "I see before me the mortal man who, sixty-five full moons ago, spared me, when he was ordered to see me slain. Ask of me what I shall give you."

In the gloom of the vault, Scrope lurched as rapidly as he could, shoulders tilted, lugging the huge weight now hanging from his right stump.

He had two holsters, one under each armpit. His Webley, with its single green bullet, was strapped under his right. Fox's piece was a beautiful Heckler & Koch VP70 with an eighteen-round clip. It was a double action semiautomatic able to fire a three-round burst. That was under his left. Fox also had owned a fountain pen that contained an injector. The needle capsules were white and black. Black was a thiocyanate compound, for humans. White contained holy water, for vampires. That was in Scrope's coat pocket. The paratrooper knife and small round stone were in his pants pockets.

These dark vaults were the national gold reserve of the City of London. Behind each barred cell door rose empty rack upon empty rack. The gold long ago had been spent, and MI4 now used the facility to store unsafe anomalies. The financial world would collapse if rumor of this leaked out. One more secret kept from the public for their sake.

The cell nearest the main vault door held no empty shelves. Nor was there any cot, sink, chamberpot. Not even a magazine to read.

Standing motionless in its center, beneath one small pale bulb, was a dark man in a fez. His tunic was ochre, and his sash was white. On the second finger of his right hand was a ring with an onyx stone adorned with the image of a scarab.

The dark man was six and a half feet tall. Half circles of fatigue and grief were scars beneath his eyes. His nose was a hook. His mouth was a sardonic slash, like a knife cut in the trunk of an oak stump. And every inch of face was wrinkled and sunken, as if his flesh were parchment a thousand years old that had been crushed and crumpled, and left in the desert to desiccate.

He stood with his hands folded over his breast, unbreathing, unmoving. The eyes were open, staring. So dark were the pits beneath those lowering brows that the whites of his eyes seemed to glow.

"Well, Lord Scrope," said the mordant voice, which hummed like a pipe organ in a cavern. "To what do I owe the honor? You know that I one day will escape this place and find your heirs, no matter how remote the generations, and kill them all. I don't expect these bars to rust and walls to rot within your lifetime. But one must be patient about these things."

Scrope spat quickly: "Ardeth Bey, Agnes Grosvenor will die unless we save her. If I free you, will you help me?"

Very slowly Imhotep raised one eyebrow. "Most interesting. Of course I agree. Until she is safe from harm, you are safe from me."

Scrope reached for the barred door, and then paused.

Imhotep did not laugh, but a slight darkening of the shadows around his eyes communicated his amusement. "You hesitate? You wonder that I am so swift to agree? Look upon yourself. The blood still wet upon your coat cries out for vengeance. You have betrayed one of your own. The limb of silver is an *ushabti*, an animate thing, crafted brilliantly, affixed clumsily. I have seen wax crocodiles made thus, or servants, but never an arm, never of so noble a metal. That you wear that stain of blood and this unliving arm speaks loudly enough."

Scrope looked down at the silver hand. In the dim light, the fingers and thumb looked perfectly made, with wrinkles at the joints, tiny black hairs on the back of the hand, and indentations of tendons and veins. The arm was solid metal and weighed at least sixty pounds. The mass was immense, making his whole body crooked.

He had never stopped regretting. Even years later, some new thing would reopen the sorrow: seeing a child twiddling his thumbs or learning how to tie his shoelaces, or glimpsing an old woman knitting, or watching an old man wind a pocket watch, or hearing people applauding a pianist—

Imhotep said, "Also I know the name of the prince of the midnight air who cleared his debt to you by bearing you here swiftly, and who adhered to you that silver arm. The hand has power over things of iron or metals mortals mine. Break the door! In a circle about my feet are the sacred words written from the *Book of Going Forth by Day*. Scuff them out."

"And you don't care to know what her danger is?"

The ancient voice was sardonic. "I slew nine acolytes who guarded the Sacred Scrolls of Thoth, printed in gold, and read the words it was forbidden men should read; and I loved a Pharaoh's sacred daughter—a virgin consecrated to Isis it was forbidden I should love—both treason and blasphemy at once. Whom would I fear?"

"I want it understood, one gentleman to another. As soon as she is safe, the truce is over."

"I quite understand. You alone, Lord Scrope, robbed me of the love and life I waited four thousand years to consummate. You will not outlive the dawn." Imhotep smiled an odd smile, his eyes half open. "The spirit in you yearns to boast that you can prevent me; but if I believed you, our alliance is stillborn. I do not. Ankhese-namon sleeps: Agnes is but her dream; Death, her waking."

"You don't want my word?"

Imhotep's eyes glittered like the eyes of a snake. "You have also killed your acolytes and betrayed your Pharaoh, have you not? By what name would you swear?"

Scrope had no answer. For the first time, he realized that he held nothing sacred.

"Make haste. The guards work the lock."

The bars felt oddly soft and brittle beneath his silver fingers. He pried the cell door out of the frame easily and sent it clanging to the floor with a noise like a train wreck.

The main vault door hissed and swung open. The light was blinding. Three men in riot gear peered over the round lip. More men, armed with pistols, were behind. Scrope leapt into the cell, to get out of the line of fire, but the sixty-pound weight of his arm made him fall heavily, almost at Imhotep's feet. There were hieroglyphs chalked on the concrete around his sandals.

Bullets struck Imhotep and rebounded. Scrope, on the ground behind him, was not hit. He spat on the nearest hieroglyph, an image of a crane, and rubbed it away with his left thumb.

That was enough. Imhotep stirred into motion, and came hugely forward. The men switched to automatic. Imhotep should have been cut in half. Instead he was driven to one knee.

With his silver hand, Scrope drew the H&K. He aimed. A trio of shots knocked the closest man backward out of the vault.

Imhotep, in wrath, strode forward, seized the other two men by their throats, held them aloft, and choked the life from them while they emptied their clips into him.

"To me!" He called to Scrope. "And close this door, lest we be whelmed!"

Scrope loped toward the door, dragging the heavy arm. When he reached the great steel plug of the vault, he merely touched it with his silver hand. It clanged shut. He rotated the central wheel, extending the radial pistons. He gripped one piston with metal fingers, preventing it from retracting.

Scrope said, "We cannot leave by the way I came in."

Imhotep threw the two men he held against the concrete wall, shattering their helmets and the skulls within them like eggs. "No matter. You know my arts."

"Do you have handy a temple to your gods built atop a sacred pool?"

"A bowel of wine consecrated to Anubis will do."

"What about whiskey?" Scrope drew out a hip flask.

Imhotep unscrewed the flask, sniffed it, and nodded. Then he bent over a corpse and fished around inside the bloody hemisphere of the helmet. Out he drew a section of skull bone, still intact, and wiped it clean of brain stuffs with his fingers. He set it on the ground and uttered a prayer. Into this impromptu bowl he poured the whiskey.

Scrope felt the vault door tremble under his metal fingers, but whatever engine they were using to crank it open was not strong enough.

Looking back, he saw the whiskey in the skull was glowing. An image formed in the depth.

Here was Agnes in her nightgown, head thrown back, lips parted, the line of her throat exposed. Her dark hair was spilled across two pillows, her bosom was not moving, and her shapely white limbs were haphazardly flung on the wrinkled sheets as if she had struggled madly to rise while the drug took effect.

The viewpoint drew back. There were eight agents and one doctor. A body bag was on the floor. A plastic sheet was under her, to prevent blood from staining the furniture.

Imhotep stared down. He spoke a word from some language

not meant for human throats, passed his hand that bore the scarab ring over the image, and then, with a ghastly grimace, he closed his fist.

One agent in the tiny image now stiffened, eyes wild. His arms and legs were as fish flung onto land, jumping and writhing frantically.

The name of the dying man was Carstairs. He was a ready man with a joke, always willing to lend a cigarette, and was going through a messy divorce just now.

Scrope said, "It takes fifteen minutes for a man to die from oxygen starvation. There is a better way. If you incapacitate one, it will take at least two healthy men to see to him. Blood-choking three for five minutes without killing them neutralizes all nine men in the amount of time it would take you to kill one."

Imhotep smiled a crooked smile. "Mercy...? Your love for her is weak. It will prove no barrier when I cast the memory of Agnes Grosvenor into oblivion."

"You know I would destroy any monster that threatened her, Ardeth Bey. Including a Manticore."

The dark gaze was magnetic, aloof. "Your *ka*, issuing from your heart like a miniature sun, and the *ka* of this arm cannot mate properly, not in the sunlit world. Tendrils of silver even now grow through your form, like the roots of a deadly *upus* tree, seeking your heart. You will die when sunlight strikes that arm, at the dawn of this day. But she will be safe by then with me." He gazed back at the wine-filled skull and made another gesture. "Even now, I force the *drugs* from her blood; I command her limbs. She rises, she walks. I call her here. You must make a path for our escape."

"Ah—I have fifteen bullets and one knife."

"You have power over cold iron, which are the bones of Geb. You may part these walls."

Madhouse Harry twisted the piston, so that it could not move. He walked over to one of the vault walls and tapped it experimentally. There had never been anything so solid and thick ever made by human beings. This vault could withstand an atomic bomb.

"Do not doubt! *She* is beyond this wall."

He did not doubt, but struck. His fingers dug in through metal slabs and reinforced concrete, and closed on a fat girder.

He closed his fist and felt the steel length, *sensing* where it was connected to the cross bracing, where it was strong, where it was weak. He pulled and...

The beam twisted in half and came free. An avalanche deafened him. Dust choked him. Imhotep tossed him through the hole.

Scrope was blind and strangling. He crawled, he stood. He began to blink and cough. Through blackest clouds, he saw a slender figure in white, half nude standing in an empty corridor. Stepping closer, he saw the cascades of dark hair; the strong, narrow face of her English father; the high cheeks; the vivid red of her lips; the wide, dark, deep eyes of her Persian mother.

It was she.

She wore only a sheer silk nightgown. Her feet were bare.

He cried out her name in joy, but when she turned, her eyes were blank, and she stared at him without recognition.

He met Agnes Grosvenor in Cairo, at the ambassador's ball, a young and willful dark-haired beauty with smoldering eyes and a silver laugh. A month later, on a rooftop of the embassy compound where they retreated to escape the oppressive heat of rooms during a power blackout, she helped him remove his jacket with its stubborn buttons, and then, to his surprise, his shirt. The shouts and gunshots of rioters rose in the distance, frightening her. He hugged her with one arm. She put her lips to his ear and said that life was brief.

They became lovers in the oven heat of an April midnight beneath the stars above a darkened city, and the wind from the great river carried the scent of jasmine from the northern plantations to their nostrils.

Unceremoniously, Scrope hoisted the nonresponsive Agnes across his shoulder, Tarzan-style, and fled. When confronted by a locked door or a blank wall that barred his way, Scrope tore out any metal beams, hinges, or locks. Imhotep followed, his face a storm cloud.

They reached the street. Snow was falling. Heading riverward, they were engulfed by a mob of partygoers in festive hats and costumes, blowing noisemakers and snapping crackers. In the distance, Big Ben read a quarter past midnight, and the merrymaking was still cresting.

Men whistled and shouted lewd advice when they saw Scrope hoisting high a shapely, callipygous girl in a flimsy nightgown, rear end first through the throng.

Imhotep towered behind. Perhaps his great height and outlandish costume, torn with bullet holes, would have attracted attention elsewhere. A man dressed as a teddy bear stared at him and so did a teen in a neon red afro, but no one else noticed.

Scrope saw three faces he recognized, glimpsed in the crowd behind. Petrie, Youngblood, Lestrange. Then he saw two, then none. Manticore was pulling back, unwilling to open fire on an inhuman target where eyes could see. That meant Monoceros was coming.

Imhotep spoke, "Release her. Your hands are unclean."

Scrope said, "*You* release her! Undo this spell!" He put her down. She stood there, as empty-eyed as a waxwork doll.

"Oh? And for what reason should I do this thing?" Imhotep smiled.

Scrope popped the top button of his shirt, pulled on a fine gold chain, and drew out a small ivory figurine of a woman crowned with the moon.

The circles beneath Imhotep's eyes grew darker as they wrinkled with sarcasm. "Your charm may be potent to prevent me from stopping your heart with a mere gesture. It has no power to dismay me. Am I one of the lesser beings of the dark world, that I should be stopped with an intersection of sticks, like some blood-drinking corpse?"

With a flip of his wrist, Scrope tossed the chain over Agnes's head. She drew in a breath, blinked, looked down at her semitransparent nightgown, looked up at Imhotep, and screamed.

Scrope seized and kissed her. He felt the tension drain out of her body. He drew his head back. Some of the yobs circling them whistled and clapped.

Those gorgeous eyes were blazing with dark fire and she said softly, "Your grip is hurting me...but...how do you have a grip?"

Imhotep said angrily, "Unhand her. You demean the pure flesh of Ankhesenamon!"

Scrope stepped back. Agnes gazed at the silver hand in awe.

"Sorry," said Scrope, "This is a...a prosthetic that...experimental...ah..."

Imhotep said, "He has drenched his soul in darkest magic, shamed to be a cripple before you. With murder he betrayed his masters, who commanded him to kill you."

Agnes said playfully, "Universal Exports asked him to commit murder? They must be very serious about trade balance."

Imhotep dropped his voice and spoke with burning urgency, "Many times he has deceived you! I have never, my princess!"

She said scornfully, "*He* never made me walk hypnotized through London in January in the snow! Barefoot! Nor tried to stab me with a behemoth horn!"

"I would have revived you, shed of mortality as a snake sheds it skin!"

She sniffed, "You were equally sure the Pharaoh would guess nothing."

"I have sacrificed all things for you!" protested Imhotep, his dark, sardonic face for the first time showing signs of helplessness, bewilderment.

"And if your *all things* are not enough? Ardeth, you are hopeless. Henry, give me your coat. Take me someplace warm. Did you think to bring a pair of shoes for me?"

Scrope doffed his coat and threw it over her shoulders. Eyes were turning toward them. He realized that both his holsters, one beneath each armpit, were visible to passersby. He wondered what was wrong with the English, that they would ignore a four-thousand-year-old Egyptian necromancer standing in their midst, but stare aghast at an armed man.

Scrope took Agnes's hand and wormed his way through the crowd, with Imhotep striding behind, cuffing partygoers out of his way.

Scrope said over the clamor, "Agnes, I've planned this out. There is a warehouse fronting the river not far from here, where I've had a boat ready...I have friends in Goa who can hide us."

She said, "Goa? It is filled with nagas. You did not think to discuss the plans with me?"

He said, "It's the Official Secrets Act. My mouth was sealed. If I told, and they found out..."

She laughed. "What would have happened? *What?* We'd be running through the streets at midnight in the snow with a crazy dead Egyptian, being hunted?"

Scrope saw a small green glitter flicker through the air. He turned his head. A dragonfly landed on Agnes's wanton black curls and twitched its forelegs.

He released her hand and swatted at the insect, uttering a stream of curses.

She said, "Watch your language, Henry! There are mummies present."

The bug was lost to sight. More specks buzzed here and there. A ladybug on the back of a man's coat, a beetle perched on the rim of a dropped beer bottle, a cluster of bees flickering as they passed through the snowy light shed by a streetlamp.

The three worked their way to the crowd's edge, turned a corner, and were suddenly alone. They ran. Barefooted in the snow, Agnes could not keep pace. Imhotep picked her up and set her on his shoulder. Now Scrope scowled.

They reached a narrow street. Frowning brick closed in one side. A row of warehouses loomed on the other. Beyond them, the dark water of the Thames glittered.

Suddenly the streetlamps and lights from windows died. From afar came the wide noise of a crowd roaring in dismay.

Scrope said, "MI20 always creates a blackout, just before they strike."

Agnes said, "Who, exactly, is coming?"

"Our first man is Criswell. He was stranded on North Sentinel Island, whose people are the last to have no contact with civilization. At least, not human civilization. The witch doctors forced a concoction of honey and larvae down his mouth and nose, and left him to die, eaten from the inside. Thanks to his study in Tibet, he made an . . . agreement . . . with the nest built in his lungs. He can command any insect, see through their eyes. Rains and winds impede him. The second of his team is Rabbi ben Bezalel who woke the golem, a living statue of clay. The third is Grendel."

Agnes said, "Who?"

Scrope said, "Don't you read the classics? One of the descendants of Cain who survived the deluge, interbred with elves and ogres and evil phantoms. Amphibious. Very strong. Charmed life, immune to fire and steel, blade and bullet. The Americans call him the Creature from the Black Lagoon."

Agnes said, "We are in luck! A thunderstorm is hitting us in a few minutes. Thundersnowstorm, I suppose."

She sat atop the shoulder of Imhotep, slender and small in the bulky overcoat, a look of innocent guilelessness on her features. "I...ah...heard it on the weather report. Earlier. It will help with the bug man."

There was a silent flash of lightning from a distant storm. In the momentary glare, three things could be seen.

The first was a hulking shape in the street before them, dressed not very convincingly in an oversized trenchcoat with a bowler hat pulled low over its slablike features. It stood bowlegged and its apelike arms fell below its knees. Slung from shoulder to hip was a voluminous bloodstained bag of lizardlike skins pebbled with bright patterns of scales, all knitted together with gold thread.

The other was behind them, closer. It was even less likely to pass for human.

It was fully nine feet tall, the brick-red face a scarred and half-melted ruin, and the skull was as pointed as a bishop's miter. Its eyes were deep-set slits that ran from midbrow, slanting down left and right to touch the corners of its mouth, giving it an aspect of ghastly misery. Its mouth was a crooked slot held shut with three iron staples running through lip and jaw. It had no chin, no neck; the skull rose directly from the shoulders. It wore dungarees and bulky sweatshirt. A knitted longshoreman's cap had been thrown across the horrid skull to disguise the shape.

Above, a pitchy cloud of insects was pouring across the streets, murmuring, spreading.

Scrope said, "That warehouse. Run."

Behind him, Imhotep ran down the dark street on silent steps, and the long hair of the girl on his shoulder was a banner. The slow golem was outdistanced, but Grendel grinned and charged on all fours, overcoat tails flapping.

The dark man gently put Agnes down. His voice trembled, "Should I perish, and if it be a thousand years more, or ten thousand, never will I cease to love you, my Ankhesenamon. I shall return to you always."

So saying, he turned and fell upon Grendel, who reared up on hind legs to meet him.

Scrope and Agnes ran on. A short concrete drive led to the warehouse. Before them was a large square garage door. He unlocked it.

The wind was rising. A snow began to fall in pelting lines,

mingled with icy rain. In the gloom behind them, two inhuman shapes grappled, cracking the pavement beneath their feet, scattering trash cans, smashing the red pillar of a postbox, and bending an unlit lamppost.

Scrope pushed her inside. He pulled the heavy door shut and locked it.

Agnes said, "It is not cricket to leave him behind."

"He will kill us as soon as—" Something was wrong. He turned, spooked.

At the building rear was a boatslip that opened onto the Thames. It allowed boats to dock inside the warehouse and load cargo directly from the lofts overhead. A door of corrugated metal hung down between the river and the warehouse. There was a single beam of light coming down from the skylight. It was falling on a small, fast, cigarette boat in the slip.

"We're sailing to India in *that*?" asked Agnes.

Scrope drew the H&K. He looked left and right, wondering what was setting his nerves on edge. "The yacht is in Calais. This is just to get us across the Channel."

Then he realized. That light was not coming from a lamp. A man was standing on the roof, looking down, torch in hand. Scrope shot a burst. He heard the noise of shattering glass and cursed himself for a fool.

A buzzing filled the air. Down through the broken panes came a cloud of flying insects. He shot again, and the light went out. But the insects swarmed him, stinging at his eyes, trying to crawl into mouth and nose.

He shoved Agnes toward the boat and ran up the creaking wooden staircase toward the door motor. He ran as fast as he could in the dark, his silver hand over his eyes, flight after flight, spitting. A hundred hot needles stung his jaws and neck, his shirt, his ankles.

Then he was at the top loft. He parted his metal fingers to peek. In the snowy moonlight, he saw no one on the roof.

Thirty feet below, Agnes, hidden in an insect cloud, ran toward the boat. She dove and vanished from sight, leaving behind a spreading pool of bugs on the surface.

His left hand and face were beginning to stiffen and swell. Scrope turned on the door motor. It was not connected to the city power grid. It sputtered to life. The river door started to lift.

Half the swarm fled Scrope and fell upon the engine, squeezing their bodies into the innards. It only took a pound of dead bugs crammed into the vents to choke it into silence. The doors halted two feet above the water, insufficient to let the boat escape.

Scrope opened the door engine housing. A gush of fumes rose. The insects were startled and flew up. He had a moment before Criswell resumed control. There was an oil-soaked rag, large as a bath towel, near the engine. He tossed it over his head, an impromptu insect net, found a tear to peer through, and down the stairs he ran.

He saw no sign of Agnes. How long could she hold her breath?

He was on the second landing when a light appeared underfoot. Into view beneath him came a thin man in a wide-brimmed hat, dark sunglasses, an overcoat. He entered from the small door leading into the warehouse office. He carried a torch and a crowbar but no pistol. A carpet of poisonous centipedes crawled after him in an endless train along with scorpions and other deadly things. Criswell had descended the fire ladder connecting the office to the roof.

Scrope raised his pistol, but the insects crawling on his hand warned Criswell, who doused his torch and threw the swarm into Scrope's face. The oily cloth on his head saved his eyes, but he did not have a shot.

He heard the sound of Criswell crowbarring open the main doors. Scrope ran down the next flight of stairs to the first landing, half blind.

A flash of lightning spilling in through the opening main door and the broken skylight painted the scene with jagged, leaping shadows.

Grendel still wore the tatters of his vast overcoat and the crushed shape of his bowler hat. His face was streaked with blood, and he was breathing heavily between his white, sharp teeth. Impatiently, he forced the doors open, yanking them from their tracks.

Behind him was Imhotep, limp as if his bones were broken, in the grip of the freakish, cone-skulled, nine-foot-tall statue-man. Imhotep did not bleed blood: instead, a thick, black oil was dripping from him.

Next to the golem was a short, fat, little man in Osprey armor, and on his back a flamethrower, and in his hand a golden scroll. Scrope recognized him as Rabbi ben Bezalel.

Criswell pointed at the water, made a gesture in sign language. Grendel loped across the concrete floor and dove. Criswell then snapped his fingers at the Rabbi and pointed at where Scrope crouched on the first landing in the pitch dark. Scrope shot at Criswell, but missed. The thin man did not even flinch as bullets ricocheted from the concrete at his feet.

The Rabbi sprayed his flamethrower against the base of the wooden staircase and then up the stairs halfway to the first landing. Black smoke rolled upward, and the heat was like a bludgeon. Scrope shot a burst into the Rabbi, igniting the flamethrower canister. The chubby man ran, trying to flee his burning back, shrieking for help, clawing at the shoulder straps.

Responding literally to his master's call, the golem dropped Imhotep. It lumbered over to where Rabbi ben Bezalel was twisting in a pool of napalm, burning, and bent over the charred, still-moving body solicitously. *"Avenge me!"*

Grendel leapt free of the water, Agnes writhing in his grip, the slick coat and sheer nightgown clinging to her.

Scrope held his breath, ran down the burning stairs. The smoke drove the insects from him, but the heat was burning through his boots, and his silver arm grew hot.

Imhotep's voice rang out over the wind of the gathering storm. *Let two hands from the Earth open my mouth: Let Seb, the Erpa of the gods, part my two jaws; let him open my two eyes which are closed, and give motion to my two hands which are powerless; and let Anubis give vigour to my legs, that I may raise myself up upon them. Be there given to me my mouth wherewith to speak, and my feet for walking; and let me have my arms wherewith to overthrow my adversaries. And may Sechit the divine one lift me up!*

And through the driving snow, the dead man stood and a thunderclap echoed from the heavens.

Scrope fell back from the heat. It did not seem fair that the mummy could raise himself from the dead, and Scrope could not even get downstairs.

The flames parted. The woe-eyed golem came toward Scrope up the burning stairs, slowly, methodically, unstoppably.

Scrope retreated, but the stairs behind him collapsed with a roar and a storm of flying sparks. He fired his six remaining bullets point-blank into the sad, ruined, worn clay face of the lifeless monster. The golem clasped him.

He felt his ribs bending and knew he was about to die. He also knew the weakness of the golem. The cabalistic letters forming the secret name of truth were written somewhere on its head. But where?

Agnes screamed. Imhotep had rescued the girl from the hands of Grendel and was driving the quaking amphibious man backward merely with the pressure of his gaze. Grendel closed his eyes and lunged. The two figures wrestled with superhuman strength. They fell into the spreading pool of napalm.

The stairs beneath the golem's feet, eaten by fire, gave way. The golem fell a dozen feet, clutching Scrope. The fall jarred the golem's grip, and Scrope managed to tear his silver arm free. He battered at the triangular, woebegone face, making dents like a sledgehammer would, but the spectacular damage he had done to metal bars and doors eluded him. The magic arm had no power over clay. But the three clamps holding the mouth shut were metal.

He pried the first clamp up with his silver fingers with a *snap*. The golem tightened his grip. Scrope's vision faded into a haze of red. *Snap!* The second clamp broke. He could no longer hear the roar of the storm, no longer feel the heat from the burning building. *Snap!* He was sure it was his bones breaking.

His silver hand pried the scowling, lipless mouth open and gripped the tongue. In the wobbly, red haze of his vision, he could see the cabalistic letters printed on it. The golem did not notice or care. It was carrying out its master's last order obediently, mindlessly. With the thumbnail of his living hand, Scrope scratched out the letter aleph. EMETH became METH, the word for *death*. Instantly, the statue perished.

He was trapped in the motionless arms. He pounded at the clay hands.

Imhotep, even with his back and one arm afire, was besting Grendel. With immense strength, the dark man threw Grendel spine-first onto a jagged stump in the midst of the burning lumber pile that had once been the staircase. Storm winds through the broken doors fanned the flames. Grendel fell. He groaned and clawed his way through the oily flames, dragging his limp and motionless legs behind him.

Imhotep now turned toward Criswell, and the light in the eyes of the Egyptian was truly a nightmarish thing.

Criswell had lost his hat, but not his sunglasses. He clutched Agnes and hid behind her, backing carefully toward the boat.

The swarms of insects closed on Imhotep, but the flames from the dry and burning body prevented them from landing. The Egyptian trod scorpions, unhurt. Agnes worked one arm free, reached behind her, and clawed Criswell's face. His sunglasses broke. The two empty eye sockets were filled the gray papery substance of wasps' nests, and half a dozen queen wasps flew up from the vacant pits.

A scream rent the air. It was not her scream, however.

With her pinned arm, Agnes had at the same time drawn from the overcoat she wore the black injector shaped like a fountain pen Scrope had left in the pocket. She flicked open the needle and drove it into the large muscle in Criswell's thigh. A mix of holy water and deadly toxins entered him. Wasps issued from his open mouth as he screamed. His feet slipped, and he fell into the water. She fell with him.

Frantic, Scrope broke off one of the clay fingers, then another. He was almost free...

Imhotep lumbered toward the water, staggering and being eaten by the flames. "My love will never die. Never. The whole dome of the sky will crack and topple to a withered, lifeless earth before I surrender her!"

All the insects in the warehouse were directionless, dispersing. Agnes had not surfaced. There were no bubbles, no motion in the water.

Grendel, by his right claw, pulled himself free of the oily flames. He was burned across his face and body. It seemed impossible that he still lived. But he held the same gold foil scroll that the Rabbi earlier had carried. It was red-hot, and Grendel's fingers sizzled when he unrolled it.

Imhotep dove into the waters, quelling his burning back. His skin grew dark and heavy and seemed to sag, but he was too buoyant to force himself below the waters.

"Ankhesenamon! *Ankhesenamon!* I will find you! Even if you are drowned, I will revive you! You shall be with me, ever living, undying, greater than the gods themselves!"

Grendel held up the scroll and spoke. His voice was a nasty, gargling croak, but the words were clear: *"In the name of Isis, I call upon the river god of Thames, Nodens, to protect against this blasphemer of the mysteries. Let him be overthrown and slaughtered. His abode is transferred to the slaughtering block of the East, his head is cut away, his neck is crushed, his thighs lopped off, he is given to the great Annihilator who resideth in the Valley that he may not ever escape from under the custody of Seb. Come, thou Crocodile of the West, who livest on the Setting Stars. Come, thou Crocodile of the East, who livest upon those who devour their own foulness. Come, thou Crocodile of the South, who livest upon impurities. Come, thou Crocodile of the North, who livest upon that which lieth between the hours."*

Four twelve-foot-long greenish shapes, like crocodiles but bearing pschents of gold and red-gold on their narrow skulls, surfaced in the waters and eyed Imhotep with strange, cruel eyes.

"*Ankhesenamon!*" Imhotep called out in a great voice. "Do not again forget me! Of all the torments of hell, that is the worst!"

"Is it?" said a deep voice from the deep waters. "Come. We shall see."

And the four crowned crocodiles seized the arms and legs of Imhotep in their teeth and, spinning, ripped his limbs from him. The black oil he used for blood spread across the water. A whirlpool formed beneath him, and the waters swallowed the dismembered man.

Grendel was now crawling, arm over arm, to where Scrope was still pinned and motionless. The monster was no more than four yards away. "The Jew told me to do that, in case he failed."

Three yards. Scrope battered frantically at the dead hands holding him. Scrope twisted and pulled, but he was caught fast.

Two yards. Grendel's claws scrabbled against the concrete. Scrope could already see the blisters on the monster sinking, the third-degree burns vanishing.

"You wish your limbs grew back, Son of Seth, do you not? But you are not a Son of Cain, and you do not have the art. Of all these wounds, I shall heal, and forget, and dance beneath the waves with the nicors and sirens. But *you* shall die. I will eat your brain like cabbage."

Scrope pulled with all the strength of his silver arm, and an immense pain shot down from his right shoulder. He had dislocated it.

Desperate, he twisted in the statue's grip and drew his Webley.

The creature saw the gun. "Why, Madhouse Harry! Are you going to stick your hand down my throat and fire? I will tell everyone in the department how bold you were up to the last!"

One yard away. The creature reared up, drew back its great claw...

Scrope fired point-blank into the thing's broad chest. The creature flinched and then laughed. But the laughter turned into a long, dry, hideous sucking sound.

"Damn you!" croaked the monster. "It is Dr. Serizawa's oxygen destroyer! Only against the blood of the sea people does it do harm! How did you—?"

His skin crinkled and flattened on his bones, as if a great vacuum were inside him. His eyes curled up like raisins, his tongue became a thin lash of flesh, his lips lost their hue. He collapsed inward on himself.

The fire was spreading. Scrope pried himself loose from Grendel's grip. Smoke filled the warehouse. Agnes had not surfaced. The corpse of Criswell was floating in the water, being busily devoured by his own insects. The winds howled, and the snow and hail poured through the broken skylight.

He hoped he would find her outside. Surely she slid away to safety under the waters.

His shoulder was a fiery vise-grip of pain where he had dislocated it, and his feet were so blistered with burns that he could barely stand, but by sheer force of will he made the silver arm rise up and shatter the sea doors. Pain shot through his whole body, and for a moment he collapsed, staring upward at the hailstones ringing through the broken skylight, at the black smoke pouring up and out.

Wearily he crawled along the lip of the concrete quay. He had to keep telling himself that if he dove in the water, the sixty-pound weight of the arm would drag him under.

He passed the body of Grendel. He carefully twisted, then tore the head free. It was dry and crumbling, and he lugged it along by the hair.

Painfully, slowly, he undid the boatlines. Painfully, slowly, he boarded and crawled aft and spun the engines to life, glad they were not clogged with dead wasps.

The slim boat slid out onto the Thames. The city was dark. The storm was fierce, but the wind was blowing out to sea, at his back. Shivering in the hail, he wished he had his jacket. He wished he had bullets. He wished a lot of things.

The wild winds blew the clouds free of the moon, and in

that pallid light he saw the ship. Crewed by thin and famished men, and some of them were dead, and some of the dead were skeletons, was the great three-masted clipper, her canvas sails torn and flapping, her hull crusted with barnacles.

Something splashed behind him. Agnes was there, her arms, shoulders and head coming up out of the water and over the gunwale of the boat. She was nude, and her long black hair clung tightly to her skull and shoulders. Her eyes were beautiful, chatoyant, and were of a dark and deeper hue than he had ever seen before. He was afraid to step across the boat to her.

She cocked her head to one side, smiling.

He said, "My coat?"

She said, "I did not really need it, but I thank you for the gesture. We don't get cold."

He just nodded. "Why did you do it?"

She said, "Because when you knelt and offered me a little square black box, I knew what it was supposed to hold. It was supposed to have a ring inside, a wedding ring. Instead it was your flat key. We did not exchange vows. We exchanged *keys*."

He felt a pounding in his head. Perhaps it was the combination of burns, dislocations, evil magic, bee stings, and a general adrenaline overdose. Perhaps it was the typical frustration of a man talking to a woman. "What—what the hell are you talking about, Agnes?"

"My name is Aglaope. Aglaope Vanderdecken."

"I wanted to know why you chose *me*?"

"Your crazy bravery! And you were in Cairo. I needed someone crazy to protect me from Imhotep. What were his last words?"

"Is that why you came back here? Not to have a last word with me?"

She giggled. "My last word with you is to ask what Imhotep said when he was carried alive to hell by Apep."

"But why didn't you ever—"

"—tell you?" She merely smiled, and his words caught in his throat.

"I was sent by the ruler of my people, Her Highness Aquareine, to spy out Manticore and your doings, because of late you grow ruthless in hunting us down, unseelie and seelie both. Other realms soon intersect with earth, ancient gates will open even we wish kept shut. I was sent to see whether you could be reasoned with. You cannot. You don't know your own hearts. Your superiors at MI4 assumed you knew I was only half human, and wanted me that way. I become a mortal woman if a man weds me in a church, and would bear him strong sons and fair daughters."

"Half human?"

She pointed. He thought he had never seen an arm so fair, so well shaped. "My father is the captain of that ship, which sailed into the night world long ago, forsaking yours. My mother is Princess Clia, who took him in her arms to comfort him; from the union sprang a porpoise and a sea bream, and the other was me. The great god of your world blows the winds against him whenever he tries to make port. I sent a signal to him earlier asking him to come up the Thames. See how simple? It is like having a storm in your pouch. It will cover my retreat."

She heaved herself up on her arms, so that her belly was at her elbow, and her naked, wet, shining breasts were visible. Between them hung the charm of Isis. She pouted and pointed at it with her chin. "May I keep this? I want to remember Imhotep, and things of your world are easy to forget. What were his last words?"

"He said his love for you will never die, even if the sky falls and earth perishes. Or something like that. He said your forgetting him was worse than all the pains of hell."

She smiled sadly. "Ah! Did he? Well, my sisters will honor me for that."

"You lure sailors to their deaths, do you?"

"Had you lured me to life, dear Henry, I would have stayed! Something is more important to you than I was. What? What do you hold sacred?" She shook her head. "We are not luring men out of the mortal world to kill them, you know. We need fighters when the time comes, and you humans are the deadliest monsters of all. But we *change* them. They can never go home again. Sunlight kills them." She nodded at the silver hand. "You know. Like that. My sisters will honor me for your death, too. You put on that deadly arm for me, didn't you? How sweet! But Imhotep was serious. You were not. *A flat key!* Imagine! And me the reincarnation of the Pharaoh's daughter!" She smiled dismissively. "Him, I shall miss. You, I shall forget."

She slipped down and sped across the dark and stormy waters more swiftly and gracefully than a dolphin toward the dark, tattered, ghost ship.

By the time he reached the English Channel, the black ship was gone, and so was the storm. The sky was pink with coming dawn, and the jolts of pain running down his silver arm to his heart were growing stronger.

He took out the severed head of Grendel, inserted the small, round stone into the dead man's mouth, and spoke the words. This time, they did not burn his throat.

The eyes opened. "I see a mortal man who has no claim on me. Our debts are paid, each to the other."

"I propose a new bargain. You are not at peace, by any means, are you? You have monsters you need hunted. I am skilled in the work, and I have it on good authority that we men are the deadliest monsters there are."

The lifeless head twisted its lips into a smile. "You wish me to be your lord? Ah, but by what name would we swear our oaths of loyalty and fealty?"

"There is one thing I hold sacred. Any monster I kill for you is one less to menace the innocent. I gave up everything for my profession. Even love. Some men are wolves and must prey on the weak; most men are sheep and never look up from the grass they graze. I am a wolfhound, and I prey on the strong. I hunt the horrors. I swear by—by *Monsterhunting!*"

Perhaps the dark voice laughed. "Then come. Say farewell to sun. I open the jaws of night to you and bring you living to my court of darkness."

The boat was later found by the Coast Guard, drifting, empty.

Trip Jones was picked for MHI's best team right out of training for a reason. He's a skilled Hunter, but more importantly the man's got a bigger heart than the rest of us put together.   —A.L.

The Dead Yard

Maurice Broaddus

When monsters want to feed, they go after the poor and the powerless first. The longer I've been with Monster Hunter International, the more true I believe this to be. What was worse: those monsters came in all shapes and sizes. I splashed water on my face before leaning heavily on the sink. I took a long, hard look in the hotel mirror.

How are you doing, Mr. John Jermain Jones? Triple J to some. Trip to friends and family. I could always tell how I knew a person by what they called me.

I zipped up my suitcase. I never bothered to unpack it at a hotel or on any mission. I hated the feeling of settling in only to uproot myself again.

My family used to be fishermen in Jamaica, but immigrated to America a few generations ago. They made a life for themselves, but we never forgot where we came from. There was a Jewish teaching that always stuck with me: *tikkun olam*—repairing the world, the damage done by myself and others, healing the broken pieces, as a way of life. It was what led me to go into teaching high school chemistry. It was also what led me to pick up a pickaxe when a zombie outbreak occurred. That was the way my world worked now. In the end, I just wanted to make a difference and keep my family safe.

So when word came to MHI about a series of killings on the island, I felt a strange familial tug to lead the investigation team—a small team of people I trust with my life: Owen Zastava Pitt and Holly Newcastle. Family took care of family.

A young man claiming to be a distant cousin, who kept greeting me as Brother Jones, ran the Sandals resort in Montego Bay. I wanted my friends to enjoy themselves, a moment in the sun before we got down to business, so my cousin comped us a night. A blast of heat let me know I was leaving the confines of the hotel lobby to enter the beachfront. The entire beach line was a series of cordoned-off resorts. Tourism was the lifeblood of the island, with tourists arriving, shedding their old lives, and doing things they wouldn't dare back home. I knew where I'd find Owen. Under the canopy of an open-air bar, shifting in his seat, never quite comfortable in his own skin. Owen was one of them dudes you'd mistake for being a jock type and never peg as having been an accountant before hooking up with MHI. That was kind of his thing, never quite being what people expected.

"What's that?" Owen stared at the beverage in his glass, an umbrella tilted to the side like an assassin poised to strike.

"An umbrella?"

"The bartender insisted that I try it. Wanted to give me a taste of the island. I'm not sure I trust any drink with an umbrella in it." Owen turned his hulking frame, fully revealing the scar on his face. My dad used to love this show called *The Rockford Files*. He told me what he loved was how the main detective got his butt kicked so often while working a case. That was Owen's go-to move in a nutshell: putting himself between danger and innocents. The scar was only one of his souvenirs from doing so. "Everything okay, Trip?"

"Yeah, why?"

"You look like you're carrying the weight of the world's problems. You know, more than usual."

"Thanks. I'll be okay." I glanced around. "Where's Holly?"

"Um...taking point on tactical surveillance." Taking a sip, nodding approvingly at the glass before carrying it with him, Owen led the way to the pool. Wearing a black-and-white-striped bikini, Holly floated on an inflatable mattress. She raised her sunglasses when she saw us.

"Getting a taste of 'resort' Jamaica before we get to 'real' Jamaica?" I asked.

"This is real enough for me." She eased back into her air

mattress to bask in the sun. All blond-haired and blue-eyed, she had a swimsuit model's body and knew it. She didn't care how people gawked at her, since she was once a stripper in Las Vegas. She had this fierce sense of self and a will nearly as strong as Owen's. Not that I'd ever tell her, but I'd always admired how she carried herself as a Hunter.

By the time I realized I was staring, Holly met my eyes. "Never see a woman in a bikini before?"

"This is the kind of hunt we need to do more often," Owen interrupted to rescue me from an awkward moment. "What are we looking at?"

"The series of murders have been localized to a single parish just outside of MoBay," I said.

"MoBay?" Holly asked.

"That's what the locals call Montego Bay," I said.

"You couldn't sound any more like a tourist if you tried," Owen said.

"I still feel a . . . connection to this place. My mother used to tell me stories her mother passed on to her about this place. You know how kids are . . . after a certain age you just tune out your parents' voice. As I got older, I realized I had no stories to tell them."

"I bet you have some now," Owen said.

"Not if I'm actually trying to get them to sleep." I scanned the area for potential eavesdroppers. "My 'aunt' is the justice of the peace of the St. James Parish. Her family, our family, is hosting the Nine Nights."

"Nine Nights?" Holly asked.

"Think of it as an extended Irish wake. Some people still refer to it as the Dead Yard. The latest victim was a baby. Nine days old, drained dry. Emotions are running high, so the Nine Nights has been closed to just family. She invited me and my family to come stay with her"—I turned to Owen—"though she wasn't real receptive to the idea of me bringing a friend."

"Wait," Holly sat up like a student still working out a math problem. "When you say family . . ."

"She wanted to meet . . . Mrs. Jones." I avoided her eyes.

"Ha!" Owen snorted. "This mission just gets better and better."

"Whose idea was this?" Holly crossed her arms.

"Apparently my aunt is very traditional. So having Owen as my wife was out."

"Why would I be the wife?" Owen asked.

"Because it's my story. So if a woman was going to come along, she'd have to be someone's wife in order to be 'under her roof' as she put it. So your cover would be either Mrs. John Jermain Jones or..."

Owen held out his arms and started humming a wedding march.

"It's like choosing between the lesser of two evils," Holly said.

"What do they think it is?" Owen asked. "Baruragaru, chupacabra, vampire, loogaroo?"

"When you hear hoofbeats, think horses not zebras. Our best guess is we're looking at some sort of undead." I was still settling into the idea of being in charge of the mission. Because it was family, Earl wanted me to lead it. Part of me enjoyed the way they turned to me as leader. Owen especially. Owen didn't do well with authority, or anyone, telling him what to do. But he listened to his friends. "Officially, we were called in as a favor to a government official."

"Favor? Not to sound too crass, but favors don't pay the bills," Owen said.

"Did I mention the victim was nine days old? Besides, as I understand it, my aunt is paying the equivalent to the PUFF herself." The Perpetual Unearthly Forces Fund was the government-issued cash bounty for monsters. Since the PUFF didn't apply out of country, someone had to foot the bills. This was a job, not a calling, after all, and it didn't get done cheap.

"So they want a low-key investigation. That all?"

"It's just...this one is personal."

"This time it's personal?" Holly lowered her glasses. "Buy me whatever Owen's drinking, Trip, and I'll let that line go."

When we exited the resort, a taxi driver snapped to attention. A bowler hat with feathers stuck in it topped his grizzled dreadlocks. Yellowed, bloodshot eyes tracked us. A strikingly well-trimmed silver mustache framed two rows of perfectly white teeth. Hardscrabble hands waved us over. "You Jones?"

"Yeah." I stepped forward.

"You a rasta?" Pulling the cigarette from his mouth, he ground it out under heel as he studied my dreadlocks.

"No, it's just...my hair."

The man made a noncommittal noise. "Come on. I have the rest of your luggage already loaded."

"Any trouble with customs?" I asked.

"Not if you know the right people." The driver half sneered at me. "Why have you come here?"

Ignoring the challenge in his voice, like I was some unwanted trespasser, I dropped into the passenger seat. "We were asked. Come to investigate some deaths under...mysterious circumstances."

"You Americans don't think we can handle our own business? You people come and stare and make fun, like we're exhibits at a zoo for your entertainment."

"I have family here. We were called in to help, not take over."

"Then you're hunting your heritage."

The taxi sped by a billboard which read DON'T BE IN A HURRY TO ENTER ETERNITY. Armed police stopped traffic at a roadside check. We were officially leaving resort Jamaica. I leaned forward to catch the eye of the taxi driver.

"No problem, man, no problem," the driver moved his hands like he was patting down the air.

One of the men pointed at Owen and demanded that he open his bag. Owen complied, revealing several shirts with loud prints on them, toiletries, and a magazine. Disappointed, the police officer waved us through.

The drive up the mountain gave a perfect view of the parish, a tableau of green hills covered by low-lying clouds. A series of potholes and edges which bled into a scree of crumbling asphalt, the road was barely wide enough to allow two cars to pass. The taxi driver stayed in the middle, honking his way around the blind curves. Only if another vehicle honked in response did he drift into his proper lane.

"I've flown in helicopters through enemy fire that was safer than this," Holly said.

"How much longer?" I asked.

"Soon come," the driver said. "Just around the corner."

A couple miles later, we stopped in front of a house. Concrete walls surrounded the property, seven feet high topped with razor wire. Metal gates jerked open. The long driveway took us past an intricate garden filled with banana, coconut, breadfruit trees along with rows of corn, tomatoes, and vegetables I didn't recognize. The main house was a pastel castle, with its thick turquoise walls trimmed with a pink-and-red-tiled roof. Metal grating painted white enclosed the portico. Each window fitted with "burglar bars"—wrought iron bars fixed to the exterior—gave the house the appearance of a prison. At least they were painted white to match the portico.

"Mind if I check my bags?" Owen stepped out of the taxi.

"No one trouble your stuff, man." The driver walked to the rear of the car and popped the trunk.

Owen opened the top chest. A couple of Jericho pistols. A Beretta 1301 Tactical, a gas-piston-operated, semiautomatic, 12-gauge shotgun. Tavor assault rifles. A Negev machine gun. Magazines of ammunition. Not our usual gear, but since we were operating in another country, we didn't know what might get caught up in customs. Or was legal. Or what we'd have to ditch on short notice. Owen strapped a Jericho to his hip and exhaled as if he'd been holding his breath the whole time. "I just wanted to make sure none of our equipment grew legs."

"Tourists. All you see are beaches and criminals. We live in between," the driver said.

"What do you think?" A short woman, five feet four tops, with recently dyed reddish-brown hair, swept her arms out as if she were responsible for the view. Straight-backed, she carried herself with authority. "Senior Justice of the Peace Carmen Hicks."

"It's so good to meet you." I hunched over awkwardly to give her a hug. A lot stronger than she appeared, she hugged me tight and kissed me on the cheek.

"I've been telling all of my people that we have important family coming from the States to stay with us. And who is this beautiful gal?"

"This is Holly. My . . . wife." I laced my fingers into hers. She squeezed my fingers as if locking them in a steel trap so they wouldn't wander.

"Come here, let me take a look at you." Brushing my hand aside like she swatted at a fly, Carmen took each of Holly's hands and held them out to better inspect her. "I have such a beautiful niece."

"Thank you," Holly said through clenched teeth, half glaring at me.

"And this is my friend, Owen." I stepped aside.

Letting go of Holly's hands, Carmen scarcely spared a glance in Owen's direction. "Yes. He can stay round back with Lord Evader. Come, let me show you around."

Entering through a mosquito-screened door, a blast from an air curtain hit us. A wide-screened HDTV filled the back wall and sat next to the array of boxes of her wifi and satellite connections. Doilies and knickknacks covered each end table and shelf surface with an elderly British mum's fussy sense of décor. Sheets of plastic covered the furniture and similar strips ran along the main walkways. Owen sat down, his chair sounding like it passed gas. He squeaked against the plastic, attempting to settle in. Carmen insisted that Holly and I take the loveseat while she stood. She barked at a maid to fetch a tray of a drink called sorrel. The maid disappeared through a door leading to the kitchen. A group of women sat around huge metal pots filled with bubbling rice. A series of pots held what smelled to be curried goat simmering on the stove. Trays and trays full of jerk chicken lined the counters. The driver leaned a stack of crates along a dolly, wheeling bottles of rum through to another room. Eyeing us, the man closed the door behind him.

"Quite the party you're preparing for," Owen said.

"Death is a chore which needed attending to," Carmen said. "The Nine Nights are a celebration of a life well lived. Our loved one no longer suffers with this life."

"But one so young," Holly said.

"You're never too young to know the sting of life. Friends soon come, not with their condolences and sad faces, but with food and drink and music. Life."

"It goes on all week?" I asked.

"On the ninth night, the family prepares the food for all who come. Some say that's the night the spirit of our loved one passes through to say goodbye."

"Spirits?" Owen perked up.

"Look how the duppy kissed me last night." Carmen turned her arm over to reveal a bruise. Then she grinned as if letting us in on some joke. "Did you have any problems with your arrival?"

"There was a police roadblock, like they were searching for something," Owen said.

"Police? Big-talk buffoons, the lot of them. If one stop you, he's just trying to get a let off. All them wanting money in return for doing their job? No, sir."

"I thought they might be looking for our guns," Holly said.

"American guns drop into Kingston like mangoes from a tree," Carmen said.

"Then what about the deaths?" I asked.

"The 'police' just collect the bodies and file a report. Natural causes." Carmen sucked her teeth.

"But our reports said the bodies had been drained?"

"No one cares about a poor, dead child." Carmen took a glass of sorrel when her maid passed her the tray.

I took a glass of sorrel. "Do you have any idea what's behind the killings? My mother used to tell stories that her mother told her . . . I only vaguely remember duppies and the spinning cow."

"Oh, that takes me back. I haven't heard or told a Br'er Nansi story in forever. Nor a . . . spinning cow." Carmen rocked back with laughter. She repeated the spinning cow reference to her maid so quickly in thick patois that I barely recognized the words as English. "I think you meant 'rollin' calf.'"

Hoping Holly and Owen didn't notice, I flushed with mild embarrassment. I took a deep sip of sorrel. It tasted like bitter fruit with a dash of ginger. Not used to it, I wanted to spit it right back into my glass. What Holly said was true: I was little more than a tourist here now.

"Did your mother ever tell you about Old Higue?"

I shook my head.

"All these gals keep going on and on about it around here when they should be working. I normally don't have time for such foo-foo nonsense."

"But you suspect something," I said.

"I've seen a lot of things. I was the first call my people made. Not the police. Not the hospital. Not their family. Me. Because my people, them know I will do whatever it takes to look out for them. I saw the body myself. Poor little child, little more than a week old, the life drained from it. Sometimes even the best people turn wrong." Her voice took on a mournful quality. "If people swear that an Old Higue stalks these parts, I'm not quick to dismiss it. Whatever it takes, me say. Whatever. Whatever. Whatever. But sometimes it's best to keep things in the family . . . so to speak."

Owen leaned forward. "I just need to know one thing: bullets, fire, or ax? If we're going to go hunting, I need to know what to pack with me."

"Je-sus." Carmen said with such emphasis, the word almost had an extra syllable. "Do you know I came home one day to find rice scattered all over the house? Them gals"—she cocked her head toward her maids—"said the community set a trap for the Old Higue. She flew about in the night looking for her next victim, drawn by the smell of asafoetida. So them pile up rice, nuh. Say that the Old Higue has to count the grains and if she loses track, she has to start over."

"Did it work?" I asked.

"You know a monster who stops its rampage to count rice grains? I told them to sweep it up and quit wasting my rice. We have a whole community to feed. Go talk to Lord Evader. He loves to chat."

"The taxi driver?"

"Driver. Handyman. Gravedigger. Used to be a reggae singer a lifetime or two ago."

"Like Bob Marley?" Owen asked.

"That's reggae for people who don't know reggae. Overproduced for easy consumption," Carmen said.

"I like Bob Marley," Owen whispered.

"You might as well order 'Rasta Pasta' back at that hotel resort." With a self-satisfied grin, Carmen waved us on our way. "It's the last night of the Nine Nights and we begin about seven. See you in the morning. If life spare."

The sky threatened to rain, the heavy air smelled of salt and damp sand. The trees crowded in, assuming thick huddles, but soon opened up. Two guard dogs barked in the distance. At the center of the clearing, a man dug a small hole. A machete poked from the earth like a marker. A tiny cardboard box filled with four bottles of Jamaican rum sat next to it. Lord Evader had changed into a denim shirt and threadbare dungarees. Hopping out of the small grave, he straightened his bowler hat, then swiped up his machete, carrying it on his shoulder like it was a backpack and he was on his way to school.

"Catch you at a bad time?" Owen crept his hand to his Jericho.

Lord Evader swaggered past the box of rum and stabbed the dirt with his machete before plopping down. He laid out an array of marijuana and papers with the sacrosanct air of preparing for communion. After rolling his spliff, he offered it up. "Do you like to blow bush tea?"

"I'm good." I held my hands up.

Lord Evader leaned his head back and let a thick plume of smoke issue from his mouth. "Me, too. Fulla vibes."

"I bet you are." Owen moved his hand away from his Jericho.

I elbowed him gently. "We hear you're the go-to guy for ghost stories. Sorry, duppy stories."

"Puppy?" Holly whispered to Owen.

"Shh," Owen said.

"Them say that duppy dead out," Lord Evader said. "The Maroons considered the cotton trees sacred. They believe duppies often danced among the branches of those rooted in graveyards."

"Carmen said you could tell us more about the . . . Old Higue?" Holly raised her voice with uncertainty.

"Old Higue. Yes, man. That what we call any old witch. I grew up around here, not two miles from this very spot. I remember when I was a boy having to walk past the house of an Old Higue. The chill that crawled up and down my back like stepping in front of Death. This haggish-looking woman. Ageless, years upon years upon years. My grandmother told me she used to provide the witch with food. Since we barely had food for our pot, it wasn't fair, I said. But my grandmother warned me that taking care of her was for our own protection. But then children started to die mysteriously. That was when we all knew what we was dealing with was a true Old Higue, but we were too scared to confront her. We just make cross marks by their house and hung a blue cross over the cradle of any new baby. But soon she disappear. One night, a fireball left her house and she was never seen again."

"A fireball?"

"Yes, man. The Old Higue waits until early morning when everyone is asleep, she sheds her skin like a snake, and then transforms into a ball of fire. Flies from her house and lands on the roof of another. If there is a baby in a cradle, she will suck it dry, dry, dry. Only then does she go home."

"So . . . vampire." Owen turned to me. "Why didn't your aunt just say 'skin-shedding vampire'?"

"This just gets better and better," Holly said.

"Old Higue would hang her skin on branches as a warning. If her skin is found before it is put back on, salt and pepper or vinegar thrown on it, that ends her."

"Rice. Salt and pepper. Vinegar. At this rate I don't know whether to cut its head off or toss a salad," Owen said.

Lord Evader continued, his yellow eyes focused on me. "She may have a raw body, skinny fingers, and red eyes, but in the end, she just an old witch. Miss Carmen knows. She thinks she hide it, but I know her mother was a powerful obeah ma. She worked the old ways, set duppies on people. People they come trouble her, all vex up about them neighbor or something. She'd work obeah on them and seldom asked for anything."

"Her mother?" I feared where this might be heading. "Her mother lives here, too?"

"When life hard, you try anything." Lord Evader stared long and hard at me. He held the burning spliff between his fingers and gestured at me. "You an obeah man, too."

"I don't think so."

"You have faith. So if an obeah man or an obeah ma try to work obeah on you, it wouldn't work. Your faith . . . it has been bruised. You've seen things and have your doubts. Like passing clouds over the sun, but the light is still there waiting to burst through."

I stood there, suddenly self-conscious of all eyes trained on me.

"Where's the guest house?" Owen chimed in, sparing me any more discomfort.

"You're there." Lord Evader cast his arms about, waving him toward the small shed. "We're back where Miss Carmen buries the things she doesn't like to think about."

"You've got to be freaking kidding me. I might as well sleep in a tree. Look, I'm securing the perimeter, you two get yourselves pretty. If this thing likes to come out before daybreak, we'll just have to hunt it down tonight before it can hit its snooze button."

I prepared to leave, but Lord Evader took me by the arm. "No one appreciates the stories like they used to. The Old Higue may be the last of her kind. After this, she may only live on in stories, but there are fewer and fewer storytellers. Like I told you, you hunting your heritage."

Aunt Carmen had small bottles of Jamaican Rum Cream set out on the dresser, which tasted like a vanilla milk shake spiked with rum. A mosquito net over the bed fluttered in the breeze. A lizard skittered across the wall, stopped, and stared at me as if I were the one intruding. Staring through the curtainless window, I rested on top of the made bed in my full body armor. Body armor was not designed for tropical climes. My fellow Monster Hunters always liked to say that I'd get used to the heat. They lied, but I did get used to the protection it offered. Despite being suited up, I felt the pressure of an incoming storm closing in. Wind swept through the leaves of the breadfruit trees which sounded like rainfall. A chirping chorus of cicadas filled the night.

"You all right?" Holly fastened the last part of her body armor as she came out of the bathroom.

"I don't know how to explain it. For a long time, I've just felt so disconnected from everything. Like I have no roots to ground me. I don't know. Maybe it's just the idea of being able to help out family."

"Even family so distant you couldn't pick them out of a lineup?" Holly asked.

"Like I said, I don't know how to explain it. I just have a hole gnawing at me, something missing. I just need to see this through." I closed my eyes. "I still have the nightmares, you know."

"About the zombies?" Holly stared at me with those blue eyes of hers that never missed anything.

It seemed like my life kept coming back to voodoo of some sort. It was a voodoo priestess who terrorized my home in Florida, stirring up zombies which I had to put down with a pickaxe. All the talk about obeah and the undead left me more on edge than I was ready to admit. "Yeah. This mission, it's just got me all turned around. Like there's a debt that I owe."

"You don't owe anyone anything, Trip." Holly sat on the edge of the bed. She put her hand on my arm. "I'm only going to say this once and if you ask me about it later, I'll deny it, but you're a good man, John Jermain Jones."

"Thank you... Mrs. John Jermain Jones."

Holly punched me in the leg.

We slipped out the back entrance of Carmen's house. A DJ had begun to spin a few dancehall tracks while people milled about in line for food. We couldn't escape all of the curious stares. Two Americans in paramilitary gear would certainly stir the rumor mill. Carmen nodded her approval. When we turned the corner, Owen was slipping a tank onto his back.

"What is that?" I asked.

"The XM42 flamethrower. These are perfectly legal to use to clear weeds. Or snow."

"Though clearing the undead is probably an off-brand use."

"Never fight high-level undead without one," Owen said.

A few scattered houses hid behind Carmen's property. Dilapidated shacks I thought abandoned, save for the furtive movement of extinguishing a gas lamp at our approach. The sounds of the Nine Nights retreated to the main house. The hillside took on a foreboding aspect at night. Its crests and tree line a series of shadows against an indigo sky full of more stars than I could ever remember seeing. We formed a skirmish line with Holly on point. She hefted the Negev machine gun like it was an extension of her arm.

"Do you hear that?" I asked.

"Hear what?" Owen said.

"Exactly. It all stopped. No birds. No cicadas. Everything's quiet."

A small path cut through the overgrown trees. Owen tromped through the woods. I used to play football in college and it would be easy to confuse Owen with a simple bruiser, but he knew how to use his bulk when he moved. His bulky frame pushed through like he dared nature to get in his way.

"Anything?" I asked into the comm link.

"Nothing yet." Holly moved further ahead of us. "Wait, I may have a trail. Leads back past the property line. Got some houses back there."

I had the undefinable feeling that we were being watched. Something stalked the woods alongside us, waiting for its time to strike. Tree branches crunched loudly underfoot, each twig snapping and echoing across the hills. I'd grabbed the Beretta 1301 Tactical shotgun and carried it at the low ready. I switched to my helmet-mounted night vision monocular. Though I had a 1,000 lumen Nitecore MH12 LED flashlight affixed to my shotgun, a second light casting the world in green was picked up by the monocular. The trees loomed tall overhead, now so thick they blocked the night sky. Anything could hide among their high limbs. Owen had the same idea, spending as much time scanning the branches above as the path in front of us.

Holly pointed to the nearest house and signaled that she was going around back. I stepped to the front door. It didn't quite fit in the frame as if the house had been assembled from spare materials.

"Let's see if anyone's home," Owen said.

The house was a small open room with two tiny windows. Broken bottles lined the shelves. In the center of the floor was a brass bowl with dried blood on it. All manner of teeth lay scattered around it. Other bowls sat on a makeshift bench, half filled with grave dirt.

"What do you think?" Owen sifted through a pile of dirt.

"Witch." Holly stood by the rear door.

"Definitely a witch," I said. I paused at a framed photo on a shelf—a picture of an older woman next to a young Carmen who could be her twin in another ten years. The air temperature dropped several degrees. I set the photograph back on the shelf with calculated care, not wanting to make any sudden movements.

"We've got company," I whispered.

A woman stood in the corner, hunched over, like a grandmother whose arthritic bones barely allowed her to stand.

"Trip? Go to white light," Holly yelled in my ear.

I flipped my monocular back and activated the Nitecore on the forearm of my shotgun. The light filled the small room with such intensity, it seared our eyes for a moment. That moment froze in time. The old woman reared, her skinless body a mass of pulsing, moist muscle and tendons. A mane of gray hair stuck to the undulating flesh of her face. Her brown eyes stared at me as if from behind a pink mask of freshly butchered meat. The Old Higue tensed, her movements slow and deliberate, her bones aged and full of ache. Her slow grind of teeth approximated a smile.

With only a hiss as warning, she sprang at me. Her bare fist struck me in the gut with the weight of having slipped on a set of brass knuckles. The blow landed deep and with such force, I nearly vomited. I doubled over and left my feet, flying into the shack wall. Plates toppled from the shelves, crashing all around me. I struggled to my feet and assumed a fighting stance. My legs unsteady beneath me, I feared I might appear drunk.

Without skin to interpret the movements of her facial muscles, her face was an emotionless, blank canvas. Her eyes refused to blink. Weaponless, I threw a series of quick jabs. She let the blows land. She kicked me in the chest. All air left my lungs. I had the sensation of plunging into deep, cold waters.

Holly opened fire. The Old Higue howled as the shells ripped into her. She threw her head back and time seemed to slow. Debris wafting in the air got caught up in an invisible stream and ignited. Her body erupted into flames before collapsing in on itself, forming a ball of flame. The incandescent ball shot upward through the roof and back the direction we came.

"Come on," I yelled.

We ran through the woods at full speed. The Old Higue landed squarely atop Lord Evader's house. It screeched. With a bottle of rum in one hand, Lord Evader stumbled out of his room, took one look at the Old Higue, and held his arms up to shield himself. I ran and tackled him, barely avoiding the swipe of one of her wizened claws. She shredded the back of my armor.

Holly provided cover fire. The creature slowed, wanting to chase after me, but needing to deal with the more immediate threat first.

"Come and get some," Holly yelled. She swung the Negev back in its direction.

I pointed Lord Evader back to Carmen's house before heading back to flank the creature. On my way, I grabbed Lord Evader's machete. I turned it over in my hands. "Just like old times."

Holly had the beams of her Nitecore trained on the Old Higue but I noticed something fluttering in the trees behind it.

"Owen, behind you. In the trees."

A low-hanging branch of a cotton tree, stark and loathsome in the dim light, had something quavered along it like thick, ropey, spider webs, tangled among its limbs. The Old Higue's skin.

"I'm all out of salt," Owen yelled. "This will have to do."

Owen let loose with the flamethrower. Streams of fire lit up the countryside. The Old Higue turned toward Owen and wailed like a mother grieving the loss of its child. Holly ceased fire as I neared the creature.

"Over here," I said.

The Old Higue turned in time to see the swing of my blade as it sliced through its throat. The blade lodged in the beast's neck. Rather than pull it free to chance another swing, I fell on top of her and drove the blade the rest of the way through. I laid on top of her, face to face, the last fetid puff of breath escaping her mouth before her head tumbled from her body.

✧　　✧　　✧

Holly and Owen carted up the remains of the Old Higue and gave Carmen and me some space for privacy.

"Thank you." Carmen watched them load the body.

"That's what family is for. To take care of one another and deal with the problems outsiders wouldn't understand."

There was another Hebrew word that always stuck with me: *mishpacha*, which means "family." I glanced at Holly and Owen, who waved me to hurry along before the police arrived with questions I didn't feel like answering. In the end, it was the people to whom you belonged, who always had your back, who were family. And family took care of family.

It is difficult to verify if this historical account is authentic or an elaborate forgery. I include it here, because if true, the ramifications are very troubling.   —A.L.

The Bride

Brad R. Torgersen

"Grandfather," the young man said, standing deferentially in the doorway to Benjamin Franklin's study.

"William," the older man said over his shoulder, his bespectacled face illuminated by the oil lamp perched on his writing desk. The quill in his hand was still poised over the parchment, upon which he'd been quickly scribbling. Now, more than ever, Benjamin Franklin's world was a whirlwind of correspondence.

"There are two gentlemen at the door," the young man said.

"Frenchmen?" the old man asked.

"No, Grandfather. Or, at least, only one of them is French. They say they're from . . . it's regarding General Washington, sir. About the Army. They say they can help."

Benjamin Franklin's spine straightened, and he slowly turned to the side, to stare at his grandson—and secretary, and personal aide—over the rims of his round glasses. It was late in the evening for such unannounced and uninvited visitors. Very odd indeed.

"Who?" the old man asked, his left eyebrow arched slightly.

"The first is Hessian, someone calling himself Van Stooburn."

"It's *von Steuben*," a French-accented voice corrected loudly, from behind William's position. "And the Baron is *Prussian*."

Two men appeared behind William, and the young man nervously clasped his hands together, looking from his grandfather's face, to the faces of the visitors, and back again. A commoner would have been promptly remonstrated for interrupting Franklin's

123

peace and quiet. But the Baron was someone already acquainted with Franklin. So the American diplomat sighed a long, tired exhale, and beckoned the two men forward.

"It's all right, William," the old man said. "Please make sure the front door is closed. I am sure whatever business the Baron has brought to me tonight can be handled expeditiously."

William dipped his chin in acknowledgment and shuffled quickly from the doorway. The Baron strode in, followed by his ever-present attaché, Louis de Pontière, who closed the study door behind them.

"The answer is still no," Franklin said, standing up from his small bench at the desk and placing the tips of his fingers into a pocket on his vest, over his ever-growing belly. The American diplomat wasn't a spring chicken any longer, and the various parlors and courts of Paris kept him well supplied with a variety of culinary delicacies. Perhaps too well supplied? Not that it mattered much. Franklin wasn't marching with Washington. He was a persuader, not a fighter. And thus far, his mission—as envoy to France—had been going extremely well. The French liked him. They liked his ideas. They liked his sense of humor. He was winning them over.

But not everyone was pleased with what Franklin had been able to tell them.

Von Steuben turned to his young aide and barked out something in guttural Deutsch.

"The Baron says he understands you won't make any promises which your Continental Congress cannot keep," Louis said, his English proficient and refined. "But the Baron also wishes to inform you that the situation has changed."

"Oh?" Ben Franklin said, taking a couple of steps forward. "In what way?"

Louis briefly translated the question for the Baron, who again replied in Deutsch.

"The Baron says he has been made aware of a terrible new weapon, being prepared by Landgrave Frederick at the direct request of King George, and which is due to set sail for America."

"A new weapon?" Franklin said, feeling the hair on the back of his neck begin to stand up. He'd heard rumors—through the Freemasons of Paris—that the Hessians had been promising the King of England something special, and for which the King might pay a princely sum. So far, Franklin had been unable to come up with anything conclusive, so he'd not bothered to get word to Washington or any of the others. But if the Baron was here tonight—rudely unannounced—it meant that the Baron was bringing more to Franklin's door than mere speculation.

"Yes," said Louis.

"What's the nature of this weapon?" Franklin asked.

Von Steuben's frown deepened, and he looked Franklin square in the face, before uttering the name, "Dippel."

Franklin closed his eyes, his mouth souring.

"Nonsense," the old American said.

Von Steuben nodded his head up and down twice in affirmation, saying "Dippel" again.

"The Baron believes you know what to do about it—that you can *stop* the new female monster."

"Female this time, eh? Perhaps," Franklin said. "But there were extenuating circumstances regarding the first example, the details of which I am not at liberty to discuss with the Baron."

Von Steuben listened while Louis made his report, then the Baron began to practically shout, gesticulating with his hands.

The young aide calmly said, "The Baron is sure that this thing is on its way to your country, sir."

"How does the Baron know that?" Franklin asked sharply.

Louis repeated the questions to his master...and translated the response.

"There are family connections involved, which are too complicated to explain to you tonight, Monsieur Franklin. The Baron hopes that you will understand the gravity of this situation. He also hopes that you will appreciate the fact that the Baron spared no time, nor expense, in bringing the matter to your attention—before it's too late."

"Ah," Franklin said. "The Baron wants in with Washington that badly, eh? There's still no money in it. Washington can't even pay his own officers, much less Prussian aristocrats seeking to make a name for themselves during a foreign campaign. Why do you think I'm in Paris in the first place, Monsieur? For vacation? For the women? It might seem to some that I am an old man on holiday, but the future of my home is at stake, and I am doing everything in my power to ensure that France remains with us during our fight against the English Crown."

Louis translated...and received a response.

"The Baron knows all this already," Louis said, "but he admires what you and Washington are doing. He deems it a righteous quarrel. He hopes that if he assists you in rendering the Hessian weapon harmless, you will in turn pass the good word to Washington regarding the Baron's value and abilities."

"Does the Baron know where this weapon is?"

"Not at the moment," Louis said. "But we believe we know where and when the weapon is due to depart overseas. We need only be there to interdict."

Franklin pulled off his spectacles and rubbed one eye with his fist.

"Like I told you, there were extenuating circumstances the first time. And if we're dealing with what I *think* we're dealing with—and what you seem to think we're dealing with, too—I don't have any alchemical weaponry, nor occult incantation, with which to send this thing back to Hell."

Louis translated. The Baron threw up his hands, eyes rolling.

"Then how, Monsieur Franklin, *did* you manage it? With the other one? With the one you call Franks?"

It was three weeks overland, or six days by ship. Both Franklin and Von Steuben agreed that the ship was preferable, though they'd need a day in Amsterdam—to cover their tracks. Which was where Franklin's connections with the Freemasons of Paris came in handy. Kings might make or break agreements at will, but the Freemasons—with their fraternity stretching throughout Enlightened homes and courts across Europe—were something else again. Franklin had but to ask and the network unfolded its rhetorical wings, spiriting him and the Baron across contested international waters, and depositing them on decidedly Teutonic shores—without either the French, nor the British, being any the wiser. For all anyone knew—and Franklin's grandson would tell—the old emissary was at home, recovering from yet another episode of gout. Well-wishers were permitted to leave gifts or notes in the foyer, but no one was allowed to see Franklin in his bed.

Now on German soil, it was the Baron who navigated deftly. If anyone in this part of the world noticed Von Steuben's dialect or accent, they didn't say it. Perhaps the Baron was simply that good at effecting a local quality, whenever he spoke? Benjamin

Franklin could not tell. And Louis de Pontière, for all his talkativeness at sea, had become practically mute now that they were moving in unfamiliar circles.

Franklin was simply reminded of the fact that he was *old*. Too old, certainly, to be undertaking such an adventure without a small host of helpers and assistants to ensure that the American diplomat was properly protected and cared for. If anything happened to him while he was away, William would be hard-pressed to explain Franklin's disappearance. The Continental Congress *had* to keep the French aligned with the Congress, and almost all of that burden rested on Franklin's shoulders.

Still, the mere mention of the name *Franks* had spurred Benjamin to action.

"He's not like any man," Franklin had explained one evening while he, the Baron, and the Baron's aide were staring over their ship's railing into the greenish depths of the sea. "When they brought him to me, he should have been *dead*. It took a direct hit from a field gun—a whole cannonball, you understand!—to neutralize Franks. When Washington's men dropped the body off with me in Philadelphia, I thought they were depositing a cadaver. Imagine my shock to discover that the torso—or what was left of it—still had a pulse, and that tiny amounts of blood, mingled with that cursed Dippel's Oil, flowed in the torso's veins. I knew then that I was dealing with something truly extraordinary."

"But how do we *stop* it?" Louis pleaded, staring past the waves, out to the clouds on the horizon.

"I told you," the old diplomat said, "in the case of Franks, it was a direct hit with a field gun. But that did not kill him. I am not even convinced that a creature such as Franks *can* be killed. Which is why I was amazed to learn—upon sewing the creature back together using fresh cadavers from the Philadelphia medical college—that Franks wished to serve the Continental Congress. Can you imagine?"

"So that was it?" Louis said, after repeating Benjamin's words to Von Steuben. "Franks is made whole again and bends his knee to your cause?"

"No," the old man said. "I knew we couldn't simply make him our slave. We have too much of that back home as it is, you know? We've entered an age when men must do away with that kind of thing. It was wrong in the time of the Pharaoh. It was wrong in the time of Caesar. It remains wrong, even if some of my countrymen disagree. Anyway, I didn't want Franks chained to us. I wanted him with us of his own accord, compacted in agreement, like a man. So we drew it up formally, with stipulations. Franks would serve the Continental Congress, and we would give Franks a cause worth fighting for—with one caveat."

"And that was?" Louis asked, after translating for the Baron.

"Franks made it clear that there would be no more like him."

"What does that mean?"

"Well, putting the poor creature back together—with flesh and bone from several different bodies—I learned enough about him, and also about Dippel's Oil, that I probably could have tried to produce a facsimile. I certainly know more about electrical fire than anyone else at home, and it's the electrical fire—combined with Dippel's Oil—that makes a thing like Franks possible. One of the two, by itself, is not sufficient. Combine them in the right ways, with enough raw tissue, and a man might create *anything.* Even something grotesquely *unlike* a man. But there's more to it, even than that."

"Yes?" Louis said, after a short pause to translate.

"I deduce that Franks first came to this Earth as a disembodied spirit."

"You mean, like a ghost?"

"Possibly, though I don't think that word is right. A ghost implies the spirit of one who has lived and died. Franks never even had the chance to live—until Johann Konrad Dippel gave him that chance. Now? Now, Baron von Steuben has learned that Dippel did not terminate his experiments after Franks' creation. The Freemasons had assumed that Dippel quit, when I was still a young man in England. But it seems Dippel did not. How or why this second creation has eluded attention, until now..."

"So we blow it up," Louis said, for his master. "Or we burn it. To pieces, or to ashes. That doesn't seem so hard."

"Washington's troops—in their graves—would disagree with that assessment."

"Do you propose to talk to it, then? This she-creature of Dippel's design?"

"I don't know, sir. Having not even seen it yet, I really don't know."

And so, the three men found themselves spying on a ship, far from any of their homes, and with only a few pistols tucked into their belts, and no real plan other than to wait and see who—or what—was taken aboard.

Yet again, Benjamin Franklin was reminded of his age. Even one night on the harbor—with the damp, cold air making beads of water on his marten fur hat—could be the death of him. The weapon he carried was one the young French aide had loaded for him. Franklin doubted he had the reflexes or the eyes enough to fire—and hit anything. Besides, a musket ball would not stop a creature like Franks any more than a flea might stop Franks. If things got desperate, the Baron proposed to set the entire ship aflame. The gunholes in the ship's side meant there should be cannon powder aboard. The Baron claimed to know a thing or two about that. Franklin did not and could not have tried to guide them to the armory. Again, he was a man of reason, not of action. Yet here he was, trying to take action, with the skimpiest of reasons.

Maybe they would get lucky, and the rumor of the Hessian weapon would turn out to be just that—rumor. They could all have a good laugh about it on the way back to Franklin's Paris home. And Franklin would write an introduction letter, on behalf of the Baron, to General Washington, anyway. Von Steuben may have been a Prussian aristocrat looking to pad his service resume, but he was not a coward. He was prepared to give his life if it meant stopping Dippel's second monster; it showed in Von Steuben's eyes. And the young French aide? He would follow his master to Hell, if necessary. So Franklin would write his letter on behalf of them both. The Revolution needed grit.

There weren't many lamps on the docks. Nor many people. Occasionally, sailors speaking half a dozen different languages wandered past the stack of barrels where Von Steuben had hidden just before dusk. There was enough space between the huge casks to watch the specific dock for the specific ship which had been named in Von Steuben's communiqués. Either his intelligence was right, or it was wrong. Either the she-monster of Johann Dippel was here tonight, or it was not. They would just have to wait and see.

"Wake up, old man," whispered Louis.

Benjamin Franklin's eyes fluttered open, and he realized he'd fallen asleep, slumping against one of the barrels. His greatcoat was wrapped tightly around him, against the chill, damp air, and he wondered how long he'd been dreaming. In his mind, he had been rebuilding Franks—over and over and over again—like assembling the grizzly pieces of a bloody, putrid puzzle. If he'd not been a man of science, Franklin doubted he'd have had the stomach for it. Even so, repeating the process *ad infinitum,* had been the most unpleasant type of bad dream.

"Is something happening?" Franklin whispered.

"*Ja,*" said Von Steuben, who was crouched, peering between the barrels.

The Prussian whispered to the Frenchman, and the Frenchman whispered to the American.

"A wagon has arrived. The dock is practically deserted. It's going to be dawn soon, but we're still in complete darkness. No one has gone aboard or left the ship in many minutes. The wagon is just sitting there. It does not appear to be a normal wagon. There are iron bars and the wood seems to be of a particularly heavy grain. A dozen different men—wearing Hessian uniforms— appear to be waiting nervously. They are armed."

Franklin absorbed the details, not bothering to look for himself. He could well imagine in his mind what it might take to transport Franks safely across country. In Franks' specific case, he had worked for the Hessians by choice—because the Hessians who had been sent to kill Franks had instead made Franks an offer. Much as Franklin himself had eventually made Franks an offer.

This new creature? Who knew what motivated it or what allegiance it felt—if any—to the nations of men.

Finally, there was some noise as if a gate had been opened.

Von Steuben continued to report, and Louis continued to translate.

"The side of the wagon has come open, finally. And there is... there is a *young* woman descending down to a footstool placed before her. She is beautiful. She does not appear to be much over a score of years old. She is dressed as a proper lady of society. Several of the Hessians are bringing out two trunks. The trunks are being carried up to the ship. The woman is being spoken to by one of the Hessian officers."

Franks, robust as he was, had still been a crude work. Stronger than a team of oxen, but also just as ugly. Either Dippel had significantly advanced his process and technique—between the two inceptions—or Franklin and the Baron had come a long way for nothing.

Ben hoped for the latter. But how to be sure?

"We have to get in close," the American whispered. "Sitting up here, taking notes, doesn't do us much good. We have to look in her eyes. They won't be quite like the eyes of any living man or woman either of you have ever seen. You will understand what I am talking about when the time comes."

Von Steuben asked and Louis translated, "How do you propose we do that with so many infantry standing about, looking nervous?"

Franklin thought about it for a moment.

"We need a distraction," the American said. "Something spectacular enough that it keeps every single Hessian occupied, until we can confront that woman."

The three men sat in silence for many moments.

Eyeing what was to either side of them, Franklin finally asked, "What's in these barrels?"

The oil was cold and viscous, and it flowed out of the bung-holes rather sluggishly. Franklin was mildly appalled at the vandalism the three of them had wrought, but none of them had had any better ideas. Once the oil caught, they had to hope it made enough of a fire that all attention would be drawn to the burning barrels. The harbor watch would muster every able body to contain the flames—oil being notoriously difficult to deal with because water would only make it spread—and this might rope the Hessians into assisting, lest they be accused of cowardice.

In the confusion and the tumult, Franklin and Von Steuben would have their chance.

Assuming the young Frenchman could get his firestarting kit to work.

"Keep trying," Franklin encouraged. They'd spent so many hours in the dark, the tiny sparks from the flint seemed alarmingly bright. The Hessians or the harbor watch might see them and come to investigate.

Von Steuben muttered something under his breath and tapped one of the muskets on his aide's waist.

"Firing a weapon would be suicide," Franklin hissed. "Even if you did ignite the oil, the noise would draw them right to us—before the flame got big enough to mask our maneuvering."

"No," Louis said, pausing, the whites of his wide eyes just barely visible. "The Baron suggests we use a bead of powder to ignite the oil."

Louis switched to his powder horn, pouring out a little line of black dust over the surface of the pooling oil. Franklin's eyes could barely make out the young man's hands as he worked.

"You two had better be well away from this when it goes," Louis said. "In fact, *far* away."

"What about you?" Franklin asked.

"Assuming I am not burned to death, or captured, I will meet you at the gangplank to the ship."

A quick relay of instructions—aide to Baron, then Baron to aide—followed.

Von Steuben clapped the Frenchman lightly on the young man's shoulder, then he was leading Franklin out into the dark, cold, exposed, night air.

The two older men walked calmly—neither pussyfooting, nor hurrying. This deep into the wee hours, there were only the few lights near the ships to worry about, and their range was limited. If anyone could see the Baron and the American moving, they would be mere shadows against the backdrop of the sea, with the harbor's black surface gently slapping against pylons and ships' hulls alike.

Suddenly, Franklin saw illumination on the side of one of the far ships. Illumination coming from behind him.

"That did it," Benjamin said, and then without having to be told, he and Von Steuben changed direction and began to angle over and down toward their destination.

At first, only one voice rang out. Then several. Every Hessian standing watch pivoted to stare up at the stack of casks which now boiled with thick, smokey flames.

Shouts turned to screams, and then the screams were drowned out by bells which began to clang loudly, again and again.

Glancing occasionally to see how bad the fire had gotten, Franklin again felt a pang of guilt: for the vandalism. He did not enjoy destruction for destruction's sake. He'd worked his whole life to build things, not ruin them. He also suddenly realized that such a fire might very well burn out of control, risking innocent lives.

The old inventor whispered fervent prayers as he and Von Steuben began to make their final, lengthy approach to the ship—praying that no innocent lives would be jeopardized this night. It was worth a lot, to halt the she-monster of Dippel in its tracks. Even the lives of the three men who'd conspired to confront and combat the beast. But that didn't mean Ben Franklin wanted anybody else to get hurt.

Suddenly, the cosmopolitan gentleman from Philadelphia felt a pang of empathy for his comrade Washington. Over on the other side of the Atlantic, George was fighting their cousins—the British—many of whom were not their enemies. Merely Englishmen and Scotsmen, Irishmen, and even Hessians, all pressed into service in the name of King George, who wouldn't let the American Colonies out of his grasp without a struggle. Washington's men had to shoot at people who might very well be blood relatives. Kin by birth and common heritage.

Then Franklin grunted and reminded himself to keep his feet moving—lest he gather so much wool, that he fall over and break something. They'd all known the Revolution couldn't be had without cost. And while Franklin had been content to serve as that Revolution's mouthpiece to Continental Europe, he'd never thought he might find himself engaging in any derring-do.

The old man picked up his feet and stayed after the Baron.

The ruse partially worked. About two thirds of the Hessian troops guarding the wagon left to go deal with the growing fire. One third stayed behind, while everyone else aboard the ships on several nearby docks—including the specific ship in question—came out on deck to see what was going on.

A few men began running down the gangplanks or climbing over nets and down the sides of their ships, to the docks, and dashing to help with the fire. What threatened one boat, threatened all boats. Other men simply gawked, as the barrels of oil were consumed in a huge geyser of flame that shot several stories into the air—a thick, angry column of black smoke curling off the top, and beginning to drift out over the docks and into the harbor town proper.

Louis de Pontière was nowhere to be seen.

As the Baron and Franklin both approached their intended destination, no eyes watched them. Everyone was gazing up at the conflagration which had ignited out of nowhere, and about which none of the several hundred men—all cobbled together into an ad hoc fire brigade—seemed to have any idea what to do about, oil being a literally slippery foe for any would-be firefighter to have to handle.

The woman, as well as her two trunks, was nowhere to be seen.

Noticing this as well, Von Steuben didn't stop. He walked right past the Hessian officer who'd been talking to her before—and who now stood gazing at the flames, occasionally shouting to his men—and proceeded up the gangplank, with the old American directly in his wake. Franklin was moving harder than he had in a long time, his blood pounding in his ears, while his breath wheezed in and out of his lungs. Not even the few nights he'd spent in bed with the women of Paris had given him such a workout. But then, the women had understood. The charming American democrat wasn't the freshest horse in the barn, even if his ideas did send the ladies swooning.

Up on deck, one of the ship's crew finally noticed strangers coming aboard and confronted the older men.

Hessian to Prussian, Von Steuben and their interlocutor argued it out.

Whatever Von Steuben managed to concoct as their reason being aboard, it satisfied the man who'd barred their path. The bearded sailor moved out of their way and allowed both Franklin and Von Steuben to make their way past several more sailors, who were all standing and watching the fire, until Von Steuben found a doorway that allowed them to take a steep flight of stairs belowdecks.

A second sailor confronted them. Guttural Deutsch flew back and forth between the men. Von Steuben was a natural in command. His demeanor broadcast authority with every syllable. He didn't just belong, he *owned*. This was *his* ship. Five minutes prior, he'd been slowly approaching the vessel like a burglar. Now Von Steuben barked orders like he was the captain himself.

Sailors came out of side passages, listened just long enough to decide they didn't want a piece of the gruff, imperious older man in the officious-looking officer's garb, and they quickly vanished back to where they'd been pretending to sleep through the alarm on the dock.

Finally, both Von Steuben and Franklin arrived at a single, closed, and apparently locked cabin door.

The Baron thumped a fist on the door proper, commanding entry.

A woman's voice—surprisingly and disarmingly pleasant, speaking perfectly in German—filtered back through the wood.

Von Steuben's face showed surprise; then he thumped the wood again and commanded entry a second time. Then he thumped the wood a third time, gave a third command and, lacking better alternatives, pulled one of the pistols from his belt and aimed it at the lock.

The pistol report—in the cramped spaces belowdecks—was deafening.

But it did get the door open, with smoke curling all around and splinters of wood and metal all over the deck beneath their feet.

Von Steuben barely got two strides into the cabin when a force of nature leapt from the shadows. A single set of candles on a tiny cabin table whooshed out, but not before Benjamin Franklin had a glimpse of the beast: arms outstretched, like a bat clawing the air, teeth bared, with eyes . . . yes, the *eyes*. There could be no mistaking it now. Dippel had returned to his fiendish work. Honing. Practicing. Apparently, perfecting?

Where Franks was a blundering buffalo, this new creation was as lithe and gorgeously ferocious as a leopard.

Von Steuben never had a chance. His surprised cry of pain was instantly snuffed out, then his body hit the floor.

Benjamin Franklin—old, still wheezing from exertion, and utterly unskilled and unprepared to defend his person—simply stood in the open doorway and waited for the end. It would be quick. It would be, hopefully, painless. He was sorry that he could not have made some kind of reconnaissance report to the Continental Congress—to let them know what they were facing. Franks had been a blunt instrument. This new one? A surgeon's scalpel.

The woman was on Franklin before he even knew what had happened. He hit the floor hard, the air rushing from his lungs, with the she-creature pinning him beneath her—legs straddling Franklin's rib cage and squeezing with astounding strength.

The words she said in German did not register and Ben's face must have shown it because the she-beast instantly switched to very fluent, very refined French.

"How did you find me? Was it the Landgrave? I'm not letting him switch his choice now. Not after all the years I gave to him!"

Franklin felt his ribs complaining and tried to speak, but could only gasp with pain.

"Tell me!" the woman, with those telltale unnatural eyes, commanded. "Are you here to claim a bounty?"

The woman raised her arm, cocking her fist back for what would surely be a jaw-crushing blow, and Franklin merely stared up at her, unable to stop her; the pistol in his belt hopelessly pinned.

"Mercy!" Benjamin Franklin finally managed to force through his lips.

"For you and your kind?" the woman spat, and then laughed—a hard, cruel, gloating noise that seemed to make the whole passageway darken with a kind of feral, ominous tension.

"Not...not...not for us," Franklin gasped. "For *you*. For... a spirit who could never be born."

The hard laughter instantly stopped. With her fist still cocked and ready to strike a killing blow, the woman's expression suddenly became confused.

"What...what did you say?"

Her legs, clamped around Franklin's ribs, loosened.

Ben Franklin drew in several long, painful breaths and laid his head back onto the deck, closing his eyes. He didn't know where Louis was. Probably dead, or caught in the act of setting the barrels on fire. The Baron? Also probably dead. And even if this she-creature let Ben live, what would the crew and the Hessians do? Franklin was positively powerless.

But he still had his words. Always, Benjamin Franklin had his words.

"I know what you are," Franklin said, opening his eyes and gazing up into the woman's face. She was remarkably beautiful, with a full mouth, lovely, well-defined cheeks, a proud bearing, and blond hair the color of soft gold.

"Don't *speak* to me of what I am," the woman hissed.

"Nevertheless," Franklin said, "I know. Because I've known one just like you. He was sent, like you're being sent, to fight us. To fight in America. He was a cudgel, but you are a rapier—the one smashes, the other slashes—hunting men, and otherly things...the demons that stalk the shadows. The ones we scholars of science sometimes dare not talk about, but we know are still waiting. He's out there right now, fighting the darkness. I think he is trying to atone. For what, I have never been quite sure. If you're like him, and I think you are, you might know better than I."

The woman stared down at Franklin, her eyes boring into his soul, searching for something, as if trying to read the pages of Benjamin Franklin's brain.

The cocked fist slowly lowered.

"I know the one of whom you speak," she said, her voice gone cold, almost monotone. "He was with us in the beginning, for the very first war. The war when it all began. Before this world existed. I was there, when he entered Dippel's golem—seizing for himself what so many of us had always wanted."

"Franks told me God commanded him to serve us," Benjamin said.

"Franks? Is that what he calls himself? How appropriate. Me? I took a very different path. Dippel was in despair after his first creation fled. The men who'd come for Franks? They took Dippel away in chains. Threw him to the floor before the court of the Landgrave. Dippel begged for his life. He promised the Landgrave anything. The Landgrave commanded Dippel to make *me*."

"As a . . . bride?" Franklin said.

"The perfect object of the Landgrave's desire. I took this body when I had the chance, but it was a gamble I learned to regret. Human beings are hard for me to relate to. I hated any man who touched me. I made a poor wife. So then I was deemed a prisoner. Tortured. Starved. Left to die. But my kind, we do not die from neglect alone. We endure. And the prisoner was eventually summoned for a new purpose, and taught manners and etiquette, and how to learn languages, and about the art of going into the courts of other houses and other lands, to seduce enemies to their beds . . . where I would finish them."

"I believe it," Franklin croaked.

"The English Crown believes if it can just get rid of a few key people in your little Revolution, the Colonies will come back. Most of the Colonists are loyal to the Crown, you know."

"I know," Franklin said. "It doesn't make any difference. We will be free, one way or another. And so too could you be, if you wish."

"To be like *him*?" she said viciously. "Your battering ram against the others who call the darkness home?"

"Or not," Franklin said. "He entered into the contract of his own free will, and we abide that contract . . . although, discovering your existence does complicate things."

"Why?"

"He will seek to destroy you," Franklin said direly. "There are to be no others like him. Ever. He may even think you are a violation of our contract and try to destroy us, too."

The woman considered, her expression turning thoughtful.

"Yes...yes, I think you just might be right about that."

"What keeps you in the service of the Hessians?" Franklin asked.

"It's all I know!" she spat. "It's the only purpose I have, beyond existing."

"We could help you find a new purpose," Franklin said, managing a small smile.

The sound of running feet in the passageways alerted both of them to the fact that whatever distraction had been provided outside, it was now ending. Von Steuben's pistol shot had drawn plenty of attention on its own.

"And we could find a way to keep Franks from finding out about you," Franklin offered, his smile broadening. "But first we have to find a way out of this mess."

The sound of running feet grew louder.

There was a tiny moment of indecision on the woman's face—sculpted, perfect, like Michelangelo would have done, but in living flesh—then she was dragging Franklin back into her cabin, slamming the door.

A man's groan alerted Franklin to the fact that Von Steuben was still alive.

"He's not hurt badly," the woman said. "but he won't be shooting the locks off of any other cabin doors anytime soon."

"We are trapped," Franklin said, "and one of our party is still missing."

"We'll look for him later," she said.

"You presume there will *be* a later," Benjamin remarked dryly.

"I have survived far worse. Just don't leave this cabin. I will take care of everything else. You just have to promise me that you're good on your word, *Monsieur Franklin*."

"How do you know who I am?"

"Now that we've been talking, I realize you are one of my intended targets."

"I think I ought to be...flattered?" Franklin said, half in jest.

"Promise!" she spat.

"I promise before God the Creator, and on my honor as a gentleman, that the Continental Congress shall make a home for you...of your own choosing and desire. A woman with your abilities could do any number of things. And Franks won't know anything about it. To him, you will not exist."

"Good. Then I agree."

Jane Yellowrock is a very successful Hunter who has worked with us at times. Surprisingly, her exploits have been chronicled in a series of bestselling novels and sold as "urban fantasy" in stores everywhere. I believe this to be some sort of MCB trick to confuse the general public.　　　　　　　　　　　　　　　　　—A.L.

She Bitch, Killer of Kits

Faith Hunter

The child was twelve, one of those gorgeous blondes with blue eyes and creamy skin, but so pale she nearly matched the white of the hospital sheets and the bandages that covered her arms. Eventually the wounds would close, the scars would heal, shrink, and fade. Maybe. Possibly. If she was allowed to live. The doctors said there was a fifty percent chance she'd go furry at the full moon. Fifty percent chance. *Crap.* Furry meant that she'd be insane, biting anything that moved. A werewolf. For the rest of her unnatural, short life.

The two suits in the hallway outside the door were to make sure that she stayed in the hospital, under observation. Their job was to put a bullet in her brain if she changed on the full moon, though no one had told her or her parents that. It had to be the most difficult job on the planet, and I wouldn't change places with the shooters for love nor money. My job was a lot easier—to track down and kill the clawed and fanged wolf that bit her. If I took the job.

"Is that all you remember, Sandra?" I asked.

Her mother's grip tightened on her hand. Mrs. Doherty was sick and tired of all the questions, all the law enforcement people traipsing in and out, and the media parked in front of the hospital, constantly trying to get inside. "That's what she said.

139

That's what she's said to every single person who's asked. That's all she remembers."

I gave her a commiserating shrug. "I know it's annoying. But memory is a crazy thing. Sometimes things jog loose and we remember more later." I knew. I remembered my youth, some one hundred seventy years ago. Skinwalkers live long. Few prosper.

I turned my eyes back to Sandra's. "Like smells. Do you remember any smells? Food? Smoke? Cigarettes? Anything."

Sandra squinted her eyes, her mouth pulling down, and I knew that the mention of scent had triggered something in her memory. My heart rate spiked. "I smelled chemicals. And meat cooking. Like when you cook steak on the grill, Daddy," she said to the silent man sitting in the chair by the window.

"All the time or only sometimes?" I asked.

"All the time when the sun was up. Most of the time at night. And...there was a lot of noise. Trucks? And...she called me Baby Girl and Punkin and Becca. *Not* my name."

As if, in the insane way of werewolves, she had been replacing a lost child. I must have given away my interest because Mr. Doherty leaned in and asked, "Is that important?" He was a small man compared to my six feet in height but he outweighed me by eighty pounds, all tight, protective muscle.

"Could be." I gave him a maybe/maybe-not look and pulled a business card from a pocket. With two fingers, I held it out to Sandra's father. "I promise to tell you when I get the thing that hurt your daughter."

"That's more than anyone else has offered," he said, taking the card. "For that alone I'll call if she remembers more."

"My thanks." I turned to leave.

"You're Jane Yellowrock, aren't you?" he said. "Cherokee woman. Vampire hunter. 'Have Stakes Will Travel.' That's your motto."

I nodded, shoved my hip-length black braid over my shoulder and left the room. I didn't stop to make nice-nice with the two guards. My Beast wanted to tear their eyes out at the very thought of them killing Sandra. But they'd be just as happy killing me if they got a whiff of what I was. Gunmen on government pay couldn't be trusted to ask first and shoot later, and few people knew the difference between a skinwalker and a were. It didn't make me safer that most skinwalkers were evil, baby-eating things called "liver-eater" or "spear finger." I was a Cherokee skinwalker, the pre-white-man version, which meant I was sane and not a *u'tlun'ta,* pronounced *hut luna.* So far. But lucky me.

I left without speaking, my scuffed Lucchese boots too loud on the hospital floors, that hollow echo that spoke of ancient death, current death, and impending death. I hated hospitals. The stink of illness and broken bodies was foul even to humans, and with my skinwalker senses, it was an overpowering, fetid stink.

I pushed through the doors of Mission Health and out into the icy night. It was late fall, which, in the mountains, meant the first snow had already fallen and another was due. I'd gotten soft in the warm damp of New Orleans, but my Beast remembered everything there was to know about stalking prey in bare trees on frozen earth. She would love a hunt this time of year, so long as I didn't get bit. I had discovered a way around going wolfy, but it wasn't an easy process, and my magic had begun to change, sometimes in dangerous ways. I'd rather not use its less predictable elements.

The doors closed behind me and I took a deep breath. The frigid air smelled of home and, for a moment that lasted a single heartbeat, I let myself grieve for the things I had lost. Then I stepped into the street and headed for my bike, Bitsa. The Harley panhead was freshly repaired, an old beauty with lots of new parts and perfect, gleaming golden paint—puma claws reaching across the fuel tank. She was parked under a security light.

I stopped. Standing beside Bitsa was a long-forgotten piece of my past. I started walking again, hating that I had hesitated, hating that he saw me hesitate. Hating him. And I didn't hate many people.

I reached the bike without slowing and he stepped back. It was that or get shoved aside. His long legs were leaner than I remembered. Blondish hair dulled by silver. Jeans and T-shirt. Shoulder holster with a .45. Scruffy beard. Jacket. He still smelled of coffee and Irish Spring soap, and something inside me somersaulted, fisted up, and growled, though I kept it all inside.

"You still ride a kickstart," he said. *Observant.*

I didn't answer, just helmeted up, my eyes on his face. More craggy. The lines deeper.

"Fine. You goin' after the wolf?"

I straddled the Harley. Again, I didn't answer. Put a foot on the start and stood tall to kick Bitsa on.

"MHI has the gig," he said, warning me off.

I paused, letting my weight settle back to my feet, still straddling the panhead. I had never said the words, never had the chance, though for years they had burned in my chest. Maybe now was the time to get some closure. "Monster Hunter International is a decent organization. Ben and Laden are okay. They came back for me when you left me to die. If they show up, I'll utilize them. If they beat me to the punch, I'll help them." I let a hint of my Beast glow into my eyes. Nomad had seen that only once and it had scared him. Bad.

"Bite me, bitch," he spat.

Inside me, my Beast sat up. *Eat human? Eat former mate?*

My lips curled up, a toothy smile. "Tried that," I said to both of them. "Tasted like chicken." I came down on the start and Bitsa roared to life, that particular Harley rhythm that can't be imitated. I eased off and out of the parking lot. In my youth I had liked the bad boys, the dangerous ones, the kind that broke a girl's heart. I had learned a lot since then. Woman scorned and all that. I had been iffy on going after the wolf. Now? She was mine.

I was out on the open road before the grindylow crawled out of my bike jacket pocket and up to my shoulder. Grindys kill weres, any were that harms a human, but they're rare on this continent and little known. This one was neon green, the size of a six-month-old kitten, with steel claws sharp as razors. She had appeared in my hotel room last night. Maybe she came through the AC vent. Maybe she walked through the walls. I didn't know. I had met grindys before, and they were cute as the kittens they appeared to be until they needed to kill. Because of the coat color, I figured she was the littermate to the ones in New Orleans and Knoxville. This one loved to ride, nose to the wind. Somehow she didn't get blown off. Grindy magic. I'd named her Bean.

I stopped at a QT gas station and pulled up a sat-map of Asheville, one already highlighted by all the werewolf sightings, child disappearances, and odd animal attacks. Wolves are territorial, stick to known hunting ranges, and form packs. I figured this one was doing just that, biting to make a family she had lost. My partners in Yellowrock Security had marked off a likely hunting range centered by the sites and I followed the terrain, checking water sources and how the sun would rise and set against the ridges of the mountains. I texted the Youngers, back in New Orleans, "Taking the gig. Site looks good. More in a.m."

I weaponed up with what little gear I had checked on the flight to Charlotte and then stored in the saddlebags. No way was I riding anywhere now without weapons. Not with Nomad around again. A girl can't be too careful.

Before I started my hunt, I pulled a small flashlight and went over the bike with fingers, eyes, and nose until I found the small GPS tracker. Nomad had positioned it up under the seat, easy to find. Thinking it was a game, Bean joined the hunt. Together we found the second one attached to a saddlebag strap. The grindy found the third one wedged into the headlight casing. Nomad was a sneaky lil bastard. I wrote him a note with the word MHI on top, folded the scrap of paper around the trackers, and placed the package on pump number one.

I hadn't seen members of Monster Hunter International since they pulled me out of the Tennessee River, half dead from my second real run-in with a rogue-vampire. Nomad's and my very first hunt had been easy—stake, behead, and payment—an experience that left me cocky. The second rogue-vamp had been a near-death disaster, the event that sent me out on my own and Nomad into the employ of Monster Hunter International. I was pretty sure that Ben and Laden, or the rest of MHI, didn't know that Nomad had tucked tail and run when the vamp and I fell off a bridge into the Tennessee River, leaving me alone, fighting the vamp, underwater. I made it a point not to think about that event. Ever.

After refueling, I took the Pisgah Highway through the dark to the tight, uphill U-turn neck that bikers love. There, I caught the scent of she-wolf, maybe two days old. I slowed and put my nose to the air, taking in everything. At the full moon, she had taken down a deer, eaten, and left the entrails and splintered bones behind. She wasn't alone. The scent patterns told me that she had a pack. One was a male cub, likely one of four missing Asheville kids.

I eased off Route 151 and onto an old logging road that hadn't seen traffic in decades. No ATV tracks, no horse scent, just old snow, matted leaves, woods, deep gullies, and ridges. A hundred yards in, I parked Bitsa behind a jagged boulder, stripped, and left my folded clothes and most of the human weapons in the saddlebags. I attached a go-bag filled with clothes, a Yellowrock Security GPS tracker, and a .380 around my neck, and sat on the rock. Bean sat on a limb, watching as if fascinated, eyes huge and glowing in the night. I was in no hurry as I slipped into a meditative state and shifted into my Beast.

Hunt killer of kits, Beast thought at me the moment we were mountain lion. *Kill pack hunter before she can make more.*

That's the idea, I thought back at her. What I'd do with a teenager in wolf form once the bitch was dead I didn't know, but no way was I killing kids. In puma concolor form, I/we padded into the night, found a rabbit warren with a dozen rabbits at the surface eating underbrush. Beast and Bean made a game of chasing them, and then ate them to restore calories lost in the shift. When we were full, we went wolf hunting.

I found werewolf scent, scat, a downed tree where they cleaned their claws, markings, and several werewolf trails that had been used often enough to indicate a den was close. There was more than one wolf-bitch. This was a pack.

With one twenty-foot leap, I took to the tree limbs, Bean on my shoulders, to keep the wolves from finding a ground trail that could lead back to me. The scent told me the bitch was young, healthy, probably turned twelve to fourteen moons past when I hunted a werewolf pack in the Appalachians. I had assumed some had gotten away, in human form, via vehicle transport. Now I knew for sure. Letting them get away made the new disappearances and deaths my fault. Guilt twisted her talons deep into me. Familiar.

But they wouldn't get away this time, no matter how much experience they had gained in the intervening months. No were could survive against a mountain cat who had hunted since the Trail of Tears. Beast growled softly, agreeing. Bean hissed, mouth close by my ear.

High in the trees, I scouted the wolves' territory, found one of their watering holes on a branch of McKinney Creek. I also caught the scent of death, weeks old, long decayed. At least one of the other missing children hadn't survived the transformation to werewolf. Beast growled, a vibration that carried through the night. *Beast kill killer of kits. Beast kill pack hunters.*

Chuffing in fury with each step, I/we followed the stink

through the treetops, over the McKinney, to the remains. They'd been strewn over a wide area by scavenger depredation. It had been too long to tell if the body was male or female by scent. But the sight of the doll beside the scattered ribs and ruffles on a small dress told me the gender. They had eaten a little girl.

Beast's growl shuddered through us, a low reverberation of sound, counterpoint to Bean's harmonious howl. The entire forest went dead silent. *Kill killer of human kit. Rip out throats. Drink blood.*

I/we memorized the location by lights in the distance, cell towers on the nearby crests of hills, and by Beast's cat awareness. Unlike most humans, Beast always knew where she was. Then we leaped thirty feet to the ground, following the scent trail, no longer caring if we were discovered by the prey we tracked. More wolf scents appeared, overlapping. Three or four males and the lone female. In my experience, females were rare.

Pack hunters close, Beast thought, as we caught a distant scent of wood smoke, garbage, and raw sewage.

Yeah. Maybe we'll get lucky. Can you take on them all?

Beast is best hunter. Kill killer of kits.

Above us, the moon appeared through the trees, a waning bulbous shape. Beast thought, *Mother moon, with kits at teats.*

She had her own names for each phase of the moon. Knowing she could be spotted in the cold clear light, she took to the limbs again and crept toward the stink of man.

In a clearing at the base of a gulley were three small mobile homes, circa 1960s. The trailers looked as if they had been dragged into the woods and set up as temporary living quarters. No running water, no septic tanks, no electricity. And no guard set. By the smell, it was currently deserted, the wolves out hunting. The pack was overconfident. That was a good thing. I/we turned back into the trees and took a different route back to Bitsa.

I changed into human form, dressed, rebraided my hip-length hair, and weaponed up. It was downright cold, and while riding leathers would be best against the wind, all I had with me were secondhand ones from a consignment bike shop in Charlotte. My good fighting leathers were back in New Orleans. Not expecting that I'd be chasing werewolves, I'd traveled light. Stupid me.

Back in town, I cleaned out a fast food restaurant's ready-made breakfasts for the calories, bought supplies, and checked into a Country Inn & Suites. Bean curled on a pillow and was instantly asleep. I made a conference call to the Youngers. After hellos, I said, "Get me contracts and liability releases. I uploaded my search from the GPS tracker. I need every bit of intel you can dig up on the owners and/or tenants of the land at the farthest point. And I don't need help. I got yahoos here I can call on if I need."

"What kind of yahoos?" Alex asked. He was the intel/hacker/background part of YS, a nineteen-year-old kid who was scary smart when it came to intel.

"People I used to know," I assured. "I'm good. Stay home. Finish the security job." I didn't need their help. Last thing I wanted was for my human partners to get bit.

"Names," Eli, the elder Younger asked. Well, demanded.

"No."

Their interest sharpened like blades on a whetstone. "Janie?" Eli asked carefully.

I took a breath and let out the rage I had held down by force of will. "They killed a child." My voice vibrated, anger stripping my throat raw. "Ate her." I swallowed and managed a breath. Got myself and my emotions under control. "I've got a grindylow. We'll be done before you could get here."

"Jane—"

"Call with info if you get it." I ended the call. I should never have mentioned yahoos. Now they'd be looking into my past. Into things that were none of their business. There were days when my big mouth still got me in trouble. I'd have to live with my slipup.

Bean was sleeping on the pillow when I left the inn. I was curious if and how she'd catch up to me. Grindys weren't magical but they often acted like it.

I didn't have enough weapons to deal with a pack, no matter what Beast thought, and I wasted a moment wishing I had the Benelli M4 and my silver-plated vamp-killers, but even without my gear, I had an ace in the hole. One of several guys who hand-packed my silver fléchette rounds lived on the French Broad between I-26 and the Blue Ridge Parkway. Old Bourbon had most anything for the right price. Old Bourbon wasn't his real name. He lived off the grid, squatting in an old school bus that he'd somehow mounted on a deck on ten-foot-high pylons at the end of a winding mud trail that routinely washed away when the French Broad flooded. Somehow his bus survived. Maybe he tossed an anchor.

Leaving Bitsa on the trail, I hiked in. Bourbon met me with the business end of a shotgun but we parted happy: Bourbon with a fistful of cash and me with two fairly well-balanced, silver-plated machetes and an ancient, bolt-action, Mossberg 12-gauge shotgun of indeterminate provenance but with excellent action. I also had a well-used leather spine rig and a pocketful of his hand-packed silver fléchette shells, which had been my main goal. I had wanted a pump shotgun, but because of hunting season, Bourbon was fresh out; the bolt was all he had left. It wasn't enough gear to take down a pack, but I had the reek of the child's decomposing body stuck in my memory and a craving for vengeance burning through me. And I had the .380. I could always throw it at the werewolf like they did in the movies.

The path to the impromptu trailer park hidden in the hills was even worse than the road to Old Bourbon's place, and it looked like it hadn't been driven on in ages. A mile in, trees were down across it, which is where I left Bitsa. The werewolves had marked their territory with piles of poo and the stink of werewolf urine. *Classy.* I figured they four-pawed it overland when they went in and out and, assuming they had any, left parked vehicles off another road somewhere. If I cared, I'd backtrack and find their parking area and access. I didn't.

I had changed boots before I left the inn, and the heavily modi-fied combat-style boots were silent as I approached the clearing along a well-used wolf trail. Wood smoke blew on the breeze, mixed with the stink of rotting meat, unwashed human, and sewage. But nothing moved. By the sun, it was around ten A.M. but a front was blowing in promising snow, the winds currently from the west.

I'd had a good image of the clearing from above before dawn, but I made a slow circumference, reconnoitering the three trailers, positioning each door, broken chairs, a bicycle in parts, a picnic table, the kind with benches built on. I learned where everything was and the fastest way around, over, and through. The smell said several wolves were here, the female and some males, two of them cubs. The eldest male needed to be taken out first. He was likely one I had missed a year past, and he'd be more experienced.

Keeping the body of Trailer One between me and the clearing, I stepped over a squat metal drum that stank of kerosene, slid the shotgun into the sheath at my back and drew the machetes. There was a stinking puddle near the door where he had been using the ground for a toilet, but it was mostly dry. I hoped that was an indication that he was asleep. The door was long gone, making entry easy as I leaped up and landed lightly, but my weight depressed the rotting floor with a soft sigh.

"Collette?" He sounded half asleep. Maybe he'd fall back asleep if I stayed silent. Sadly, the wind changed and wolf noises decreed that luck wasn't with me. A low rumble filled the trailer, reverberating off the mildewed walls. I heard the distinctive sound of bones breaking, reshaping.

I dashed in, leaped over a broken recliner, bounded across a mattress on the floor, and down the narrow hallway. He was the fastest shifter I had ever seen, already mostly wolf when my machete came down across him, cutting deep into his right shoulder, an inch off from the perfect strike point. The machete had more heft than a vamp-killer, and less balance. And a less-honed edge. The blade stopped before hitting the cervical spine, avulsing the dozens of neck and upper shoulder muscles. The trapezius and the sterno-cleidomastoids peeled back like the skin of a fruit. The werewolf screamed, a strangled dog cry. I whipped the machete out of the mess of muscle, blood pulsing as the blade tore through the carotid.

I cut down with the other machete, using more muscle than I usually needed, but this time hitting the exact spot at the proper angle. The swing carried down, momentum burying the blade in the spinal processes. The wolf went silent. Too late. One full backswing downstroke and his head was on the floor.

He was a bloody mess of flesh, bone, and fur, still wearing the flannel pajama bottoms he'd slept in as a human. I spun, blades out, throwing a circular spatter pattern across the walls. The missed initial cut had cost me, and I heard howls from across the compound. I wiped the machetes on the bare mattress and slid them into the unfamiliar sheaths at my thighs. Losing precious time. I pulled the shotgun. Stalked through the mess and filth and leaped to the ground. I raised the gun, drawing on Beast's strength. I wasn't a shooter, I preferred blades for my work, but a mantra taught me by a sensei I had studied with had been, "The right tool at the right time."

A reddish blur flew through the air at me. Time did that little slow-dance effect and I focused on his open maw, black lips snarling, two-inch fangs, razor sharp on the inside edge. I raised the shotgun. Fired point-blank into his open mouth. I could almost see the silver fléchette shot as it flew. I worked the bolt, the cartridge spinning to the side. Thrust another shell into place for firing. Worked the bolt, reloading and firing twice more, until his torso was bloody meat and silver.

To the side, Bean was in a gory, furious fight with another reddish wolf, yowling and growling that I could hear over my concussion deafness. Bean's abnormally long canines latched under his jaw, claws slashing his throat. The were couldn't get to her, even with the odd joints that gave him further reach than real wolves. Bean shredded his throat to the spine before he rolled over, dead.

I got a glimpse of two black-furred wolf forms taking off into the woods. I swore softly, breathing heavy. There was nothing left to kill. I had let two get away. Worse, Bean was injured. Her blood was an emerald green, darker than her fur. She mewled piteously and I lifted her gently into my gear bag, relieved to see flesh knitting about a thousand times faster than a human's. "You do not have permission to die on me," I said. She glared at me, catlike, before closing her eyes.

In my world, the only true-dead paranormal is one without a head, so I took all the heads.

I took photos of the heads and dead wolves for proof of payment, sent them to YS for processing, and pulled the bodies into the smoking fire pit. I doused them with kerosene from the drum in back and they burst into spectacular green and yellow flames. I took more photos as they burned.

Over the reek of burning were, I smelled something else. And heard a faint whimper as my hearing returned.

I entered Trailer Two, which was trashed but empty. It had been used as a den and mating nest by the bitch. In Trailer Three, I found two teenagers—juvenile werewolves—chained to the floor, raving, psychotic, forever insane. My heart plummeted. I don't kill kids. No matter what. But I knew the wolves had to be put down. I opened my official cell phone, the one my boss could track me on, and spun the contact list to the N's. There it was in all its never-deleted glory. I debated for a whole thirty seconds, then dialed the number.

"Nomad."

"There was a pack. I got three." My breath stopped. I forced myself to go on. "Leaving two teens chained in a trailer at this GPS. They're all yours." I disconnected, texted him my GPS, resettled my gear, downed a bottle of water, and headed into the woods. I didn't answer his callback.

I followed their trail to the watering hole on the branch of McKinney Creek, and then downstream to the creek itself. The McKinney roared, clear and greened by the season, full of snow-melt and downed trees. It splashed almost playfully, but temps and underwater strainers could be deadly. The wolves had swum across and muddied the far bank.

From upstream, water thundered, likely through a micro canyon. I hoisted the unfamiliar gear higher and trekked up. The crossing at the micro canyon wasn't much better, except for a leaning pine hanging on by a tangle of roots. I drew on my skinwalker energies and finished the job that some recent storm had started, pushed my bridge over, where it bounced on the far shore. I'm stronger than I look.

High on the ridge, I followed the wolf scent and tracks in the snow, a hard up-and-downhill hike. I heard it before I smelled it. Bikes. Lots of bikes. Roaring along 151. The bitch had circled back to the highway adored by bikers. Sandra Doherty had said she heard trucks. But... maybe motorcycles? And the meat smell meant a biker grill. *Collette had two dens.*

Half a mile down the road I found tracks of wolves, barefoot humans, boot tracks, and bike tracks. I checked the sat-maps and texted both my YS partners and, more reluctantly, Nomad. "Pig-It-Your-Way, three miles from my twenty. Bitch is on a bike." Then I made the trek back to Bitsa. Temps dropped and it started to snow. Nothing was ever easy.

I wheeled from snow-covered mud trail to snow-covered asphalt. It was past sunset and I was starving. No surprise there. Some of the best chow in the world—or at least the most acid-inducing—could be found at biker bars, so I pulled in at Pig-It-Your-Way and killed the engine about fifty feet from the door. I smelled gas, oil, and that heated distinctive scent of big

Harley. There were eighteen bikes in the lot and a dozen trucks. Country music blasted through the walls. The picture window was full of neon beer signs. Grease, beef, and spicy wings laced the air, the best perfume God ever created.

Somewhere under the mélange was the stink of werewolves. They had been here days ago, maybe weeks ago, but they weren't here now. This wasn't the den. Disappointment threaded through me.

I unhelmeted and made my way inside, where I stepped quickly to the side of the door burger menu, beer on tap, neon beer signs, all kinds of bikers and biker chicks, from the discreetly armed, upper management Hell's Angels at the back booth, to the weekend riders at the opposing corner. There was no bouncer, but the interest of the bartender was predatory, and I had a feeling he kept lots of pretties back there. He was tall, had prison tats mixed with some really good ink. Black hair, long and greasy, acne, knobby knuckles.

I gave him a steady stare and a nod that told him I'd be starting no problems, acknowledging his dominant position. He relaxed and nodded back before I took a two-person booth that would place my back to the bar and me facing the door. I gave my order to the barmaid, made a trip to the Ladies, positioned the shotgun on the bench beside me, and waited for my meal as bikers roared up and the joint filled with Friday night partygoers. The food was every bit as delish as I expected, and I was wiping my greasy hands when the door opened and the stink of were and something chemical-based, like battery acid mixed with drain cleaner and antifreeze swirled inside. I pulled the shotgun across my legs, but with the place full, there was no clear shot. Collateral damage. Polite phrase for dead and mangled humans. Bitten humans who might have to be put down. *Crap.*

The bitch walked in, movements limber, wearing high-end biker boots, black leathers, and scarlet lipstick. She was tiny, sharp-featured, and crazy-eyed, with wind-tousled dark hair. I could take her in my sleep. Except that she was followed by three huge werewolf males, armed to the teeth. Too much potential collateral damage. I needed to get this outside. Fast.

Behind them stepped Ben, Laden, and Nomad, dressed in high-tech MHI armor, visible through open coats. Relief flashed through me. Laden spotted me and his eyebrows went up a millimeter or so. Laden was a minimalist, like other former military I know, buzz cut and the bluest eyes on the face of the earth. I winked at him and glanced out the picture window to the parking lot. He nodded.

The wolves-in-human-form caught my scent and all four stopped, sniffing the air. I don't smell human. The pack turned slowly toward me. Too late to get this fight outside, so I had to end it fast. I grinned at her, showing teeth, and laughed, giving MHI time to get into position.

The MHI Hunters moved into a semicircle around the males, but out of my line of fire. I stood up, slammed a machete onto the table with a loud *thwhack*, braced the shotgun, and aimed it at the bitch. Seemed like I had lied to the bartender.

The place fell dead silent and I said, my words ringing, "Hey bitch. I killed a few of your old men today. Now it's your turn." She screamed and launched herself at me. Time did that odd slow-down thing it did in battle. With all the time in the world, I bent my knees to take the hit. Adjusted the weapon up, left-handed, to cover the males, just in case. Lifted the machete to counter her lunge.

Clawed hands reached out, grabbing the barrel. Her teeth elongated, fur on her face and hands. I let her grip the weapon and start the torque that intended to take the shotgun from my hand. Bringing up the machete in my right, slightly curved point slanting toward her twisted torso. Dropped my left shoulder and swept outward with the barrel, opening up her reach, exposing her belly. Stealing her balance.

The machete entered just below her breastbone. Slightly to the right. Cut deep. Rotation and angle pulled the blade. Through her body, hard left. Blood spattered over my arm. Across the bar. Distantly, I heard screams. The *pop-pop-pop* of small arms. The *boom* of something bigger. Her torso twisted. Hit my left arm. Pushing the shotgun. I let it. Put muscle behind the cut. Severed the descending aorta in a release of pressure. Blood in a gush. The blade snagged on tendons in left hip and thigh before they gave way. Her rotation yanked the machete from my bloodied grip. She landed hard and rolled, guts spilling.

I thought about shooting, but drew the remaining machete. Glanced at the others.

Ben was taking off a wolf's head.

Laden was shoving another's head through the jukebox, glass shattering.

Nomad was down, wolf fangs latched tight on his right arm.

Buried in Dyneema or Zylon. I could smell the stuff. A fourth had joined the fray and ripped at Nomad's booted foot. A green blur flew through the air. Landed on the wolf on Nomad's arm. Steel claws slicing deep. *Bean attack.* I laughed, an unexpected sound in the chaos. Raised the machete. The bitch's belly was already trying to knit. Her face and body were mostly werewolf—fangs, claws, and oversized jaws.

Drawing on Beast's strength and speed, I brought the blade down. Hitting her just below the mandible. Severing carotid and jugular. Blood erupted, under pressure. I cut again. And again. Her head rolled over to the floor, tongue hanging out.

I smelled smoke. The flames of a grease fire roiled from the kitchen. Dead wolves. Laden and Ben were cutting the jukebox wolf into pieces. Bean was gone. Nomad was bleeding badly. Out cold. Dang it. The rest of the bar had emptied.

I gathered my weapons, took a quick burst of pics across the bar scene. Bent and lifted Nomad into a fireman's carry. I left the bar, Laden and Ben behind me.

"You got pics of the wolves?" Laden asked, his voice as casual as if we were discussing roses at a garden party.

"I got 'em," I said, not quite as easy. "You got bandages?"

"You're the girl. Got sanitary napkins?" Ben asked.

I sighed. I had forgotten the crudity of some MHI. "No, but I saw some in the Ladies. Back in a sec." I dumped the weapons and Nomad onto him and raced into the smoke, which had filled the bar. I beat open the vending machine in the Ladies and stuck a variety of absorbent materials down my shirt. Smoke curled in under the door.

I heard a frightened cry. Spotted a small handle with a lock, hinges. *Trap door.*

Adrenaline pumping, I wrenched open the door, the small lock flying. Two children were in the cramped space. Tears and mucous on their faces. I didn't ask. I just reached in and took an arm in each hand. Hauled them up against me.

Coughed my way outside.

MHI were behind a rusted U-Haul that hadn't been there earlier, taking cover, applying pressure to Nomad's wounds. They stared at the children and me, open-mouthed. I remembered the chemical smell on the werewolves and Sandra Doherty's testimony. "The U-Haul smells like a mobile meth lab," I said.

The men looked from me to the U-Haul. There was something odd in their expressions, and Ben said, "That stuff flammable?"

"Pretty much," I said.

From out front, engines roared, Harleys, at least ten bikes, heading in. I figured the bikers, who had vamoosed, were on the way back with reinforcements. Not good. But then, nothing had ever been easy around Nomad. He was my own personal Murphy's Law.

Behind me I heard the distinctive *schlacking* sound of a shotgun. "Move and die."

I glanced around. It was the greasy-haired, acned barkeep, who kinda looked like a meth dealer.

"We need outta here," Ben warned.

"Flaming fun on the way," Laden added, too casual.

I figured that meant they had called in an airstrike on the bar.

"You ain't going nowhere," Greasy said.

I was still holding the kids. Greasy was too close to miss and too far away to jump before he fired. Yeah. Murphy's Law. "Easy there," I said.

"You killed Collette."

"You were banging the werewolf chick?" Ben said. "Damn stupid."

Greasy turned the weapon on him. I leaped away. Laden shot, a three-tap. Greasy fell.

"Now!" Laden shouted. Ben picked up Nomad, Laden the weapons, and we raced away. Overhead, something roared. The ground shook. The air thundered. The U-Haul exploded outward. Heat like a furnace blasted me. I glanced back.

The bar and the U-Haul were gone. The bikers wheeled and roared away.

A helo landed. Medics took over Nomad and the kids.

It's over. I closed my eyes and remembered to breathe.

In the aftermath, Ben slipped a business card into my palm with the words, "For a good time call..."

I chuckled and checked to see that he had given me his number. I said, "I'll send you the pics. The bitch is mine."

"Pleasure doing business with you, Yellowrock. 'Have Stakes Will Travel.'" My motto. MHI had been keeping tabs on me since they fished me, naked and bleeding, out of the Tennessee River. *Interesting.*

Before law enforcement showed up and started asking questions, I puttered away from the melee, happy that I had parked far away from the Pig-It-Your-Way. Bitsa and I tootled through Asheville. I called the Dohertys with my promised update, then checked my balance at an ATM. My account had been credited with three kills so far. A good start. Satisfied, I took the road south.

Sometimes, I loved my job.

The US government has a long history of drafting people—and things—into its war against unearthly forces. From what I've heard, it is a tough gig.   —A.L.

Mr. Natural

Jody Lynn Nye

Bobbie Hubert swung the machete with a practiced hand for the thirtieth or fortieth time; she'd lost count. A swathe of huge, lush green vines fell at her feet, and she stepped over it. While the other soldiers of Detachment Lutefisk carried on hacking at the unnatural growth, she stopped to wipe her sweating and sticky face with the back of her glove. The combat nurse's ochre canvas trousers and khaki uniform shirt stuck to her body under her black cloth-covered armor, and her braid of brown hair under her black helmet was a wet rattail down her back. Green sap covered their uniforms, ran down their faces and glued their machetes into their gloves. The Huey helicopter that had dropped them in the clearing lifted off behind them, blasting them with gusts of chlorophyll-scented air.

"God, I'm going to dehydrate!" she said. "It's like being back in 'Nam!"

Ex-Army Captain Carl Pipkin stepped up beside her to yank down a massive, writhing vine. The big-shouldered blond man stomped on it with his heavy, steel-toed boot. The remains shuddered and went limp.

"Wrong color. This don't look like 'Nam. My mother had a garden every year from the time I can remember. This is the right green for a springtime pea shoot, but it's a million times bigger than it ought to be."

A winding tendril from a nearby vine reached for his neck.

He hacked it off with a practiced blow and beckoned for Bobbie to follow. The rest of the company kept on slicing away at the undergrowth to clear the roadway to a forty-yard diameter. Under their feet was paved tarmacadam with a white stripe down the middle. According to their briefing, the road and most of the surrounding countryside had been completely grown over in the last four days, an instant jungle in the Le Sueur valley of Minnesota. Check, check and double-check on the jungle. They needed to get it cleared wide enough to create a landing zone from which to bring the hostages out—providing the poor SOBs were still alive.

The vast, fertile countryside around Blue Earth was famous as a growing area for a giant vegetable-producing corporation. Bobbie and most of the others from Detachment Lutefisk lived about thirty miles east in the Twin Cities and their suburbs. She felt another frisson go down her neck. This was the first time they'd been called out on a monster hunt so close to home.

Why am I not in a nice hospital somewhere shaking down thermometers, instead of pruning a road? Bobbie asked herself. But the question had more than one answer, all of them definitive, as far as she was concerned. One: Doctors were assholes who treated nurses, even army nurses, even nurses with decades more experience than they had, like ignoramuses. Two: Patients in the hospitals might be nice, normal human beings, or they might be antiwar protesters who felt smug about spitting in the faces of returning servicemen and support staff, most of whom had no goddamned *choice* about going to Vietnam in the first place. Three: MCB paid a whole hell of a lot better than hospitals or even private care facilities. And God knew they paid head and shoulders above the Veterans Administration for staff. All she had to do was risk her life every time she went out into the field.

And four: They basically had no choice. They all had had to join MCB. It was better than any of the alternatives, and it gave them someone to talk to about their shared experiences.

She felt a chill every time she thought of that first time. The 72nd Mobile Army Surgical Hospital had just been moved into the Da Krong Valley in mid-1972, a stretch of overgrown jungle not unlike the place she was ripping into. The unit was a lot closer to the action than it had been before, meaning that the army unit that ought to have been backing up the marines on the front line was split, half helping to keep the Viet Cong from overrunning the camp and slaughtering the patients and medical staff. One bright moonlit night, she'd been on her way back from the latrines when a company of them burst into the camp. At their head was a saffron-robed monk with a shaved head. This was no peaceful Buddhist. His hands were flying around like he was trying to swat a million bugs. Light lanced out from his fingers, and it fed into a spiky man-shaped *thing* that grew larger with every bolt. She had been the one to raise the alarm. And somehow they had managed to kill the demon by treating it like a lightning hazard in the camp, something they *had* had experience with. The monk had gotten away.

But the real problems started when they were cleaning up, mourning over the messy deaths of several of the medics and the support troops in the literal firefight. A company of MCB agents came out of the jungle, prepared to deal with anyone in the MASH who had seen the demon. They'd been so surprised that the servicemen on the ground had disposed of the monster, they had called off the air strike that would have taken out any surviving witnesses to the demon's appearance. Instead, they offered the few remaining soldiers and Bobbie jobs in the Bureau after their terms of service were over.

At first, Bobbie had turned them down. Then, when they arrived home, she had to deal with the long-haired draft dodgers who spat at them in the streets of St. Paul. She and all the vets suffered mistreatment from all quarters for going to a war they never supported. She had started a job at St. Paul General, then quit after a month. She made the call, as had most of her unit.

The truth was, most of them really liked monster hunting, partly because they never got over the adrenaline rush of being in the war zone. They hated civilian life. They'd been treated badly by the general population, neglected by the government, but they had each other. And someone to shoot at.

All but her, of course. Bobbie's job description was to stay alive and help the team and any rescuees stay alive, too. If those rescuees weren't too freaked out by their experience, or if they had seen too much of the reported demon, meaning Captain Pipkin was going to have to make a decision on whether to save them or bring them in for hypnosis, or ... triage them. Her heart sank. She hated it when civilians got into the mess. Worry made her hack faster.

"Incoming!" shouted Dwight Johansen. The balding former sergeant from Duluth dropped his machete and dragged his M16 around. "Here comes another bunch!" He fired off a fusillade of shots at the little round green demons bounding over the top of the hedge.

Bobbie crouched down and pulled her own M16 off her shoulder just in time.

Except for their size, the weird little creatures looked like gigantic green peas, nearly perfect spheres except for a sharp little beak. On a pea, that was the sprouting edge. These monsters used it to gouge and tear. Poor Helton, laid out on the ground near the perimeter waiting for a body bag, had his gut split open. Bobbie put a round into a pea bouncing toward her. It spurted thick green goo like a pimple bursting. Bobbie had to fight down her gorge. She looked back over her shoulder.

"Shina! Don't just stand there! Do something! This ought to be easy for you!"

The michabo gave her a dirty look. The eight-foot, brown-furred rabbit spirit, revered by local Native Americans, didn't want to be there, since he already had his PUFF exemption, but the bureau must have had enough pull to haul him up out of his burrow for this mission. Bobbie reached for the pistol at her left hip. The hollowpoints loaded in it had their tips filled with salt blessed by a local Ojibwa chief, which she was assured by MCB would keep the unruly demon in line, and take him out if he decided to team up with the monster in the valley. On her right hip was a pistol loaded with cartridges that had the bullets filled with acid blessed by a bishop with magical abilities back in the Twin Cities. That had been an effective weapon against some demons they'd faced. She had to be careful not to get the two confused, but either would have given Shina a serious psychic burn.

"Lightning and thunder curse you, Bobbie Hubert!" Shina snarled, showing a couple of front incisors the size of kitchen tiles.

He leaped into the air, intercepting two of the green peas. With his powerful paws, he smashed them together into paste and went for another pair. Fragments of vegetation sprayed the whole company. Corporal Tom Worth blasted at another pod's worth that tried to land on the men chopping at the crazy undergrowth.

"Hubert!" the captain barked. "See if you can find anybody!"

Bobbie glanced around. The report had said that the commune

where Randy Barlow lived was at these coordinates. It took a while to spot the hand-hewn timbers of the cottages under the mass of creepers. The door of one shack stood ajar. With her rifle leveled to protect against the peas, she and a couple of the ex-noncoms, Fred Loftus and Elmo Blanchard, edged through the undergrowth and pushed the creaking portal aside.

"Hello?" she called. "Anyone in there?"

A narrow shadow toward the rear of the one-room hut rose. A white man with a long, thin face decorated with a long, shaggy brown beard and waist-length hair parted in the middle stared blankly at them. He wore jeans and a chambray work shirt with a long suede vest over it. His face had a patina of grime as if being close to the earth meant smearing it on himself.

"Damn it to hell," Fred said. "Hippies!"

"Shut up," Bobbie said. "We've got to get him out of here, too. Excuse me, sir, do you know Randy Barlow?"

The man worked his jaw as if he was going to spit at them. Bobbie growled low under her breath. Not again! Then he opened his mouth, shooting a gout of flame toward them. She and the soldiers jumped out of the way just in time.

"That's new," she said.

"Easy, fellah! Stand down!" Fred shouted, leveling his M16 at the skinny man.

The hippie bellowed out something incoherent and scrambled for the door, hands outstretched. Bobbie jumped out of his way. Fred and Elmo grabbed for his arms. With surprising strength, the hippie threw them off and shoved Elmo into a rickety wall. Fred, who had been trained in karate, twisted the man's wrist and flattened him on the ground. The hippie collapsed on the bare earth, sobbing. Smoke curled from his lips. When he looked up at them again, there seemed to be some intelligence behind his eyes.

"Sir, do you know where you are?" Bobbie asked.

"Home," the man said. "Commune. Oh, God, you've got guns! Don't kill it!"

"We're here to protect you," Elmo said, his big dark face sincere. "What's 'it'?"

"The earth spirit, man!" The hippie's face filled with wonder. "The one who made this place burgeon like the Garden of Eden!"

"We're looking for Randy Barlow," Bobbie said. "His parents are worried about him."

"Stonesinger?" The hippie frowned and wrinkled his forehead, as though having a couple of men in armor sitting on his back was no big deal. Fred handcuffed him behind his back and hauled him to his feet. "Last I saw him, he was down by the brook. What's today?"

"Tuesday," Bobbie said. "Take us to the brook."

"God, it's all so beautiful, isn't it?" the man said, ducking under a tomato vine thicker than Bobbie's wrist. She shoved greenery out of her face. She couldn't figure out how the hippie, who called himself Appleseed, could tell where he was going. Their compasses were going haywire. The only direction they could see for any distance was up. They threshed blindly in Appleseed's wake. He seemed too out of it to be leading them into a trap, but monsters were cunning. They had enough to deal with from the vines, which kept trying to catch them, but left Appleseed alone. Maybe they thought he was one of them.

"On a smaller scale," Carl said dryly. He held up a fist. The group halted, weapons at the ready. Carl touched his ear. Everyone listened, but they didn't have to strain to hear. Loud humming, like a million bees, issued from beyond the wall of greenery. Appleseed started humming in response. Fred flicked him in the arm.

"Wake up!"

"Oh, yeah!" Appleseed said, blinking. "Just got caught up in it, man. Don't you dig it?"

"What the hell are you and Randy doing here?" Bobbie asked.

"We work for the growers," Appleseed said. "We got done with the planting a few weeks ago. They pay us for picking all season long. It keeps us closer to Mother Nature than you robots who live in the city."

"Watch it, pal," Elmo snarled. "I ain't nobody's robot."

"Not trying to ruin your vibes, man," Appleseed said pleasantly.

"Why does Randy Barlow need to pick vegetables?" Bobbie asked. "His folk records sell millions of copies!"

"He doesn't need that green when he's got this, man," Appleseed said.

Bobbie knew what the others were thinking. If their target had the rest of the commune under its spell, maybe all of Minnesota was in danger.

"How come another monster moved in here?" Elmo asked. "What happened to the Jolly Green Giant?"

"He's a myth," the hippie said. "We've been chanting, trying to get him to manifest, but this guy turned up instead. He's green, too. Plants just leap up out of the ground for him. We worship him, man. We've got so much to learn from his wisdom!"

"Don't tell me you're growing those peas we saw back there!" Carl exclaimed.

"Peas, carrots, string beans, potatoes—everything!" Appleseed confirmed, his face a mask of bliss.

Bobbie blanched. All of them had done the readings on the Green Men of Europe. It was the brass's guess that this creature was probably related, a demon that gained its power from living things.

Even if they couldn't see far, they were moving steadily downhill. Under the humming, the trickle of running water came through. Even louder was the sound of chewing. Bobbie spun on her heel to catch Shina hunkered down over a mass of sprouting shoots, munching away.

"Hey! Later!"

"But I'm hungry," Shina complained, opening his big, dark brown eyes and pasting his tall ears back over his skull to look pathetic.

"Are you sure this stuff is safe for you to eat?" Bobbie asked.

"What do you care whether a demon gets food poisoning or not?" Fred asked.

"Because I do," Bobbie said, stung. "Some of the stuff they put on crops is worse than Agent Orange."

"Hey, we use only organic pesticides and fertilizers!" Appleseed protested. "Mr. Natural wouldn't have it any other way. We *care* about the land. You baby-killers don't get it."

Bobbie grabbed him by the collar of his filthy shirt.

"We were exposed to that stuff, freak. We do get it, more than you ever will."

Appleseed recoiled a little.

"It's cool, ma'am. Our crops are healthy. Come on. You'll see. Mr. Natural is going to revolutionize organic farming. The future is green, baby!"

The humming got louder the deeper in they went. Tomatoes as big as her head hung among frilled leaves longer than her torso. Asparagus half the height of telephone poles poked up through the undergrowth. Bobbie felt as though she was in the Vietnam jungle, but a lot weirder. She hated having been scared all the time. None of their other MCB missions had made her feel like she was back there again, and she resented the hell out of it.

Carl called a halt again...and beckoned. Lutefisk edged up carefully to take a look.

"Holy flaming shit," Fred whispered. "So that's Mr. Natural."

Bobbie pushed aside the greenery...and gawked.

They had found the source of the humming, all right. In the middle of the fast-moving stream that Appleseed had mentioned, it looked like a tree was growing. The monster stretched green-festooned limbs and hair up to the sky. It swayed from side to side as if it could hear music. On the gigantic trunk at its center was a face with glowing green eyes and a wide, moss-fringed maw. It did look like the living spirit of Nature. If it hadn't taken over a chunk of the state of Minnesota and engendered killer peas, Bobbie might even have thought it was beautiful.

Around it, dancing and bowing on the banks and right in the water with it were dozens of long-haired men and women. Mud covered most of their bodies, making it difficult to see if they were wearing clothes or not. Bobbie felt disgust. They were abasing themselves before an unnatural creature. Didn't they have any sense or self-respect? Once in a while, they'd breathe fire on the giant. Instead of hurting it, the flames made the huge creature sprout more leaves. And when it burgeoned, the foliage around it got thicker and taller. Other hippies tended to the enormous plants, digging around pods nearly as large as they were.

"Damn it," Elmo said, hacking at the sprouting greens with his machete. "This is probably swallowing our LZ, too!"

"We'll deal with that when we evacuate our target," Carl said. "Now, where is he?"

In the midst of the happy, chanting group, Bobbie spotted their quarry. Randy Barlow was a big man, with thick, wavy red hair that he wore in a long braid down his back, like his hero Willie Nelson. He wore only a pair of much-patched blue jeans. His pale skin had been scorched red by the sun, but he didn't seem to care. He was singing and blowing flames like it was the most ordinary thing in the world.

"Down there, Cap," she said.

"He's your priority, Hubert," Carl said. "The rest of you, two teams, five and fifteen. One moves those civilians out of the way and gets them back to the landing strip. As soon as they're clear, team two takes out that giant. When the monster's down, we call for evacuation. And look out for those pods! Got it? Three, two, one, go!"

Prodding Shina and Appleseed ahead of her, Bobbie stumbled down the slope with team one. The whole valley smelled over-poweringly of plants, compost and fireborne halitosis. Bobbie coughed, trying to clear the miasma out of her throat.

"See the humans! They have given their minds over to the giant!" Shina's squeaky voice was full of scorn.

"Shut up," Bobbie gritted. "Keep between me and the monster. I have to get Barlow out of there."

"He's all right," Appleseed said cheerfully. "See! He's doing the dance of life!"

Bobbie edged her way into the circle of dancing hippies. A couple of bare-breasted women joined hands around her and pranced like they were playing London Bridge. Their pupils were pinpoints, probably from the fumes in the air. She took their wrists and tried to pull them apart. They shrieked in fury and shot flames at her. Shina grabbed her by the back of her armored vest and lifted her out of the literal line of fire. The women's faces softened into idiotic bliss, and they danced away.

"There," Shina said. "Do not let yourself be trapped again."

He sounded so smug Bobbie wanted to put a salt plug in his big fluffy tail. Instead, she searched the circle for her quarry.

Barlow frolicked at the feet of Mr. Natural, looking happy and carefree. The monster itself seemed pretty benign. In fact, Bobbie felt a kind of peaceful vibe in its presence. The closer she got to it, the more relaxed she felt.

Why run? she thought. *Why not just dance with the others?* Her gun was so heavy. A man with long black hair and sharp cheekbones like her maternal grandfather's reached out a hand to her. Why shouldn't she dance with him? She started to put the rifle down. Something heavy hit her in the back. Her temper flaring, she spun to level the gun at her attacker.

"That's twice I have saved your life!" Shina said, tapping one massive foot on the ground. "And are you grateful? No!"

Bobbie glowered at him, but he was right. She had to tap the well of anger she carried to keep from becoming one of the hippie freaks in the circle.

Concentrating, she homed in on Barlow. He tried to take her hands, but she evaded them and hooked her hand through his arm. He smelled to high heaven, and his clothes were filthy and greasy.

"Come on, sir," she said. "We've got to get you home."

All of a sudden, the beatific expression changed, and his mouth dropped open like a nutcracker's. Bobbie ducked sideways as flames shot out of the folk singer's jaws. Her helmet kept her from getting roasted.

All around her, team one was having the same problem with their targets. The hippies wouldn't go quietly. They were fighting and flaming their would-be rescuers all over the valley. But Lutefisk had had one success with Appleseed. Bobbie needed to break Mr. Natural's hold over Barlow. As filthy and disgusting as he looked, he was still a human being. As he belted out another stream of fire, she rammed herself up against his chest, hooked a heel behind his foot, and tripped him to the ground. They both fell with a thud.

Fire shot into the air like the top of a volcano. Bobbie held on tightly as he struggled. In a moment, Barlow went limp and started to sob like a baby.

"Come on. You're okay," she said, stroking his face.

"Where am I?" he asked. "It was all so beautiful!" He looked up over her shoulder. The giant had stopped swaying and seemed to be listening. It hummed louder than she had heard it before. "What's *that*?"

"That's been holding you hostage for weeks," Bobbie said. Barlow shook his head.

"Hostage? No! He's beautiful. He loves us. He *cares* about us... Oh, God, he's going to eat us!" Barlow threw her off and frantically scrabbled toward the slope. Bobbie fell heavily to the earth. She turned just in time to see a hand formed of gigantic green branches reaching toward her. She rolled out of its way. The fingers fumbled over the ground, trying to close on her.

"Help me!" she called.

The only ones close enough to hear her were three of the hippies. At the sound of her voice their faces contorted into gorgon masks. They closed in, spewing fire at her. Behind them, Bobbie saw Fred leveling his M16 at their backs, ready to kill them to save her.

"No, don't hurt them!" she shouted. "They're still human!"

The massive hand scraped toward her, dislodging rocks and gravel on the sodden riverbank. Bobbie managed to stay away from it, but a fire-breathing woman in a fringe-lined suede minidress wasn't so lucky. The branches closed around her and lifted her high into the air. She sang a trill of joy that turned into screams as it brought her up above its mouth and dropped her in. Her cries were immediately silenced. Bobbie almost threw up in horror.

Most of the hippies were too busy dancing to notice, but a few of them were looking up when it happened. Their pupils widened, and they froze.

"That could happen to you!" Bobbie yelled. "Come with me! We have to get away!"

Some of them dithered, but at least a couple snapped out of their trance. They stood blinking in confusion.

"Get out!" she shouted. "Save yourselves! Hurry!"

Fred and Elmo ran over and urged them up the hill toward the fast-closing corridor in the mass of vines.

Bobbie was glad to see them escaping. She picked herself up to follow, but she heard more sinister rustling noises behind her. Her voice had drawn the attention of the giant. It came out of the water, hands and even some of its long green hair reaching for her. She tried to climb up onto the shallow bank, but the grass was slippery. She kept falling back.

"Come on, lady!" Appleseed appeared above her on the bank. He grabbed a stone and threw it at the giant. "Bug off, man! She's trying to help Stonesinger!"

"Yeah!" said a black man with a tan vest just barely fastened around a massive barrel chest. He came running down the grassy bank and took Bobbie's arm. "She's good! She wouldn't harm you!" He dragged her over the rise and onto the slope. Bobbie banged both knees and one elbow on the way up. Appleseed threw more stones. The giant raised its arms to protect the face on its trunk.

With the giant's attention distracted, one hippie after another started waking up from the trance it had put them into. One by one, they stopped breathing fire at the soldiers. Some of them ran away, but others came to form a chain to get Bobbie up the hillside with her heavy pack. Barlow was at the top.

"Are you okay, ma'am?" he asked. "I dunno what was going on with that thing, but you snapped me out of it!"

"We have to get out of here now," Bobbie said, urging him toward the narrowing path. "There are more men up there who will take it out, but we have to get clear. We're going to evacuate you."

"You heard the lady," Barlow shouted to his friends. "This isn't the Eden we made! Come on!"

"Stonesinger, I ain't going nowhere with the establishment!" a woman in ragged blue jeans protested.

"Lena, they're here to help," Appleseed said, gesturing to her. "Come on. We don't have to believe in their politics."

"Well, all right," Lena said, but she looked doubtful.

They all began to run, with team one behind them, firing their rifles and grenade launchers.

As it lost more and more followers, the giant began to collapse in on itself, screeching like a scalded cat. The pleasant humming turned into a fierce whistle that made Bobbie clap her hands over her ears. It stumbled up the hill after them.

The hippies fled, pulling Bobbie along with them, helping her whenever her heavy boots caught on a root or a rock.

Bobbie was astonished. These weren't the selfish antiestablishment loafers that she had come to loathe. They were as concerned with her safety as she was with theirs! As Barlow gave her an arm to help her, they heard a ripping noise like boards being torn by saws. Fred pointed.

"The pods! They're hatching!"

Surrounding the river valley, acres upon acres of pea pods the size of human beings began to split open. From the green sacs, killer peas by the dozen bounded out and began to attack the fleeing people. Bobbie brought her rifle around, potting one huge green sphere after another. Fred and the others loosed off covering fire, backing up the slope. The peas bounded after them. They landed on Fred. He bellowed in pain. Only Shina's kicks knocked them back. Blood spurted from Fred's shoulder. He'd been gashed right through his armor. Bobbie ran to support him, with Appleseed on the other side.

"Hold on, Fred," she pleaded, pressing her hand into the wound to try and stop the bleeding. Warm red seeped over her knuckles and into her sleeve.

"I'm sorry, man," Barlow said over and over again. "I'm really sorry."

"Head toward the LZ!" Elmo yelled. "We'll be right behind you!"

As they plunged into the undergrowth, mortar shells blasted past them. Carl and team two began the destruction of the valley. Their machine-gun fire raked the peas, making them explode in bursts of green goo. The giant staggered as it took heavy fire.

"No, don't kill it!" Barlow pleaded with the captain. "It's a natural creature!"

"It's you or it, buddy," Carl said, with an unsympathetic glare. "Get out of here so we can save your miserable lives! I'm calling in the air strike and evac helos. How many locals?"

"Nineteen," Elmo said. Carl barked an order into the big black walkie-talkie radio. Team one herded the hippies in the direction of the rescue coordinates.

Team two filled the air with machine-gun fire and grenades. Two of the men hauled the 3.5 inch M28-1 bazooka forward and loaded a rocket into it.

They could hear the giant only yards behind them. Bobbie glanced back. To her horror, it stepped right over the weapons, stomping one of the gunners into the ground. Carl and the others began firing on it. It let out a shriek that rose into the stratosphere and began laying about itself with all of its limbs. Bobbie could tell it was getting weaker, as more of its human acolytes woke up and smelled the coffee. At thirty feet tall, it was still big enough to cause problems.

It wailed in hunger as it threshed knee-high through the mass of vines, raking up yards of jungle with every step. Dwight Johansen leaped into its way with a bazooka on his shoulder. Pete Jenkins loaded in a round. It blasted into the giant's trunk, knocking a burning hole in it. It still kept coming.

"You just made it mad!" Elmo shouted. "Dwight, look out!"

Johansen leaped sideways into the undergrowth as the branch-fingers reached for him. Unfortunately, one of the hippies was close enough to catch. He yelled for help as the giant scooped him up and deposited him in its maw.

"All organic," Fred quipped.

"You're sick," Bobbie said. Hot tears burned their way down her cheeks. The man who died had helped her up when she fell.

The roar of helicopter engines was as welcome as a lullaby as the Huey gunships came in from the east. Bobbie waved an arm, hoping they could see her through the jungle. No such luck. The pilots took one look at the not-so-jolly green giant lurching toward them and veered off, coming back around with their miniguns roaring. It stood at bay, swinging at the streams of bullets as if they were mosquitoes. Bobbie held her breath. The thing had *fast* reflexes. It almost got one of the birds as it came around again. The black craft lifted just in time. The giant threshed after it, heading straight for the crowd of screaming hippies. Bobbie and team one crouched over them, weapons out, hoping they wouldn't be hit by friendly fire from team two.

From the forest, white phosphorous mortar shells burst on the tree-being's body, the explosions setting some of it ablaze. It bellowed in fury, but fire didn't weaken it—it strengthened it. It grew new leaves and shoots with every new canister that hit.

"Stop!" Shina shouted, bounding into the midst of the firefight. "You are making this harder! Kill it but do not use fire!"

"We can't!" Bobbie said. "We weakened it, but it's not enough. It's going to kill us!"

The enormous rabbit clicked his tongue. "And I must rescue you yet again. Oh, well." He squeezed his eyes and mouth shut and clenched his paws. Bobbie watched in amazement as the eight-foot rabbit became ten feet tall, then twelve, then sixteen. He opened his eyes and grinned down at the nurse.

"Now you see why I am honored by the Ojibwa people," he said.

With one leap, he bounded into the giant's path.

The tree-being windmilled to a halt. It was surprised, but only for a moment. It let out a trilling hum, trying to bring the michabo under its spell. For answer, Shina leaped into the air and scissor-kicked it with his huge feet. It staggered backward, then let out a horrifying roar. The hippies at Bobbie's knee wailed in fear. She wished she could cover them with a solid armored dome.

Shina leaped up again and again, kicking at the giant. It retreated a yard or so with every blow, but the rabbit spirit could not seem to knock it over.

"It is rooted deeply in the earth!" he cried. "Destroy the base!"

"What?" the radio in Fred's pouch crackled to life. "What's he saying?"

Bobbie grabbed it and pushed the toggle. "He's saying, knock the ground out from under it."

The helicopters must have gotten the word, because all three swung around and came in high. They fired high-explosive rockets into the undergrowth, blowing it into a massive green cloud. Shina and the giant disappeared. All Bobbie could hear was whistling and shrieking and Shina's war cries and yelps of pain.

Within a few minutes, silence fell. The remains of the jungle settled around them into a three-foot-deep mass of chopped salad. A green haze still hung in the air.

"Well, it's too bad," Appleseed said, his expression rueful. "It was paradise while it lasted. I'm gonna miss those six-foot carrots."

"We'd better get moving," Bobbie said, reaching for her machete. "Let's get out to the county road. Someone will pick us up there."

"I can lead us," Randy Barlow said. The mud had dried on his reddened skin. "Sorry about your rabbit friend. I'll write a song about him and Mr. Natural. Holding back on the rabbit part, of course."

"Why?" Shina asked, appearing through the cloud. He had shrunk down to his normal size. In his paw was a long stick covered with ivy leaves which he munched on happily. The mist began to clear. Here and there an enormous branch, one or another of the giant's limbs stuck up. "Am I not wonderful enough to be honored in song as I am, without Mr. Natural?"

"You're all right!" Bobbie cried, beaming at him in relief.

"Of course," the michabo said, twitching his nose at her. "I am the superior fighter. I am far better than any of you puny humans. I knew you would have to use my strength. You are not fast enough or clever enough to deal with a real threat."

Bobbie groaned. She couldn't take it any longer. She took the pistol off her left hip and plugged the rabbit spirit one in his two-foot-wide fluffy tail.

"Ow! You're a healer! Why did you do that?" Shina bellowed, hopping around and batting at the burned spot in his fur.

"Because you're also more insufferable than any human," Bobbie said. "I had to. It was the natural thing to do."

All of us got our start in this business somehow. Sometimes you blunder into your first monster, and other times Hunters are born into it. And in rare cases, both.   —A.L.

Sons of the Father

Quincy J. Allen

"Mom's gonna kick the shit out of us if she finds out," Kyle Schaeffer hollered over the grumbling dirt bikes.

He and his brother were in the middle of breaking the only Law laid down by their mother from when they were toddlers: *never* go to the Goblin Hills. No reason was ever offered, only the titanium-clad warning.

The telltale shadows of goblins reached out to them across the Utah desert. A jagged pattern of dusty arroyos spread out before them, pale sandstone layered with ruddy streaks and dark shadows. Kyle lifted his goggles, settling them over the brim of his helmet.

Jared, eldest of the twins by a couple of minutes, twisted the throttle, the scream of his motor echoing across the hills. As the engine settled into a grumble, he turned with a mischievous grin. "Mom can't kick the shit out of us anymore."

Kyle raised a dubious eyebrow.

"Not both of us at the same time, anyway." Jared chuckled, but the doubt in his voice carried the simple truth that their mother probably still had a few tricks up her sleeve. She was that sneaky... *and* that good. "And besides," he carried on with more bravado, "we turn eighteen tomorrow. She'd *never* kick our asses on our birthday."

"Maybe," Kyle muttered.

"What's that?" Jared shouted as he revved his engine again.

"Nuthin'."

Kyle put his goggles back on, revved his engine, and let a smile crimp his face. He popped the clutch and wheelied down the rocky slope, leaving his brother in the dust.

"*WHOOP!*" Jared shouted and gave chase.

Jared drifted his back tire around a massive outcropping of rocks, a boot dragging through the dirt as his engine screamed.

A dark SUV loomed dead ahead.

"SHIT!" he shouted.

He jerked the handlebars, rose out of the turn, and angled for a small mound of dirt at full speed. He popped his knees up and yanked on the handlebars as he sailed over the SUV. His back tire skidded across the roof, and then he slammed down on the far side. Grabbing a handful of brake, he came to a wrenching halt, his heart pounding.

He turned to see his brother skid around the far side of the SUV, his knee grazing the rear fender.

"You okay?" Kyle yelled.

Jared nodded with a thumbs-up. Then he noticed the SUV. It was a gray Santa Fe, with all the windows shattered. A small, pink, stuffed kitten dangled from the rearview mirror, swaying in the breeze. A weathered Ford Focus sat parked a short distance off, but all its windows were intact.

"What the hell?" Kyle asked. "Isn't that Cindy Wilson's Santa Fe?"

"Sure looks like it."

"Jared...*look.*" Kyle pointed past the SUV at what remained of a campsite, dread filling his voice.

Three tan tents lay flattened and slashed to pieces. The nylon of one was spattered with droplets and streaks of what could only be dried blood. Clothing and gear lay scattered across the ground.

"*Jesus...*" Kyle whispered. He killed his motor and laid the bike down as he climbed off. Jared followed suit, and they stepped into the campsite.

"Oh my god," Jared kneeled down before a large patch of dried blood soaked into the dusty earth. "It looks like someone gutted an antelope." Fear filled his voice.

"Who is Cindy dating these days?" Kyle asked worriedly as he walked around what remained of the tents.

"Ashad...*something*...I think." Jared rose and lifted the flap of a tent. "You know, that big defensive back from Caineville."

"Oh yeah. I remember him. Any idea who might have been with them?"

"No clue. I don't recognize the Ford back there, either."

Kyle stopped in his tracks and groaned. "There's another big patch of blood over here. And a whole bunch of tracks headed off that way." He pointed toward a maze of narrow, winding canyons to the west.

"Who could do something like this?" Jared asked. A wave of nausea washed over him.

"The Devil's Dealers, maybe?" Kyle offered doubtfully.

It was the only thing he could think of. They'd crossed paths with the biker gang a few times over the years, mostly at their baseball games or a local bar afterward. The bikers, usually drunk, occasionally picked fights with people.

The Schaeffer brothers always stepped in. And it always ended badly for the bikers, assuming there weren't more than six or seven of them. With their mother's training as well as everything they learned from their father's best friend, Wiley, the two brothers could hold their own against long odds.

"This isn't their style. Not by a long shot." Jared couldn't figure why a low-rent biker gang would slaughter teenagers.

"We gotta tell Sheriff Picket."

"What?" Jared asked harshly. "Tell Picket that we were out here illegally, *on dirt bikes*, and we just happened upon a slaughter. After he arrests us, Mom *will* kick the shit out of us...one at a time as she bails us out of the pokey."

"But, Jared, we can't just—"

"No, thank you!" Jared crossed his arms as he cut his brother off. "We call Wiley, and we sort this out ourselves. If the Dealers did this, I see no reason to let them go to jail, let alone keep breathing. Cindy is a *friend*. Ashad too."

"You serious?"

"As a heart attack." Jared stepped over to his bike. "I say we go get the four-wheeler, some gear, and our guns. We follow those tracks until we find who did this. We'll call Wiley and he can bring in some heavy artillery, if that will make you feel better, but we'll sort this out the way Dad would have." Their father had died in the Middle East on some secret mission a few months before they were born. Their mother never spoke about it, but over the years, Wiley gave them enough scraps of information to know their father died a hero. "Wiley will take some convincing, but I think I can turn him around."

"Wiley, we've got a problem." Jared sounded nervous, and his brother looked even worse. If Wiley said not to go, they wouldn't have much choice. The brothers *talked* about their mother kicking their asses. But she never actually had to. Wiley, on the other hand, had been a drill sergeant to them since they were old enough to do front kicks. He was hard as nails and mean as piss when the boys screwed up. And even at sixty years old, the whole town knew he was a BAMF. Wiley was the one who taught them how to think fast, shoot straight, and fight dirty. He demanded their best and was a real ballbuster any time they came up short.

"Jared?" Wiley's graveled voice fluttered in and out across a weak cell signal. "What's wro—?...Is Kyle oka—..."

"Kyle's fine. We're both fine." Jared took a dep breath. "We found a campsite. Somebody tore it to pieces. No bodies, but lots of blood. At least a couple of them are friends of ours. And we found tracks."

"Where are y—...?" Wiley sounded worried. Probably worried about what the boys might do next.

"Umm..." Jared started slowly. "We're..." He gulped, finding that he was more worried about Wiley's reaction than his mother's. Wiley knew all about the Goblin Hills Law.

"Tell him," Kyle urged.

"We're in the Goblin Hills," Jared blurted. "We think the Devil's Dealers have stepped up their game or something. And we're going after them."

Silence.

Jared waited, nervous that Wiley would fly off the handle— tell them to come home that second and let the police handle it. Even a tongue-lashing from Wiley was a thing to be avoided.

Finally, Wiley said the one word Jared didn't expect.

"Okay." The word came through loud and clear, and there was a strange resolve in Wiley's voice. As if something long pent up had finally been set free. "But it wasn't the Dealers...Not out there..." Wiley's voice broke up, thick with static.

The expression on Jared's face was enigmatic enough for Kyle to poke him and ask, "So what'd he say?"

Jared shook his head, held up a silencing finger, and checked his signal. It was down to one flickering bar. He put the phone back to his ear "Wiley, how do you know it wasn't the Dealers?"

"—u're breaking up." Wiley's sounded urgent. "...you to hook the bikes up to the four-wheeler...—d track these fuckers like I taught y—...Arm for bear........know where you're headed.... —ime you boys got your hands......—irthright......—eet you at the entrance....—ait till I get there. Copy that?"

Jared did, mostly. Wiley had given them the green light. The pieces he'd picked up also meant he and Wiley thought a lot alike, which gave him a strange sense of validation.

"Most of it. Arm for bear. Follow the tracks. Wait at the entrance..." Jared wondered what the hell Wiley might be talking about. "Whatever that means," he added quietly.

"Trust me," Wiley added and then ended the call.

Jared rubbed his jaw thoughtfully, feeling the thickening stubble that was a relatively new concept to him. There was more going on than he understood, and Wiley's reaction seemed peculiar.

"What fucking entrance?" Kyle's face twisted into a knot of confusion.

"I have no idea." Jared slid his phone beneath the motocross armor and into a shirt pocket. He turned and looked at the trailered dirt bikes hooked up to the four-wheeled ATV.

He opened the door of their pickup and grabbed his 7mm Browning BAR Short Trac. Quickly checking the load and the safety, he slung it over his shoulder. He pulled out his brother's Remington 750 Woodsmaster .30-06 and handed it over. Kyle automatically checked the chamber and safety as Jared walked to the bike trailer and gave it a shove with his boot. All four five-gallon gas containers sloshed nearly full in their brackets on the trailer. The cooler, strapped in place with bungie cords, didn't budge, and the old army footlocker with their camping and baseball gear jammed inside barely shifted from where he'd wedged it next to the cooler. They were as ready as they could be. A duffle bag with more of their supplies sat in the back seat of the ATV.

Kyle stepped up next to his brother, and the scope of what they were about to do hit them both. "This is some real shit, isn't it," Kyle asked. Awe, excitement, and nervousness filled his voice.

"Yeah." Jared rubbed the back of his neck again. "You ready?"

Kyle nodded. "It's like you said. Cindy, Ashad...they're *friends* of ours." There was a trace of scared rabbit in his words, but the resolve propping up each syllable made Jared proud. They'd been trained to handle themselves. They both knew there might be consequences, but facing down whoever took their friends, maybe even killed them ... It just felt *right*.

"All right." Jared looked at his brother. Lean, armed, and armored in white camo motocross gear. His own set was green camo. He couldn't decide if they looked super cool or just plain stupid. Either way, they'd face this together ... like always.

"You take the hood. You're a better tracker than I am," Jared said, getting into the driver's seat of the ATV.

"Roger that." Kyle hopped up onto the plastic hood, clutching his rifle in one hand and holding himself in place with the other. It was awkward, but it put his nose only a couple feet off the ground. "Fire it up!"

Jared eased the clutch and sent them rolling slowly over a barren patch of rock. "Don't lose your grip," he droned.

"*Yes, Mommy!*" Kyle shot back. His nervous laughter sounded hollow in his ears. Jared's did too. They were headed for trouble, and the stakes were life and death. In the past it was all spur-of-the-moment, bare-knuckle brawling. This time they had plenty of time to think about what they were doing, and it really put a kink in their cojones.

"*Christ!* What is that smell?" Kyle covered his nose as they approached a nasty-looking lump of something to the side of the trail they'd followed for nearly two miles through twisting canyons.

The trail itself wasn't hard to miss. The footprints were a mix of boots, something like moccasins, and the bare feet of a mob of tiny individuals with disturbingly long toenails. Most of the prints were smaller, but there was at least one bruiser in the mix who had to be a staggering giant. Either that or a really fat clown. The tracks looked as if Shaquille O'Neal had led a cub scout troop on a hike to push landmarks over in the park.

"I don't smell anyth—" Jared's eyes got wide and he covered his nose. "Holy shit!"

As the four-wheeler approached the dark mass, Kyle realized his brother's assessment was accurate. It was shit. Even with his mouth and nose covered, the stench pressed into him, into his face, into his skin. It clawed at him like hell's version of every beer-shit and bloated roadside corpse he'd ever got a whiff of. Part of him wanted to cover his eyes as they rolled by, but the seventeen-year-old boy in him couldn't tear his eyes away.

And then he saw it. Amidst the black mass of what had to be the nastiest pile of shit he'd ever seen, he saw something that chilled his blood.

"Jared..." Kyle called out nervously over the motor. "I don't think these are bikers..."

"Yeah?" Jared eyeballed the turd from behind the steering wheel as they rolled by. Jared wanted to believe it *had* to be the Dealers, but his brother's tone sounded like a terrified chummer insisting on a bigger boat. "Well, who then?" was all he could manage.

"Dude! I don't know, but it sure as hell isn't bikers!"

"How can you be so sure?"

Kyle rolled on his side and locked eyes with his brother. "The Dealers don't eat *people*."

Jared's face froze with shock. "What?"

"There was a fingernail back there, man," Kyle cut in. "Pink. Perfect... Except for the bite taken out of it."

Jared's mouth dropped open. All Kyle could do was nod his head slowly, eyes wide.

"What the fuck?" Jared whispered. The whole thing seemed unreal.

"You sure you want do this?" Kyle asked, clutching his rifle a bit nervously. "I mean, I'm not sure I wanna get eaten today, man." Kyle was the thoughtful one, looking to the long-term consequences. It didn't take a rocket scientist to figure that if they got their asses kicked, they were next on the menu.

Jared stopped the ATV, cocked his head, and thought about it. His eyes darted back and forth as he pictured Cindy and Ashad and whoever else might still be alive. He and his brother had always protected the other kids. From kindergarten through high school. Every place on earth has people who think it's okay to prey on the weak. And the Schaeffer brothers stepped up time and time again, taking their beatings but dishing it out twice as hard. It was what their mother had taught them—what Wiley had beaten into them—as if the brothers were carbon steel in a crucible.

He turned his gaze to Kyle and held it there. "It doesn't change a goddamn thing." At least two of his friends might already be dead, maybe more. "These sons of bitches must pay,

Kyle." He looked at his brother, searching for the same resolve he felt within himself. "You know?"

Slowly, Kyle nodded his head. "Yeah. Yeah, I know." He took a deep breath and let it out slowly. "You're right." He sniffed once hard, tightened his jaw, and rolled over onto the hood of the ATV. "Let's get this party started," he called over his shoulder.

Jared hit the gas. They rolled down the canyon as fast as they could and still track whatever it was they hunted. And it *was* a hunt.

They rolled around a tight corner, and Kyle held up a closed fist. Jared hit the brakes. The ATV kicked up gravel and small dust clouds that drifted by them.

They'd reached a dead-end arroyo filled with jagged rocks scattered and stacked up in big piles along the canyon floor. Most of the Goblin Hills were weathered sandstone, but this area held a fair amount of hard-angled rubble, much of it darker than the surrounding landscape.

It looked as if someone had dug an immense hole in the ground nearby and dumped the tailings straight into the canyon. But there was no hole, only a dead end with high canyon walls.

The big cluster of the odd footprints ended right up against a canyon wall. And there was that smell again . . . somewhere nearby . . . but neither brother was interested in finding it.

Jared cut the engine, grabbed his rifle, and stood up in the seat, poking through the roll cage. Clutching his own rifle, Kyle rolled off the hood, came up in a crouch to get a closer look at the footprints.

They were the same ones they'd been tracking. Rising slowly, he paced around the pattern, looking for any sign of a mass exodus. As he drew closer to the back of the dead end, the stench grew stronger, so he knew where the shit had to be. But if anything, the tracks thinned out in that direction. Kyle made two full circles, an increasingly puzzled look on his face. He finally stopped in front of the ATV and shrugged.

"They came in here," he said flatly, "and they didn't leave."

Jared scanned every inch of the canyon walls above them, looking for any way a mob of cannibalistic cub scouts and a giant, man-eating troop leader could have escaped.

There were declivities and protrusions, even a large, dark

opening about twenty-five feet off the ground a short distance further along the canyon wall, but the tracks didn't go there.

"Well, shit, what are we supposed to do now?" Jared wanted to shoot something. Or punch something. Or kick it. Anything would be better than sitting around wondering what they should do next. And for the life of him, he couldn't figure out how Wiley could find them in the middle of the Goblin Hills.

Kyle sat on the hood and rubbed the peach fuzz on his jaw thoughtfully. "Well, what would Wiley do?"

Jared's answer was immediate: "He'd look at the evidence and follow where it leads." He couldn't keep sarcasm from creeping into his words. "You *know* that. And we did that. It led us *here*." He waved his hands at the barren sandstone walls and shook his head.

"Right," Kyle continued, undaunted. "So, what evidence do we have?"

Jared sighed. "Near as I can tell, just the tracks."

"And where do they lead?"

"To a *dead end*."

"Exactly," Kyle said with a smile.

"What?" Jared's thought process derailed like a commuter train in a *kaiju* movie.

"The tracks led us here and don't lead anyplace else. The people we're after aren't here, so it *can't* be a dead end. There *must* be another way out."

"Riiiight," Jared droned. "So, what? There's a secret door around here somewhere."

"I don't know." Kyle got down on his hands and knees. "Let's find out." Placing his nose practically in the dirt, he moved toward the canyon wall and examined the tracks, looking for the big set. He figured the owner might just be in charge, and if so, he might be the one to keep the group moving.

Jared crossed his arms. "Come on, Kyle. That's just *stupid*. Secret doors don't exist."

Picking through the footprints, Kyle finally found the big footprints layered on top of all the little ones. The big set walked straight in and... Jared peered at a small rock on the canyon floor, set up against the wall. The rock was rounded and protruded from the sandy earth around it by about three inches.

Kyle made out a clear imprint of the big boot *around* where the rock stuck up, as if the boot had pressed into the ground without the rock being there. He reached out and pressed the stone. The thing gave slightly under his pressure. He stood slowly and motioned for his brother to step over.

"Bring the Browning," he called over his shoulder nervously. He unslung his Remington and flipped the safety off. Jared approached and released the safety on his own rifle.

The boys' hearts raced inside their chests, and Kyle could taste copper as a very rational fear slunk through his body like some reptilian predator in tall grass. Swallowing, he stepped on the rock and pressed down.

Click. Clunk! CLANK!

The rock face shivered once and swung inwards with the clatter of rusty cogs and grinding stone.

A dark passage opened up beyond the door, one large enough to accommodate a tall basketball guard. The stench that wafted out of the darkness hammered into them, assaulting their senses with equal parts shit, carrion, sweaty locker rooms, and the rotting feet of soggy corpses.

"Jesus, that's *rank*!" Jared said. He turned sideways, covering his mouth as he fought the urge to vomit.

"Damn it," Kyle said, staring into the darkness. "We need the headlamps." He moved toward the trailer. "Watch the tunnel," he said over his shoulder. He propped his Remington against the frame and opened the footlocker. Their baseball bats and gloves hit the ground first, then the sleeping bags and tent. He pulled out the headlamps, tossing one to his brother. He slipped his own over his head, clicked it on, and put the Remington into the footlocker. A dark cave meant close quarters, so he pulled out a pistol-grip Mossberg 12-gauge, pumped it once to chamber a round, and then flipped the safety off.

He cracked open a box of shells, slammed one home into the Mossy's receiver, and filled his pants pockets with as many shells as he could fit.

"So, ummm...Wiley said to wait at the entrance," Jared said slowly. The unspoken suggestion in his voice wasn't wasted on his brother. Adrenaline pumped through them. They were worried about their friends. "I'm still wondering how the fuck he knew about this place."

"Well, it can't hurt to take a quick reconnoiter, can it?" Kyle asked. "I mean, Cindy and the others might still be alive."

Jared's smile was wicked. "I'm thinking it's a long shot, but we gotta try." He motioned for his brother to proceed. "You've got the shotty. You go first."

Reason and fear struggled against adrenaline and dreams of payback. Kyle hesitated for a few moments but then thought about what he'd been taught. The shotgun was the natural weapon to lead with.

He nodded and stepped silently into the cave, straining to hear anything further in the cave as his heart pounded in his ears. They now hunted on someone else's turf, and those someones were more dangerous than anything they'd ever faced. Silence was their best friend and would be right up until the shooting started.

Jared followed him in, reminding himself that in the cavern he'd have to *really* check his targets. Not only was his brother in front of him, but their friends might still be alive somewhere.

The passage opened before them, rough-hewn and changing in size from about two meters to almost three in places. They moved forward slowly, the passage descending with a slight curve to the left.

"You know, there's something I don't get," Jared whispered.

"What's that?"

"Why the fuck would anyone be down in a cave in the middle of the fucking desert?" He shook his head. "Something doesn't smell right."

"No shit," Kyle replied, trying not to suck in the foul air still pressing into his nostrils.

"I'm beginning to think these aren't people we're dealing with."

"What do you mean, 'not people'?" Confusion twisted Kyle's face into a knot. "What then?"

"I don't know. Cultists or something? I mean like *real* psychos.... They sure as hell smell bad, whatever they are," Jared muttered.

About forty meters in, they encountered what had to have been a cave-in. The walls seemed scorched, as if explosives brought the ceiling down rather than time or pressure. Jagged chunks of rock littered the floor, and someone had reinforced the widened area above them with rough, iron struts and irregular timbers. The cave-in continued for another twenty meters and then ended, with the passage going back to rough-cut stone.

They continued creeping along, and it was clear they were in a large, spiraling tunnel that looped deeper into the earth.

"What do you think Mom will do when she finds out we came in here?"

"Well, assuming we make it out, you know, as opposed to being eaten by psychotic cannibalistic cultists, I'm pretty sure she'll take the escrima sticks to us both." Jared shrugged. "Whether or not she beats us to death remains to be seen."

"Yeah..." Kyle whispered. He couldn't disagree. "I think—"

A grunt of some kind—like a big animal—echoed up toward them along the passage.

Kyle froze in his tracks and held up a fist.

Slowly, he reached up and switched off his headlamp. Turning, he pointed to his brother and pointed at the ground, indicating he wanted his brother to stay put. Then he pointed to fingers at his own eyes.

Jared nodded, tightened his grip on the Browning, and set the stock into his shoulder so he could cover Kyle as he scouted ahead.

Kyle lowered into a crouch and moved forward, listening intently as he inched along. He held the shotgun at waist level, his finger poised on the trigger guard and the barrel aimed straight ahead at waist level. As he proceeded, pale light seeped around the bend, a faint, flickering glow that grew in intensity as he drew near.

Then he heard the voices.

But they weren't in any language he'd ever heard. They were guttural, rough, and the sounds reminded him of dogs or pigs or something, only deeper...more menacing. As he approached, the stench of carrion increased, mixed in with the smell of a slaughterhouse—butchered flesh and spilled blood. There was also the smell of roasting meat, but not any meat he recognized.

And they were just around the corner.

Kyle turned. His brother's headlamp was barely in view around the curve of the rock. He tapped his headlamp, made a cutting motion with his hand, and motioned for his brother to come forward.

When his brother came up, he moved forward. Side by side, they inched along. The darkness around them faded, and the passageway opened a dozen meters ahead into a torchlit cavern. They turned the corner together and froze in their tracks.

A single torch protruded between two unfamiliar teenagers who were hung on the far wall. The boy and girl had been stripped bare, their hands cuffed in dark, metal shackles hooked on pins anchored to the wall above them. Their feet dangled a foot off the ground. Their throats had been slit, and blood covered the front of their bodies to pool beneath them and run off in a trench along the wall. Additionally, the boy's left leg had been hacked off at the hip.

But that isn't what terrified the brothers.

Off to the left squatted five humanoid creatures about four feet tall with greenish-black skin, broad shoulders, spindly limbs, and dark, matted fur. Their faces were piglike, with short snouts and inch-long tusks protruding up from their lower jaws. Beady eyes in deep-set sockets glowed with an inner, reddish light.

The things wore a mishmash of hide clothing, cast-iron bracers, and greaves. A couple of them also wore odd pieces of filthy human clothing that looked like they belonged in the 1980s. Each had a badly crafted weapon of some sort lying on the stone floor within easy reach, including a couple of hand axes, a battered sword, and one larger, double-bitted axe that belonged to the largest of the five.

They conversed in their strange, grunting language as the larger one rotated a severed human leg on a spit over the campfire.

Rage blossomed in Kyle's chest.

"WHAT THE FUCK?" he growled.

All five creatures turned surprised faces toward the Schaeffer brothers.

BOOM! Turkey-shot from Kyle's Mossberg turned the nearest pig-face into a red, meaty cloud that spattered across two pig-faces behind him. The headless corpse flew backward and slammed into another pig-thing.

The four monsters still breathing squealed in unison, grabbing their weapons as they rose.

Jared aimed at the next one in line and fired twice. The first round caught it in the chest, forcing it backward. The second hit it in the face, sent a burst of brains out the back, and hammered into the shoulder of the next one in line. A single shot from the Browning sent that one to the floor in a heap.

The big one roared a challenge and rushed forward, double-bit axe held high.

Kyle pumped the action and fired again, catching the thing square in the chest. Jared followed up with a shot through its throat. It tumbled backward to slam onto the stone.

The last one screeched in terror, turned, and bolted for the passage on the far side of the cave.

Both brothers shot it in the back. The thing slammed into the rock face next to the passage it had run for. Kyle took two steps, pumping the action of the Mossy again. He took aim, pulled the trigger, and blew the head off the last pig-face. The body slid to the ground and tipped onto its side, one of its legs twitching.

Silence filled the room, broken only by the adrenaline-fueled panting of the brothers. Gunpowder filled their nostrils, and the ringing in their ears reminded them why shooters wear earplugs at ranges. Half in shock, they stared down at the carnage as smoke dissipated on a current of nauseating air drifting up from below.

The pig-faces' blood was nearly black and almost as thick as honey.

"Holy shit..." Jared reached into his pocket and loaded a fresh mag into the Browning. He chambered it, hit the safety, and then slid four more rounds in.

"What the hell are those things?" Kyle asked, slipping fresh shells into the Mossberg. "And what were they doing here?"

"I'm guessing they were guards." Jared shrugged. "But I'm more worried about where the rest of them—" A deep drumming sound caught his ear. "Do you hear that?"

The ringing in their ears had faded, and now that they were listening for it, the sound of distant drums and grunting chants drifted up to them from the downside passage.

"We should keep going, but if we run into many more of these things, I'm thinking we need to get the hell out of here. We only have five rounds each."

"Yeah. Well, if we run into more, you shoot the ones on the left. I'll shoot the ones on the right, and we'll work toward the middle. That way we don't waste ammo."

Jared nodded. "Good thinking." He hefted his rifle and motioned for Kyle to take point again.

The brothers moved forward more quickly this time, moving deeper down the spiraling passage. They passed one single side tunnel that angled back and up at a steep angle. It was narrower than the main passage, but still large enough for something large to move through.

With the sound of the drums and chanting growing, they continued on. Jared glanced back occasionally to check their six. They made one more loop downward, the drums and chanting rising to a deafening level and the tempo quickening with each heartbeat.

The brothers killed their headlamps again, revealing a growing brightness in the passage ahead. They crouched low and inched toward a widening section of passage that opened up into a massive cavern brightly lit by torches and a huge bonfire. They got down on their bellies and crawled forward, rifles ready.

The path split before them, branching off to the left and right along the cave wall. A rocky lip stuck up that gave them perfect cover to look down into the cavern onto whatever lay below.

Kyle gasped.

Off to the left, Ashad's gutted body turned slowly on a spit. Two small pig-things worked the spit, straining to keep the body rotating over open flame. To the right, a row of large pig-faces in identical hides and war paint hammered on great drums. In the middle of the room, a mob of the pig-things stomped and grunted to the quickening beat. On the far side, Cindy lay trussed upon a large stone altar, her unconscious body restrained by four pig-things. Just beyond, a bruiser of a pig-face nearly seven feet tall in dark plates of armor stood next to a large cave opening, holding a massive iron mattock.

Then something moved inside the cave. The brothers watched in horror as a giant spider nearly ten feet long leapt out of the cave and pierced Cindy's chest with its foot-long fangs. The girl screamed once and then went limp.

Kyle, blind with rage, started to get up, ready to unload into the crowd, but his brother grabbed his arm and held him down.

"NO!" Jared hissed.

"But—" Kyle strained against his brother's grip.

"There's nothing we can do for them now!" Jared's voice was urgent. "But these motherfuckers must pay...." He locked eyes with his brothers. "*All* of them."

"How do we do that?"

"We're gonna need bigger guns."

An idea popped into Kyle's head. "Yeah, and maybe something else," he added with malice.

"What are you thinking?"

"Trust me." He crawled backward as silently as he could. "I have an idea."

"I'm pretty sure I said, 'Wait for me at the entrance.'" Wiley scowled at the brothers as they walked out into the night.

"Oh, shit," Kyle mumbled.

"We thought we might be able to save them," Jared said quickly. "They're dead, Wiley...Our friends. They're all dead."

Wiley sat on the hood of their ATV, his trusty LAR-47 cradled in one arm and two large duffle bags on the ground a few feet away. The old man wore a camo boonie-rat hat, his bushy gray ponytail protruding down his back. The boys stopped short, in part because Wiley was there, but mostly because he had on a set of combat armor they'd never seen before. It covered his whole body, and there was a strange logo on the right shoulder guard.

His Jeep CJ-5 was parked behind their ATV.

"Is Mom back?" Kyle asked anxiously, trying to change the subject. He could still see those two teenagers hanging on the wall.

Wiley winced, knowing full well what Kyle was doing. It was an old dance for both of them. Kyle was the more sensitive of the two boys. "No. She's still in Vegas seeing an old friend and getting you your birthday presents."

"Old friend?" Kyle asked. "Who—?"

"So," Wiley interrupted, "how many of those pig-faced fuckers did you kill?"

"How did you—?" Jared blurted.

"Not my first rodeo," Wiley said simply. "Look, boys. There's a lot you don't know, and your mother may not forgive me, but this is more important than my sorry old ass."

"What do you mean?" Kyle asked.

"I'll tell you everything tomorrow. Okay?"

Both boys nodded.

"Gimme a status report," Wiley ordered, groaning slightly as he got off the hood. He left his rifle leaning against the ATV and limped forward a step. He'd limped for as long as the boys had known him. He'd said he'd taken a hit during the war, but it didn't keep him from kicking their butts during training.

Jared quickly filled him in on what had happened, worried that the mob down below might discover the dead pig-faces.

Wiley nodded when Jared finished up. "Well, boys, we've got two choices." He stepped up to the duffle bags. "We can either call in the cavalry or"—he reached down, picked up the bags, and dropped them in front of the brothers—"you two can go back down there and take care of the bastards that killed your friends."

"There's an awful lot of them," Kyle said doubtfully.

Wiley reached into a vest pocket and tossed a box at Kyle. It was brown cardboard and looked like an ammunition box.

Kyle caught it. It was heavier than he expected, and it had a military-style label.

"Wiley..." Kyle stared at the old man. "These are—"

Wiley nodded slowly. The grin on his face would have made the Devil proud. "Yep."

"Aren't these like super illegal?" Kyle showed the box to his brother, whose face went wide with surprise.

"I won't tell anyone if you don't," Wiley said. His chuckle got both boys smiling.

"Even with those," Jared chimed in, "I don't see how we can get them all."

"You haven't seen what's in the bags," Wiley said.

The boys bent down and opened the bags at their feet.

"Holy shit!" Jared blurted as he pulled out an FN FAL. The battle rifle had been modified with a larger flash suppressor, a laser sight, and what appeared to be a custom-built stock.

"That was your father's," Wiley said.

"Is this a—?" Kyle said quietly when he opened his bag. He couldn't believe his eyes as he pulled out a solid-framed monstrosity.

"An AA-12 auto shotgun," Wiley finished. "I bought that for you shortly after you and your brother were born. There are Colt Commandos in there for you both as well as a shit-ton of special ammo perfect for what's down there. And you got your father's pistol, Kyle." Wiley crossed his arms and smiled at both boys... *men,* he corrected in his head. Today they were men. "I figured you both deserved one of your father's weapons, and those two saw him through quite a few shit storms. It's your birthright."

"So what's this?" Jared asked, pulling out the upper portion of combat armor virtually identical to Wiley's.

"You both get a set," Wiley said with pride. "Also your father's." He looked a little embarrassed. "I'm afraid they might be tight. You two are a bit larger than he was. But for tonight, I figured they might come in handy."

"What the hell is all this stuff?" Kyle asked. He pulled out his own armor and examined the emblem on the shoulder. It was a cartoonish version of Elvis smoking a big cigar on an olive green background.

"Well, the emblem is for Team Vegas."

"What?" the brothers asked in unison.

"Look, all I can tell you right now is that those things down there are the ones who killed your father. Three months before you were born. Back then there was an army of them. We thought we got them all and sealed up the cave, but apparently we missed a few."

"Dad?" Kyle asked, shocked.

"Who's 'we'?" Jared asked.

"It's a long story, boys," Wiley said tiredly. "And you have to get down there and finish what we started."

"I don't know," Jared said uneasily. "Even with all this firepower, there must be nearly a hundred of those ... *things* down there."

"Hobgoblins," Wiley clarified. "They're called hobgoblins—mean as piss and twice as rank."

"Whatever you call them," Jared continued, "I don't see how we can get them all."

Kyle looked at the ammo box Wiley had tossed to him and eyed the gas containers on the trailer.

"Did we bring all those Styrofoam plates?" he asked, looking at his brother.

"Yeah," Jared replied. "Three big bags of them."

"Then I have an idea." Kyle's grin was malevolent.

Wiley's eyebrow went up, paired with an appreciative grin. "You got a mean streak, son," he said.

"Gee," Kyle said sweetly, locking eyes with Wiley. "I wonder where I got that from."

He strode over to the back seat of the ATV and rummaged through a duffle bag filled with their camp gear. "Now help me put these plates to good use."

The drums had settled into a steady throb that echoed up the spiraling passage. The seven bodies—two human and five hobgoblin—had been right where the brothers were forced to leave them.

Now at the bottom of the passage, Kyle peered over the lip, his heart pounding in his chest. Little had changed from the last time he looked at the hobgoblin party. The bulk of them were grouped up between the lip and the altar, stomping and grunting to the drums. The only real difference was that a handful of what Kyle guessed were females surrounded the obviously sated spider, rubbing red paint over its legs. Cindy's shriveled corpse, still prone on the altar, looked like a gray raisin, her limbs twisted at awkward angles.

Kyle adjusted the wheel chock he'd set against the rocky lip, lining it up between the passage and the altar. He crawled back and rose to a kneeling position just inside the passage. He took a deep breath and relaxed his muscles. The trick to skeet shooting was to let the barrel lead the target and fire.

With a glance over his shoulder, he gave a thumbs-up and waited.

Further into the passage, Jared kicked the starter and fired up the dirt bike. He revved the engine once, dropped the clutch, and raced down the passage.

Kyle rose, took a step to the side, and moved to the lip. He didn't see a sea of startled pig-faces look up at the commotion. He didn't see the spider kick the females aside and move toward the altar. All he saw was the shot he was about to make. He visualized it. His finger drifted toward the trigger of the heavy weapon in his hands. He'd never even fired the thing before. And if this didn't work, he and his brother were dead meat.

Jared shifted into second gear, goosed the throttle, and pushed off the back of the bike as hard as he could, making sure to clear the gas cans strapped on either side of the rear seat.

The hobgoblins squealed and howled their rage.

The spider hissed.

The bike hit the chock hard, bouncing the front tire up and then the rear one, sending it into a forward tumble as it sailed through the air.

Jared pulled the trigger on his AA-12 and held it down.

Boom! Boom! Boom!

The white phosphorous rounds Wiley had given him hammered into the dirt bike, burning everything it touched at five thousand degrees. The already tumbling motorcycle twisted in midair.

Whoofff! The gas tank detonated, sending flaming gasoline in a spiral pattern.

Boom!—WHOOFFFF!!

All four gas cans detonated simultaneously. The Styrofoam-gasoline mixture inside blossomed into a sticky cloud raining liquid hell upon the shrieking pig-faces, burning a swath thirty feet wide across living flesh.

The dirt bike, a spinning ball of flame, slammed into the

giant spider, caving in most of its thorax as it sent the ruined creature hurtling into the rock wall. The big hobgoblin dove to the side, flames licking along its armor.

Kyle drifted the barrel down into the line of drummers and let his own twenty-round drum of Willie Petes beat out its own rhythm. The drummers burned as they scattered.

Jared grabbed his father's FN and stepped up behind his brother, and he held his fire.

The last drummer went down screaming when the AA-12 clicked empty.

"SWITCH!" Kyle shouted and stepped back.

Jared stepped up to the lip, staring at a pit of flaming carnage. The incinerated heap of the spider twitched, and most of the hobgoblins in the middle writhed within the flames of a now smoke-filled cavern. Through the haze swam a mob of hateful goblin faces, all turned up toward the brothers.

Jared pictured the dead faces of his friends and did what came naturally. He leveled the FN at a crowd of pig-faces on the left as they surged forward.

THUD!-THUD!-THUD!-THUD!-THUD!

The HE rounds Wiley had provided ripped the hobgoblins to pieces. Great chunks of meat blew out their backs. Limbs tore free, driving the mob back.

The FN clicked empty.

"SWITCH!" he shouted and stepped backward.

Kyle stepped in, leveled the AA-12, and opened up. White hot death poured into the hobgoblins who now scrambled over one another to find cover. "On the right!" he shouted over his shoulder.

Jared stepped forward, pulled the bolt back, and poured a thirty-round magazine into the handful of pig-faces moving toward him. He spotted the bruiser stepping out of the cave, its fur singed. The thing bellowed something in its own language and the hobgoblins around the boys began to retreat. Twenty or thirty remained, scrambling back as smoke burned the boys' eyes and lungs.

"Fall back!" Jared yelled.

One at a time, they reloaded with the last magazine and drum as they backed out of the passage, straining to hear any sort of pursuit as they moved.

A couple minutes later, the big one roared, and a stampede of little feet echoed around the passage.

"Here they come!" Kyle shouted.

A mob of small, raging hobgoblins raced around the corner, all brandishing their ill-crafted weapons. At twenty feet the boys opened up to the left and right as they'd agreed. In perfect syncopation, the brothers mowed down the onslaught—one-shot-one-kill-one-shot-one-kill. The hobgoblins scrambled over their fallen comrades, and then the big one came into view. Finally, Kyle blasted the face off the last of the small ones as Jared took aim at the bruiser. He pulled the trigger.

Click!

The bruiser smiled.

Kyle raised the shotgun and aimed. It was too far of a shot to guarantee a kill, but the bruiser got the message. He scowled and disappeared around the curve.

"Keep going," Kyle hissed.

As they moved backwards, Jared asked, "Why didn't you take the shot?"

"Because there isn't one. I'm empty."

"What about the pistol?" Jared accused.

Kyle looked embarrassed, realizing that it was holstered at his hip. Then he frowned. "What about yours?"

Jared got a sheepish grin. "Guess we're a little new at this, huh?"

"I guess so."

Making sure the bruiser didn't follow, they emerged from the passage to find Wiley on the phone. "Yeah, boss. It's time you met 'em.... Vegas, huh? I thought she might be coming to see you... All right. I'll see you soon."

He slipped the phone into his pocket and smiled at them.

"Good news, boys. I just—"

A massive shadow dropped from above and landed in front of Wiley.

The giant hobgoblin roared and swung its mattock, a hammering blow that caught Wiley in the chest and sent the old man sailing into the darkness. The brothers heard the old man slam into a canyon wall and drop.

The bruiser spun, raising the mattock above his head.

The Schaeffer brothers moved in unison. The Colts slipped

free of their holsters, the hammers clicked back, and a thundering hailstorm of .45 ACP blasted into the giant hobgoblin. A few rounds ricocheted off its armor, but most found gaps at elbow and neck.

Finally, Jared aimed at its forehead and put his last round dead between the bruiser's eyes.

The mattock dropped to the ground and the monster tumbled backward with a tremendous thud.

Something moved in the darkness. Kyle dove for the baseball bats they'd left on the ground and came up in a fighting stance.

"Easy, Kyle," Wiley said, wheezing. "Oh, shit that hurts."

"You all right?" Jared asked.

"Some broken ribs, to be sure, and one hell of a lump on my skull, but I've had worse." Wiley stepped up and gave the boys an appraising eye. "You boys are gonna do just fine."

Jared and Kyle sat on their living room sofa, worried looks on their faces as their mother paced back and forth like an angry tigress. They'd just told her the entire story. Wiley sat on one arm, wincing with every breath and picking at the medical tape wrapped around his chest.

"How could you?" she screamed at all three of them. "Especially *you*, Wiley, after what happened to Jimmy!"

"That wasn't your fault, Heather," Wiley said gently. "You couldn't help being pregnant any more than either of you could help getting into this business." He took off his hat and dropped it on the coffee table. "We are what we are, and sometimes the choice is taken away from us."

"I never said I thought it was my fault."

"Yeah, you did, Heather. Not in so many words, but it was always there—the guilt you felt because you weren't there to watch Jimmy's back."

"I don't know..." She stopped pacing. "Maybe..."

"Heather, I know you may hate me for all of this, but this was fate. You *know* how it works in this business. Your sons are naturals. Just like you and Jimmy were." She got an agonized look on her face. "Together, there wasn't a thing you two couldn't handle. You were unstoppable. It's the same for your sons. They were *born* for this. And born to avenge their father."

"Boys," Wiley turning to them, "there's a man outside who I

think you should meet. Feds are gonna be here in a while, and he can help you get through the debriefing."

"Debriefing?" Jared asked.

"Just go talk to him. Your mother and I need to talk."

Kyle nodded and got up off the sofa. His brother followed him out into the driveway where a lean, average-sized man with sandy-blond hair leaned against Wiley's jeep, smoking a cigarette. Putting the cigarette out under a dusty boot, he stepped up to them with a slight smile.

"Evening, boys. Or should I say good morning?" He held out a hand. "I'm Earl Harbinger, and I knew your father." He shook hands with the speechless brothers, and then his ears perked up. Turning, he stared down the long dusty drive that led from town to the Schaeffer house. Two black sedans were headed their way, brimming with spooks.

"Listen to me very carefully because I don't have much time, and you need to get this right. Those agents are gonna grill you pretty hard about what happened in the desert today. Tell them the whole story, *especially* about how many of those things you killed. Stay cool and swear to keep quiet about what you saw." He reached into his brown leather jacket and pulled out a pack of cigarettes. Pulling one out, he said, "Oh, one other thing." Producing a Zippo from his pocket, he lit the cigarette. "They'll probably ask what you would have done if you ran into humans rather than monsters. Just tell them you didn't think that far ahead. Remind them that you're just kids, after all."

He turned and walked off toward the open desert, a trail of smoke drifting around his head. Harbinger paused for a moment and turned, giving them a wolfish grin, "And keep in mind, after today, you boys are gonna be rich."

Since the secret government program Which Shall Not Be Named has been "under new management," MHI has teamed up with them a few times. These events take place after Operation Siege. —A.L.

The Troll Factory

Alex Shvartsman

When the zombies rushed our position, I froze up.

They moved fast—nothing like the shambling dim-witted creatures from the movies—a half dozen of them coming straight for us. My fellow Newbies didn't hesitate. To my left, Carl fired methodically, a lit cigarette dangling forgotten from the corner of his mouth. Paula whooped and cackled as she let loose with her 12-gauge shotgun. I was certain others were in their element too, having finally been given a chance to take down real baddies after months of training. Me, I stared at the ugly critters through the scope of my rifle and couldn't bring myself to pull the trigger.

It's not that I had any qualms about eradicating the unnatural things. Far from it. I'd joined Monster Hunter International to do just that. But when push came to shove, this wasn't like video games or shooting ranges. All I could think of was the night my life got ruined.

We had just gotten married, Audrey and me, and were honeymooning in Florida. The newly minted Mr. and Mrs. Mike Cantor enjoyed a few days of hiking and camping in the Apalachicola National Forest. We were setting up a tent for the night when a half-man half-spider *thing* attacked us.

To this day, I only recall flashes. The monster's sharp claws ripping into my flesh, its fangs dripping with venom...I got between it and Audrey and fought back, armed with nothing but a small hatchet and aluminum tent pole. I screamed for her to run, but she stayed and fought by my side until it pinned me with its legs and bit, its venom burning like molten led as it paralyzed my body.

I woke up in a hospital. I was lucky, I was told. The team of Hunters had pursued this rare Philippine spider demon for days, and caught up to it before it finished me off. Audrey... wasn't so lucky. We had to have a closed-casket funeral.

It took me weeks to recover, physically. Mentally was another story. At the hospital they had told me I had some form of PTSD. Not a night went by without me waking up in cold sweat from nightmares featuring giant spiders.

The two remaining zombies were almost upon us. I could see the rotting flesh of their faces, could smell the stench of their decay. Still, I was unable to shoot. I'd joined MHI because I couldn't go back to my past life, the life where everything reminded me of the happiness I could have had with Audrey. Instead, I figured I'd dedicate myself to eradicating demons, vampires, and zombies so other couples could go on honeymoons and live to tell the tale. The world around me felt like it was in slow motion as I willed my finger to pull the trigger. It wouldn't cooperate. Instead, the hairy, disgusting spiders ran rampant through my mind.

A blast from Paula's shotgun blew a zombie's head like a watermelon. Carl put a pair of bullets through the eye socket of another. Just like that, it was over. I lowered my gun and looked around, ashamed and afraid. But it seemed the others had been too busy fighting to notice how epically I had choked. There was much celebrating and high-fiving. I did my best to imitate everyone else's excitement.

When we climbed into the SUVs, I pulled my cap over my eyes and pretended to sleep all the way back to Cazador, Alabama.

The next morning Carl woke me from yet another nightmare. "You okay, man? You were sweating and moaning, like Casper the Friendly Ghost on LSD."

I rubbed my eyes and mumbled something intentionally incomprehensible.

Carl shrugged. "Harbinger wants to see you, so maybe splash some water on your face, eh?"

Well, crap. That didn't bode well. Surely the boss had some experienced Hunters watch our first outing. Surely they'd seen me fail. I cleaned myself up and got dressed, all while trying to figure out how to maintain my dignity as I got booted from the ranks. Inside my mind, the spiders scratched in earnest.

When I got there, Earl Harbinger was chatting with a pretty redhead I didn't recognize. "Mike," Harbinger said amicably. "Meet Heather Kerkonen."

The lady and I shook hands. She had a solid grip. I wondered if she was a PR person who conducted exit interviews.

"You used to be a computer hacker before you joined up, right?" asked Heather.

I never cared for that term. "Not exactly. I was a network security expert. So, really, the opposite."

"I see." She sized me up. "Do a lot of security experts have aliases, Black Neo?"

"Neo used to be my handle on a pro video game circuit. But then there was another Neo, and the guys..." I pointed at my face and shrugged. "The name stuck."

The spiders scratching at my brain reminded me that I never really fit in. Not growing up as a mixed-ethnicity inner city kid in the Bronx, not among the mostly entitled suburban teenagers at gaming tournaments, and not with my fellow IT nerds at work... And now I was finding out I may not be a good fit as a Hunter.

"Either way," said Harbinger, "Mike is our top computer expert." He turned to me. "We could use your help."

Maybe they weren't going to fire me. But were they going to stick me in the server room somewhere? Not a lot of monster-slaying potential, unless you count an occasional computer virus.

"There's a corporate data center in Podolsk, Russia," said Harbinger, "and in that data center, they employ several trolls."

He didn't sound like he was passing judgment, nor should he. MHI cooperated with orcs and elves and other nonhumans, and even had its own troll running the IT department.

"This didn't work out well for them," said Heather. "The trolls have run amok, taken over the facility, and eaten their corporate overlords. Local Hunters have been retained to clean up the mess."

"There's a company near Moscow. We worked with them last year," said Harbinger. "It turns out they're all right." Harbinger seemed to divide all Monster Hunter outlets into two groups: those that were *assholes* and those that were *all right*. The *all right* ones you could trust with your life.

"Problem is, there's some sensitive data stored at that facility," said Heather. "I'm going to lead a small team to liaise with the Russians and retrieve that data." She nodded at me. "That's where you come in."

"We don't usually loan out our Hunters," said Harbinger, "but for you I'm willing to make an exception." He smiled at Heather warmly. "So long as you promise to take real good care of 'em."

An international mission sounded splendid, especially in light of what I'd been expecting to happen. It seemed Harbinger didn't know that I choked after all. I felt a strange mixture of relief and shame for getting rewarded with a cool assignment despite my screwup. I wondered who else was going. Would I get the chance to work with Owen Pitt, or Holly Newcastle, or someone equally cool from Team Harbinger? But those guys weren't IT experts. In which case...

"Is Melvin coming, too?"

Harbinger frowned. "Son, you don't send a troll to a troll revolt. He might think it's a party."

Instead of Melvin, Harbinger assigned my buddy Carl to round out the team. Carl's computer skills were limited to playing Candy Crush and losing, but he was interested in joining one of the international teams, and I guess Harbinger didn't mind sending two Newbies on such a training-wheels mission.

After nearly a day spent in planes, trains, and automobiles, we arrived at the Russian Hunters' headquarters, somewhere on the outskirts of Moscow. It looked like the private dacha of some Communist big shot, fallen into disrepair in the decades since perestroika but fixed up recently. You could see the fresh patches of paint and concrete in places. It was large and offered as much privacy as any estate this close to Russia's capital might provide.

Heather headed off to meet with the Russian Hunters' boss, some man named Krasnov, while Carl and I were ushered into the cafeteria for some refreshments. There were several Hunters in the room, gregarious and loud; they were just like our guys back in Alabama.

Carl and I grabbed some bread and cold cuts from the cornucopia of food. Seriously, the tables were groaning with the weight of deli meats, potato, herring, and other dishes, not to mention vodka and beer. Owen and some of the others would have had a field day; their Vegas buffet exploits were legendary.

The Russians kept stealing glances at us, but none approached.

"They probably ain't never seen a black Jew before." Carl waved his sandwich at me. With his blond hair and blue eyes, he fit right in with the local crew. "Or maybe they're stunned by my good looks and winning personality."

The largest of the Russians broke from the group and made his way toward us. He was nearly seven feet tall and made of solid muscle; basically Ivan Drago's big brother. He grinned. "We see vampyr, goblin, and kikimora every other week," he said in heavily accented English. "After this, different skin color is not big deal, *da*?"

I smiled politely while Carl laughed uproariously. The Russian extended his hand. "Hi, I'm Sergey. But you call me Ponchik. Everyone else does."

"Mike," I said. "And that's Carl."

"Hey, is that ChronoRex 500?" He pointed at my smartwatch, the latest and greatest on the market.

Turned out, Ponchik was almost as much of a gadgethead as me. Our conversation quickly descended into technobabble, prompting Carl to flee and try his luck with Hunters whose foreign language was Cyrillic rather than Nerd.

We chatted for hours. The spiders in my mind scratched less loudly. I felt welcomed and my anxiety remained in check. I told Ponchik stories about my time on the pro gaming circuit and he educated me on the history of monster hunting in Russia.

Back in the Soviet days, it was a government-controlled thing. The Commies brutally exterminated anything that wasn't human. When the USSR collapsed, Russia still had its version of the MCB, but all sorts of private outfits—cooperatives, as Ponchik called them—sprouted to fill the void. The current government attitude toward monsters wasn't quite as extreme. They were happy to employ the agreeable ones, or look the other way when corporations who paid the bribes did the same.

"We knew about Troll Factory for years," said Ponchik.

"The troll factory?" I raised an eyebrow.

"Not real factory. Is just what we call it. Big, boring office. They use trolls for corporate spying, propaganda, to write bad reviews of competitor products on internet, stuff like this. But we, how you say, had bigger fish to cook. Trolls behave, not kill anyone, so we don't bother. Now they misbehave, we go to work; it will be piece of pie to defeat them." For a guy without an ounce of fat on him, Ponchik sure seemed fond of slightly askew food metaphors.

We entered the Troll Factory at dawn. Heather, Carl, and I followed a team of twelve Russian Hunters armed to the teeth. The factory was a four-story office building, drab and gray and so ordinary it might as well have been in Jersey.

Heather had expressed some concern about going in light, but the Russians all seemed as confident as Ponchik. "It's only a few trolls," said their leader Oleg. "What we've got here is overkill."

He was wrong.

The trolls waited until we got past the foyer and ventured deeper into the bowels of the building. We hoped to surprise them—instead, they ambushed us. They attacked en masse, at least two dozen of them pouring out of offices and down staircases. Eight-foot-tall green humanoids with unnaturally long limbs, they were a terrifying sight.

We retreated through a maze of cubicles and corridors, cramped spaces preventing the Hunters from taking full advantage of their guns. The Russians left at least two mauled bodies behind. A door burst open and a troll came at me with a nasty club that had large nails embedded at its business end, creating a makeshift morning star. I moved to duck but he was too fast. Just as the club was about to brain me, someone yanked me backward. The club missed my head by inches and its nails bit into the gray sheetrock of the wall. As I landed ungracefully on my ass, I saw Ponchik tackle the green bastard before he could recover his balance. The Russian landed on top of the troll and drove a big, mean-looking knife through his misshapen head.

He got up and turned to me, bits of the troll's brain on his blade. "Something wrong here."

"No shit," I said. "There are a lot more than a few trolls."

"Yes." Ponchik moved fast and half dragged me along as he spoke. "But also trolls act strange. Fearless. They swarm, not care if first ones get shot."

Come to think of it, they seemed to act just like the zombies from the other day: trying to overwhelm us with numbers, not caring for their individual safety. I thought trolls were supposed to be smart. But then, we also expected there to be only a few of them. There must've been a lot of vacant real estate under Russia's bridges.

We turned the corner and came face to face with four more of the damn things.

"*Blin!*" Ponchik cursed. He shoved me back in the direction we'd come from. "Run."

But I wasn't going to abandon him. I wasn't going to freeze up again, not this time. I pulled my pistol, aiming to get at least a few shots in before Ponchik, who rushed ahead like a cartoon character attacking a much larger force all by himself, closed the gap. But before I raised the gun, one of the trolls threw something baseball-sized at my head with a speed and accuracy that would make Cy Young jealous.

It felt like I'd just been punched by Muhammad Ali wearing metal gloves. Then the world went black.

I woke up with the mother of all headaches—and anyone who thinks that's just a cliché hasn't been knocked unconscious by a hit to the head. I was lying in the corridor, right next to my gun and the broken remnants of a plaster paperweight, which must've been what the troll got me with. It was quiet; no sounds of fighting and gunfire.

I groaned and pulled myself up. There was a pair of dead trolls. No sign of Ponchik or the other two, though cracked sheetrock and blood splatter on the drop ceiling suggested they'd taken the battle farther down the corridor.

Nauseous and in pain, I checked my watch. I'd been out for nearly an hour, which didn't bode well; contrary to what they show in the movies, most knockouts last seconds, or minutes at most. I figured the surviving Hunters must've retreated. If so, they'd be back soon with reinforcements. I had to decide which was safer: to try and sneak out of the building or to find a hiding spot and wait for the cavalry. I settled on the latter and made for the office door farthest down the dead-end corridor. My ears were ringing, which is why I didn't realize it was occupied.

I opened the door and five pairs of yellow troll eyes zeroed in on me. They sat at computer desks separated by cubiclelike dividers. On their screens were images burned into my retina over the years of competitive gaming: the Dust2 map. The trolls were playing Counter-Strike.

There was no way I could outrun them, and I sure as hell couldn't outfight them. So I did the only thing I could think of that stood a chance of me not ending up as troll chow. I pointed at a vacant computer and issued a challenge no true gamer could resist. "Wanna scrim?"

The trolls said nothing, but they didn't attack, either. I moved toward the PC, taking care not to make any sudden moves, and powered it on.

They were good, like way better than an average player. But not as good as a pro gamer who supported himself through college by competing on e-sport tournament circuits. Mike Cantor stood no chance against five trolls, but Black Neo could dispatch their avatars in-game all day long, despite suffering from a concussion.

We played a bunch of quick three-on-three matches, with me leading my team to victory almost every time. Two of the trolls cheered and laughed while the other three became progressively more salty. I made sure to reshuffle the teams after a while to keep everyone happy.

The trolls were dedicated gamers. Under better circumstances, playing with them might've been fun. They chugged energy drinks and munched potato chips, and acted pretty much like every human gamer I ever met. It was hard to reconcile this behavior with the murderous rage I'd witnessed earlier. I stole a glance at my watch, uncertain as to what the trolls would do to me when the Hunters returned.

Soon, I got to find out. Before I could figure a way out of that mess, gunfire erupted outside. The trolls sat up straight. Their demeanor and body language changed as though evil new souls inhabited each body. They were suddenly menacing and scary as hell. And they studied me, almost as though they were surprised I was there.

Two of them grabbed me, disarmed me, and dragged me out of the room.

The trolls brought me into a security office in the basement. There were monitors hung up on the wall, showing dozens of camera feeds from inside and outside the building. And in the chair watching them sat . . . *something.*

The swivel chair turned and I was face to face with a demon. I may not have been MHI's best trainee when it came to shooting at things, but I'd hit the books hard. I recognized what he was from a picture in the training manual: a man-sized, scruffy-looking bearded creep with reddish, blotchy skin and two small protrusions for horns. He might've passed for an especially ugly satyr but he didn't have goat legs and he sure as hell wasn't jolly. Also, he smelled like vomit. He was a *bies*—a rare Russian demon with mind-control powers.

So that was why the trolls behaved so strangely! An average bies could enthrall one or two people at a time. This one must've been crazy powerful to control an entire army of trolls.

The bies studied me intently. "Interesting," he said. He didn't speak out loud; instead I heard his creepy, raspy voice inside my head. "Your mind won't obey me." He leaned forward. "Your mind has been touched by another."

The spiders inside my mind scurried and scuttled like no one's business. Only a few months after learning about the supernatural and I'm facing my second rare kind of demon. Must just be lucky, I guess. What's more, they seem to have a mutual admiration society going. I tried to come up with something brave and defiant to say to mask my overwhelming fear.

"It was touched by your mother," I said. Yeah, it was mega lame. I challenge you to do better, under the circumstances.

The bies ignored my attempted burn. "No matter," he said. "Your friends will make better slaves. Especially the werewolf."

Before I could ask "What werewolf?" the trolls tossed me into a corner and proceeded to beat the crap out of me.

Another troll played with the controls of the security system, and the biggest screen displayed an image of Heather and Carl and several Russians in the lobby. I could see them watching a monitor there, which showed the two trolls taking out their frustrations on me. Then their screen displayed the floor map of the basement level, with the security office highlighted in red.

Surely, the Hunters would know I was bait. But they didn't know about the bies. Best as I recalled from the manual, a bies needed to be in close proximity to enthrall someone, but then it could control them from a greater distance afterward. My would-be rescuers had no idea of the danger awaiting them, and there was nothing I could do but watch. At least the trolls ceased hitting me once the Hunters got the message and moved on from the monitor.

The security feeds showed forty or more Russian Hunters entering the building and methodically clearing it, room by room. Meanwhile, a smaller team fought its way toward the basement. The trolls didn't make it easy on them, probably so the trap would look less suspicious.

I watched as Heather transformed, her bones twisting, thick reddish fur covering her skin. In moments she was a wolf and her fangs ripped troll flesh like it was cotton candy. I had no idea she was a werewolf, and I wondered if Harbinger knew. But he trusted her and that was good enough for me.

Soon Heather burst into the room, followed by Carl, Ponchik, and two more Hunters. The bies stared at them and they froze as though someone clicked Pause. Then the Hunters stood at attention, like so many marionettes, and the werewolf sat, muscles playing under her fur, like a German shepherd awaiting its master's command.

I tried to help, to do something, but I could barely move. It felt like they broke a few of my ribs during the beating. I coughed up some blood onto the carpet.

Then another Hunter, a woman in her thirties with a single long plait of blond hair swept over her camo shirt, ran into the room. One of the enthralled Russians turned toward the newcomer and calmly shot her in the head.

I let everyone down, just like I let my Audrey down, and now I watched my friends become subjugated by this evil bastard. The mix of frustration, fear, pain, anger, and shame reached its pinnacle, and I screamed.

Then the terrifying spiders from my dreams were there, corporeal, each the size of a spaniel and rampaging in what had become a very crowded room.

The bies screamed as venomous fangs bit into his ruddy flesh. I counted at least seven spiders swarming over the demon's body as he thrashed on the floor. The Hunters and the trolls looked as though they'd just woken up from deep sleep. They didn't have time to gather their wits: once done with the bies, the spiders attacked them, indiscriminately and with ferocity.

"No," I croaked. I didn't know how I'd summoned the creatures, but when I willed them to stand down, to leave my friends alone, they ignored me.

Hunters and trolls fought together against the new threat. The spiders seemed to have lost their focus once they dispatched the bies, and while they attacked anything that moved, they were more manageable individually. One by one, they were all put down, but not before they managed to inject a troll and several of the Hunters with their venom.

After the fight ended, the werewolf transformed back into Heather, her eyes gradually losing the golden glow as her bones re-formed into human shape. Some of the Russians were polite enough to avert their eyes as Carl handed her his trench coat.

Last thing I remembered was Carl and Heather crouching over me and calling for a medic. Then I faded out, and I'm pretty sure it was for much longer than an hour that time.

I woke up in a large infirmary, my ribs sore and tightly bandaged. There were a dozen beds, half of them occupied. I recognized some of the Hunters from earlier. Ponchik was one of them.

"How are you feeling?" Heather asked from the bedside chair, lowering the book she'd been reading. Carl was there, too, sitting on an empty bed. He rushed over.

"Kill me," I whispered.

"What?" they said in unison.

"I summoned those spiders somehow, and I couldn't control them. No telling when or how I'll summon them again."

"It's admirable that you're willing to sacrifice yourself," said Heather, "but there's a better way." She glanced around and lowered her voice. "I work *with* MHI, but I work *for* a government agency that employs people with special powers, like me. We can help you learn to cope with your ability. To control it."

I processed this new information.

"STFU," Carl told me.

"I didn't say anything."

He smirked. "They're called Special Task Force Unicorn. Not what I would name such an illustrious group, but there you have it."

"We wanted access to some of the data stored at the Troll Factory," said Heather. "But, given the current political climate, Russian authorities weren't going to let a federal agent waltz in and take it. Working through MHI was...expedient."

"Once you took down the demon and the trolls were freed from its control, they practically fell over themselves to give us everything we needed," said Carl.

"A year ago I wouldn't have suggested this, but STFU is under new management these days and it's well on its way to becoming an organization it should have always been. I really think this would be a good fit for you. So, what do you say," asked Heather. "Wanna work for Uncle Sam?"

My head felt very heavy. I wasn't sure if I was feeling the scratching of the phantom spiders again, or if it was just the aftereffect of my injuries. "I need to think about this. And to rest."

They let me be.

I closed my eyes and pondered my situation for a while. I'd failed so many times recently; I was barely qualified to be a Hunter, and now I was a walking disaster waiting to happen. Who was to say I'd succeed at gaining control over my scary power? How could I trust myself? How could I risk the safety of others? There were so many difficult questions...and so few answers.

Ponchik was awake. He was reading something on a tablet, his long frame barely fitting on the bed. He shifted and the blanket slid from his left leg: it was purple and huge, an aftereffect of the venom I recognized from my own past encounter with the spider demon.

I made my way over to him, feeling the damn ribs with every step I took.

"I hope you feel better than you look," he said.

"I'm sorry," I said. "Your injury...It's my fault."

"What?" he asked.

I told him everything. About the spiders residing in my head, about my failing at my first mission, even about STFU, though I'm sure Heather wouldn't have been happy about that. But I had to tell someone, and Ponchik had saved my life at least twice at the Troll Factory.

He listened intently to my story. "You can't give up," he said. "You must try to control your magic power. Use it to fight evil."

"I don't know if I can do it," I said.

He pursed his lips. "Do you know what Ponchik means in Russian?" he asked.

"What?"

"It means 'doughnut.' I was soft and flabby kid."

I looked at his rock-solid biceps skeptically.

"I was very depressed. No friends. Alcoholic parents who gave no support. I had to fight hard to change. Kept nickname after, as reminder." Ponchik patted my shoulder. "We all have inner demons to fight. Even if yours is actual demon." He smiled. "You can't let demon win, Mike."

Despite all my doubts, despite my fears, I knew he was right.

"Besides," said Ponchik, "you are kid from New York and you got powers after you get bit by spider! Know what it makes you?"

He was still laughing at his own joke when I limped back to my bed.

For the first time in months, I slept through the night.

This story is hard to confirm because it comes by way of an MCB leak. With those guys you can never tell if something is true or they're just messing with you. —A.L.

Keep Kaiju Weird

Kim May

Kumiko reached across her chest to the phone strapped on her left bicep and turned up the volume. She smiled and ran a bit faster, her favorite J-pop song blasting through her earbuds. This track had a very catchy dance beat that made it easier to keep pace up the steep hill.

The PUFF exemption tag around her neck shrugged itself loose and began to bounce annoyingly with every step. Kumiko quickly tucked it back into her sports bra and hoped, rather than expected, it would stay there.

Sweat trickled down her bare midriff, and her thighs ached as she rounded the third and final switchback on the narrow, tree-lined street. Kumiko was tempted to cheat a bit. A quick twitch of her five fox tails and she could soar effortlessly to the top. Of course, that would require removing the veil of invisibility around her tails, which would attract a lot of attention—attention that would threaten her PUFF exemption.

Sometimes it sucked being a kitsune. Especially when bureaucracy knew how take the fun out of immortality.

With a growl, Kumiko ran faster—past the houses and parked cars, past the other joggers, and finally past the firs that marked the end of her route. There, the road leveled and wound around the Rocky Butte viewpoint.

The viewpoint proper rose from the center of the small plateau like a basalt layer cake. The bottom layer was a twelve-foot-high wall of rough-hewn stone. The top layer resembled a crown because of the electric lanterns and decorative stone railing. A radio tower stood in the middle, almost like a giant birthday candle. Jogging around the viewpoint reminded Kumiko of chasing her littermates around the base of the original Nagoya castle as a kit.

Kumiko turned off her music and stretched on the side of the road. The sun beat down on her long black hair. It was uncomfortably warm at the summit, and the soft breeze didn't provide much relief.

She pulled out her earbuds, then shook her head to dispel the pinching cramp that set in whenever she wore them too long. It didn't work this time. Instead of dissipating, the cramp was replaced by a rhythmic *chink chink* sound that aggravated her sensitive kitsune ears.

That wasn't a normal sound for this area. Kumiko looked around, perplexed. She didn't see anything on this side of the butte that could have caused it, but it was definitely close.

The breeze shifted, carrying with it the scent of sweaty men and stone dust. Someone was carving into the butte. *Vandals again?*

As soon as she thought it, Kumiko realized her assumption didn't make sense. If it were vandals, why weren't they spray-painting the stone? Carving was more work than any tagger would care to exert. There wasn't a park service vehicle around so that ruled out site maintenance, too.

Something about this didn't feel right.

Kumiko ducked into the tree line behind her. Blackberry brambles scraped her shins, and twigs snapped with every step. The second Kumiko was out of sight she dropped the veil and stripped. She placed her folded clothes and phone on top of her shoes under a large rhododendron.

Then, with an instinctual inflection of will, Kumiko shifted into her fox form—her true form. Her silky white fur seemed to glow in the shade. She backtracked to the road, her dainty black paws moving silently through the underbrush.

Kumiko sniffed the air. No humans, other than those she'd smelled earlier. Kumiko threw a veil around herself just in case, and leapt out of the trees, moving so fast her paws barely touched the ground. She jumped on top of the base layer and crept around the bend.

Fifteen feet away, Kumiko found two men kneeling on the

stone. One of them carved a strange symbol into the base of the top tier with a hammer and chisel. Kumiko's ears twitched every time the chisel struck the stone. The other worked about three feet away from his partner. He held a piece of paper to the stone and used a piece of white chalk to outline a different symbol onto the rock. Both of the symbols were similar to Nordic runes but with jagged points that made every curve and line look like a claw mark.

Pain emanated from the stone, sharp on Kumiko's heightened awareness. The feeling wasn't caused by the chisel cuts though. It came from the dark, otherworldly energy that gathered around the symbol itself. In fact, the longer she stared at the symbol, the more she felt as if someone watched her...

Kumiko growled and bared her teeth at the *other* who spied from beyond.

That's my job, asshole, she mentally projected to it.

A sensation of amusement was its only response.

The carver suddenly fell back in fright, nearly dropping his tools. "Did you hear that?" he said.

"For the hundredth time, no," the sketcher replied. "I don't care what you hear. He can't come through until we perform the ceremony. Now get back to work. I want to be done before noon. It's hot up here."

Kumiko retraced her steps, inspecting the butte. Three feet away she found another symbol. It looked different from those the men presently worked on, but it was clearly the same unearthly language. As she continued around, she found more, each emanating the same entity's malevolent amusement.

That made it official. It was time for Kumiko to make the call.

She leapt down and dashed into the trees—faster than the human eye could perceive. Her fox form definitely had its advantages. Kumiko landed beside the rhododendron and shifted back to human form. Rather than dress, she grabbed her phone and pressed four on speed dial. The other side picked up on the first ring, but didn't say anything in greeting.

"Franks," Kumiko said quietly. "How fast can you get to Portland, Oregon? Cultists are prepping a site for a summoning."

"Where?" the other side grumbled—a deep, almost inhuman bass.

A newbie might have babbled a lot of useless details. Kumiko suspected this was one of the reasons why so many of Franks' co-workers sported broken noses. Either that, or they weren't smart enough to stay out of striking distance. She kept it simple and to the point.

"Rocky Butte. It's an extinct volcano."

"On our way."

Seven hours later, Kumiko stood outside the Air National Guard installation at the Portland airport, waiting for Franks. He was an imposing wall of a man, almost as wide as he was tall, and made of raw sinew tougher than iron. When she saw him through the glass exit, she smoothed out the black pantsuit she'd changed into for formal business.

Franks walked out, accompanied by a handsome human carrying a duffle bag with their gear. The human must have been the poor bastard assigned to be Franks' latest partner.

The smell hit Kumiko's nose instantly. *Too much Dolce and Gabbana,* she thought. His black suit was of excellent quality, and judging by his cocky strut, he was proud of it, too. Any twenty-first-century American woman might have been impressed. Kumiko merely *tsked* in the back of her mind.

"Armani?" she asked, just a touch tongue in cheek.

"Lastrucci," the human said, correcting her with a forced smile.

Kumiko suspected Franks' partner wasn't happy about being caught wearing something just shy of top of the line.

"You must be the informant," the human said.

Kumiko nodded.

"Thank you for your help," Franks' partner continued. "We'll take over from here."

"She's coming with us," Franks announced, deadpan. The partner's steps faltered.

Kumiko didn't bother to hide her grin. "I'll brief you on the way."

She led them to where she'd parked at the back of the lot. There weren't very many cars back here, and the partner automatically gravitated to the largest: a black Dodge Ram Quad Cab. He was visibly shocked when—instead—she keylessly unlocked the doors to her cobalt Scion FR-S.

"Uh...we are *not* going to fit," the human said dubiously.

"It's bigger than you think," Kumiko replied in all honesty.

"But—"

"Shut up, Grant," Franks said.

Kumiko opened the door with a flourish and watched as the human—Grant—peered in, then rubbed his eyes, and peered in again. From the outside, the car looked no different than it had when it left the factory. However, once she opened the door, the *substantially* expanded interior was clearly visible.

"How can it be *bigger* on the inside?" Grant asked.

"She's a kitsune," Franks said as he pushed Grant into the car.

"We're very good at warping space," she said.

Grant fell into the back seat. Franks sat in the passenger seat, and stretched his legs. Since Grant was aware of her true nature now, Kumiko dropped the veil—and casually jumped over the car, her now-visible tails flared around the vehicle. She glided into the driver's seat and closed the door. In the rearview mirror, Grant's jaw dropped.

Franks watched out of the corner of his eye as she arranged her tails on the back seat, next to Grant.

"Still can't shift into a form without tails?" Franks asked.

"No. Most don't gain that ability until they're six hundred."

"Six hundred... what? *Years?*" Grant sputtered.

"I know," Kumiko said, mock pouting. "It's unfair for a five-hundred-and-thirty-seven-year-old to look thirty." She turned over the engine and sped into traffic. "It's the curse of being Japanese. I won't look my age until I'm a thousand."

Kumiko stayed on the side streets. There was no way they'd get there in time if she took the freeway. Not in rush hour traffic, anyway.

"I spent the day following the cultists I told you about," Kumiko said as she whipped the car around a slowpoke Prius. "They reported to their leader at Demonicon, a demon-themed convention being held downtown."

Grant leaned forward. "And the fact that there was a demon-themed convention planned this weekend wasn't enough of a reason to call us?"

"This is *Portland*," Kumiko said, as if that were explanation enough.

The stale yellow light that Kumiko hoped would last two seconds longer changed to red. She floored the gas and blasted through the intersection, nearly hitting a cyclist.

"There's always something demon-themed going on," Kumiko

said. "Three months ago it was CthulhuCon, before that it was some horror writers' conference, and before that it was the Lovecraft film festival...the people here like weird shit, but they're usually harmless."

"Damn hippies." Franks interjected.

Kumiko nodded. "The local Wiccan community usually prevents dangerous groups from entering the city. I don't know how this cult slipped past."

Kumiko turned onto a quiet neighborhood street and floored it. She ignored the angry granny on the corner waving a KIDS AT PLAY sign. There was very little traffic here, and no signals to slow them down. Besides, depending on how the next hour went, there might not be a neighborhood *left* to play in.

"I still don't know who they plan to bring through," Kumiko continued. "I did sense them at the site. They're powerful and have a chip bigger than you on their shoulder."

"That doesn't narrow it down," Franks grumbled.

Kumiko figured he'd say that. "They've also stolen pages from a convention guest artist's sketchbook to turn into a corporeal vessel."

Franks turned to her. "Who?"

"It was Paul Komoda's sketchbook."

"Fuck," Franks said.

Grant leaned forward again. *"Why* fuck??"

"Well," Kumiko said with a mischievous gleam in her eyes, "when a bird and a bee love each other very much—"

"Ha ha," Grant huffed indignantly and leaned as far away from her as he could. Somehow he managed to be both handsome and petulant at the same time. *Now that's a God-given gift,* Kumiko thought.

Kumiko answered Grant's valid question. "Paul draws and sculpts really *detailed* demons and monsters."

Kumiko parked by a church at the bottom of the hill.

"We're still a mile away from the site," she said.

Grant leaned forward. "You can't get us any closer?"

"Are you going to replace my car if it gets trashed in the fight?"

He flashed Kumiko a smile that had probably moistened many seats. "Well, I can give you a ride..."

Kumiko rolled her eyes and gave Franks a pleading look. He shrugged. In the blink of an eye, Kumiko created a realistic illusion of herself twisted around in her seat, holding a gun three inches from Grant's face. For added effect Kumiko threw in the twined scents of blued steel and fresh CLP.

"Get this through your head now," Kumiko said, "I am not some hot thing you can woo while reloading. All those pickup lines and kinky positions flitting through your mind? I tired of them before your ancestors sailed to this country."

"You can't threaten me!" Grant sputtered. "You'll lose your exemption for that!"

Kumiko released the illusion, showing that she still faced forward in the driver's seat, no firearm in sight. "How could I have threatened you? I haven't moved."

Kumiko and Franks got out of the car. While they waited for Grant to make up his mind about whether he trusted her or not, she opened the trunk and pulled out a long bundle in a lavender silk bag with a drawstring at the top. Franks raised his eyebrow when he saw it. She untied the string and slid out a katana with a black lacquered wood scabbard, and a leaf-green silk cord wrapped around the handle.

Franks nodded in acknowledgement: not to her, but to the sword. It startled her that he not only recognized the Honjo Masamune, but greeted the holy blade as an . . . actually, she wasn't sure. As an equal? An old friend?

Grant, who decided to join the party after all, stepped out of the car carrying the duffle and pulled out a heavy load-bearing vest with bulletproof plating. Both men were already armed with the federal-issue sidearms they'd brought with them. The vest, however, had small demo charges, aka "MCB Specials," strapped to it. The charges were often used to blow heavy doors or altars, so they'd work well on the symbols. Grant strapped on the vest and made sure his Glock had a full mag.

Kumiko wrapped her free arm around Grant's waist, flared her tails, and leapt forward, propelling them up the hill as fast as any sprinter. Beside her, Franks ran at the same pace. When they reached the top, Franks wasn't even winded, but Grant looked a touch pale as she deposited him on the pavement.

Smoke rose from the viewpoint, and Kumiko could faintly hear chanting. The symbols around the summit glowed dark violet and pulsed like a heart beating. *Chikushou! They've already started!*

Kumiko closed her eyes and gathered as much energy from

the earth as she could. There wasn't much in this place. Not the kind she needed anyway. She focused what she could gather into a sphere that vibrated and pulsed on the tip of the Honjo's scabbard. Kumiko then took a deep breath and channeled that energy into a thick veil.

With a flick of her wrist, the hazy veil streaked out. It followed the tree line around the summit and back to her again. The completed veil was only twenty feet high, with no ceiling, but that would be enough.

Kumiko had to take a knee to catch her breath. The effort it took to project the veil caused her human form to slip a little. Twin sets of fox fangs protruded from her mouth, and her eyes had changed from normal human brown to glowing amber. Franks paid her no mind.

Grant, however, had his Glock pointed at her. Kumiko could almost feel the red dot on her head, as seen through Grant's scope-tunneled point of view.

"That veil will prevent the neighbors from seeing or hearing anything," she explained.

Grant lowered his Glock. "You should have warned me."

Kumiko sensed Grant was speaking to Franks, as well as herself.

"I didn't need to," Kumiko said, inclining her head toward Franks' back. "He trusts me. That should have been enough."

Kumiko got to her feet and trotted up the gravel service ramp that led to the south entrance, with Franks and Grant close behind. They flanked the entrance—Kumiko and Franks on one side, Grant on the other. From here, they had a clear view of the entire viewpoint.

The place looked like a Rob Zombie video set. Nine men and four women in knee-length white tunics surrounded a salt circle around the base of the radio tower. Their clothing was freshly stained with goat's blood, the body of which lay motionless in the salt circle. The grass inside the circle smoldered. Bits of ash swirled in the thin tendrils of smoke that probed the air like tentacles.

The stolen drawings—three small and one large—were taped to the tower, one drawing per side. Crimson sparks danced around the edges of the small drawings, while the large one pulsed with the same violet light as the symbols. The presence of the entity that laughed at her this morning was everywhere but it was strongest on the large drawing.

Kumiko didn't recognize the language the cultists chanted, but from the extra grim expression on Franks' face, it seemed that he did.

"Orders?" she asked softly.

"Symbols," Franks replied. "Then cultists."

Kumiko and Grant pulled earplugs from their pockets and put them in. They nodded when they were ready. Grant placed a charge on the nearest symbol while Kumiko and Franks headed for those on the far side.

They didn't get far. The symbol flared suddenly. A violet tendril of hateful energy slithered out of the symbol and wrapped around the charge. It pulled the explosive into the stone. Grant hit the remote detonator but it was too late. The tendrils and the MCB Special were well into the void, beyond the signal's reach.

Another tendril lashed out and wound around Franks' arm. Franks smashed the symbol with his free hand. The tendril sputtered before dissipating, releasing the big man's arm. Sharp gunshots from Grant's side instantly silenced the chanting. He must have opened fire on the cultists. It was just as well since his Glock would be useless on the stone.

"Go," Franks barked.

Kumiko ran to the next symbol and smashed it with the Honjo's scabbard before it lashed her. Her strike removed only half of the symbol. Light seeped out of the other half like a drunken snake. She swung the sword around and smashed the other side.

They were about to move to the next set when a ball of fire— rising in the air—made them pause. Kumiko and Franks climbed up the wall and peered over the ledge. Her eyes grew big.

Three pudgy figures with squat legs, round bellies, and lizard-like heads, waddled through the mud and ash. *The drawings are alive,* Kumiko thought in horrid fascination. The creatures each took position at triangular points along the edge of the circle. As one, they sucked in a deep breath, then released a stream of fire on the center. Heat waves blurred the entire site, and the base of the antenna started glowing a dull orange.

Kumiko and Franks pulled themselves up all the way. She raised her sword in a defensive pose. Franks, on the other hand, pulled out his cell phone and hit a number on speed dial.

"Stand by," he said before hanging up.

"Reinforcements?" she asked.

"F-15 Strike Eagles," he answered.

Kumiko nodded. There was a squadron stationed at the Air National Guard facility attached to the Portland airport. If they needed air support, the Eagles could be here in less then five minutes.

Grant entered from the south entrance, his Glock aimed at the nearest cultist. Before Grant could make the shot, the steel tower shrieked and groaned. The base now glowed bright white, from the fire demons' effort. The metal buckled under its own weight and fell across the south entrance.

Sparks filled the air as an electrical line was ripped in two. The lamps flanking the entrance both exploded, sending glass in all directions. The cultists scattered. One wasn't quick enough and was pinned under the searing hot metal. His screams excited the demons, who continued to blow flame at the center of the circle. The blackened ground cracked open. Molten rock pooled below the surface; the deep orange glow cast sinister shadows on the demons' alien faces.

"I don't see Grant," Kumiko said, trying to peer through the wreckage.

"He dodged it," Franks grunted.

On cue, Grant's head popped over the wall's edge a few feet from the wreckage. He seemed to have difficulty climbing up but he still managed to get over the top without humiliating the MCB. Thin tendrils of smoke rose from his shoulders where sparks singed the fabric of his pricey suit, but other than that he looked unharmed.

The cultists, having regrouped, charged them.

Franks introduced himself, with bullets spitting out the muzzle of his gargantuan slide-action pistol—from the looks of it, a .454, though Kumiko had only ever seen that caliber in revolver form. An ordinary man would have found such a beastly weapon impossible to wield. Franks handled it like it was a mere M9. The high-power shots tore their targets practically in half.

Kumiko charged one of the women—a petite redhead—and swung the still sheathed Honjo behind the woman's knees. The redhead fell, and Kumiko brought the Honjo around and hit the redhead laterally across the chest, cracking ribs and collarbone.

Not a killing blow by any means but Kumiko preferred it that way. She'd seen too much needless death in her long life.

With this in mind, Kumiko turned her attention to the three demons at the center. She picked up a stone and flicked it at the salt circle. The stone bounced off an invisible barrier of power.

Chikushou! I can't reach them without breaking the circle.

The ground roiled beneath their feet. Kumiko had to use her tails to keep her balance. If that tremor meant what she thought it meant, the circle wasn't going to contain the final form of the summoning.

She started to unsheathe the Honjo when something pulled her back. Kumiko looked over her shoulder. Three of the male cultists had grabbed her tails. With a growl, Kumiko spun around and slammed the trio against the circle's barrier. One of the men, dazed from the strike, fell to the ground and disturbed the circle just enough to break the barrier.

"*Arigatou.*"

Kumiko shook off the other two men and darted into the circle proper. The second she crossed what was the threshold, the ground shook again. This time, it knocked Kumiko onto her back. The earth opened at her feet, and an enormous hand with leathery fingers tipped with two-foot-long ebony talons reached out of the fissure.

Kumiko scrambled back, and Grant had to help her to her feet. A slight rumble was all the warning they got before the ground split again, this time across the entire width of the viewpoint. They ran to the perimeter wall, gaping in horror at what came forth.

A head the size of a house with four glowing eyes rose above them. Long spikes ran down the back of the monster's head. The creature rose and rose...twenty feet, thirty feet, fifty feet...

When it finally stepped out of the chasm, the titan was at least eighty feet tall and completely pissed off.

"Oh, my Buddha!" Kumiko whispered.

An older man—the nominal cult leader—dropped to his knees, chanting "Hail, Valumneb!" The weird accent on the vowels made it sound like, *Hail, volume knob!*

"A massive German guy, a Japanese girl, and me against a frickin' Kaiju," Grant said as he reloaded his Glock with a fresh mag. "I feel like I'm in a damned movie!"

"If you're the jackass Australian, then yes," Kumiko said, still staring in awe at their new foe.

Kumiko realized that what she thought were spikes, jutting from the monster's back, were actually appendages: a row of long, humanlike arms ran down the Kaiju's spine, each moving independently of the others. Both titanic legs were covered in scales, and there was a secondary mouth in the center of its belly. It bared three rows of shark teeth and roared into the sky.

Kumiko unsheathed the Honjo. She looked through the chaos and found Franks. The cult's elderly leader was now on Franks' back, trying to use the sacrificial knife to slit Franks' throat. Franks threw himself like a wrestler, body slamming the leader against the ground. Even at a distance, Kumiko heard the leader's ribs crunch under Franks' considerable weight. Franks casually got up, straightened his suit jacket, and put a bullet between the leader's eyes.

Franks met Kumiko's gaze across the fractured plateau. He noticed the unsheathed blade in her right hand and the brandished scabbard in her left. Franks pulled out his phone and hit speed dial again.

"Go," Franks mouthed. His eyes never left hers when he said it.

She nodded to affirm that she understood what he had set into motion. Kumiko launched into the air, tails working hard, and landed on the fallen radio tower. The warm metal groaned under her weight and the thick smoke made it hard to see. That was good. What her veil couldn't hide from the public the smoke would.

The Kaiju—seemingly oblivious to merely man-sized threats—turned and started to walk toward downtown. A rush of panic sent fresh adrenaline through Kumiko's veins. No matter what, she couldn't allow that monster to leave the butte.

Remember me, asshole? Kumiko shouted with her mind.

The Kaiju stopped midstride. It turned to stare at her and growled. Yep. It definitely remembered.

Kumiko tossed the scabbard behind her, gripping the Honjo tightly in both hands, and jumped over the Kaiju's head. Her tails lifted her higher into the air. She raised the sword high above her head, and when gravity brought her down behind the beast, she sliced off the first three spine-arms. The Kaiju screeched, and black ichor squirted from the stumps.

One of the lower spine-arms grabbed Kumiko by the ankles and swung her around like a rag doll. With a grunt, Kumiko tucked her knees to her chest, bringing her sword close enough to cut through the wrist. The hand still clutched her fast. She frantically pried herself loose while using her tails to slow her fall.

Below, Franks pulled the arms off of one of the three fire demons, while Grant emptied a mag into a second. A smoldering lump at the base of the tower was all that remained of the third.

I need to buy them a little more time.

Kumiko focused her consciousness and condensed the static in the air into a massive lightning bolt. She raised the Honjo high again, and the bolt surged along the blade, making the *tatara* steel glow.

With a fierce cry, she sliced the blade through the air and sent the bolt arcing across the plateau. It struck the Kaiju in the shoulder, searing through its unearthly flesh and rendering shield-sized scales to ash.

The second Kumiko's feet touched the ground, she leapt again—tails going all-out—and landed on the Kaiju's head. Before it could reach for her, she sliced across both of the beast's huge, feral eyes. The Kaiju roared with rage.

"Iku yo!" Franks shouted from below. *Let's go!*

Kumiko glanced north. She heard more than saw that the F-15s were close. She jumped off the beast's head—tails steadying and softening her plummet—and followed Franks through the protective veil and quickly down the hill. The Kaiju spun and stomped furiously in its blinded state. In her periphery, Kumiko saw Grant dart into the woods.

Kumiko stopped short, about twenty feet downhill, and turned around. *Gotta work fast!* She got down on her knees, facing the summit, and focused her will into the veil. Kumiko thickened it into a blast shield against the Strike Eagles' precision-guided munitions.

"C'mon baby, hold together," she whispered.

The planes shot past the site, one directly after the other—a deafening sound that blotted out even the screams of the Kaiju. Even with ear protection, the concussion of the two bunker busters hitting one second apart was almost too much for Kumiko's sensitive ears.

She felt the Kaiju fall. Magma and debris rolled downhill. The shield bowed and wavered from the stress. Kumiko poured more energy into it, forcing it to hold. Eventually, the magma cooled enough that it no longer threatened the homes on the hillside. She dropped the shield with a sigh of relief.

Franks stepped up behind her. Demon blood dripped off his hands. Together they watched the motionless carcass of the Kaiju sink into the earth. Out of the earth it had come and into the earth it returned. Franks wiped a palm on his pants, then put his phone to his face and gave an all-clear to the jets—who did a flyby just in case before returning to base.

"How will the MCB explain this?" Kumiko asked, her own voice sounding muffled and far away.

"A small eruption," Franks mouthed.

She raised an eyebrow. "For a long-extinct cinder cone?"

"They're very convincing." Grant said, stomping out of the woods. He handed her the Honjo's scabbard.

Kumiko sat down on the ground next to Franks and laid the Honjo across her knees. She ripped a piece off her ruined jacket and used it to wipe the ichor off the blade. Kumiko incinerated the fabric with a flash of foxfire.

Kumiko sheathed the blade and stood. "Let's get back to the car. Now that the veil is down, it won't be long before the press shows up."

Grant looked down at his ruined suit. "For once I agree with you."

The Vatican's Hunters are a secretive bunch, but there have been rumors that they have a supernatural heavy hitter of their own. —A.L.

The Gift

Steve Diamond

Present Day

We stood in front of La Iglesia de San Fernando in Guaymas, Sonora. It only took us a few hours to drive to the port town after the jet touched down in Hermosillo. By the time we had arrived, it was well past midnight. As late as it was, the heat and humidity were oppressive.

The church, while dating back to 1750, had obviously been recently restored. The new gray and white stonework of the building shone in the moonlight. The cathedral was impressive, and in the daytime I knew it would shine even more brightly.

The sight should have filled me with peace.

Instead, my skin crawled.

Michael Gutterres, Knight of the Secret Guard of the Blessed Order of St. Hubert the Protector, was shaking his head, the movement drawing my attention. "Something is wrong, Fedele."

I was sensitive to the ebbs and flows of supernatural power—the product of having the bones of a saint grafted to my own. I'd taken to calling that process "the Gift." Due to the Gift, I'd been alive for half a millennium dealing with the monsters of this world and others.

The feeling of wrongness in the church wasn't overwhelming to the point where it would be obvious for a normal individual. This wasn't the first time I'd wondered if there was more to Gutterres than being a standard Knight of the Secret Guard. No one

225

knew much about him other than he worked for the Vatican and his instincts were always right.

"You have a hunch or something?" I asked.

"Or something," he replied, then circled around to the trunk of the car. He opened the trunk and pulled out an armored vest and pulled it over his head. He also pulled out a Sig 556 rifle, standard issue for the Secret Guard.

I opened the back door to the sedan and opened the bag I'd brought with me. I pulled out my own rifle, a Crusader Templar. The name—while I found it appropriate—was a happy coincidence. It was a beautiful AR-15 and had served me well the last year. Below that was my own tactical armored vest. Just because I was faster and tougher than any human—not to mention more than a few of the supernatural regulars—didn't mean I didn't appreciate body armor. I slipped it over my head and adjusted it. The last item in the bag, besides two dozen magazines for the Templar, was a long, sheathed sword. I'd carried a sword for centuries, even as I had taken to modern firearms. Swords don't run out of ammo.

I pulled the blade free from the scabbard. The hilt and cross-guard were simple black. The blade itself had the appearance of a skinny falchion, with the last foot of the blade widening out to add some extra weight to the swing. I pushed the blade back into the scabbard and belted it around my waist.

Gutterres pulled a phone from his pocket and dialed a number. As the phone rang, he kept his eyes on the cathedral. This wasn't the first time on this trip he'd made the call. He shook his head and put the phone back in his pocket. "Our priest still isn't picking up, Fedele. He should have by now."

"Are we going to find him inside?" I asked.

"Only one way to find out."

We moved to the entrance, eyes constantly searching for threats. Nothing moved around us. Nothing. This was wrong. There should have at least been drunks, animals, or teenagers. The only sounds I could hear were distant.

In all my years on this earth, finding the front door to a building unexpectedly open has never been a good omen. To my right, Gutterres sighed softly, probably thinking the same thing.

As carefully and silently as I could, I pushed the large wooden door open while Gutterres covered me. The hinges squealed a bit, and in the quiet, the sound carried a sinister note. We pushed in, moonlight spilling in through the open threshold behind us. I didn't need much light to see by, which saved me from having to rely on night-vision goggles. Gutterres didn't seem to be having any trouble either. Interesting.

A line of pews—a mix of old and new—lined the left and right sides of the chapel with a path running between them to where a pulpit stood. A confessional box hung open to the right, the front of it ripped off and turned into kindling. The floor at the front of the chapel was littered with broken candles and glass. Without the candlelight, deep pools of shadows clung to every corner so dark that even my eyes couldn't penetrate.

Gutterres held up a hand and pointed to his ear.

I paused and listened as he had directed.

Drip. Dripdrip. Drip.

I couldn't tell where the sound was coming from. It seemed to echo...move around. We were halfway up the aisle to the front of the chapel when I noticed abandoned belongings on the pews.

Drip. Dripdrip. Drip.

The feeling of unease and wrongness was replaced by a wave of evil. Of *other*. It was made all the worse because we stood in a church sanctified to God. Gutterres grunted as if the force of it had been a physical blow.

Drip. Dripdrip. Drip.

The coppery, rancid smell of old blood hit my nose as something wet pattered down on my head. I reached up and felt the wetness in my hair, then looked at my fingers. Red.

I looked up.

Twenty or so bodies hung, ignoring gravity, pressed to the vaulted ceiling. In their center was the priest, his mouth moving in a silent *help me*. Each time it opened, blood dripped from it.

Help me.

Drip. Dripdrip. Drip.

Help me.

Drip. Dripdrip. Drip.

The bodies shifted all at once, then fell.

Gutterres dove to the right while I dove to the left. Bodies thudded to the floor around us and hit pews with the crunching of bones and rending of flesh. Blood splashed over us from the multiple impacts.

As I tried wiping the blood from my eyes, I caught a glimpse of a single figure walking out of the cathedral, framed in the moonlight. The blurred figure's silhouette turned to look back at us and presented me briefly with a profile. A thread of familiarity ran through me at the sight and I tried to clear the rest of the blood from my vision. When I opened my eyes again, the figure was gone.

"Fedele," Gutterres said, "I think we have a problem."

I tore my gaze away from the doorway and looked to the Knight. His eyes were locked on the twitching, broken body that hung across the pew in front of him. I wiped at my eyes again and was able to clearly see the dead body. It wasn't twitching in death.

It was twitching as if something was trying to push free of the skin and bones it was imprisoned in.

His eyes met mine, and in that instant no verbal communication was needed. Simultaneously, we shouldered our rifles and opened fire on the corpses. Hesitation at shooting the broken bodies was not something we had a problem with. God already had the souls of these individuals in his embrace. He would forgive us for destroying the flesh before us, and neither Gutterres nor I wanted to see what was trying to escape the bodies.

I don't remember running dry, but soon all my mags were empty and discarded on the floor of the church, and I was hacking at the bodies with my sword. My throat hurt from a prolonged scream. Not one of the bodies was in a piece bigger than a collection plate. Gutterres had out a pair of long knives and had attacked the corpses like I had.

The loss of control we both had experienced was...frightening. Something truly primal had taken hold of our minds and bodies, driving us to the slaughter we had enacted upon these bodies. And yet...I felt as if I had done right by them.

"You okay, Fedele?"

"Yeah," I replied. My words were hoarse and my breathing heavier than it had been in a long time. "You?"

"I think so."

I looked around at the devastation we had wrought. "I don't think we can clean this up, Gutterres."

He nodded in agreement and with a shaking, bloody hand pulled his phone from a pocket. He tapped out a number, then held the phone to his ear. After a moment he said, "This is

Gutterres. Requesting permission to burn our location. The grounds are no longer sanctified and are beyond the help of... anyone." He paused, listening. "Yes, that includes the Pope." He listened again. "Thank you." He returned the phone to his pocket, then took a few calming breaths before meeting my eyes.

"Fire was sanctioned?"

"Sanctioned and endorsed."

I looked around at the cathedral, once a beautiful and holy building sanctified to God. Even before it had been remodeled, it had been a bright and hopeful place. A refuge against the storms of the world. Now it was a tomb of violence and... *other*. None of the bodies moved anymore, and nothing had spilled from their insides as we hacked at them. Whatever had been about to happen, we'd stopped.

For now.

The vision of that profile in the doorway fluttered back to my awareness. A hawkish nose and the hint of a cruel smile. Thousands of people had those features but...

"Fedele?"

I let out the breath I'd been holding and nodded. "Let's burn it down."

Twenty-one Hours Earlier

"You don't look happy to see me, Fedele."

I looked over my shoulder, purposely taking my time and letting my eyes linger on the wall-hanging clock. The hands showed it was three in the morning. Having made my point, I returned my gaze to my visitor, Michael Gutterres.

"What do you want, Michael? It's late."

"Or early," Gutterres suggested. "It's not like you were asleep."

Funny guy, Gutterres. Though he had a point. I don't sleep. Haven't since 1533, when I was given the Gift. But the intrusion still bothered me. This was my time. Time when I could relax my mind and meditate.

And when Gutterres made a house call, it was always bad news.

I sighed and stepped aside. "Come in."

His ordinary-looking face split into a bright smile. Michael Gutterres was the type of man who could disappear into any crowd: not overly tall or short, his features a blend of Asian and

Caucasian, his clothes nondescript. The only thing preventing him from being completely unnoticeable was his parked Ducati I glimpsed in front of my home. It looked new.

"Did you throw your money away on another new motorcycle, Michael?"

"My last one didn't survive an encounter with the Fallen."

"I heard about that business with Franks."

"I imagine you have."

"And he was not exterminated? I admit my . . . surprise . . . that he kept his covenants."

"Is that respect I hear in your voice, Fedele? I thought you found him—oh, what was your exact word?—*unholy*? You two are more alike than you like to admit."

I ignored his barb. I knew he didn't mean it. Franks and I were nothing alike. I was the product of a more *blessed* creation. But still . . . I was almost impressed that Franks had kept his end of the deal. "You could have called me."

"You were busy with the Sons of Anak in New Zealand. We handled the Fallen. God was with us."

"He always is," I said and closed the front door. "Now, why are you here? Does the Secret Guard have a mission for me?"

"For us."

"Us?" If the Vatican wanted or needed my help, the situation was potentially dire.

"Yes. Try not to look too put out."

"What's the mission?"

Gutterres smiled. "When was the last time you visited Mexico?"

Within an hour we'd left my New York home and were on a private jet heading to Hermosillo, Sonora. My last visit to that particular region of Mexico happened nearly twenty years ago.

Gutterres was asleep within moments, leaving me to my thoughts. How I would love to sleep. To dream. It's been so very long since I've had that type of respite. In these moments, my memories always seem to take me back to the time when I was made into the man I am today—to the Gift.

Some product of the Gift makes sleeping impossible. My own theory is that my body, on the cellular level, has no need for it anymore. If I am able to live for centuries without hardly aging a day, then why would I need sleep?

I heal faster than normal humans—and faster than many of the supernatural creatures that wander the earth—but the scars I carry from the day the Gift was given to me have never faded. Neither have the memories.

That morning—for the procedure was carried out with the dawn—the stones of the monastery were cold upon my naked back. One of the monks performing the Lord's will could heal any person or creature he laid his hands upon. I've not seen many of his kind since...the occasional faith healer; most were frauds.

I remember his face as he knelt over me. A hawkish nose set in a severe—almost cruel—face. His dark eyes burned with a terrifying intensity.

His assistants would cut deep into my arm first, down to the bone. I can still feel the scraping of that blade. Two other monks would hold the incision open while the healer would take a piece of bone—barely a sliver—and heal it in place. The bone was from a saint, they said.

To my right was the pile of bones from that saint. I have no reason to doubt the veracity of the claim now, but at the time I wondered how much of a fool I had been to commit the small theft that put me in the hands of the monks.

For each bone in my body, they cut a sliver of bone from the skeleton. The process was long, bloody, and painful. The times I passed out they paused in their work to slap my cheeks until I was awake. They said my consciousness was vital to the process. It went the full day until completed the following dawn. Though the monk healed me after each blood-dripping cut into my body, I lapsed into unconsciousness for the next three days in what would now be identified as a coma.

The number of days for recovery, they insisted, was not happenstance.

The bones of that saint—a name I have never been able to discover—are grafted into my own. I'd been given a unique gift, *the* Gift, and though I haven't been perfect—far from it—I've tried my best to let my abilities be of good use to the Vatican and to the world.

The monk who conducted the procedure died shortly after the working his...magic. As far as I can tell, I haven't aged a day since 1533. Most people would think that the memory of the pain I experienced that day would have long since faded.

Pain like that doesn't go away... ever. It is the sharpest memory I have. It kept me going when I was "young" and still learning my new place in this world.

I mostly work for the Secret Guard at the Vatican, though I've never been to their headquarters. I work through intermediaries, like the Knight, Gutterres. I suppose the Secret Guard want their deniability, too. Or just an added layer of safety. I understand, and I approve.

I felt Gutterres' gaze on me. "Have you finished sleeping, then?"

"Some of us still need it, Fedele. What occupies your mind?"

"Memories."

"Of those I'm sure you have many. Any in particular?"

"Of the Gift."

"Ah. I see."

Gutterres and I rarely spoke of the Gift. The subject made him uncomfortable, though I never understood why. He'd seen more than most people in the world. He could hunt vampires by himself, and he'd fought the Fallen. Yet the mere mention of the Gift killed any conversation.

"Are you ready to tell me what mission we have set upon?"

Gutterres nodded and stretched in his seat before speaking. "Mass disappearances."

"How many is 'mass'?"

"We don't even have an accurate number. At first it was a person here and there, which could easily be attributed to cartels and the like. Then, starting last month, people began disappearing in higher quantities. Several at a time. Then last week an entire neighborhood."

"And we are just now being called in?"

"No one noticed until hardly anyone showed up to Mass yesterday. The local priest put the pieces together and called us directly." Gutterres shrugged and let out a long sigh. "There once was a time when something like this would never have gone unnoticed. Communities spent time together, knew when the simplest of things was wrong in their areas. Now people keep their heads down and keep to themselves, afraid that the perpetual outrage and hostility of the world will unmake them. I'm sorry, Fedele. There are times when even my faith is tested by discouragement... the adversary at work."

I waved his apology away. "When you live as long as I have,

you see this sort of thing come and go in cycles. I was in Salem in the 1600s when the citizens where murdering women and men wholesale on the presumption of witchcraft. Like now, many people kept their heads buried in the sand for fear of their lives."

"What were you doing in Salem?"

I smiled. "Hunting the real witches. They were amongst the most vocal accusers of the innocent and had wrought spells to make the minds of the masses more suggestible. That was my first encounter with true and powerful witchcraft. I was relatively young at the time. I had not yet learned humility. I nearly lost my life."

"I've never heard this version of events in the official records of the Secret Guard."

"Those were my 'Freelance Exorcist' days."

"Ah. Did you save any of the falsely accused?"

"One," I answered. "Her name was Sarah. She went on to marry and have a family. I still keep an eye on her descendants."

"Their very own guardian angel?"

I smiled. "Back to the disappearances. Any theories?"

"Not as of yet." Gutterres smiled and pointed a finger at me. "That's what you are here for. The Secret Guard doesn't typically go in blind. They don't have your particular skill set."

"So, essentially, you are expecting things to go as poorly as possible, and I'm here so you don't lose any more men and women."

Gutterres spread his hands in front of him. "Sounds fun, no?"

Of all my Secret Guard liaisons over the centuries, I liked Michael Gutterres the best. He was the closest thing to a friend I'd had in over two hundred years.

I smiled.

Present Day

As we drove south to the outskirts of Guaymas, Gutterres called the Secret Guard for backup. We both knew, without putting voice to the words, they would never arrive in time to be of any practical help, but it was protocol.

We left the burning wreckage of the cathedral behind us. Both Gutterres and I felt the pain of lighting a church aflame, but we also knew it was the only way to properly cleanse away the stain inside it.

"I need a shower," I said.

"Me too," Gutterres agreed. "And a map."

"Why the map?"

"With our contact gone, we have no way of knowing where to go next. I'm hoping we can chart out the disappearances, where possible, and use that data to find a likely spot where the people are being taken."

"You don't think it was the church?" I asked.

He shook his head, keeping his eyes on the road ahead of us. He obviously knew where he was going, but I didn't bother asking the destination. "Those kills were fresh, and they felt more like a message. A hastily scrawled message, but ultimately clear."

"Stay away?"

"Pretty much."

"So somewhere out here is another den of abducted individuals?"

"I think so. But I have the feeling that it will be far worse once we find them."

We drove southwest for another twenty minutes, the road changing from paved to dirt. It was after three A.M. I was drained both physically and mentally, but the real weariness was on a deeper, more emotional level. The events in the cathedral had figuratively scraped me raw. Every time I closed my eyes, I saw the bodies twitching, and I knew it was wrong on every level. Evil. But it also seemed familiar in a way I couldn't explain. And that silhouette...I couldn't shake the memory.

"We're here."

I hadn't even noticed the car stopping. I rubbed a hand across my eyes, took a calming breath, and then pushed the passenger-side door open. Three in the morning, and it still seemed I was being boiled alive in the heat and humidity. Gutterres pushed himself out of the car, and I could tell he was wearier than I. That man still needed rest in the traditional way. He pulled at the back of his shirt where it stuck to his skin.

"Do you think a dry heat would be better than this humidity? It has to be, right?"

Gutterres. Always trying to bring a bit of calmness and levity to the situation. He was a good man. "I imagine the people in the dry heat say the same thing about humidity. 'The humidity has to be better, right?'"

He smiled, then pointed at the humble home in front of us.

"This is where we rest. It's a safe house the Secret Guard keeps. We have maps inside. And water."

"I could use a shower."

"I never said *running* water." He walked by me into the small home.

I pulled my belongings from the car and followed him in, closing the door behind me. Gutterres was already at a small table in the center of an empty kitchen, map spread out before him. The water he had mentioned was in the form of several stacked, one-gallon bottles of purified water. I walked straight to the stack and pulled the top container off. I tore off the cap and drank straight from the bottle. It was a messy business, but at the moment I didn't really care.

Gutterres was mumbling to himself like he did when working out a problem. I found it an annoying habit, but it worked. He was marking areas on the map with a black Sharpie. "These are the places we know—or think we know—where abductions took place, according to the priest." He motioned me over. "I need you to look at this and tell me what you see."

I watched as he marked more and more places. He pulled out his phone, checking it for any more information, and then marked a few more. The pattern was fairly obvious.

"San Carlos."

He nodded his agreement. Nearly every abduction reported by credible sources formed an equidistant arc from Guaymas and its surrounding communities around the rich retirement community of San Carlos. It was hard to miss.

"No one else noticed this?" I asked.

"Some of this information is coming in right now in real time. Our little request to burn down a cathedral has garnered some attention. But you are right. There is enough here to have given anyone from the Order a good idea of where to go."

"Are they in the business of withholding information?"

"Not usually."

"So you think this looks like a trap, too?"

"You are suggesting the Secret Guard has a mole that is setting us up?"

"I'm not suggesting anything," I replied. "I'm reading the situation and making my best determination as to how much danger we are walking into."

"I see." His mind was spinning, that much was easy to read. He nodded and looked at me. "Your evaluation then?"

"Once we are done here, you may need to do some house-cleaning."

"You don't recommend we abort?" Gutterres asked. "Even though this is obviously a trap?"

"Where's the fun in that?"

"Remember, O most glorious Virgin Mary," I prayed, reciting the Memorare on my knees with Gutterres at my side, "that never was it known that anyone who fled to thy protection, implored thy help, or sought thy intercession was left unaided. Inspired with this confidence, I fly to thee, O Virgin of virgins, my Mother; to thee do I come; before thee I stand, sinful and sorrowful. O Mother of the Word Incarnate, despise not my petitions, but in thy mercy hear me and answer me. Amen."

"Amen," Gutterres echoed. We stood, embraced, then with our prayer still fresh on my lips, we drove in faith, hoping to be led to the evil before us.

Due to the Gift, I'm drawn to the supernatural. This happens regardless of where I travel. I have been led to vampires, sandmen, giant spiders, revenants, and all other manner of creatures from this world and from others. I've used this spiritual compass to guide me to lost children, to taken women, and to hiding men. Usually it's just a tingle that tells me I'm close, and it becomes stronger as I get closer to the source.

The instant we crossed into San Carlos, I knew we were in the right place. This time I didn't have a tingle. It was more like lightning coursing through my blood—no...through my *bones*. I could feel them humming inside me. I'd never felt it this way before. I lifted my hands and turned them over and back again thinking that perhaps I would be able to see them vibrating.

At the first intersection in the town, Gutterres looked at me with a cocked eyebrow.

"Try right," I said.

He turned the wheel and we headed north. Gradually the humming in my bones lessened, and I directed Gutterres to turn around. We proceeded like this for half an hour before Gutterres suddenly sat up slightly straighter.

"We're getting close," he said. The Knight of the Secret Guard was full of surprises. One of these days he and I were going to have a talk. Until then, I was content knowing he was on my side.

I'd never felt the presence of the otherworldly like I had at this moment. Whatever this power or entity was, it was calling to me. Gutterres was right: we were very close.

"Let's go on foot from here," I suggested.

He pulled to the side of the road at the base of a small hill lined on either side with huge homes. The sky was growing lighter with the approaching dawn, and with it, I could feel the already stifling heat becoming worse with the gulf breeze doing nothing to help. We exited our rental car and again geared up for whatever supernatural power was pulling us toward it. I put on my vest again, belted on my sword, and slung my rifle over my shoulders. The extra mags I could carry were all reloaded, and I strapped an extra pair of long knives to my thighs. A wise man once told me that a man can never have too many knives.

We headed up the hill, drawn by the power. We both instinctively knew which way to go at this point. After a few minutes of walking, we found ourselves at the very top of the neighborhood hill facing a massive home that had been painted orange. It was a standard three-story home where the top floor was the entry and the other floors descending down the hill it stood upon. With its white shutters and ceramic, pleated roof, the home looked like most of the others surrounding it.

But we both knew this was the one.

Even as we stood unmoving in front of the home, I could feel that the power inside was growing. I was done waiting. I was done sneaking. I shouldered my rifle and nodded for Gutterres to breach the front.

Gutterres pulled a flash-bang from a pouch on his vest, pulled the pin, then kicked in the front door and tossed the grenade inside. We waited two seconds for the detonation, then rushed inside.

Three men and a woman writhed on the floor. They wore the dark, generic robes of cultists. I hated cultists. I sighted and put three rounds each into the woman and one of the men. Gutterres took the others. From the hallway off of the main entry room, more cultists began streaming in. They stacked up perfectly for us, and our overlapping fire tore through them like paper targets. Blood hit the walls in rapid bursts. As they fell, I could see a stairwell behind them.

I led the way, Gutterres covering my back. There were two doors on the right side of the hallway, and we kicked them open in turn, laying waste to the cultists inside who were apparently waking up from all the gunfire. I dropped my first expended mag and slammed home a fresh one.

We pushed down the stairs to the second of three floors. Here all semblance of a normal home left. The floors and walls were cracked and completely barren of decoration except for strange symbols painted on every surface. Just looking at them hurt my eyes.

"Fedele, these ... these are ..." Gutterres looked on in revulsion.

"Symbols of a cult dedicated to the Old Ones," I finished for him. "This is bad."

"Very," I agreed.

At that moment, there was a faint tremble in the floor beneath our feet. We exchanged worried glances.

"Still think walking into an obvious trap was a good idea?" Gutterres asked.

I spotted another set of descending stairs on the opposite side of the room and pointed to them. "We need to get down there, now!"

I sprinted to their top, my Gift-enhanced muscles taking me there in a heartbeat. I risked a quick glance over my shoulder and found Gutterres just a few steps behind. Good. I had to trust that however he was supernaturally endowed as a Knight, he would be able to keep up. I could feel in my bones—almost a resonance—that we were running out of time until *something* horrible would happen.

Not bothering to run down the steps, I planted my left hand on the rail and vaulted over and down. Most men would have broken ankles and legs. Those men are weak.

I hit the bottom of the stairs and rushed forward, finger pulling the trigger on my rifle as cultists rose from murky candlelight. Spraying blood was illuminated in my muzzle flashes. A second rifle—Gutterres'—joined the music of my own, as we massacred men and women cultists alike.

When none were left standing, I fired single shots into the heads of any that moved. God doesn't have mercy for sinners like these, and I do my best to follow His example.

My rifle went dry again, and I realized I'd gone through four mags in the firefight already. I didn't have many more. I pushed a fresh one into place. Ahead was a closed door with a sickly, guttering yellowish-orange light leaking out from the space under it.

Gutterres, God bless him, stalked forward, holy anger filling him. In two steps he was at a full sprint, and he collided with the door, tearing it off its hinges. I was right behind him. We both pulled up short at the sight greeting us.

The room was long, and both ends were lined with beds upon which rested sleeping forms. I assumed they were the abducted people we had been looking for. A long tube snaked from the back of the head of each individual. My eyes followed the tube from the nearest...

...all the way into a huge portal at the opposite end of the room from which the yellowish-orange light was pulsing.

The cultists had opened a portal into the realm of the Old Ones.

Next to the portal stood a man in robes blacker than midnight. He turned to face us, a small smile on his lips. I recognized the face, though it was impossible. It was the face I saw in my memories of the day in which the monk had turned me into what I am today.

"Hello, my child," he said to me. "I am so happy to see you. I was assured that you would be assigned to investigate these 'abductions.' How pleased I am to see some of my efforts paying off."

I couldn't speak. This man was dead. How could he have survived all these centuries?

"Who is this man, Fedele?"

"Fedele?" The monk looked at me with a smile. "Is that the name you chose for yourself after I made you? I approve. Now, I'd love to stay and converse with the both of you, but I must take my leave. I've been ordered to have you killed, Fedele. My masters typically don't care about humanity at all, as you are less than parasites to them. But for some reason they want you dead." He winked at me. "I suppose maybe they see too much of themselves in you."

Without another word, he stepped through the portal. As I made to follow him, the abductees in the beds began to move. It looked like what we'd experienced in the cathedral, but their motions were more violent. I looked at the sleeping form closest to me—a woman in her early twenties—and saw her skin rippling.

Her face contorted in absolute agony, and her back arched until only her head and heels were on the bed. Then she fell back to the bed, absolutely still.

I took a step closer to examine her, shouldering my rifle.

Her body exploded in a shower of blood and flesh.

All around Gutterres and me, the bodies of the abducted ripped apart in violent geysers of gore. When finally I could see around the carnage, in place of the human bodies were pulsing masses of eyes, flesh, bone, and writhing tentacles. The tubes that had been attached to the heads of the people were still connected to the monstrosities, and now I could see in the pulsing light that the tubes were translucent and fleshy, like umbilical cords.

The question that frightened me more than the things about to kill us was: what were these things connected to?

Gutterres opened up on the nearest monster, the deafening sound of gunfire slapping me back into action. I fired my Templar as fast as I could pull the trigger, punching holes into three of the nearest monsters. At this range, accuracy was a formality, and black ichor spurted from the wounds without doing anything to slow the creatures down.

A tentacle lashed out and wrapped around my leg, then yanked my feet out from under me. I hit the ground hard, and as the tendril tightened around my leg, I felt multiple sharp pains as something pierced my skin. I fired into the seething mass of eyes until my mag ran dry, then reached back and pulled my sword free.

I hacked at the tentacle, severing it. The severed stump flailed in the air, spraying more dark ichor in black arcs around the room. The lifeless piece wrapped around my leg fell away, revealing the sharp barbs that had stabbed into me. I got to my feet, looked around, and saw Gutterres with a two-foot-long kukri chopping into the monster nearest to him. One of the things enveloped his hand in a tentacle, pulling him backwards.

I spun in a quick circle, slicing pieces from half a dozen attacking tendrils to give myself a moment of freedom. I unsheathed one of the knives strapped to my thigh and hurled it into the creature closest to Gutterres' left hand. He pulled the blade free, turned, and yanked it through the tentacle imprisoning his hand.

I dove past one of the monsters just as its face split open into a wet maw of bones and teeth, and brought my sword up and through the umbilical connecting it to whatever was through the portal. From beyond the pulsing glow came a deep, maddening roar of pain.

A monster launched itself at me only to have its movement arrested by the thudding of my knife being thrown back toward me. I lifted a boot and kicked the knife as hard as I could, driving the blade and hilt all the way into the round mass of eye-ridden flesh. It shivered and collapsed. I cut the umbilical from it, eliciting another roar from the portal. This time the portal itself seemed to jitter and stutter.

"Cut the cords!" I yelled.

As I turned to cut another attacking tentacle, Gutterres nimbly danced around another monster and chopped down into the cord snaking from it. I yanked my other knife free and threw it, pinning a tentacle to the wall that was making for his neck from behind. Gutterres spun, pulled the knife free, and threw it back my way, severing the umbilical of one of the monsters before hacking at another one that had paused when the thing beyond the portal shrieked.

Tentacles lashed at me, opening long gashes across my arms and legs. One hit me across the forehead and blood poured into my eyes. I moved on instinct, dodging and cutting with my sword. When I could, I grabbed the knife and would stab into the monsters before throwing it back to Gutterres, who would do the same. He looked in worse shape than I, and his movements were becoming slower as fatigue gripped him.

I cut another cord, then another. I saw Gutterres pull a grenade from his vest, pull the pin with his teeth, and throw it like a baseball into the open maw of a monster ahead of us by the portal. The mouth closed on reflex, then the grenade detonated, showering us with more bits of bone and streams of ichor. Still more monsters came. They took an astonishing amount of abuse before dying. The only thing keeping us alive was supernatural speed and toughness.

With every cord cut, the portal guttered more and more, becoming unstable.

There was another roar of pain and unfathomable anger, and then a massive tentacle, bigger around than our rental car, pushed through the portal.

I grabbed the knife from the face of a nearby monster and threw it at the massive, questing tentacle. It hit point first, but bounced off harmlessly. Gutterres cut another cord, then another before one of the creatures landed a blow to the back of his head that sent him crashing to the blood-and-gore-covered floor, unconscious.

I grabbed a severed tentacle and hurled it at one of the things before it could devour Gutterres, giving me the moment I needed to get close and cut through it from top to bottom with a two-handed slash.

One more umbilical cut. Then one more.

The creatures with their cords removed were now dropping to the floor, twitching. The portal flickered and its edge cut a deep gash into the side of the massive tentacle that was now reaching for me, only a few feet away. I stood over Gutterres' limp form and cut into another spawn of the Old Ones while keeping the tentacles away.

With one more umbilical cut, the thing reaching through the portal shrieked louder than ever before, and it seemed my head would burst from the sound. The portal shook violently, then with a *whoosh*, it collapsed, severing the remaining umbilicals. The massive tentacle fell to the floor with an impact like a miniature earthquake.

The other monsters opened their own maws and screamed with inhuman sounds before dropping. Without the umbilical cords, their flesh began melting away until nothing was left but piles of bone.

I looked at those piles of bone and felt something break inside me.

My consciousness was thrown back into the past and I lay there again on the cold, stone floor. The hawk-nosed monk knelt over me, knife in hand. He motioned to the pile of bones behind him and one of his assistants cut a sliver from one. Those bones. I'd always thought them holy. I'd always thought my creation was somehow ordained by God.

The vision of the past collided with the present. The images of those piles of bones meshed and became one. Now I understood the monk's last words. *I suppose maybe they see too much of themselves in you.*

I wasn't made from the bones of a saint, but from the bones of a minion of the Old Ones.

I bent over and retched.

✧   ✧   ✧

"I've known for a while now," Gutterres said as we watched the charnel house burn. "The Vatican monitors you like we do Franks."

"You should have told me," I said, trying not to think how very similar Franks and I really were...and failing.

"Probably. And then what? What would you have done?"

"I don't know, Gutterres. For the first time in centuries, I just don't know what to do." I glanced sidelong at my friend. "To think I called this a 'Gift' all this time."

"Isn't it, though?" When he saw my questioning expression he continued, "A gift isn't what was intended by the giver, but what is done with it by the receiver. Every child knows this, Fedele. Give it time, you'll figure it out. And I'll help."

"You have enough going on with the Secret Guard. You have a house to put in order."

"Indeed. And I will cast the guilty out like Christ did with the moneylenders in the temple...only with more violence and guns. I could use your help."

"You want my help? I'm literally an unholy monster. A very, very bad one."

"I'll make you a deal," he said and held out a hand. "You help me with this, and I will help you hunt down that monk. I have faith in you, Fedele."

I looked as his offered hand. I was still trying to wrap my mind around what had just happened and what I had discovered about myself. I pushed down my revulsion at myself again, determined not to show my friend my weakness, not to show him my fear at myself. Gutterres was the closest thing to a friend I had in this world. *A gift isn't what was intended by the giver, but what is done with it by the receiver. Every child knows this, Fedele.* I took a deep breath and nodded, then gripped his hand.

"Deal."

Chad Gardenier was a well-known Hunter in the Eighties and Nineties, and he wrote detailed memoirs about his experiences. The first two have already been released. This is an excerpt from his third volume, which will be titled *Monster Hunter Memoirs: Saints.* —A.L.

The Case of the Ghastly Spectre

John Ringo

"Is sir in?" Remi asked.

It was winter in England. Most people hate English winters. After two years in New Orleans, I loved the rain and the cold. But it wasn't weather to leave people on the doorstep. On the other hand . . .

"Depends on who is calling upon sir," I said, turning over some notes I'd found regarding the second Dutch expedition to destroy the Indonesian *mava*. They were internal memos of the Dutch colonial administration. I had to wonder how Oxford came up with them. I'd also had to learn Dutch but, eh, Dutch, Deutsch, whatever.

"They would not vouchsafe their identities, sir, but I would tend to surmise members of Her Majesty's government," Remi replied. "Some version of MCB would be most likely, sir."

"MI4," I said with a sigh. "Please tell me they made it as far as the parlor and are not on the stoop."

"I rather considered sending them to the servants' entrance, sir." He'd had to nurse me back to health after the beat-down and wasn't favoring government entities at the moment.

"Show them in, Remi. We're playing nice with these assholes."

✧　　✧　　✧

"Mr. Gardenier," the lead officer said, shaking my hand. "Senior Officer Gordon and Officer Frye, MI4."

Senior Officer Gordon was short and stocky with thinning hair and a multiply broken nose. His suit was rumpled and he was wearing a trench coat that reminded me vaguely of that Colombo character on TV. He looked more like one of those long-term London street bobbies who'd somehow wandered into being a detective and had the confused look you'd expect.

I was going to be watching him very carefully. You didn't become a "senior officer" of MI4, equivalent to an MCB special agent, if you were dumb.

Frye was Briscoe with a few years on him. Medium height, brown eyes, shaved head, very wide shoulders, Popeye forearms. Clearly some sort of Brit special operations background.

I shook his hand too and gestured to wing-backed chairs.

"Nice place," Frye said, looking around.

The small mansion had come complete with decorations.

"Rental," I said. "Not as nice as my one in New Orleans. You know that. To what do I owe the pleasure of a visit by England's Finest?"

"I hear you're an expert on gnoll," Gordon said.

"I've written a dictionary on American gnoll," I said, shrugging. "The expert is probably Dr. Witherspoon-Bunders. But..."

"He's retired," Gordon said. "We need a gnoll expert who's still capable of fieldwork."

"Why?"

"There are various immigrant fey groups turning up in England," Frye said. "Mostly refugees from Eastern Europe. We don't have language with all of them. In some cases, even our contacts in the same species don't have language in common with some of them."

"Stuff's coming in from the hills that hasn't been seen in a thousand years," Gordon said, growling. "It's worse on the Continent but we've got our fair share."

"Something's hunting gnolls in Manchester," Frye said. "Normally we don't bother with...supernatural internal disputes. But it's spilling over to humans."

"Killing them or eating them?"

"Killing them," Gordon said. "What would eat a gnoll?"

"Don't ask a master's candidate at Oxford a question like

that," I said, smiling. "Giant spiders come to mind. I take it you've autopsied the humans. Cause of death?"

"Unknown," Frye said. "Best our doctors can say is heart failure. No wounds, no toxins, soul was not stripped. No clear indicators of death magic. You're aware that there is a spiritual mark left from something like, say, a voodoo doll."

"I work in New Orleans," I said drily. "Normally."

"All of them just…died from natural causes. Same apparent cause of death in the gnolls. However, given the fact that one of the dead was a healthy twenty-three-year-old and there have been three sewer workers who died all in the same four-block area, either it's some sort of disease that's spreading from the gnolls to humans or it's the same supernatural entity.

"While some of the gnolls are Brit gnolls, ones we can communicate with, they don't know what the entity is. They can't even detect it. But they know, somehow, that another group knows what it is. That group, unfortunately, doesn't have a common language and are very…clannish. We're not even sure where they came from. They've also have an ongoing territorial dispute with the local gnolls. The locals suspect they brought down this curse on them. We need to determine if that is the case and what the nature of the entity is. To do that, we need to talk to them, which we cannot do."

"So you're asking me to get the foreign gnolls to confess to murder," I said. "I take it you'll have the usual sort of response to that: Kill them all; God will know his own."

"We just need to get the killings stopped," Frye said. "And they need to know that there are rules about that sort of thing here. If some of them need to die to get that across, some of them need to die. But to find out, we need to find out what is causing the deaths."

"So you'd like me to go up to Manchester and try to figure out their language, talk to them, and find out what they know about this killing 'thing,'" I said.

"He's not as dumb as he looks," Gordon said.

"Neither are you," I said. "What you're probably looking at is an incorporeal, given the cause of death. Some sort of wraith. I can see several potential issues to this mission in no particular order. The first that springs to mind is whether you're going to believe me if I say that it's not the fault of the foreign gnolls. It's possible it's something that followed them here or they're completely unconnected. Simple coincidence. As you noted, you've had various 'ferenners' coming over from the East. This could be part of that. The second that springs to mind is that I'm sure as hell not going on an op unarmed. And you Brits get all weanie about people being armed. The third is that assuming an incorporeal, we're not only going to have to find out what it is, but how to destroy it. The gnolls may not know that. They're not particularly into the occult per se. They don't even have shamans."

"From last to first," Frye said, nodding. "Find out what it is and we'll figure out how to destroy it. As to the second, we'll send in a support team to cover you."

"Nice knowing you, gentlemen," I said, standing up. "Remi will get your coats."

"Look, you," Gordon growled.

"Two issues," I said. "First, gnolls under the best of circumstance are skittish. If they're being hunted they're going to be even more skittish. One person is the best choice to make contact under those conditions. Second, the best way to protect a person is for them to protect themselves. Third. I don't know the backup team and I trust about as little as any person you've ever met— both assurance that they'll do their job if the shit hits the fan and assurance that they're competent to do it.

"I'm not knocking your people but I have a different view of what 'competent' means and even competence has different meanings. Are they going to follow my fire/no-fire order? You'll notice I haven't thrown in 'how am I getting paid for this?' I'm going to be armed for my own protection, I'm going to be either solo or with at most one other person at my back or you'll need to find another linguist. As to my fee, standard rates for this sort of thing. Much less than I usually get paid, I'll add. But the *conditions* are firm. I *will* be prepped for battle. Or find another linguist."

"It is illegal to arm a foreign national for this sort of thing," Frye said placatingly.

"It is illegal under British law to do more than half the sorts of things that are your daily bread and butter," I said, sitting down. "Ditto US law for the MCB. Strawman argument. Gentlemen, I'm not going to go all cowboy on your turf. I don't know what sort of exaggerations you've been getting from the MCB but I am, generally, discreet, and when I am not, I have a damned good reason. So let's work something out. Or find another linguist."

"Wait," Gordon said, holding up a hand to Frye. "We'll work

something out. As to the believability... you do know what we do for a living, right? This job is like the Mad Hatter's bloody Tea Party. You have to believe ten impossible things before breakfast. So... we'll arrange to get your toys. But only for this op. No wandering Oxford dressed for a bloody op."

"Agreed," I said.

"Find out what's killing people," Gordon said. "We'll detach Briscoe for your backup. He's a good lad and steady. Give him some field experience in something other than monster killing. Find out what it is. We'll probably know how to dispatch it and Bob's your uncle."

"Sure," I said, grinning. "It's always that easy."

The next bit was making contact with the gnolls and learning their language. I wrote the details of how to do that already in the first memoir. So I'll gloss over most of it. Because the enemy was more interesting.

Turned out the gnolls were from deep inside the Soviet Union. Their language was a gnollish variant of Permian. Not the geologic record—the tribal group. The Permian tribes are an offshoot of the Finnish-Ugric lingual group which is also called "Uralic." In the human languages, there are about two hundred phonemes shared between several tribal languages, Finnish-Ugric-Permian and some with Samoyedic.

Before going to visit them I'd boned up on every known variant of gnoll in Dr. Witherspoon-Bunders' seminal *Gnoll Dialects of the World*. The man had to have had no sense of smell to collect all the variants he collected. But he had missed a few. Despite claiming that it was "a complete collection of all gnollish dialects with etymological tree," he'd missed pretty much every type of gnoll I'd ever dealt with. Really it should have been entitled *Gnoll Dialects of England, France, Germany, and Scandinavia with a bit of rudimentary Finnish picked up thirdhand*. That is *not* everywhere that gnolls are found.

Fortunately, the Finnish section had some similarity and from there I was able to build enough of a basis to communicate. Took about a week.

The Permian gnoll tribe mostly hung out around Hulme Park; Briscoe and I had many a fine adventure suiting up and clambering down into the sewers in the area. From time to time I'd have a lorry of garbage collected to make friends and get some intelligent, for gnolls, conversation. Finally I had the thing pieced together, and we arranged to meet up with Gordon and Frye again.

"Right," I said, taking a pull on my beer. "Item the first. Not the fault of these gnolls. At least not directly."

The nice thing about working with the English is unless you're forced to go "downtown," you can pretty much figure the meeting will be in a pub. The British, bless their tyrannical hearts, even have a pub in every police station. Right in there. No need to go out to get hammered. It's better than Germany that way.

"So they say," Gordon said.

"As I mentioned, trust and belief," I said. "According to them, their tribe was cursed by a Baba Yaga a long time ago. Don't ask me how long a long time is. They don't have a calendar. In the time of their forefathers, before any living gnoll in the tribe. Gnoll average age is about two hundred, so long time. Best I got. The curse was to be haunted by some sort of specter. They leave gifts for it to keep it away. There's probably been a certain amount of pilfering of food, drink, and tobacco in the area as well. I've passed on the proper propitiation to the other gnolls so they're not going to get killed anymore. But you're either going to have to get the sewer workers to leave out some Guinness and Prince Albert along with their sandwiches or we've got to get rid of *it*."

"What's it called?" Frye asked. "We're fairly good at this sort of pest control."

"You're joking, right?" I said. "It's called *ub!tah po hahfack!* All that means is 'evil night spirit.' It's a previously *unknown dialect* of gnoll, Officer Frye! There probably is a name for it. It is probably a recognized spirit. We might be able to figure it out. But just knowing what the gnolls call it isn't much use. And it is definitely incorporeal. But that's about as much as I could get. There's not a lot of terms in their language for boogeymen."

"I hate this sort of crap," Gordon said.

"Tell me about it," I said, sighing.

"This is a Finnish-Ugric linguistic group, yes?" Briscoe said.

"Yes," I said, shrugging. "Gnoll variant but yes."

"Then will their 'boogeymen' be Finnish-Ugric as well?" Briscoe asked.

"Possibly," I said, frowning. "There's only one battle cry at this point, gentlemen."

"To the Unseen Library!" Briscoe said.

"A para who enjoys research," I said, shaking my head. "Will wonders never cease."

"A Marine who can read," Briscoe replied. "Will wonders never cease..."

"I had to talk the librarian into letting me leave with this," Briscoe said, slamming a heavy tome onto my desk. "Is it me, or does he look *just* like an orangutan?"

"He looks just like an orangutan," I said, still grading papers. "Balding red hair, long arms, flat face. Where y'at?"

"What?" Briscoe said.

"What do you have for me?" There were times I still missed New Orleans.

I'd more or less deputized him as my... deputy. Research assistant, maybe. I had papers to grade. That sort of thing was what undergrads—and junior MI4 officers—were for.

"Piru," he said.

"You're welcome," I said, then frowned. "You weren't saying thank you?"

"No," Briscoe said.

"It's 'thank you' in a rather obscure Indian language," I said. "Also a type of evil night spirit of Slavic derivation."

"And the master is beaten," Briscoe said. "Uralic, not Slavic. Or it was originally Uralic and got transferred to Slavic according to this."

I picked up the book and looked at the title page. "*Spirits, Myths, Heroes and Devils of the Finno-Uralic Tribes.* So that's saying piru—which I'd sort of put aside as being Slavic, not Uralic—is Uralic?"

"According to this," Briscoe said, grinning.

"So how do you banish it?" I asked. "Does it say?"

"Uh..." Briscoe said, then frowned. "No. Do you know?"

"No," I said. "We haven't covered Slavic or Uralic in incorporeal creatures. And I don't usually get into them since they're not PUFF-applicable. Guess you've got more research coming your way."

"Drat," Briscoe said, picking up the book.

I went back to grading papers. Bloody essays. *Everything* at Oxford was bloody essays, and of course the TAs had to grade them. And, no, the students were no better at writing them than American students. I was running out of red pens.

✧   ✧   ✧

"I've found a book which is said to have various spells and incantations for dispelling Slavic and Uralic spirits," Briscoe said, dropping the book on my desk again. It was another weighty tome.

"So how do we dispel it?" I asked. "You could have just done notes."

"I don't do runes," Briscoe said. "It seems that the Germans were having trouble with Slavic and Uralic supernatural entities going *way* back. This was written in the eleven hundreds in Germany, but it simply transcribed the Elder Futhark runes for the spells assuming that anyone who was reading it also read Elder Futhark."

"Go down to the linguistics department," I said with a sigh. "Ask Professor Furnbauer for his Elder Futhark dictionary with my kind thanks. I'll need to bone up."

"Oh, you have got to be fucking kidding me..." I said as I finished the translation. Maybe I was wrong? I'd have to get a second opinion. Was Professor Furnbauer read in?

He was. And the translation was right. Bloody hell. This was going to be complicated...and my orals were coming up. On the other hand, the book was interesting and this was shaping up to be a great paper. I was considering translating the whole thing since it had dozens of wards, traps, dispellations, and charms I'd never run across anywhere else. Publish or perish had serious meaning in our job.

Two days later I grabbed Briscoe as he was leaving class.

"Go down to the geology department," I said. "Ask them about some sort of crystal or stone that changes color between 'firelight and sunlight.' One color in sunlight, different color in firelight. Only found in the Ural Mountains."

"If so, it'll be bloody hard to get our hands on," Briscoe said.

"Worse, we'll need one the size of 'the last joint of a tall man's thumb,'" I said. "Just find out what it is."

"You're not going to like this," Briscoe said.

"I'm not liking anything about this," I said. "I'm not liking having to depend for information on eleventh century alchemists, gnolls whose language I think I'm translating right and an undergrad para who has enough trouble with English much less any other language."

"Thanks for the vote of confidence," Briscoe said.

"What am I not going to like?" I asked.

"Alexandrite," Briscoe said. "Extremely rare color change variant of chrysoberyl. Changes color from green in sunlight to red-purple in artificial light. Named after Tzar Alexander the Second. Only mined in a few areas: the Northern Urals, Sri Lanka, and Brazil."

"We'll need the Urals' one to be sure," I said, frowning. "Bit of a trick what with that being the Soviet Union. And a good, clear, pure-quality one."

"More of a trick than you think," Briscoe said. "The Russian deposits were the finest in the world...*were* being the important word. They were all mined out in the 1950s. 'Of the size of a large man's thumb' is about ten carats. I asked Professor Shelley how much that would cost and he said, 'Oh, about a hundred.'"

"Hundred dollars?" I asked.

"Hundred *thousand*," Briscoe said. "Pounds."

"Not my problem," I said, grinning. "That's on MI4."

"You're bloody insane," Gordon said. "A hundred thousand pounds?" He patted his pockets for a moment. "Here, let me just *pull it out of my arse,* why don't I?"

"The night creature is a piru," I said. "Or at least a Uralic version of the piru. It's found in Slavic folklore as well. Previously—and I've checked with Professor Henderson—there was no known way to dispel or entrap one. According to the book Briscoe turned up, there is a way using a Ural alexandrite and a spell. The fact that they're rare is unsurprising given that piru are really nasty spirits. As I said, Professor Henderson had no answer to how to dispel them or kill them. Generally you do what the gnolls are doing, which is propitiate them. But if you want to dispel it, you're going to need a big alexandrite. And it will be destroyed in the spell so you won't even be able to sell it afterwards."

"Bloody hell, there goes my budget," Gordon said. "We've got the area blocked off for now. I'll have to get back to you. That really is a bit of a budget item for us at the moment."

"Feel free," I said. "I've got exams coming up."

"That do?" Gordon said, setting a large reddish purple gem on my desk.

I'd done well on my orals. Now all I had to do was pass the

written portion and turn in my thesis and I'd have my second master's.

"Pretty," I said. The stone was deeply colored, cut in an oval and just beautiful. "Hate to ruin it."

I pulled out a loupe and checked the alluvia to be sure. I'd followed up on pretty much everything Briscoe had brought to me and there was a way to check if it was a Russian stone.

"Bit of a budget line item," I said, dropping it in a pocket.

"I had to call in a favor," Gordon growled.

"Favor from whom might I ask?" I asked.

"MI6," Gordon said. "Let's just say it didn't come out of my budget. Or theirs. I had to get authorization but it came pretty quickly. Seems this beasty has gotten out of the sewers. Two people were found dead from natural causes in the area in the last few days. Both were in the prime of their lives. And MI6 had to burn a cell. So this had better work."

"I tried out some of the white incantations from the book," I said. "They worked well enough. Only one way to find out. And if it doesn't, you won't have my ass to chew if you know what I mean."

"When can you get started?" Gordon said.

I had exams all week. If I missed one, there went my master's. And I really needed to bone up before each of them. Not to mention sleep.

Death is lighter than a feather. And I could sleep when I was dead.

"Tonight."

"You don't really need to be here," I said.

The capture and destruction of a piru takes more than just an alexandrite. First, the piru must be attracted and fed. They liked expensive food, drink, and drugs. Yes, drugs. Tobacco will do but opium has much the same effect on them as on humans for some reason. We were banking on heroin for that. You could find it on various street corners in Manchester, and it wasn't like we were in danger of getting arrested. On the other hand, MI4 could just get it out of an evidence locker, which they had.

We were doing the rite in an alleyway off of The Sanctuary, which I thought rather ironic in the circumstances. It was where the now three people had died of "natural causes," one each night.

You bring them in by burning tobacco and alcohol. Then set up a little tableau with the various comestibles laid out. Checking the police reports, all three had been smokers; if young enough, that shouldn't have caused their deaths, and all three had been drinking. So they'd "called" the piru but hadn't offered to share. Die, humans, die. Handy tip: always be unselfish if you're being tracked by a wraith. If one shows up when you're smoking and drinking, offer them a fag and a shot. Or else.

"Rather want to see what we've been chasing," Briscoe said.

We laid out a brass tray with some shots of rum, a prime cut of lamb, and a small brazier. Then we lit the gin and dropped pipe tobacco on the coals in the brazier.

We were right by a storm drain and it took about fifteen minutes for the piru to appear, following the scent of burning alcohol and tobacco. It was just a darker shadow amongst the shadows, a tenebrous fog rising from the storm grating.

The piru floated closer. It was difficult to see in the moonlit darkness even with the help of the streetlights. It moved from shadow to shadow. We'd placed the tray in shadow, knowing it would avoid any sort of light. It was generally bipedal, but I'm fairly sure it wasn't anything derived from human. You get a certain feeling around human ghosts and this was definitively unearthly.

The wraith floated to the tray and into the smoke from the tobacco and the burning essence of the rum. It was clear it was feeding in some way. Maybe it just liked the aroma. But it also made contact with the lamb. I'd gotten a tissue sample and I intended to check the differences between the original and the sacrificed. I was pretty sure that the people who had "died of natural causes" had died of some sort of loss of something. Phosphate, calcium ... something. It would be easier to find between the two versions of lamb.

Since we were properly propitiating it, we weren't in any danger at this point, so I took as careful notes as I could. I knew there was no way to photograph it but I wish I could have.

The gin had burned out so Briscoe lit another shot. Give the guy credit, para or not he wasn't fazed by an otherwordly spirit being.

Once the piru was feasting, I opened up the nickel bag of heroin and dropped that on the brazier.

The result wasn't immediate. The thing wasn't moving real fast as it was, but it slowly ... slowed until it was simply hanging there in the smoke from the fire like a black sheet on a clothesline.

I got out my notes and the irreplaceable gem. I laid the gem on the tray, in contact with some of its tendrils of shadow, and began to read.

The toughest part of the whole thing had been finding the proper pronunciation for some of the Uralic and Germanic in the incantation. Dean Carruthers had put me in contact with a traditional Uralic speaker and that had helped. Some of the words were close enough to tribal Tibetan I had to wonder if there was a racial connection.

I began the incantation, calling upon the owl spirit and the moon spirit and the spirit of the gem to bind and entrap this creature of darkness. Three repetitions and I could see it starting to sink into the stone. It also was starting to move, so I gestured at the second heroin packet and Briscoe tossed it in. Good little wizard's apprentice.

It took nine repetitions of the incantation but finally the piru sank into the stone completely.

I picked the stone up with a pair of tongs and winced.

"Let's hope this works," I said and dropped it into the brazier.

Nothing happened at first but then a sound started to emit from the stone. It was so high-pitched at first that it wasn't even audible but dogs started barking in all the flats nearby. Then it was in the audible range, for me at least, and I started to get the whole *banshee cry* thing. Horrible sound, eerie and painful to the ears despite being surprisingly quiet. A bit like what a hamster would sound like if it was being slowing burned to death. At least a bizarre space hamster.

Finally, with one last tortured wail, the priceless gem shattered amongst the charcoal bricks and it was done.

"Did we get it?" Briscoe asked.

"Only way to know is if nobody dies tonight," I said. "Let's pack up. We've both got exams in the morning."

Nobody died that night nor in the subsequent weeks. A guy died of a heart attack three weeks afterwards in the area but he was a risk case, so all good.

The lamb samples were subsequently bent, folded and mutilated by MI4's labs. There was a significant difference in the levels of isoleucine, an amino acid, between the two samples. Notably less in the one that the piru had touched. So apparently, besides liking to get high, pirus steal isoleucine. The pathologist who gave the report started to explain about isoleucine and I asked him not to. I've got enough stuff stuffed in my head. I'll leave that to the medical professionals. Bottom line, not enough will kill you.

I later went back and translated the book of incantations and traps for various Slavic and Siberian entities as well as adding quite a few others from Europe and Eurasia. The three-book set: *Identification of, Protections Against, and Traps for Supernatural Entities of the Slavic, Siberian, Balkans and Eurasian Spirit Tribes* by Oliver Chadwick Gardenier, PhD, is available from Oxford University Press...if you have the clearance. There's a complete copy in the MHI library as well.

Now to explain why I added all that to my memoirs besides as a commercial plug...

My *teacher* hat is on at this point so bear with me with the pro-tip. One reason for this long explanation of tracking down one minor entity is this is stuff you're going to have to learn at some point. You can't always depend on someone else to do your research for you. I don't mean you have to learn proto Uralic. But you do need to learn the Dewey Decimal System.

It's also about teaching itself. I could have taken the time to go look all this stuff up myself. But part of why Briscoe was at Oxford was to learn how to do the research. So I *delegated*. And that, too, is part of your job once you get past "me dumb grunt." He learned how to find some very obscure stuff in the sometimes baroque library system. For that matter, he found the tome that had exactly the right information. I might not have. Why? I knew where to look, he didn't. Sometimes sending out the person who doesn't know the "right" answer is the right answer. Sometimes it's not. But until that day, we didn't have an answer to piru. We found it because Briscoe went and looked in what was basically the wrong place.

Most of this particular memoir, for one reason or another, has been about the *background* of hunting. Everyone likes the big fight scenes. But hunting is about *more*. Once you're over "me dumb grunt," learn the more.

For God's sake, at least learn Latin and crack a book once in a while. Don't just expect me or Milo or Ray or whoever is the equivalent in your day and age to do all the work.

No matter how tough you think you are, Hunters need vacations, too. Sadly, when you make a living pissing off the forces of evil, that doesn't always work out.   —A.L.

Huffman Strikes Back

Bryan Thomas Schmidt & Julie Frost

Every time he watched the video of his brother Cecil's death, Glen Huffman's chest grew tighter and tighter until he was forced to cough for air.

A friend with connections had gotten him footage from the building's security cameras after some wheeling and dealing. The Feds had confiscated it, but then MHI had gotten copies and a lot of Hunters were having good old laughs at his brother's expense. So Glen had paid good money for a copy of his own.

Cecil had been sitting naked in his office when Owen Zastava Pitt walked in. Cecil was a successful executive—hard-working, dedicated, a family man—working in the fourteenth-floor finance department of Hansen Industries, Inc., in Dallas. Pitt was some tall, fat loser with a cocky attitude—a cause of many of Cecil's woes, he'd told Glen.

They started arguing. There was no audio to hear what they said, but it was obvious from their body language on screen that Pitt held Cecil in contempt. Pitt sneered with every word, his eyes rolling and widening as if everything his boss said was ridiculous or over the top.

Sure, Cecil was naked. That was unusual, but he was the man's boss. Pitt, of course, had no way of knowing what Cecil had been going through. Wouldn't have mattered. The man had no respect and no honor. They had their argument, then Cecil got righteously angry—Glen watched him tense on the video, leaning forward. Pitt uttered some kind of threat, then Cecil was changing—the fur, the twisting flesh as his arms and feet formed claws, his face warping into fangs, a long snout.

Cecil had been ready to teach the lazy sonuvabitch who was boss. That's all.

Then that moronic, selfish, fat brute Owen Pitt had broken Cecil's neck and thrown him out of a window.

Owen Zastava Pitt had murdered Glen's brother in cold blood!

Glen had to fight to control his own anger and inner beast just watching it over and over, cursing to himself, fighting back tears for his brother. He'd mourned enough. Now was the time for revenge.

The Huffmans had just returned, a few weeks before Cecil's murder, from a family camping trip to Yellowstone National Park, a return to an old favorite from their childhoods they hadn't visited in two decades. After their father died, Cecil and Glen swore they'd take their own kids there and give them the same experience they'd had with their father as boys. And so they did. Only, a couple things had happened, and it hadn't been quite the same experience.

For one, Cecil's wife had gotten herself eaten by a werewolf. The campsite had an A rating from the rangers. It was supposed to be one of the safest. Nita had left the tent to defecate in the woods. Her screams awoke everyone, followed by growling, a terrible sound of ripping flesh, and the warm, metallic smell of blood. Glen and Cecil had rushed out and found a werewolf chewing on her arm, her intestines ripped out of her stomach.

To say this was shocking would be a bit understated. And Cecil had gone nuts. In all his miserable life, Nita had been his center, his anchor, the one thing that kept him sane and happy no matter what. Glen's brother was a bit moody, one might say—angry at the injustices which slowed his advance at work, frustrated with lazy, no-good employees, bored with his job—but not when Nita was around. With her, he smiled, laughed, and lived a mostly calm, happy existence. Home was his sanctuary. And now some moth-erfucking werewolf had taken that away in an instant.

Glen wouldn't have said his brother was weak or even harmless—but he'd had absolutely no idea he was Rambo.

Cecil screamed at the monster, ripping it off his wife's body, and then pounding at it with fallen logs and branches from nearby—all the while shouting for Glen or the boys to get the guns from the truck. The boys ran; Glen was too stunned and just stood there, staring, while his wife and daughter screamed beside him.

Cecil just kept attacking the wolf, who howled and growled and swiped at him with its claws, ripping into his flesh. He didn't seem to care—he was a man possessed.

But then the werewolf dropped Nita's arm and went after Cecil, biting into him with a bloodcurdling roar. He didn't stand a chance. His own blood mixed with his dead wife's as the monster howled and chomped.

Glen fired his rifle, round after round, but while it pissed the monster off, it didn't take it down. In fact, after a bit, the wounds started healing right before Glen's eyes. He hoped to save Cecil, but then got a good look at him—a bloody mass, flesh ripped, eyes shiny, wide, but dead. He was a goner.

The werewolf rushed Glen and bit into his arm like a shark on a swimmer—an arc of agonizing pain tearing through him like fire on gasoline. Glen screamed and cursed and hit at it with the rifle stock, his eyes watering under the assault of the rancid, rotting-meat-laced breath. He managed to turn the rifle around and fired point-blank at the wolf's head, hitting it once in the forehead and once each in the nose and paw.

The werewolf roared and smacked Glen with the back of its other paw, knocking the rifle free and into a spin. It flew ten feet and landed in view atop the leaves and decay that formed the forest floor.

Glen fell back, landing on his ass, his arm bleeding something awful, and then gasped for breath before scooting away backward on all fours, trying to get away from the monster. Its forehead, paw, and nose bled, its bones and flesh looking like the creature had fallen off a mountain. The wolf just stared at Glen, glaring evilly, its teeth a snarly grimace as he shook his head, trying to recover focus.

Glen's hands touched metal as he spider-crawled backward, and he recognized the rifle. Somehow, he managed to grab it and jump to his feet, then turned and ran for the car as fast as he could.

Brush crackled, bark tore, and howling filled his ears as the monster raced after him. But thankfully, Virginia, Glen's wife, had gotten the car started. Jessica, his daughter, screamed at him and pushed the door open. He slid inside, slamming it even as the wheels starting turning, spinning on dirt and leaves seeking purchase, until the car finally lurched ahead and Virginia tore up the road.

That cursed monster chased them for a mile or two but Virginia drove like some kind of Danica Patrick. He'd never known she could handle a car like that. She hit every turn with squealing tires and slammed the wheel just right to get the car straight and steady again, all the while gaining speed. She never yelled once, just stared ahead with intense focus and drove the shit out of that minivan.

Made Glen damn proud of her.

Cecil's boys and Glen's daughter were sobbing messes, of course. He just sat in the seat, exhausted from the adrenaline rush and tension, while Virginia got them the hell outta there in no time flat.

Glen figured he'd never see Cecil again...until he showed up the next night at their hotel, naked, not a scratch on him.

That was the night their lives changed forever.

A few weeks later, his brother was dead—fallen out of a skyrise to the street below, then taken by some government agents—hauled away like some lab-animal study, whatever those bastards did.

Glen would never get over it, though he tried to get on with life, learn to live with it. He'd made progress, too, he thought.

Then that fucking video showed up.

The others were actually laughing—enjoying the sight of his brother falling to the street. Fucking monsters—brutal, uncultured, cruel bastards, all of them. But he needed them. They were the key to his revenge, so he ignored it, despite the pain it caused.

The group had been hand-chosen for their unique abilities and broad experience. All had solid reputations as reliable and had been trusted by Glen's close friends. And he needed a special team to ensure his mission's success. All also wanted revenge on MHI, and taking out one of their star Hunters was the perfect opportunity.

He looked them over now. The first didn't look like much beyond your standard garden gnome—short legs and arms covered by bright-colored clothes and a white cone hat with an equally long, white beard covering his face. In fact, until he moved, no one could tell if Björn Smallhands was a statue or alive. But when he did, you'd better pray he wasn't moving after you. He'd lost two brothers battling Hunters a few years back, but until Glen had offered money, he'd resisted. Gnomes would take any job for money. Fortunately, Glen's success in finance had left him quite rich in resources—both money and other kinds... so he could offer amounts that were hard to refuse.

The second had bumpy, mottled-green skin, bald with wispy white hair. His nose was squat with a slightly raised snoutlike tip, and tusklike teeth protruded from his mouth. He stared at the others with yellow eyes set under thick bone ridges on a short forehead, piercings of bone and steel covering his cheeks and chin, as the orc's sharp teeth spread in a laugh. His name was unpronounceable to Glen but everyone just called him "Happy," because for an orc, he had a rather pleasant disposition, even when he was killing someone or something. He'd been outcast from his tribe who had been adopted by MHI, and he wanted to hurt them and their allies. It was about respect, self-worth, and the joy of rejecting those who'd rejected him.

The third was a minotaur, though calling him that would end in your death. The Bullman had a black spot over one eye, and stood eight feet tall, head bigger than a buffalo and brute muscle all over his hairy body. He preferred being addressed by his full name, Andrew Jackson Fuller Smith, and he was prone to being quite pissed off at anyone who forgot. He had a permanent limp and scars on his neck and chest from his last encounter with MHI. Vanity alone made that cause for revenge—but after his son's death in a building Hunters had set ablaze during a mission, he was doubly motivated.

After their laughter subsided, the Bullman spoke in a deep, booming voice, "Y'all want us to take out this Owen Pitt, is that right?" Being from Texas, most Bullmen spoke like redneck cowboys, accent and all.

"Yes," Glen said.

"He has quite a reputation amongst the Hunters, dawg," Björn said.

Andrew Jackson Fuller Smith frowned and whirled to glare at the gnome. "Who you calling dawg, Lawnman?"

Björn rolled his eyes and glared back. "Glen here, you Hereford. Relax."

"I am no Hereford!" the Bullman objected. Glen and Happy stepped between them.

"Calm down, both of you," Glen said.

"Yes. No worry. Be happy," Happy said, grinning.

None of the others showed the slightest amusement at his joke. After a moment, the Bullman and gnome relaxed and everyone breathed again.

"I know his reputation, but we're going to take him alone," Glen continued. "You saw what he did to my brother. He'd do that to any of us."

"I'm not against harming any Hunter, of course, suh," Andrew Jackson Fuller Smith said and smiled. "They've earned it many times over. Even if it does require working with lesser ground dwellers." He aimed the last at Björn and smirked, looking down at the tiny gnome to be sure he'd heard.

"Chill, dawg. Just keep those clodbusting hooves of yours clear o' me," Björn replied, hands crossed over his chest. "Why should we trust a human against a human anyway?"

Glen locked gazes with the gnome and let his wolf eyes shine through—yellow, piercing—emitting a growl. "Because I am not human anymore."

He knew from their reaction then that he had them all, and planning began.

For reasons Glen didn't know or care about, his sources in the unofficial Monster Information Network, as Glen liked to call it, reported Owen Pitt had come to a private cabin in the woods south of Knoxville, Tennessee, on some kind of retreat. Just off Lake Santeetlah near Robbinsville, North Carolina, the cabin was supposedly owned by an old friend of Earl Harbinger's. It was small, remote, and rustic. The perfect setting for an ambush, and Glen had sent a local friend to scout it out, who reported back that Pitt was alone. Perfect.

Glen himself went down ahead of his team and staked the place out for a couple days. Owen Pitt looked disgusting—a couple of years ago he'd been an accountant working for a boring corporation, with a single, drab existence. Now he was a badass, murdering, monster killer with a hot wife, the kind who should have been unattainable for a schlub like him. He was on top of the world. Motherfucker. Accountant boy would pay. His top of the world was going to hit rock bottom. Glen would see to that and enjoy every minute.

❖   ❖   ❖

Owen stood in the kitchen in his socks, spooning shortening into the deep-fat fryer so he could cook up some fries to go with the burgers he was getting ready to grill. The fat crackled and began melting in the heating Fry Daddy. Owen smiled with satisfaction. After the sheer crazy of the past several months, the simple act of preparing a meal in a cabin in the woods was like a pleasant detour back to basics. Mmmmmm. Did he even remember what it was like to have a normal day anymore?

The cabin was rustic but well appointed, with woodsy décor such as antler lamps, log furniture, and high, rough-hewn ceiling beams. There was even a moose head hanging on the wall above the fireplace, where Owen had kindled a cheery blaze to keep the early evening fall chill at bay. Abomination, recently fieldstripped, cleaned, oiled, and reassembled, lay gleaming on the coffee table in the living room.

"Best of all, it's quiet," he told Julie on the phone, talking to her as he dumped the julienned potatoes into the bubbling fat. "No one for miles around." Julie was with the team investigating an odd attack in Greeneville, Tennessee, not far north, but they must have finished because he heard the whirring hum of chopper blades in the background as they talked.

"Careful." She laughed. "You'll jinx it. Next thing you know the missionaries will come knocking on your door."

"Wouldn't that be typical." He carried the meat out the kitchen door to the back patio, where the charcoal had settled into perfect cooking coals in the barbeque, and set the patties across the grill. "Maybe next time you can join me."

Julie emitted a sound of pleasure on the other end that almost caused Owen to drop the meat. He recovered just in time and took a breath, whispering silent praises to whatever God above had given him this woman.

Glen twitched when Björn appeared out of thin air after reconnoitering the situation. "He don't suspect a thing, dawg," the gnome said. Honestly, the canine metaphors were getting old. "Fat, dumb, and *tall*," he almost spat the third word, "talking to some broad on the phone and cooking dinner. Very domestic."

"Excellent. Now remember," Glen said, "he's my meat. Immobilize him. Injure him all you like, but I get the kill."

"Long as y'all don't dillydally around," the Bullman said, flexing his enormous hands. He'd decided to go into battle unarmed. He was a weapon; he didn't need to carry one. Glen felt the same way. Teeth and claws would teach Pitt a lesson, along with all those other MHI bastards. No one messed with him and his.

Happy didn't speak; he just did a figure-eight spin with the mace he carried, which was basically a big spiked ball on a stick. Björn checked a pair of semiauto pistols—Glen didn't know what kind they were and didn't care as long as they weren't loaded with silver—and nodded with satisfaction, baring a long, sharp fang. "Let's go," he growled.

They deployed through the woods with Andrew taking point. The Bullman would break down the front door, Björn planned on appearing directly into the kitchen, and Happy would go in the back. Glen followed Happy, since that seemed to be where Pitt was concentrating his activity. For a moment, Glen was distracted by the smell of cooking meat, but then Happy burst through the back door into the kitchen and all hell broke loose.

Owen set the phone down, still talking to Julie, while he kept an eye on the potatoes, fried up some bacon, and sliced a tomato. When a gnome popped into being on the counter, armed to the teeth, he had a bare half-second to react. He did so by swearing, scooping up the frying pan to use as a shield, shoving backward, and ducking as the gnome growled and raised two pistols. Owen also kept hold of the—thankfully very sharp and also double-pointed—tomato knife. A pair of bullets whistled past his ears, the sounds of the shots incredibly loud in the enclosed space.

Owen swung the frying pan on instinct, as the gnome fired again. The pan pinged and a dent appeared as a bullet ricocheted into a nearby beam, cracking the wood.

The back door splintered open to reveal an orc carrying a nasty-looking mace. At the same time, Owen caught sight of the front door smashing in and a Bullman shaking the remains of it from his horns. A guy who looked human but probably wasn't, because Owen wasn't that lucky, followed the orc—but he, at least, didn't appear to be carrying any weapons.

His first thought was: God damn it, I'm on vacation! What the fuck? But shortly after, Owen realized he was deeply, eminently, and urgently screwed.

Nothing for it, he attacked, because fuck them if they thought he'd go down without a fight. The gnome, who was closest, fired two more shots; one hit the frying pan and the other clipped his left shoulder. Owen leapt forward and swatted the gnome with the pan, sending him flying into the wall. Owen stabbed him right through the center of mass before the stunned gnome could get out of the way. The two-pointed blade was great for cutting tomatoes and even more useful as a gnome skewer; he lifted the flailing creature off the counter and plunged him headfirst into the deep-fat fryer, which made the boiling oil practically explode in a crackling, Yellowstone-esque geyser.

From the corner of his eye, Owen caught sight of the mace swinging and instinctively ducked and rolled under a stroke that would have smashed in his head like a pumpkin if he'd been stupid enough to let it connect. Ducking, he reached up a hand and pulled his knife with a sucking sound from the fried gnome, so he at least still had that available.

His roll across the cramped floor space fetched him up against a cabinet, as the pan clattered to the floor and the orc just kept on coming. Owen dove between its legs as the mace came down again, thunking deeply into the hardwood floor, the spikes sticking long enough for him to regain his feet and look for something to throw. The floor split and crackled, opening in a widening fissure.

Oh, hello, deep-fried gnome. Owen picked up the fryer, yanking the cord from the wall in the process, and flung it in a spraying arc at the back of the orc's head. It connected with a satisfying clang and the hiss and stink of cooking orc meat while Owen leapt into the living area and the orc roared with agonized rage.

He wasn't much better off there, honestly, although at least he was closer to Abomination. The Bullman bellowed and charged. Owen was not nearly small enough to "flit," but he made a fair attempt to jump aside. A horn caught him in passing on his right arm, opening a deep gash and causing him to drop the knife with a grunt of pain. Not that it would have done him any good against, well, *that*, but it was the principle of the thing. The Bullman spun on his hooves to face him, and Owen stumbled backward, slipped on a throw rug, and fell on his ass, bleeding and cursing.

Yep, still fucked.

Oh, sunuvabitch! This was what Glen got for not just doing the job himself. Good help was so hard to find. He got to the living area just in time to see Andrew Jackson Fuller Smith yank a mounted moose head from over the fireplace and fling it bodily at Pitt, on his back on the floor. He yelped and kicked his legs up in time to deflect it away from his head, though it bounced and came back down against his outstretched hands. There was a nasty *crack* as Pitt's thumb caught the brunt of the snout and bent backward at an odd angle.

Well, he supposed he hadn't said they couldn't break Pitt, just no killing. Happy loped past Glen, mace upraised, and Pitt shoved himself back. This brought him within arm's reach of the coffee table, where—

No! No, no, no, no, *no*. What the hell was that damn gun loaded with anyway? Whatever it was, it blew an amazingly huge hole right through Happy's chest and out his back, spattering orc innards all over Glen and nearly deafening him to boot. Happy staggered and fell, dropping his mace, which fell on Glen's foot, causing him to howl as its spikes tore into his flesh through his boot.

"No worry. Be—" The orc croaked then lay still, his death a punchline to the joke that was once Glen's master revenge.

The Bullman wasn't idle in the midst of all this, nor was he a coward. Even though he'd seen what the gun had done to Happy, he bellowed and charged right at Pitt before he could shift aim. Wrapping a massive hand around the weapon's barrel, he twisted hard and yanked at the same time.

The two wrestled and rolled, grunting and growling for control of the weapon. The Bullman tossed Pitt around like a rag doll, but the man managed to keep a stubborn grip on his weapon. Then the muscles in the minotaur's neck and shoulders bulged and throbbed as he threw more effort into it and finally got a solid grip with both hands on the weapon. Pitt's face crinkled and his mouth twisted. He was no match for a minotaur. Pitt held for a minute, the weapon shaking between them, but Andrew Jackson Fuller Smith finally managed to overpower him and yank the shotgun away. Unfortunately, the Bullman pulled the barrel right toward himself rather than to the side. Pitt gave a frantic push, shoving the barrel right up into one of the minotaur's nostrils, where it went off, blowing his snout to pieces and piercing his brain. He stumbled back, an expression of bovine stupidity on his face, and collapsed into the blazing fireplace, sending burning logs flying. Sparks set curtains and furniture alight.

"Of all the lucky fucking shots!" Glen growled.

He didn't care anymore. It was him and Pitt, just like it should have been in the first damn place. Pitt's gun had ended up out of reach due to the Bullman's tight grip even in death—he'd taken it with him as he fell—and Owen was down and helpless. The reek of Pitt's blood nearly made Glen lose control and shift, but he *wanted* to be himself for this, needed to see Pitt suffer and die for what he'd done to Cecil.

Pitt coughed and looked up at him, grinning through his pain. "This place was beautiful until you four arrived to fugly it up."

Glen growled, baring his fangs. In his anger, he couldn't really help a partial shift. He stalked forward with a bestial growl, claws extended. Pitt scooted away, or tried, anyway—as banged up as he'd been by the Bullman, he couldn't go very far.

"Who the hell are you?"

"Glen Huffman. You murdered my brother"—Glen's shoulders bunched—"and you're going to pay for that."

Pitt actually laughed. *Laughed*, the bastard, even though Glen could see he was hurting. "He tried to kill me first. You can see exactly how far it got him."

"He put you in the hospital. I'm going to put you in the ground."

Pitt's gaze swept around the room, at the burning furniture, the bodies, his too-far-away gun. Glen let him assess the odds and tick over logistics, and savored Pitt's dawning realization that he wouldn't survive this encounter. "You're welcome to try," Pitt sneered.

"There's no fourteenth story here, Pitt," Glen growled, then he sprang.

Owen lunged sideways and grasped the moose head by an antler with his good hand. Groaning with the effort, aided by a spike of adrenaline, he swung it at Huffman and connected with his body in mid-leap.

Not that it did him much good. Huffman was deflected, barely, but it was enough for Owen to get the trophy between himself and the werewolf, who had half shifted. "Damn," Owen grunted, "you're even uglier than your brother."

Huffman snarled, and his face elongated more. He aimed a snap at Owen, but his teeth sank into the moose's nose instead. He wrenched his head and tore away part of the hide and a hunk of the polyurethane foam beneath, then dove in again.

Owen held him off desperately, jabbing a palmate antler at his eyes, connecting with a glancing blow that at least seemed to hurt him. Huffman shook his head, and Owen caught sight of the orc's mace, closer than Abomination, which lay just beyond it. He dropped the moose and scrambled that way, picking the spiked weapon up and swinging it one-handed just in time to crash it into Huffman's snout.

"Hey, at least you aren't naked," Owen said.

Which, of course, was when Huffman shifted completely—*bam*—just like that, and shook out of his shredded clothes. Pure animal malice shone from his yellow eyes, nothing human in them anymore.

Owen backhanded the mace into Huffman's head, this time just trying to hold him off. A set of four claws ripped down his body from collarbone to beltline before Owen smacked him yet again, knocking him aside with as much force as he could muster...

...Which, honestly, wasn't much. The werewolf was healing nearly as fast as Owen was dealing damage, while Owen was leaking precious bodily fluids all over the place. He'd better finish this before it finished him.

Huffman came at him again, jaws wide. With exquisite timing, Owen shoved the mace clear down into his open throat. "Choke on that, you mangy cur," he panted. Abomination was just a couple of feet away, and he rolled toward it, scooping it up, bringing it around, pulling the trigger—

And missing.

Huffman had divested himself of the mace and was in midair, descending toward Owen like some kind of awful, fanged bird of prey, talons outstretched to engulf him. Owen slapped the bayonet release and braced. The werewolf impaled himself on the silvered blade, unfazed, because it missed his heart—of course it missed his heart, Owen could never be that lucky. Huffman strained toward him while Owen shoved upward on the gun. He managed to hold the jaws far enough away, but the claws were another matter, and they sank into his shoulders, ripping flesh.

Abomination slipped. He pulled the trigger again, but the

enraged wolf didn't even seem to notice the sudden giant hole blown through him. Owen was dreadfully handicapped and losing blood. He stared his own death in the fangs and had time to think, *I'm sorry, Julie—*

A deafening *BOOM* sounded from behind Huffman, and his head disappeared in a spray of bone, meat, and red mist. He collapsed bonelessly, in a bloody, furry mass.

Letting Abomination drop sideways with the body still spiked on it, Owen blinked several times, then wiped the gore off his face. Julie Shackleford stood there like a tall, gorgeous, avenging angel with long dark hair, holding a smoking shotgun and looking pissed. "Owen?"

"I. You. Julie?" Yes, Owen, very smooth. He would've rolled his eyes at himself if he had the energy. "How did you—?"

"I heard the door break down over the phone, and lots of crashing and swearing." Julie strode over and knelt beside him, examining him like a worried hen with breathtaking brown eyes through her slanted, oval-framed glasses. "It sounded worse than when you usually cook. I'd been planning to have Skippy drop me here to surprise you after we finished at Greeneville anyway, and we were already on the way, so Skippy redlined the chopper." She brushed the side of his face with her fingertips. "Looks like we arrived just in time."

Owen let himself sink the rest of the way to the floor. "Thanks." His eyes slid shut. "Oh my God, I hate werewolves."

"Earl will be so glad to hear that," Julie said with a grin.

Owen looked up at her and croaked weakly, "You know what I meant."

"Now that your vacation's over, we have another mission."

"A *mission?*" Owen whimpered. "No, I think I'm broken. I need Gretchen."

Julie rolled her eyes as smoke from the burning cabin wreathed her head. "I swear you are such a lightweight. It was just a werewolf and a minotaur…"

"And an orc and a very angry gnome," Owen added. Then their eyes met and she grinned. She was totally fucking with him.

"Let's get out of here before the place burns down around our ears." She leaned down and pulled his good arm over her shoulder. "Lean into me as you stand, okay?"

Trip Jones and Holly Newcastle appeared and grabbed Owen

from her, Trip draping Owen's arm over his shoulder and leaning into him as the two women wrapped arms around his waist
and shoulders. They all helped him toward the helicopter where
Skippy was waiting. Seeing another orc face sent shivers through
Owen. Thank God this one was his friend.

"Don't worry," Julie whispered, as they helped him tenderly
onto the helicopter and every cell in Owen's broken body still
cried out. "Skippy, take us to Gretchen," she called.

Skippy nodded and grinned. "Gretchen, yes."

The helicopter vibrated and lifted up as Owen watched the
burning cabin recede into the distance. Owen realized he'd forgotten his things, then he turned his head and saw Abomination
cradled in Holly's hands. He sighed. Well, that was what was
important. He hoped someone would come to put the fire out
before it set the woods ablaze.

And then his eyes began fading, his vision hazy, as Julie
cradled his head in her lap and Owen drifted off into the nether
of sleep. Just another day at MHI.

Julie Shackleford practically runs MHI now, so it is hard to imagine that she was once an inexperienced kid. She's currently compiling a more in-depth report which will be titled *Monster Hunter Guardian*, chronicling her experiences and a few recent events.　　—A.L.

Hunter Born

Sarah A. Hoyt

Some families volunteer at soup kitchens. Some families do arts and crafts together. My family kills monsters.

"Mooooooom," I said, and despised the sound of my own voice, all whiney and annoying, like the way other kids talk to their parents. I tried very hard not to do that because my parents were both too awesome for sass. I'd seen them kill horrible things to save the world since I was about five.

But at sixteen, this was the first time I was going on a date to a school dance, and Mom was driving me insane.

My name is Julie Shackleford and my parents are Monster Hunters. The government... or sometimes other people... pay a bounty for every monster caught, and that's the family business, started by my great-great-grandfather, and still carried on by my family today. I started by helping out with spotting and stuff before I was in school.

In first grade, when I had to do an essay about what we did on the weekend, I wrote about the family hunting vampires. The teacher called my mom and told her not to let me watch horror movies. Mom had told me not to talk about our business in school, but sometimes things slipped out.

I love my family and I love the business. It's not just a way of making a living, but we're doing good, too. Only sometimes I really wish I could be a normal girl. Like right then. Kyle

Armistead had invited me to the senior prom, and all the girls in tenth grade were really jealous of me for the first time ever.

For one night, for just one night, I wanted to be the sixteen-year-old who got to go out with the kicker for the football team, okay? That's all I wanted. Dance a little, maybe a kiss.

Which is probably why I was whining like a regular sixteen-year-old while Mom, who is really pretty and used to be a beauty queen, adjusted my dress. The dress had been a fight too, because I wanted this simple black dress that made me look grown-up but Mom said it wasn't right for someone my age, so I had this white eyelet lace thing. Very pretty, but it didn't feel like me.

"Now remember," Mom said, "no drinking, and your dad has told Kyle he wants you home by eleven, tops. And why aren't you wearing your glasses?"

I lifted my little purse, which was more like a purselet and made me nervous because I never carried anything but my school backpack and I lost that often enough. "They're in here," I said. "I can see enough to eat and dance without them, Mom."

Mom started to open her mouth, then snapped it shut. Probably going to tell me I couldn't shoot without them. She didn't ask if I was armed, either.

The school had gotten all funny about weapons on school grounds. One of my friends had gotten in trouble because she had a knife and was stupid enough to let someone see it.

I had a knife, too. Two, actually, concealed. And I had a Semmerling LM4 in the purselet, which probably made the purselet a fairly good flail, since the thing weighed a pound and a quarter.

The Semmerling wasn't my weapon of choice, but it was small. My brother Ray is a massive fan of F. Paul Wilson's Repairman Jack books, and had gotten Dad to give him the pistol just to be like the guy in the books. He left it behind in his desk drawer, because Dad had told him he could only have it if he promised not to try to use it to Monster Hunt. Though it was a five-shot .45 ACP, and no peashooter, it required you to work the action manually between shots. So it was great for one shot, but cumbersome after that, particularly in a rapid-fire situation. Ray had plenty of other weapons he could use. So I grabbed the Semmerling from his room with no problems.

As to why I wanted the Semmerling...well, my imaginary

friend had appeared in my dreams and told me I was running into danger.

Other kids have cool imaginary friends—kids, actors, cartoon characters—and in the case of my younger brother, an imaginary llama whom he took everywhere and fed imaginary oats.

My imaginary friend when I was four was called Mr. Trash Bags. He was a big blob, with a lot of eyes, and a bit dumb. I mean, I offered him my stuffed bunny, so he called *me* Cuddle Bunny. There were mice and small rocks who were brighter than Mr. Trash Bags.

But I was kind of a lonely kid, and he was very real to me. He was kind and sweet and we used to play hide and seek and catch and stuff. I'd been devastated when he disappeared, which was also weird, since I don't think imaginary friends are supposed to move away. I guess I was a weird kid.

But what was really weird was that he had showed up in my dream the night before I was supposed to go to the prom with Kyle, and he'd said, "CUDDLE BUNNY, beware. What seems isn't. Beware. PLEASURE EATER DANGEROUS BEWARE."

Now, I know it seems stupid that I should pay attention to the warnings of something that didn't even exist outside my imagination, but I'd woken up with a bad feeling and I'd decided I needed a gun in addition to my knives. No, I'm not sure what I expected, but it wouldn't be the first time that a high school prom got attacked. Monsters don't mind at all being clichéd and they don't watch slasher movies. Well, most of them don't. So they'll do the same hokey things you've seen in movies forever.

Kyle knocked at the door a couple of minutes after Mom had stopped fussing with my dress and my hair.

He was not one of the best-looking guys in the school. What I mean is, there were guys who were bigger, more broad-shouldered, definitely more handsome than Kyle, but he had something. He was tall, but not the tallest in the class, dark-haired with a handsome face, dark eyes, and a way of smiling that made all the girls melt. You could look at him and say he was nothing special, but once you put it all together, he was more than the sum of his looks.

When he came in, in his dark tux, and bowed over Mom's

hand, murmuring, "Mrs. Shackleford," even Mom seemed to be affected. At least I'd never heard her giggle like that before. She watched as he bowed to me and said, "Julie," before kissing the back of my hand. I swear an electrical tingle ran all the way up to my shoulder.

"If you permit me," he said. He brought out a little box, all tied with silver ribbon, and opened it, to show me a white rose-and-pearls corsage, which he helped put over my wrist. It felt very warm there, as if it were a living thing.

Kyle led me down the steps, with my hand resting on his arm and feeling all grown up, opened the door for me, and helped me into my seat.

The car was a convertible—I didn't recognize the make—white and sleek, with white leather seats, walnut dashboard, and way more lights and blinking things than I'd ever seen in a car, even in the vehicles we used on monster hunts.

He smiled as he got behind the wheel. "Do you like it?" he asked.

I have no idea what I answered. Since I'd put that corsage on my wrist and walked out of the house on his arm, I felt as though I were in a dream, or as if I were a little drunk. Not that I had any idea what getting drunk felt like, but I'd heard a girl at school talk about getting tipsy on champagne and how it felt like a lot of little bubbles rising up inside you, making you happy. That's what I felt like. Like there were little bubbles of happiness and joy bursting all around me, and like I was so lucky to be out with Kyle. After all, he could have picked any other girl. There were tons of seniors who'd be delighted to go out with him, yet here he was, taking little sophomore me.

Whatever I said made him smile. "It's my dad's car," he said. "But he let me borrow it because I told him I'd invited a special girl to the prom."

I couldn't believe he'd said that and, for that matter, couldn't believe I was out with a boy old enough to drive at night on his own. Last thing like a date I'd gone on was back in ninth grade, and my mom had driven me and Bobby Jones down to the ice cream store for waffle cones. Sure, very exciting for a ninth grader, but not a real date, like this was.

We drove down the tree-lined roads, and after a while I realized something was wrong. "Aren't we supposed to go to the school?" I said.

He gave me a little sideways glance and smiled. "Oh, I'm sorry. I should have asked. If you don't mind, I'd like to drive you by my place and introduce you to my parents? It's just a few minutes away."

I felt myself frown before I realized I was doing it. After all, he was right. I knew he lived in a nearby development north of Cazador because last year we'd come home on the same bus and got out there. Which meant he couldn't take me more than a few minutes out of my way. Half an hour, tops. But something bothered me. I said slowly, trying to reason through my feelings, "Well, you're right, you should have asked."

He smiled more. "Yeah. I'm sorry. I really should have." He reached over and just touched the petals on the corsage. "Sorry."

Golden bubbles of happiness exploded in me and around me. After all, I was making a big fuss out of nothing. So he hadn't asked. But that he wanted to show me to his family was good, right? I mean, not that I was serious, as in wanting to date, much less marry. For one, I was way too young; for another, when I met someone I thought I wanted to marry, it better be someone who would get along with and work with my family.

But if Kyle liked me, that would mean that all the normal kids at school, the average kids who'd never beheaded a vampire on the weekend, would like me. Or at least they'd be envious of me. I might still be the weird and spooky girl, but if Kyle liked me, that would mean I was the *cool* weird and spooky girl. And he wouldn't take me home to introduce me to his parents if he didn't like me, right?

I nodded and smiled.

For a moment, for just a moment, it seemed to me I heard Mr. Trash Bags' voice, *"NO, CUDDLE BUNNY."*

I mean, I didn't see him or hear him as such. I wasn't given to seeing what wasn't there. Things that were there were often bad enough, but I kind of felt like I remembered seeing him and hearing him, which was weird and sort of put a dent on the warm glow of happiness. I wondered why I was thinking of Mr. Trash Bags all of a sudden.

I suspected my teachers would say that it was all about leaving childhood behind and being a young woman, but I didn't think so. I mean, adults make up all sorts of stuff to explain things, but I thought that, yeah, I knew adult life could be difficult and dangerous, and that I was a little nervous about it. But I wasn't that nervous about the date with Kyle. Excited, sure. Nervous, no.

Or at least I hadn't been before the dream last night.

"Can't I wait in the car," I asked, "and have them come out to meet me?" I knew it sounded terribly rude, but for some reason, I really didn't want to get out of the car. The Armistead house was big and white, a pretend antebellum mansion that looked like it had come from a movie set.

Kyle had pulled into the circular driveway, shaded by trees, and we were now parked in the part of the driveway directly facing the house. I could hear the sound of music from inside, and laughter and—I swear, even though it was kind of far away—the clink of glasses.

Kyle leaned over a little. "Oh, come on," he said. "They'll want to take pictures of us together and all. It's much easier if you come inside." And then he leaned over and kissed me, just a soft touch of lips to my cheek.

Then he walked around the car and gave me his arm.

And all the while I was caught in this strange cycle. The kiss had sent more golden bubbles of happiness through me but then there was, not seeing or hearing Mr. Trash Bags, but remembering seeing and hearing Mr. Trash Bags. And my memory of the voice I hadn't heard was *"PLEASURE EATER!!!! CUDDLE BUNNY DON'T GO!"* at an almost hysterical pitch, while the Mr. Trash Bags I hadn't seen was trying to keep me in the car.

It made no sense, and again, what could I say? *My dumb imaginary friend that disappeared years ago is warning me against you?* The year before, my family had had to fight someone who thought they had a guardian angel. It wasn't really an angel... and it had ended badly. But at least what they'd seen was this big creature with white wings. What kind of guardian angel looked like a bunch of stuffed trash bags, with a lot of creepy eyes? What sense did that even make?

So I let Kyle lead me by the arm, out of the car and along this little path to his front door. The path, between the driveway and the door, was flanked with all these little trees supported by metal stakes. I thought they must have been planted recently, and the stakes were to steady them until they rooted properly. It seemed weird to plant that many trees that close to the house, but who was I to say.

At the door, Kyle took his arm from mine, and opened it. I expected him to push it open and then to hold my arm again and lead me in. But instead, he pushed it open and stood aside a little.

Inside, the house looked much better done than ours, the floors gleaming, the furniture antiques. Facing the door, on the wall inside, was this big, polished mirror with a golden frame, like something out of a palace.

And on the mirror, for just a moment, I saw Mr. Trash Bags shaking his head, that is to say, the lump with the most eyes and mouths on it, and saying *"NO. CUDDLE BUNNY. No go in. PLEASURE EATER. BAD."*

I froze... and now all I could see in the mirror was my own reflection and the reflection of the door. Something felt wrong.

"Please do go in," Kyle said.

And then I realized it. Though he'd stepped slightly to the side, he should still be visible in the mirror. But he wasn't. All I could see in the mirror was my own reflection, in my little white dress, with the purselet at my shoulder, and the corsage on my arm.

And I swear the sounds of a party were all from inside the mirror. The rest of the house was deadly silent, which I supposed explained why his family hadn't come out to meet us.

The corsage was radiating this bubbly warmth, and I wanted to feel the golden bubbles of happiness, but I couldn't stop thinking.

I'd done enough fighting to know what they said about vampires was true. You couldn't see them in the mirror. But there was more to it. Mirrors are weird things. All sorts of creatures don't show up in mirrors. And mirrors often serve as portals to other places... or ways of seeing into other places and times. If Kyle and his family were vampires, why would they have a mirror on their front hall?

I took a step back, then another. "No," I said. "I don't think so. I've changed my mind. I don't want to go in."

He smiled, and for sure it must just be my lack of glasses because his smile looked weird and... pointy. It wasn't like a boy smiling at a girl. It was like a boy smiling at a steak. I took three steps back, very fast. His expression changed. "In," he said. "You'll go in. They're all waiting. You have to go in."

He came down the path toward me. He moved very fast. I

reached for one of my thigh sheaths, pulled out a knife. "Don't come any nearer," I said. Which was stupid. And not. You can't really kill a vampire with a knife, but you can delay him long enough so you can cut his head off...maybe. Only I wasn't sure he was a vampire. Vampires had to be invited over the threshold. They didn't invite you over the threshold. And if his family were vampires, why weren't they coming out after me?

He reached for me. I slashed at him with the knife, but I wasn't willing to let him get close enough to me, or to get close enough to him, for the knife to be effective. If he got close and I didn't kill him with the knife, I'd be done. So I shoved the knife into the little eyelet belt on my dress, which was totally not ideal, and turned and ran. He ran after me, down the curving driveway. I heard a sound of wings...and turned. It looked like Kyle had wings. Big brown bat wings that had somehow ripped through his tux, over the shoulders. He grinned at me. All his attractiveness had turned into this concentrated hunger, and he was salivating like a dog. The effect was *yuck.*

I got into the purselet and got the gun. "Don't come closer or I'll shoot." Look, it was a sure thing he wasn't a vampire. Vampires don't act like that. I was sure if I checked the archives at Monster Hunter International, they could tell me exactly what kind of a creature this was, but what I really wanted to know was how to kill it. While there are many ways to kill many different monsters, a .45 might not do it, though it would put a dent in this one's attitude.

At least I was encouraged by the fact that he hesitated for a moment before saying, "Pretty Julie, good Julie, put down the gun."

Bubbles of warm happiness shot through me, and my fingers tried to open to release the gun, but I clamped my other hand on it and said, "No."

I took aim and shot. The shot went wide. I could see the leaves of the tree it went through. I worked the action, wishing I'd gotten something better than a stupid Semmerling, and shot again.

He looked confused. His mind control would have worked if, all the time, in the back of my mind, I hadn't had an image of Mr. Trash Bags going wild and telling me to be careful. "Ah, well," Kyle said and somehow his smile managed to be both attractive and repulsive at once. I could see in it the echo of my classmate's smile, but he seemed to have too many teeth and there was all that saliva, and then I realized his eyes had no white, but were yellow, and there was a vertical pupil. I was sure his eyes had been normal and dark before. He reached out and his hand made contact with the corsage.

Without dropping the gun, I realized there was something to the corsage. It was making me stupid and bubbly. I didn't need bubbly. I didn't know what Kyle was, but I didn't think golden bubbles of champagne happiness were the right reaction to something with bat wings. Even if that was just my stupid eyes acting up.

With one hand I tore at the corsage. I think I expected it to resist me, but it didn't. It was more like when I grabbed at it to pull it off, I felt like I was a terrible person and hurting someone or something. I didn't care. I tore it off, threw it at Kyle or at whatever Kyle really was, and he dodged it. And then I realized he had talons, and he was stretching a long-clawed hand for me. "Come on, my dear," he said. "I'll carry you inside."

While he was dodging it, I jumped further away, reached into my purselet and got my glasses. I hate it when Mom is right.

With my glasses on I looked up and almost dropped the gun. Kyle was a monstrosity with snake eyes, this long sinuous body, a tail that ended in a pointy thing, and wings... and were those horns?

He spoke through too large teeth, in this wet slurpy voice, as drool dripped down his chin, "You'll love what I'll do to you."

That was when I shot him. This time with glasses. And I knew I aimed right. The shot went into him like nothing. The bullet didn't even slow down. I heard it hit a window; at least, I heard glass break and shatter. I hoped whoever was in the house or in the mirror wasn't coming out.

I worked the slide again, shot again, and then repeated. He drooled and slurped and went into full raving demon mode—what was with demons and bragging about how long they'd been alive and how many people they'd killed?—and I was out of ammo. I backed away, and he pushed toward me. I didn't know why he wasn't jumping me, but it looked like he was trying to do something—perhaps command me mentally?—and I simply wasn't obeying. His face looked like he was both concentrating and very puzzled. In my mind, Mr. Trash Bags jumped up down screaming "BAD PLEASURE EATER WANTS TO EAT CUDDLE BUNNY. NO BAD. CUDDLE BUNNY, SHE'S MADE OF STARS."

I was sweating, but I felt really cold. I didn't know exactly where I was, but I knew these houses had huge lots. My only hope was to make it to the closest house. I wasn't prepared to fight a creature like this on my own. Dad would know what to do. If I got Dad, he'd kill Kyle's ass, and his family's too.

"Come on, Julie," he said. He was making his voice all seductive and stuff. "Sweet, sweet Julie."

I thought I could glimpse lights of the next house, behind and kind of to the left of the Armistead place. If I just ran forward, toward the house, but not toward the door, it would surprise Kyle enough that he wouldn't take off after me immediately. And once I was in the middle of those newly planted trees, I could dodge to the right, hit the lawn area, and keep running till I got to the neighbor's house.

It was worth a try, though I had a feeling I had a snowball's chance in hell.

But I ran for the track team, and frankly, running is one of those things my family approved of. Sure, we hunted monsters, but sometimes the monsters turned the tables and sometimes what saves you is being able to run really fast. One of the first things my family had taught me was that there was no shame in running away, because if you were dead, you couldn't fight the monster.

I threw my knife at him, not expecting it to do anything, and even though I turned right away, I could verify that, yep, like the bullets, it just went through him. Right through his heart. He laughed. He clearly had been watching slasher movies. It was that sort of laugh.

I heard it behind me as I ran. I made it to the newly planted trees. Then I heard the sound of leathery wings and Kyle was there, landing between the trees, just a foot from me, "Come on, Julie, you can't resist my seductive charms. You're just a little mortal girl. What do you know against someone with centuries of experience? Come on, surrender. I won't hurt you. And you'll like it. Ah, your high schools are such fertile hunting grounds for someone with my experience."

That was when I tried to back up and tripped. I fell next to one of the newly planted trees, and Kyle grinned. He reached over and touched just my ankle, making crazy bubbles of golden happiness burst all through me. Seduction. I remembered there was some demon or other—incubus—whose main power was to seduce you . . . before eating your willpower and life force.

I read a lot of mythology—one of the things my classmates thought was weird, but it was a tool of the trade.

He was running his hands lightly along my ankle, "Come on, Julie. Give in."

And even though he had leathery wings and snake eyes, I wanted to obey. Only Mr. Trash Bags was still screaming in my head, and my hand found a metal stake nearby, cool, hard, and sharp. I yanked on it and it came up easily. Really easily. I kicked up and away with my foot. Kyle staggered back. For a moment my mind was clear.

Perhaps what I'd been doing wrong was not the weapons I was using but where I was stabbing whatever it was that Kyle was just didn't work. Nor did the bullets. And I'd been aiming for the heart.

You stabbed vampires through the heart. There was a reason for this, since the heart was the connecting center that processed the blood they lived on. For an incubus . . . incubi lived on sex, sexual attraction, sexual seduction, and everything related to sex.

It took me maybe a second to think through this. I brought the spike up and aimed at his groin. There was . . . it looked like there was a skeleton hand grasping the stake, the part that had been in the ground. I didn't know whose it was and I didn't care. I shook the bones off. "I need this more than you do," I said as I aimed the spike at the center of what would be an incubus' glamour, right between the legs. This is when Kyle decided to jump on top of me, aided by his little bat wings. I guess if he'd got on top of me, I was cooked.

As it was, I had to reaim and thrust. And then as he fell, gravity did the work and pushed the stake all the way in.

There was a scream, and black blood poured out, and he was on top of me, covering me. He felt cold and limp. It was sort of like being covered in stinking garbage. He did stink, too, like he'd rotted instantly. I crawled from beneath him, gagging and trying not to throw up.

Behind me, the house exploded in screams, too. I ran for the neighbors. I had to call my parents. I just had to.

"I think he was trying to kidnap you," my mother said, as I sat sipping hot chocolate, after a bath had gotten me rid of all the demon blood. I could still smell a little demon stink, and Mom said the dress was done for and had put it in the trash. "To use you as a pawn against us. You know, leave me and my family alone or your daughter gets it."

"But why would he need a pawn?" I asked.

"Because he and his family fed on the life force of young girls. Virgins. You know, the demon thing. So far, they'd been hunting them in the city and bringing them here. All those trees had bodies buried under them. I suppose they thought sooner or later we'd find out and do something about it. They wanted to have a hostage, so they could continue doing it."

"It doesn't explain everything," I said. It particularly didn't explain Mr. Trash Bags' warnings, after all this time. Not that I'd told Mom about them, because one thing was the supernatural and the other just a dumb nonexistent imaginary friend. I still wondered how he knew.

"No," my mother said. "We might never know why they chose here and now to manifest. And, frankly, why a centuries-old creature would want to attend high school and stalk young girls is not clear. Seems incredibly stupid, even if they feed on virgins. As I said, we might never know. Or we might find out. Sometimes I hate when we find out."

I did, too. But for a moment, for just a moment, I thought that while the evening hadn't turned out as I hoped, it had in a way been exciting. Very exciting.

I hadn't managed to have a normal date, but I'd managed to bag my own monster, and Dad thought there would be a nice bounty on it, given the damage the incubus had done.

Okay, so kissing—I thought of what Kyle had really looked like and gagged—was out, as was dancing. But maybe someday I would find a nice boy who would like to kill monsters alongside my family.

Until then, I could do without the normal. I was a Monster Hunter . . . born to the trade . . . and I belonged.

I'm not ashamed to admit Special Agent Franks scares the hell out of me.

—A.L.

Hitler's Dog

Jonathan Maberry

– 1 –

Drancy Internment Camp
Northeastern France
October 31, 1941

Noah Karoutchi knew that he was walking to his death. No one who had been taken to the commandant's office had ever come back. Karoutchi had seen other inmates loading bodies onto the back of a flatbed truck and two of those corpses had been in the same bunkhouse with him. Both had been summoned to the office. The math was simple.

It was also there to be read on the faces of the soldiers at the front door and stationed outside of the commandant's office. Their eyes were dead and promised as much; their mouths wore cruel little smiles. If sympathy had ever lived in such men, it had been hunted down and killed, leaving only husks that moved and spoke and pretended to be human, but which were not. Maybe it was true that everyone in Drancy was already dead in one way or another. The guards and their officers were dead in their souls; the inmates walked and worked, toiled and suffered in a plant that was no doubt their tomb. Death had come to France beneath the crooked black cross of the Nazi machine and it was killing everything.

It was killing the Jews most of all.

Karoutchi knew it and when his family had been rounded up on August 20 of that year, he could feel some of his own life force

285

wither, crack off, and fall dead to the ground. When they separated him from his two daughters, his son-in-law, and the little one, Jacob, not even a year old ... more of Karoutchi had perished.

Now he was going to see the Angel of Death himself, the camp commandant, SS *Hauptsturmführer* Theodor Dannecker, the very man who had organized the roundups of French Jews.

Karoutchi was flanked by another pair of smirking soldiers, and they handled him roughly, shoving him where they wanted him to go, slapping him for not knowing the way, making obscene comments about Jews in general and Karoutchi's daughters in particular. Karoutchi tried to block out their words, tried not to believe the appalling things they said about what had been happening to his girls since they came to the camp. He tried, but hope was as dead here as life itself here in what was surely *Sheol*—hell, or something as close to it as anyone could possibly imagine.

"Stop here," snapped one of the guards and emphasized the command with a hard elbow in Karoutchi's chest. It staggered him and Karoutchi the scientist nearly fell. His body was wasted and weak from small rations and endless hard labor; however, the second guard caught his arm and steadied him roughly.

They stood before the closed door of Dannecker's office, under the eyes of the soldiers posted there.

"Wait," said one of the sentries, directing that single word to the two escorting soldiers. Then the door opened and an old man dressed in a heavy tweed suit beckoned them in.

"No," said the old man, "the Jew only. The rest of you wait out here."

The soldiers hesitated and then nodded. They shoved Karoutchi forward but not before one of them leaned close and whispered in his ear. "Behave yourself or I will feed your grandson to the pigs."

Karoutchi nearly cried out but the soldiers thrust him into the room. The man in tweed stepped aside to allow the prisoner to enter and then closed the door.

The office was elegant, dark, paneled in hardwood and hung with expensive paintings that Karoutchi was sure belonged to museums or private collections before the fall of Paris. There were two men in the room. One was Dannecker, who sat scowling behind a massive desk. The other was the old bearded man who had opened the door. He was extravagantly bearded, wore wire-framed spectacles, and looked amused. Intelligence sparkled in his eyes.

"Sit down," said the man, indicating a chair that had been placed before the commandant's desk.

Karoutchi did not move, fearing a trick or trap, but the bearded man insisted and pushed him gently toward the chair. The prisoner lowered himself carefully and perched on the edge. The man in tweed sat on the edge of the commandant's desk.

"Your name is Karoutchi?" asked the bearded man.

"Yes, sir."

"That is not a French name. Or a Jewish one."

"I was born in Morocco."

"But you *are* a Jew, yes?"

Karoutchi cleared his throat and mumbled that he was.

"You are also a scientist?" asked the man. "A specialist in bacteria and related fields of research."

"I was," said Karoutchi. "I am unable to continue my work."

He tried very hard not to make his words sound as caustic as he wanted. It would surely earn him a beating.

"Do you know who I am?" asked the bearded man.

Karoutchi shook his head.

"Speak up."

"No ... I mean, no, sir. I have never met you before."

"Perhaps you have read one of my papers," said the man. "I co-authored it with my colleague Rudolf Otto Neumann. The *Atlas und Grundriss der Bakteriologie und Lehrbuch der Speziellen Bakteriologischen Diagnostik?* Ah, I see you have heard of it, as I thought you might. You are also a noted bacteriologist, Herr Karoutchi. I have read all of your papers, including the unpublished one you were writing at the time of your arrest."

"I ... I don't understand," said Karoutchi. "The *Atlas* was written by Neumann and Lehmann, and Dr. Lehmann is dead. He died in January of last year."

The bearded man smiled and spread his hands. "Do I look dead?"

"But ... I ..."

Lehmann chuckled. "I have allowed my public persona to perish," he said, "for the sake of convenience, expedience, and security."

Karoutchi said nothing.

"Because we are colleagues, Herr Doktor Karoutchi, I will be frank with you," said Lehmann. "You know that the world is changing. Even a Jew who has no history of political involvement must have read the writing on the wall. The Third Reich has risen and we are in the process of creating a new world order. A better one. A cleaner one."

Karoutchi said nothing.

"You have probably heard the rumors of what happens to those elements of society that have been deemed antithetical to this world order. Gypsies, homosexuals, Jews... Have you heard those rumors, Herr Doktor? Have you heard the talk about extermination camps? About firing squads and gas chambers and incinerators?"

A tear broke from the corner of Karoutchi's eye and rolled down his dirty cheek.

"Yes," said Lehmann, "I see that you have. Well, let me tell you, my friend, the rumors, as ghastly at they are, speak only a fragment of the truth."

Karoutchi stiffened and stared at the bearded scientist in abject horror.

"We hold this world in our hand," said Lehmann, "and we will shape it like clay. We will mold it into something new and wonderful. And in that new world there will be no place for the impure."

"God..." the word escaped Karoutchi's lips before he could stop it.

"God is on *our* side," said Lehmann. "Read your own Torah for proof. He is a vicious, murderous, unstoppable killer and everything God does is to remove the stains from the fabric of the world. Or... that is the propaganda shouted by my friends in the party. Purification is the rallying cry." Lehmann turned and spat onto the bearskin rug. Dannecker began to rise, opened his mouth to cry out in protest, but he stopped himself. Instead, the commandant cut a wary, frightened look at the old scientist and sat back down. Lehmann slowly wiped his mouth with the pads of his thumb and forefinger. "I am not a political person, Herr Doktor. Like you, I am a scientist. Like you, I have family about whom I care deeply. Like you, I have knowledge and skills that make me—my life—more useful to the Reich than my death would ever be. I even *gave* them my death because it was more important for me to continue to be alive, even if in secret. Do you understand?"

Karoutchi stared, unable to speak.

"Then let me explain," said Lehmann. "Having read your papers I know that you are a very talented scientist. Ahead of your time in many ways. Your research into galvanic regeneration of tissues in order to reverse necrosis is astounding work. Had this inconvenient war not interrupted you, I have no doubt that you would have gone on to become one of history's greatest biologists, on a par with Pasteur, Mendel, Jenner, and, of course, Antoine van Leeuwenhoek. I, too, have had some successes, though sadly most of my greatest work cannot and will never be published. That is a side effect of my involvement in a very secret cabal of top researchers. We are making history every day, Herr Doktor. Every single day."

"I don't understand."

"No, of course not," said Lehmann, "but you will. I had you brought here today because I am going to offer you something that no one else alive in this world can offer. I will offer you your life. And I will offer the lives of your daughters and your grandson. Your son-in-law, alas, is not part of that bargain. He has already gone off to one of the other camps and by now is compost in a field."

Karoutchi flinched and gagged.

"You can still save the rest of your family, my friend," said Lehmann. "All you need to do is answer three questions. You must answer them truthfully and you must answer them completely. And, you must answer them now."

Karoutchi blinked tears from his eyes and in that moment he knew that there was nothing—absolutely nothing—that he would not do to save his children. Nothing.

"Ask your questions," he said, his voice hoarse and unrecognizable.

Lehmann smiled like a happy child and turned to the commandant. "You see? I told you that he would cooperate without you indulging yourself in anything gaudy or messy. Subtlety has not become extinct."

Dannecker scowled. "If you are satisfied with his answers, then by all means take him and go. His sluts of daughters, too. I'll be happy to be rid of their stink."

Lehmann turned back to Karoutchi. "Ignore him, my friend. He is a barbarian. We are scientists and therefore more evolved."

"What are your questions?" croaked Karoutchi. "What do you need to know so I can keep my family safe?"

The old man leaned closer and smiled. "There are three things I need to know. Answer them in any order, yes?"

Karoutchi nodded.

"First, have you ever heard of the *Thule-Gesellschaft*?" asked the old scientist, "Second, have you ever heard of *La Bèstia de Gavaudan*? And third—and this is most important of all—to what lengths would you be willing to go to save your daughters and grandson?"

– 2 –

Les Égouts de Paris
(The Sewers of Paris)
August 20, 1943

Franks looked up and saw three of them on the stone walkway. Big men, if they were men at all. They carried no rifles—only fools fired guns in the methane-rich sewers—but they had Mauser K98 bayonets in their gloved hands.

"There it is," said the tallest of the three.

It, not he. It was supposed to be an insult.

Franks was quietly amused. He had an M1918 trench knife that had brass knuckles fitted to the handle. It was a piece-of-shit knife, with a blade that would probably snap if he did anything more than stab, but the knuckle-dusters were fun. He liked those, even if his thick fingers barely fit through the holes. Franks showed the knife. Not as a threat, more as a half salute and half promise. With his other hand, he gave them a small come-on flip of his fingers.

They came.

The broadest of the three had shoulders like a gorilla and a face like a gargoyle, and he growled like a mastiff as he leapt down into the water to try and take Franks through sheer force. The third man, thinner and wiry, jumped after, dodging to one side, using his companion's bulk as a shield for a low, vicious attack to Franks' groin.

That was the plan, and they moved with the oiled ease and confidence of a pair of killers long practiced in the maneuver. Most opponents would try to back away or—if they had more balls than brains—would cut right and attempt to engage the smaller man. But the wiry Nazi was the better fighter of the two, and Franks knew it.

So he went right at the gargoyle-faced German, slapping the stabbing arm aside with such force that it pivoted the man in mid-air, turning him sharply toward his companion and blocking the sneak attack. Franks simultaneously slammed the brass knuckles into the big man's face, crunching bone, putting all of his own considerable mass into the savage blow. The impetus of the killer's leap and the raw power of Franks' punch was sharply concentrated into the unbreakable rings of the knuckle-duster and shattered more than teeth. The big man's head snapped backward and there was a huge, wet *crack* as his vertebrae blew apart inside his hairy hide.

Franks shoved the dying man hard against the slender fighter, using the mass to drive the wiry man into the water. Then Franks darted out a foot and caught the third attacker in the meat of the front of his thigh as he tried to use the confusion of the fight to conceal a blindside attack. That kick had the same effect as if the third killer had walked into a closed garden gate. His lower half jolted to a stop and the bulk of his upper body bent abruptly forward. Franks grabbed the man by the ears and jerked his hands back and down with such sudden, tearing force that both ears ripped loose in a spray of blood. Franks grinned and flung the ears in the man's pain-twisted face and followed up with a punch to the Adam's apple with his other hand. Franks had his body set against the slimy concrete beneath the foul water and he pivoted with knees and hips, waist and shoulders, creating so much torque that he crushed the hyoid bone and the trachea, and pulped muscles and meat all the way to the knobbed bones at the back of the neck. The killer reeled back, fingers tearing at his throat as he tried to drag in a thimbleful of air through crushed junk. His eyes bulged and his face went red and then purple and black. Franks could have finished him off, carved off a sliver of mercy. But . . . fuck it. Instead he turned to the other men, drew his knife, and made damn sure they were as dead as their leader.

Silence reclaimed the tunnel except for the soft lap of sewer water against the walls, a persistent slow, heavy drip somewhere out of sight.

Franks sneered at the corpses as he cleaned the blade and knuckles of his knife, slid it into its sheath, unzipped, and took a long piss on the corpses.

Then suddenly Franks was falling.

Falling.

Falling . . .

The sewer seemed to reel and spin around him and the foul water rushed up to smash him in the face.

The world—his world—went black.

Absolutely black.

And into that black, Franks fell and fell and fell.

- 3 -

Margeride Mountains of Lozère
Massif Central, France
April 20, 1943

"Did it work?"

Noah Karoutchi stood looking down at the little rabbi. He had remained silent for hours while the rabbi worked, watching as the man dug in the dirt, scooping it up from the floor of the shed, shaping it, patting it firm, muttering prayers throughout. The others in the shed—all of them thin, all of them looking like the pale ghosts of the men they had been—watched with him. Except for the prayer and the sound of wet hands on mud, there had been no sound at all. Outside, the rain fell as heavily as before but the thunder was fading as if the giants of the weather were giving up and walking away into the night.

The rabbi did not answer. Not at first. He kept working, kept praying.

Karoutchi licked his dry lips and felt his heart hammer in his chest. His head ached from tension. From dread. From the certain knowledge of what would happen to him, to all of them, if the soldiers discovered that they were no longer in their bunks. It would not take them long to discover the tunnel beneath the privy, or to follow it the thirty yards to this disused shed. Discovery was inevitable. The other scientists who had made similar tunnels had each been discovered. The bodies of their families still hung from the walls, and the heads of the scientists were slowly rotting away at the head of the mess hall tables: a grim and terrible warning.

The threat, though, had not worked as the Nazis had intended. Instead of cowing the prisoners, it made them more ferocious, more determined to escape. More inventive. More daring.

Daring in so many ways.

The tunnel had been Kinski's idea, and the Polish anatomist had begun digging before their small cabal had been fully formed. The others—Brunner, Kaplan, Hagermann, and Shulte—had all contributed ideas and done much of the manual layers, giving up hours of precious sleep to labor in their pit. The shed had been Karoutchi's suggestion. He had planned to use it to store food, extra clothes, and some makeshift weapons the cabal had made when the soldiers thought they were designing scientific instruments.

It was the rabbi—a frail shell of the robust professor of zoology—who suggested an alternative to armed escape.

"We are not strong enough," he told the cabal when they all met in the dark on a winter night late last year. "We are not fighters and we are not enough. The Thule have too many soldiers here, and they have the dogs."

At the use of that word Karoutchi shuddered. They all did. *Dogs* was the closest word that could be used to describe the things that roamed the no-man's-land between the double row of heavy chain-link fence. The guards in the tall watchtowers kept one set of guns trained on the prison yard and another set on those *dogs*.

"We have a bold plan," the rabbi continued, "and we have made such fine weapons. Clubs and crude spears, two small knives. That is what we will use to fight our way past fifty guards and those six creatures we have made for Herr Doktor Lehmann? Do you think that this is how we will save ourselves and our families? Do you think that men such as we, armed with weapons such as that, will triumph over the foot soldiers of the devil and those hellhounds? Are we to believe that we could triumph over that cursed *thing* we have been laboring over these last two years? That abomination? Will we escape *it*? Even if we got past the hounds and the soldiers and made it to the forest, do you believe that we can outrun it and not be hunted down and torn apart by the thing we made? Tell me, my friends, is that what you believe?"

"It is our only hope," said Shulte. "Why else are we digging this godforsaken tunnel?"

Which is when the rabbi smiled. The man was old and sad and nearly broken, but in that moment, in that dark hour in the pit, Karoutchi could see a ghost of the vibrant man again. And perhaps something more. A dangerous man. Not a man to use his fists, or even a scientist wielding knowledge. No, this was another kind of power altogether.

The rabbi had looked at each man in turn, fixing them with

a penetrating stare. "Tell me, my friends, have you ever heard of the legend of the *golem*?"

There had been laughter... at first. Disbelief and mockery... at first.

Now, as April rains fell in endless sheets, the cabal stood together in the shadows of the shed and watched the rabbi fashion a man out of mud and clay and his own bitter tears.

– 4 –

Les Égouts de Paris
(The Sewers of Paris)
August 20, 1943

Franks dreamed of being dead.

He understood death. He had courted the cold witch, had held her close, been her lover and her slave and ultimately her friend. During the long years of his life, he had offered up a lot of souls to the queen of the pit.

Now he slept in her icy white arms and was lost in a dream of his own death. It was not something Franks often fretted over and which he never feared. Mortality sat only lightly on him and was better suited to other kinds of men—to actual men. Franks knew that his inclusion in that brotherhood was tentative and uneasy. He was okay with that. Being regarded as a human being was an occasional convenience but it wasn't something he needed.

He did not want to be dead, though. Not a dead man or a dead thing.

Except that in his dreams his heart did not beat, his chest did not rise and fall with breath, his limbs were heavy and cold and still. He was a corpse.

No.

As his dreaming mind reached out to sense the nature of his body, he realized that this was not death. Not exactly.

He was nothing.

No flesh. No bone.

Nothing.

Except...

He felt something. A touch. Hands on him. On his arms and legs. Palms running over his chest. Fingers pressing at the contours of his face.

And a voice.

Faint. Muttering. No...praying.

Not in French, though. Nor German.

Hebrew?

Yes, thought Franks and he concentrated to be able to understand the words. It was definitely Hebrew, but an older form of it. Ancient. The words ran together like mumbled prayers, but they were not the right prayers. These were not prayers of deliverance from the evils of the world, or for the blessing of a birth, or even for the burial of the dead. No, and although his body was dead, Franks felt a shudder pass through him because the voice spoke a prayer that was long forgotten, long forbidden.

A prayer of consecration and invocation.

The praying voice called to God and begged forgiveness in the same breath. It pleaded for help and apologized for sins.

Another shudder swept through Franks' body, and he realized that he felt it twice...at the same time and yet in two different bodies.

Wait...

Two?

His mind rebelled at that, dismissing it as stupid, impossible, absurd. His body was there in the cold, foul water in the sewers beneath Paris, surrounded by the corpses of the men he had just killed.

So why did he know with absolute clarity that he was also on the floor of a shed in the mountains far from here, surrounded by living men, and touched by one man who knelt and prayed? Franks could not make sense of it.

And yet he was sure he was in both places.

Just as he was sure he was dead in both places. In each reality his body was a lifeless hulk and inhuman mass that had been forged into something approximating man-shape.

The prayers filled his head.

Shudders continued to ripple through him.

Then deep inside his chest, buried down at the core of who—or what—he was, Franks felt something new. A spark. A tiny flash of electrical current.

A heartbeat.

Franks opened his eyes. There was light.

There was light. There were faces—pale, dark-eyed, haunted,

terrified—staring down at him. A circle of emaciated men in dirty, striped, prison clothes. One man—the only one who wore a beard—knelt beside him. He was older than the rest, his face covered with old scars and new bruises. Without knowing how he knew it, Franks was certain this was the man who had been praying.

This was the man who had called him back from the land of the dead.

Franks tried to speak but he had no voice. He raised a hand to grab the man, needing and wanting to shake answers out of him. But the hand that rose into view was not his own. It was not a hand of flesh and blood. It was the same size as his own, the same shape, but it was made of mud.

– 5 –

Margeride Mountains of Lozère
Massif Central, France
April 20, 1943

They huddled together, all of them except the rabbi, pressed back against the far wall of the shed. Their eyes were filled with mad lights, with a terror that stole from them any possibility of coherent speech.

Franks could understand that. He was pretty goddamn spooked himself. Even him. Even after all that he had seen and all that he knew about the world. The shadows and the things that moved in them. The darkness in his own soul. Franks was not a deeply emotional man, not an expressive one, but he was philosophical in his way. The world was bigger, older, darker, and more complicated than most of the people who lived in it knew. It was stranger than the stories told around campfires, and more magical than what was alluded to in old poems.

Case in point.

He sat cross-legged on the floor like some barbarian chieftain, heavy arms resting on knees, chin sunk low as he listened to what the rabbi told him. All of that was true but it was also an illusion of some kind. His own body was floating in a river of shit and piss, probably being nibbled on by rats, hundreds of miles from this chateau in the mountains.

The body he wore now was not his own, but it was familiar.

A golem, a creature made from the dirt, shaped like a man, with life breathed into him with equal measures of reverence, despair, desperation, and hatred. No one—not even the rabbi—offered an apology. The world was burning and "please" and "thank you" carried as little weight as "I'm sorry."

"This is about a fucking dog?" grumbled Franks. His new voice—now that it, like he, had awakened—was a bass rumble. It was frightening. Franks liked it. It was the only thing he liked, but it was something.

"It's not a dog," said the rabbi.

"You just said it was."

The rabbi looked uncertain and turned to one of the silent men. "Karoutchi, you understand it better than I do."

The man named Karoutchi said nothing. Sweat ran down his face in crooked lines and he clearly did not want to say anything. Franks pointed a muddy finger at him.

"You," he growled. "Talk."

Karoutchi shook his head.

"Don't make me ask again," said Franks. "I am not having a good day and you guys are way up on my shit list. Talk while you still have teeth."

"Please, Karoutchi," begged the rabbi. "Tell him."

When the man still hesitated, the rabbi turned back to Franks. "They are terrified."

"No shit. This is what? A Nazi prison camp?"

"Worse," said the rabbi. "This is hell."

"Since when do Jews believe in Hell?"

"Since the Thule Society proved to us that it exists," said Karoutchi, speaking for the first time.

Franks looked at him. "The Thule Society?"

"Y-yes. You have heard of them?"

"Yeah," said Franks. "And *they* have heard of me." He chuckled. It was not a nice sound, even to his own ears. The rabbi and his companions flinched to hear it. Fair enough. Franks raised his hands. "You assholes took a big damn risk to sneak out here and work some magic to try and raise a golem. Well, here's the news, boys—you did. Just not the way you expected. You see, I'm not some earth spirit you conjured. This body is, but not me. What you idiots managed to do was somehow pull my spirit into this mud-man form. I'm not happy about that, and I'd better hear that you can put me back in my own body very damn soon."

"I..." began the rabbi; then he took a breath and tried again. "I do not know how it works. The magic is supposed to last for one night, but what happens then..."

"Shit."

"We *need* your help," said the rabbi.

"To help you escape?"

"No," said Karoutchi, "that isn't why we did this. We did this to save our families. The Thule bastards have them. Everyone we love."

"I don't care," said Franks. "They're no family to me."

"Is mankind family to you?" demanded the rabbi.

"Not all that much, no."

"You live in the world," said Karoutchi bitterly. "You have to at least care about your own life."

"That'll matter if I go back to my own body."

"Maybe you will. Maybe all of this is for nothing," said Karoutchi. "Maybe we have risked the lives of our families as well as our own lives for nothing. Maybe you are nothing more than a monster conjured through black magic, and maybe we're all doomed anyway." He came and knelt beside Franks, his face alight with desperate intensity. "Listen to me...you are not the first monster we have made. And you are not the most terrible."

"The dog, right. You guys keep skating the edge of that but so far you haven't told me shit about it. *What* goddamn dog? You're all some kind of scientists, right? Well, I've known some scientists in my days. Mad as the moon. I know that they can cook up worse things than better bombs and mustard gas bombs. I even heard there's a race on to make some kind of bomb that will blow up a whole city. Imagine that, just one bomb."

"This is worse," said Karoutchi.

"Worse?"

All of the men nodded.

"Much worse," said the rabbi.

Franks grabbed Karoutchi by the throat and pulled him close. "What the fuck did you make?"

He allowed the man just enough air to croak out a few hoarse words.

Karoutchi told him what they'd made.

– 6 –
Château de Brejean
Margeride Mountains of Lozère
Massif Central, France
April 20, 1943

Franks stood in the rain. He had no nerve endings; there was no skin to turn to gooseflesh in the cold downpour. He stared unblinking into the night sky. Being in this form brought back old, old memories. He remembered things he had long wanted to forget. Damn those skinny bastards for doing this to him.

Damn everyone here.

The shed was hard against the edge of the fence, fifty yards from the closest watchtower. Strange dogs walked up and down between the fences, but they did not bark at him or raise a cry of alarm. Why would they? He was made of mud and stone and the roots of trees. He was nothing to them. Not yet.

The guards in the tower swept the spotlight back and forth, and Franks stood silent and still as the light passed over him. They did not see him because he stood close to the shed and he did not look like a man. If it hadn't been raining, maybe they would have spotted him. He doubted they would understand what they saw. Not until it was too late, and even then, maybe not.

The light passed by and Franks began walking through the darkness toward the château. It was a large, sprawling house that had belonged to an aging vintner and his family. The vintner was dead; so were his wife and their sons. The two daughters worked in the house, cleaning it, trying not to be noticed by the monsters in black uniforms. Trying, but seldom succeeding.

The thought of the dog troubled Franks.

Not in terms of his own safety, but in how such a thing could change the course of the war. If the scientists were telling the truth. If they were not exaggerating, or perhaps all driven mad by the horrors of what their lives had become.

The Dog. The hound. The whatever-the-hell-it-was.

Karoutchi and the rabbi had given it a name. *La Bèstia de Gavaudan.*

The Beast of Gévaudan. Franks had heard of it back when he was running with the Hessians. He'd had an arrangement with them that he could kill anything unearthly, but his path never intercepted that creature. As he moved toward the house, he pulled details of the tale from the back closets of his mind. The animal's species was never determined, and theories ranged from an oversized gray wolf to a tiger someone had imported from Siberia. However, because most eyewitness accounts described something houndlike, the members of the Thule Society referred to it as a dog: specifically Hitler's dog—*Der Führer Hund.*

Whatever the thing was, the beast was undeniably bloodthirsty, attacking more than two hundred people and slaughtering one hundred and thirteen and badly injuring forty-nine. These attacks began in the summer of 1764 and lasted. Examination by officials sent by the King of France found ample evidence of savage teeth and claws, and many of the victims had their throats torn out. The beast not only killed and maimed, but the remains showed that it partially devoured them. Some dog, thought Franks. The creature had staked out a hunting ground that stretched fifty by fifty-six miles. The local government and constabulary were unable to stop it and so King Louis XV sent soldiers, nobles who had reputations for trophy hunting, groups of armed civilians, and a number of royal huntsmen. Many of them died, too. The killings went on, despite the slaughter of many large wolves, and then abruptly stopped when a local hunter named Jean Chastel shot a massive wolf on June 19, 1767. Legend held that Chastel brought the creature down with a silver bullet and that when he cut the thing's stomach open, human remains spilled out.

That was the legend. Most such stories are lies stitched together with a slender thread of truth. The full reality was even more disturbing than the legend, though, which was something that was becoming increasingly common. The world was bigger, stranger, less safe and far less sane than he had thought, and that was saying quite a lot considering Franks' own complex and troubled origins. Most days *he* was the worst monster he could think of. Now there was this damn thing.

He flexed his hands, feeling the "bones" made of oak root and stone beneath the muddy skin. Would that be enough to take on a creature like that? It was flesh and bone, sure, but also more than that. It was alive, and that technically meant that it could bleed. Whatever could bleed could die. The math, at least, was in his favor.

Maybe.

Or maybe not. Bare knuckles against something like that? Empty hands against something the scientist slaves of the Thule Society had labored over for two years? Going unarmed against a creature that was designed to slaughter whole platoons of highly trained and well-equipped soldiers at a time?

"Well," he said very quietly to the night, "should be interesting."

He kept walking.

The closer he got to the house, the more lights spilled unhelpful illumination down through the rain. He began moving in a zigzag pattern, dodging light in order to not have to dodge bullets. Not because he thought those rounds would hurt him, but because the noise would do him no good at all.

The last patch of open ground was the U-shaped gravel turn-around in front of the main steps. Two guards walked slowly back and forth, their jackboots crunching on the crushed stone, their slung machine guns barrel down and partly covered by the gleaming rain ponchos they wore. Franks studied the guards' pattern and picked his moment. There was a single point where they crossed each other on each of their forward and backward passes. He waited until the next one and then went for them, crossing fifteen feet of open ground at a dead run, his footfalls partly muffled by rain and by the sounds of the two patrolling guards.

One of them caught sight of him out of the corner of his eye. He gasped, eyes going wide even as he pivoted, began raising the weapon, letting his poncho fall away, mouth opening to shout an alert. All of that happened in half a second.

Which was a quarter of a second too long.

Franks slammed into them, his bulk smashing them backward and down, his massive fists crunching into their faces. Blood and bits of teeth flew into the downpour. Franks heard one neck break. He felt the whole front of the other man's skull collapse inward. The impact of the rush sent them skidding and sliding over the gravel and when they stopped, neither moved. Not so much as a twitch.

Franks stood for a moment, startled at the effect of his punches. In his real body he was powerful enough to kill with a single blow, but he had destroyed these two men. They lay in rag-doll sprawls. Franks considered taking their weapons. The Nazis were assholes but they made excellent firearms. His fingers were much thicker than his true ones and he doubted he could squeeze one through the trigger guard, and that was a goddamn shame. Going in guns blazing might be fun. Unchain some hell on the Thule commanders and their thugs and then go looking for the beast. He looked down at the two clenched fists of this new—hopefully temporary—body. Mud and root, packed dirt and rock. Three jagged pieces of teeth were deeply embedded into his unreal flesh.

Then he bent and pressed both fists into the ground, onto the gravel. He punched the ground once, twice, a third time, driving the sharp stones more deeply into his knuckles with each impact. Then he rose and examined his work. The knuckles and backs of both hands were gloved in fragments of razor-sharp rock.

He nodded slowly.

He turned toward the house.

"Here, doggie-doggie," he murmured.

- 7 -

Château de Brejean
Margeride Mountains of Lozère
Massif Central, France
April 21, 1943

The house bells were striking midnight as Franks entered the big house.

Between the turnaround outside and the entrance foyer, he had encountered five guards. They were stationed well apart so that they could command a useful view of the porch, the entrance, and the hall. Franks respected the threat posed by trained sentries, but he also knew the malaise that often came upon them from boredom. This château was too remote, too well protected, too overstaffed for there to be any credible threat, even with the likelihood of an Allied invasion of France sometime this year. Summer, perhaps, or the fall. It was inevitable but it had not yet happened, and so these guards had allowed themselves to become dulled by the monotony of guarding an installation so remote and secret that no one knew about it.

Franks made them pay for that inattention.

One by one, with fists of stones and crushing hands, he made them pay. He was quick, he was silent, but he was not nice about it. Not one of them got off a shot . . . nor a scream. The storm muffled the sound of smashed skulls and crushed throats. There would be a time for something louder, but not yet.

Franks never lost his smile. His monster face seemed to enjoy that smile, which felt strange because Franks rarely smiled, but now it seemed frozen there. Once he caught sight of himself in a hallway mirror. He was a heap of a thing, with features from a nightmare, eyes that blazed with actual fire, and a jack-o'-lantern grin.

Nice.

So nice.

Karoutchi and the rabbi had drawn a map for him in the dirt floor of the shed and Franks had memorized it before the running rainwater dissolved it. The laboratory was in the basement, which had once been used as a dungeon for prisoners during the Reign of Terror. Of course. Where else would someone build a monster except in the dungeon whose very nature was defined by slaughter. The Thule master must have thought it an appropriate joke.

Joke's on them, mused Franks as he killed another guard and took his keys. The guard slumped down to the floor, legs and arms twitching, head twisted around as if to look for a way out. There was none.

The fifth key he tried opened the door, and as soon as he stepped onto the top step, he could smell it.

It.

There was no other way to describe the scent. Franks had been all over the world, from the cold forests of Russia to the steamy jungles of South America. He'd hunted humans and animals of every kind, but nothing smelled like this. Not a great cat, not a wolf, not a bear or a lion.

Nothing.

He drank in the scent with whatever strange senses had been gifted him with this new body. He could smell the paint on the walls, the iron in the nails of the stairs, the different kinds of wood used to build this house, the glue on the wallpaper, the coppery stink of blood. He smelled more and was aware of more than ever before, and on some odd level, he could identify each and every scent. But nothing in that catalog of odors put a name to the thing that was downstairs.

It gave him pause and for a moment he lingered at the top

of the steps and wondered whether going down there was such a wise idea after all. What would happen if it truly was the unstoppable weapon the Thule masters had wanted? What if this *hund von Hitler* was something even he could not fight?

He flexed his fists.

"Fuck it," he told the night.

And went down.

– 8 –

The Dungeon
Château de Brejean
Margeride Mountains of Lozère
Massif Central, France
April 21, 1943

There was a greasy yellow light at the bottom of the stairs and the sound of men speaking in low tones.

No. Not speaking.

Chanting.

Franks paused halfway down the stairs and listened. Male voices, but not speaking in either German or French. He strained to hear and grunted in surprise. The language was something very old and he only caught fragments of it. Words he'd read in old books and had seldom heard spoken because the language was a dead one. It was Sumerian, the language of ancient, lost Mesopotamia.

The words he caught were the names of old gods: Ereshkigal, the name of the queen of the underworld; and Ninurta, god of war.

Each time their names were mentioned there was a sound. Not a response, and not from a human throat. When Ereshkigal's name was mentioned, there was a purr that was long, deep, and almost sexual. When Ninurta was mentioned, that purr changed to a rumbling growl filled with hate and hunger.

Franks understood now.

The *Thule-Gesellschaft* were probably all insane but they were far from fools. They had to know that the war was lost and, when it was over, the whole world was going to bend Germany over a barrel and take turns. Justly so. Hitler's mad dream had ruined Europe and nothing would ever be the same again. It couldn't be. The Nazi tacticians had made too many critical errors. Trying to eradicate the Jews, turning on their Russian allies, pissing off the Americans and British . . . and a laundry list of other offenses. The invasion of France was coming. The end was coming. And so, wisdom had given way to desperation . . . to more bad choices.

Instead of trying to form new alliances or rethinking their military strategies, the Thule Society had looked elsewhere for a weapon. They had looked backward in time to cultures long dead, they had looked in shadows, they had stepped down into the outer rings of hell. When tanks and soldiers and bullets would not stop the incoming tide, they had made a monster.

Franks came down the last few steps and peered around the corner into madness and horror.

There were thirteen members of the Thule Society. They were naked, their bodies painted with cabalistic and alchemical symbols from half a hundred faiths. The Egyptian *ankh* and medieval roaring lion, the arrow of Artemis and the dragon of China, the Norse lightning bolt of Odin and the Arabic *hamsa*. And many others. Combinations of letters and numbers, runes, the elements, and parts of spells. The only one Franks did not see was the swastika, which he found amusing. More spells and symbols were painted on the floors, the walls, and on both sides of a heavy circle of salt that had been carefully laid around the *thing* to which they bowed and chanted and prayed.

The beast.

"Oh, shit," said Franks.

He said it just a little too loud because caution had been smashed away by shock. The chanting stopped and every head whipped around toward him. All thirteen naked priests of Thule. And the massive head of the beast.

For beast it was.

Not a dog at all. Never a dog.

It was more like a great bull, at least in size, though it was the most massive thing he had ever seen. A bull in shape but as big as an elephant. A pair of massive horns arched over its misshapen head and below them were eyes as red as flame. A mane hung from its neck, but instead of hair, each strand was a wriggling worm with a fanged, gaping mouth. The chest of the creature was massive and deep, with rippling muscles and plates like those of an alligator, but darker and flecked with black and red. The body was tattooed with swirling stars and planets and burning comets as if to suggest that its power was infinite. Instead of hooves, the front legs ended in thick paws from which sprouted claws as long as bayonets. Everywhere he looked he saw lines of stitches, old and new: the marks of radical surgery that had been commanded by madmen and carried out by the damned. Karoutchi and the others had been forced to create an abomination. It was a perverse brand of science Franks knew all too well, though he had thought that his own misshapen form—the one that lay drowning in Paris—was the most fearsome example of that kind of insanity. He was wrong. The body of this beast was an affront to everything holy and sane.

But its face...

That was so much worse.

Even Franks felt a thrill of awe when he stared into that face. It was shaped like a bull's but the teeth were like spikes of polished steel and from them dripped a clear drool that hissed and burned into the stone of the cellar floor. The monster threw back its head and uttered a roar that was the loudest sound Franks had ever heard. It was like a solid blow that plucked him off his feet and slammed him into the wall of the stairwell. He hit, rebounded, and fell to his knees.

The Thule masters were scattered like leaves by the roar, but they scrambled back to their feet. They gaped at Franks with shock as great as he felt at seeing the monster, and he could understand why. After all, he was not something they had ever seen before.

One of them, obviously the leader, pointed to him and uttered a single word. He spat it with mingled horror and contempt.

"*Golem.*"

Then he turned and looked up at the ceiling, as if he could see the shacks of prisoners and spoke another word.

"*Juden.*"

He spat on the floor.

Franks rose to his feet and flexed his rocky fists.

"Fuck you," he said.

"*Töte ihn,*" snarled the Thule leader. "*Schützen sie das Tier.*" *Kill him. Protect the beast.*

With a howl of fury, the Thule masters snatched up sacrificial knives and rushed at him.

Franks did not wait to be overwhelmed. With a howl of his own, he took the fight to them, wading into a storm of blades. He felt the thud and chunk of sharp edges and knifepoints, but he had no flesh that could scream, no nerve endings to shriek, no blood to flow. Nice. He swung a blow at the face of the first of his attackers, pivoting all the way up from the floor, putting five hundred pounds of mass into a blow that exploded the man's skull and spattered the five closest men around him with blood and pulped brain matter. Then he pivoted and backhanded another, catching him in the chest and splintering bone. The others tried. They tried.

But they were trying to kill an unkillable thing.

He did not have the same problem.

They were flesh. They were bone. They were alive.

Until they were not.

Franks waded through the chamber, letting knives catch on the roots in his arms and chest, letting the steel snap on the rocks that were his bones. He laughed aloud as he smashed skulls and snapped spines and mashed internal organs to jelly. When he thought about the poor bastards in the shed and their wives and children, it made the sound of pain, the screams for mercy all the sweeter for he had brought no mercy down here with him.

But one other thing burned in his brain as he fought: the words of the leader.

"Schützen sie das Tier."

Protect the beast.

Protect it?

As he killed another man, he saw the beast rear and tear at the air with its claws. How in hell would that thing ever need protection? And . . . protection from what? It was designed as a living engine of mass murder. A living, breathing, indestructible tank that fed on its victims and which—if the science that created it was anything like the science that had created *him*—could not truly be killed. Not in any normal sense of that word.

Protect it?

The leader of the Thule swung an axe at him and the blade bit deep into Franks' neck and for one minute he was falling.

No.

Drowning.

He felt his chest spasm as filthy water filled his lungs. He smelled the stink of shit and dead fish and rat droppings.

His eyes blinked as they looked up through rippling water and he knew that he was back in the sewers beneath Paris.

And then he was back in the underground chamber . . . on his knees, feeling the jerk as the leader tore the axe free and raised it for another blow. Franks looked and saw that the axe was engraved with dark spells and terrible words of power.

He can kill me with that.

Franks knew it to be true. Both of them did. All around him, the other Thule were dead or dying, but the leader, splashed in the blood of his brethren, had a look of red joy on his face as he raised that sacred axe. Maybe it was something they had made or—more likely, Franks knew—it was an object of power looted from some sacked tomb or church or shrine. A bronze blade and a handle of hawthorn wood. A weapon kept here... why? Surely not as a protection against the improbable invasion by a supernatural construct like a *golem*.

There was the circle of salt and the spells of protection traced on either side of them. Yes. The Thule had commissioned the construction of the beast but they were not its masters. Perhaps they might have been had whatever ritual they were chanting been completed. Now the masters of the cult lay in pieces. Only the leader remained... and the beast inside the conjuring circle.

It all made sense to Franks.

And it gave him a clear map of what had to be done.

All of this flashed through his mind in the fragment of a second it took for the leader to raise the sacred axe. Normally Franks preferred sending a lot of ordnance downrange when faced with a real threat, but he didn't have a gun. So instead he drove one of his rock-studded fists as far into the man's crotch as he could manage.

He put outrage into the punch.

He put fury into it.

And he put every ounce of the body the desperate men upstairs had made for him.

It exploded the leader. The Thule killer flew apart as surely as if he had been drawn and quartered. Arms and legs tore away from the ruin of his groin. The spine shattered and twisted the torso into a goblin shape. The leader tried to scream, but the shock of the blow burst his lungs and the only thing that came from his mouth was a torrent of dark blood.

The beast howled with fury, driven mad by the smell of all that blood.

Franks sagged back, avoiding the fall of the sacred axe, which landed inches in front of where he knelt.

The howl of the monster went on and on.

The room seemed to shimmer and Franks could feel the foul water lapping at him. He touched a hand to the deep wound in his neck and it came away wet, smelling of sewer filth. Amazingly, impossibly, he was bleeding water from where his body floated all those hundreds of miles away.

"Fuck it," he snarled and snatched up the axe. The hawthorn wood burned his fingers. It hurt flesh that had no nerve endings. Franks swore at that, too, but he rose with the axe in his hand.

The beast stopped howling and watched him approach, its red eyes suddenly narrow and wary. Franks' feet felt leaden as if the axe weighed a thousand pounds.

"Fuck it," Franks mumbled, his speech becoming slurred. He stopped at the outer edge of the salt circle and stared the enormous monster in the face. It bared its teeth at him. "Yeah, and fuck you, too."

Frank swung the axe.

– 9 –

Les Égouts de Paris
(The Sewers of Paris)
(August 21, 1943)

He floated for a long time. More dead than alive, more gone than here.

Then he blinked himself awake. His mouth opened and he drew in a double lungful of vile water, then came porpoising up, wretched, coughing, spitting it out. He fought and thrashed his way to the edge of the walkway and clung there, weak, shaken.

Alive.

Alive?

He looked at the arms that hung over the slimy bricks. The faintness of old stitching and the scars of a thousand battlefields were there to be seen. A roadmap of the places he'd been and the things—the truly terrible things—which had been done to him. Things he had paid back.

He had never felt weaker.

For a moment, he thought he could hear the echo of some great beast crying out in fear and surprise and agony.

Franks smiled at the darkness around him...and in him.

AFTERWORD

I originally decided to write *Monster Hunter International* because I was a gun nut who loved horror movies. With most monster flicks, the majority of characters are clueless victims, but my favorite protagonists were the ones who fought back, used their brains, and found a way to triumph at the end. I really wanted to tell the story of what happened to all of those survivors after their monster encounters.

Also, it is kind of a running joke that a monster movie starring one of my people would be boring because we'd just blast the critter in the first few minutes, roll credits. So if you're going to have a story about capable, smart, well-armed heroes, that means you're going to need tougher monsters, or lots of them.

Then it stands to reason that if monsters are real, they're a recurring menace, and you've already proven you're good at hunting them, you should be able to make a decent living at it.

And thus MHI was born.

Luckily for me, it turns out that there were a lot more people who wanted to read that kind of story than I ever dreamed of. The Monster Hunter series has been popular and successful, and I've been given the opportunity to write several more books set in this world since.

When editor Bryan Thomas Schmidt approached me about putting together an anthology of stories set in the MHI universe, I figured that maybe some authors would be interested in telling these kinds of stories, too. I was humbled by the response we got from so many top-notch, talented storytellers.

This collection features some of my favorite authors. I hope you enjoyed reading their stories as much as I did.

—Larry Correia

BIOGRAPHIES

Co-editor and creator of the Monster Hunter Universe, **Larry Correia** is the *New York Times* bestselling author of the Monster Hunter International series, the Grimnoir Chronicles, the Saga of the Forgotten Warrior, the Dead Six thrillers with Mike Kupari, the *Adventures of Tom Stranger Interdimensional Insurance Agent*, novels set in the Warmachine universe, and a whole lot of short fiction. Before becoming an author, Larry was an accountant, a gun dealer, and a firearms instructor. Any similarity between his resume and Owen Z. Pitt's is purely coincidental. Larry lives in Yard Moose Mountain, Utah, with his very patient wife and children.

Jim Butcher is the author of the Dresden Files, the Codex Alera, and a new steampunk series, the Cinder Spires. His resume includes a laundry list of skills which were useful a couple of centuries ago, and he plays guitar quite badly. An avid gamer, he plays tabletop games in varying systems, a variety of video games on PC and console, and LARPs whenever he can make time for it. Jim currently resides mostly inside his own head, but his head can generally be found in his home town of Independence, Missouri.

A former Explosive Ordnance Disposal technician in the US Air Force, **Mike Kupari** is a veteran of Afghanistan, previously worked in the Middle East as a security contractor, and was a firearms instructor. He's worked as an unexploded ordnance technician, clearing former military ranges of explosive hazards, and continued his career in the chemical weapon demilitarization program. His first book, *Dead Six*, cowritten with Larry Correia, was published in 2011, when Mike was still deployed. The sequel, *Swords of Exodus*, was released in 2013. The conclusion to the trilogy, *Alliance of Shadows*, hit bookstores in Fall 2016. His first solo novel, *Her Brother's Keeper*, debuted in 2015, and a sequel is in the works.

Mike has lived in many places, but frequently travels the country with his dog and bird.

Jessica Day George is the *New York Times* bestselling author of over a dozen young adult and middle-grade fantasy books, including *Silver in the Blood, Sun and Moon, Ice and Snow*, the Dragon Slippers trilogy, and the Castle Glower series. She feels very fortunate to be a fantasy author, since her degree in Humanities and Comparative Literature, with a minor in Scandinavian Studies, means her only other career path is being a museum docent, and she doesn't like being quiet. She collects garden gnomes and also has gnome pajamas and socks. She likes dark chocolate, knitting, Disney vacations, and eating her weight in popcorn at the movies. Originally from Idaho, she has lived in Delaware and New Jersey, and now resides outside of Salt Lake City, Utah, with her husband, three children, and a puffy white dog.

John C. Wright is a retired attorney, newspaperman and newspaper editor, who was only once on the lam and forced to hide from the police who did not admire his newspaper. In 1984, he graduated from St. John's College in Annapolis, home of the "Great Books" program. In 1987, he graduated from the College of William and Mary's Law School (going from the third oldest to the second oldest school in continuous use in the United States), and was admitted to the practice of law in three jurisdictions (New York, May 1989; Maryland, December 1990; DC, January 1994). His law practice was unsuccessful enough to drive him into bankruptcy soon thereafter. His stint as a newspaperman for the *St. Mary's Today* was more rewarding spiritually, but, alas, also a failure financially. He presently works (successfully) as a writer in Virginia, where he lives in fairy-talelike happiness with his wife, the authoress L. Jagi Lamplighter, and their three children: Orville, Wilbur, and Just Wright.

Maurice Broaddus is the author of the Knights of Breton Court urban fantasy trilogy: *King Maker, King's Justice*, and *King's War* (Angry Robot Books). His fiction has been published in numerous magazines and anthologies, including *Asimov's Science Fiction, Lightspeed Magazine, Cemetery Dance, Apex Magazine*, and *Weird Tales* Magazine. Some of his stories are being collected in the upcoming *Voices of the Martyrs* (Rosarium Publishing). He co-edited *Streets of Shadows* (Alliteration Ink) and the Dark Faith anthology series (Apex Books). You can keep up with him at his web site, www.MauriceBroaddus.com.

Brad R. Torgersen is a multiple-award-winning and award-nominated science fiction author, who is a healthcare information technology geek by day, and a United States Army Reserve Chief Warrant Officer on the weekend. His short fiction appears frequently in the pages of *Analog* magazine and *Orson Scott Card's InterGalactic Medicine Show* magazine, while his novels are published by Baen Books. Recently returned from military deployment to the Middle East, Brad has been married for over two decades, has one daughter, one cat, one dog, and lives in Utah. Find him online at www.bradrtorgersen.com.

New York Times bestselling fantasy author **Faith Hunter** was born in Louisiana and raised all over the south. She writes two contemporary Urban Fantasy series: the Jane Yellowrock series, featuring a Cherokee skinwalker who hunts rogue vampires, and the Soulwood series, featuring earth magic user Nell Ingram. Her Rogue Mage novels are a dark, post-apocalyptic, fantasy series featuring Thorn St. Croix, a stone mage. The roleplaying game based on the series is Rogue Mage, RPG. Find her online via her website: www.faithhunter.net, on Twitter as @hunterfaith, and at www.yellowrocksecurities.com and www.gwenhunter.net.

Jody Lynn Nye lists her main career activity as "spoiling cats." She lives northwest of Chicago with one of the above and her husband, author and packager Bill Fawcett. She has written over forty books, including *The Ship Who Won* with Anne McCaffrey, eight books with Robert Asprin, a humorous anthology about mothers, *Don't Forget Your Spacesuit, Dear!,* and over 140 short stories. Her latest books are *Rhythm of the Imperium* (Baen Books), *Wishing On a Star* (Arc Manor Publishing), and *Myth-Fits* (Ace Books), the 20th novel in the Myth-Adventures series begun by Robert Asprin. Jody also reviews fiction for *Galaxy's Edge* magazine and teaches the intensive writers' workshop at DragonCon. Jody can be found at www.jodylynnnye.com, on Facebook at www.facebook.com/jodylynn.nye, on Goodreads at "Books by Jody Lynn Nye (Author of The Dragonlover's Guide to Pern)" and on Twitter @JodyLynnNye.

Quincy J. Allen, a cross-genre author, has been published in multiple anthologies, magazines, and one omnibus. His first novel *Chemical Burn* was a finalist in the RMFW Colorado Gold Contest. He made his first pro sale in 2014 with the story "Jimmy Krinkle-pot and the White Rebels of Hayberry," included in WordFire's *A Fantastic Holiday Season: The Gift of Stories.* He's written for the internet show *RadioSteam,* and his first short-story collection *Out Through the Attic* came out in 2014 from 7DS Books. His latest novel, *Blood Ties,* Book 1 in the Blood War Chronicles, is now available in print and digital editions on Amazon and digital format on Kobo, Barnes & Noble, iBooks, and Smashwords. The sequel *Blood Curse,* Book 2 of the Blood War Chronicles, debuted at Comicpalooza and Denver Comic Con in June of 2016 and is also available in print and digital formats.

He works as a Warehouse and Booth Manager for WordFire Press by day, does book design and eBook conversions by night, and lives in a cozy house in Colorado that he considers his very own sanctuary—think Bat Cave, but with fewer flying mammals and more sunlight.

Alex Shvartsman is a writer, anthologist, translator, and game designer from Brooklyn, NY. He's the winner of the 2014 WSFA Small Press Award for Short Fiction and a finalist for the 2015 Canopus Award for Excellence in Interstellar Writing. His short stories have appeared in *Nature, Intergalactic Medicine Show, Daily Science Fiction, Galaxy's Edge,* and a variety of other magazines and anthologies. His collection, *Explaining Cthulhu to Grandma and Other Stories*, and his steampunk humor novella *H. G. Wells, Secret Agent* were published in 2015.

Alex is the editor of the Unidentified Funny Objects series of humorous science fiction and fantasy. In addition to the UFO series, he has edited the *Funny Science Fiction, Funny Fantasy, Coffee: 14 Caffeinated Tales of the Fantastic* and *Dark Expanse: Surviving the Collapse* anthologies. His website is www.alexshvartsman.com.

Kim May has been a dancer, competitive swimmer, actor, singer, model, bald spot duster, and slug licker. Sadly, she wasn't paid for any of it so she gave it all up in favor of spending her days working at one of the oldest independent bookstores in Oregon, and spending her nights writing. True to form, Kim writes a bit of everything: sci-fi, fantasy, steampunk, thrillers, young adult, and tie-in fiction. The one consistency is that she often draws inspiration from her Japanese heritage. In fact, in 2013 she won The Named Lands Poetry Contest with a haiku. You can find her short stories in *Eclipse Phase: After the Fall*, and in multiple volumes of *Fiction River*. Find out more about Kim May at her blog: http://ninjakeyboard.blogspot.com.

Steve Diamond founded and runs the review site, Elitist Book Reviews (www.elitistbookreviews.com), which was nominated for the Hugo Award in 2013, 2014, and 2015. He is a Hugo-nominated author and writes for Ragnarok, Baen, Privateer Press, and numerous small publications. *Residue*, a YA supernatural thriller/horror novel, is his first novel-length published work. He is also the editor of the horror anthology, *Shared Nightmares*. Find out more about Steve at http://thethroneofbooks.com.

John Ringo had visited twenty-three countries and attended fourteen schools by the time he graduated high school. This left him with a wonderful appreciation of the oneness of humanity and a permanent aversion to foreign food. He chose to study marine biology and really liked it. Unfortunately, the pay was for beans, so he turned to database management.

But then Fate took a hand: John was offered the "rich and famous contract" and became a professional author. Over the course of time, he has published numerous novels at a prolific rate and thus made his publisher rich and famous. The author's method of work is to sit on his porch, think big thoughts, consume amazing quantities of caffeine and nicotine, then hallucinate his way through a novel. All of his books are available in deadtree as hardcovers or paperbacks in any local or internet bookstore and in electronic form.

Co-editor/contributor **Bryan Thomas Schmidt** is an author and Hugo-nominated editor of adult and children's speculative fiction. His debut novel, *The Worker Prince,* received Honorable Mention on Barnes & Noble Book Club's Year's Best Science Fiction Releases. His short stories include entries in *The X-Files, Predator,* Larry Correia's *Monster Hunter International,* and *Decipher's WARS,* among others. He can be found online as bryanthomass at Facebook and Twitter or via his website www.bryanthomasschmidt.net.

Julie Frost grew up as an Army brat, traveling the globe. She thought she might settle down after she got married, but then she wed a pilot and moved six times in seven years. She's finally settled in Utah with her family, which consists of five guinea pigs, three humans, a tripod calico cat, and a kitten who thinks she's a warrior princess as well as a collection of anteaters and Oaxacan carvings, some of which intersect. She utilizes her degree in biology to write werewolf fiction and to completely ignore the physics of a protagonist who triples in mass. Her short fiction has appeared in *Writers of the Future, StarShipSofa, Cosmos, Unlikely Story, Plasma Frequency, Stupefying Stories,* and many other venues. Her first novel, *Pack Dynamics,* was released in 2015 by WordFire Press. She whines about writing—a lot—at http://agilebrit.livejournal.com.

Sarah A. Hoyt has published over two dozen novels in science fiction, fantasy, mystery and historical fiction. She has published over one hundred short stories in magazines such as *Asimov's,*

Analog, and *Weird Tales* as well as in many anthologies. Her first novel, *Ill Met by Moonlight* was a finalist for the Mythopoeic Award. Her novel *Darkship Thieves* won the Prometheus Award. She was born and raised in Portugal and now lives in Colorado with her husband and sons. And oh, yeah, she gets to collaborate with Larry on *MHI Guardian,* Julie's story.

Jonathan Maberry is a *New York Times* bestselling novelist, five-time Bram Stoker Award winner, and comic book writer. He writes the Joe Ledger thrillers, the Rot & Ruin series, the Nightsiders series, the Dead of Night series, as well as stand-alone novels in multiple genres. He is the editor of many anthologies including *The X-Files, Scary Out There, Out Of Tune,* and *V-Wars.* His comic book works include, among others, *Captain America,* the Bram Stoker Award-winning *Bad Blood, Rot & Ruin, V-Wars,* the *New York Times* bestselling *Marvel Zombies Return,* and others. His books *Extinction Machine, V-Wars* and *Mars One* are in development for TV/film. A board game version of *V-Wars* was released in early 2016. He is the founder of the Writers Coffeehouse and the co-founder of The Liars Club. He is one third of the very popular and mildly weird *Three Guys with Beards* pop-culture podcast. Jonathan lives in Del Mar, California, with his wife, Sara Jo. www.jonathanmaberry.com.